A Sunday Times Thriller of the M...

'... er stalwart on the *Today* prog ... ...ington is as good ... politics as he is on the UK's ambiguous role east of Suez, ... cels, too, at character portraits of figures such as the British am...ssador. There are nods to John le Carré, but his impressive ... is its own thing, with three radio men at its centre, not ...ks or civil servants' *The Sunday Times*

'...ghtful, atmospheric and grippingly plotted' *Guardian*

'I... a pleasure to welcome *A Dying Breed*, an impressive debut b... Peter Hanington. The multi-layered plot, set in Afghanistan a... BBC headquarters, moves excitingly and entertainingly but a... raises serious current issues about dodgy political and c...mercial interference with the search for truth by journalists ... Hanington has true talent' *The Times*

'Gra...am Greene-lite but rings true, like an episode of *Homeland* s...ed with a bit of *Spooks*' *Esquire*

'A...emendous novel – shot-through with great authenticity and in...er knowledge – wholly compelling and shrewdly wise' William Boyd

'...*Dying Breed* is an enthralling page-turner, and, as befits an au...or steeped in newsgathering, there's a real sense of authority a... authenticity at work in this quality thriller' Michael Palin

'*A Dying Breed* is a gripping, fast-moving tale of shifting loyalties and creeping betrayal . . . It is a world in which your closest friends turn out to be your most treacherous enemies – and all written with an effortless, liquidly-drinkable prose style. A page turner from the first line'

Allan Little, former BBC foreign correspondent

'A gripping story, taking the reader from the politics of the BBC newsroom to the politics of a complex and changing Afghanistan. Peter Hanington's clear, assured voice shines out from every page'

Mishal Husain, *Today* presenter

'An intelligent thriller set in present day Afghanistan. By focussing on journalists and their work it avoids a lot of the guns and gunplay aspects of many thrillers set in this part of the world. And informed by Peter Hanington's many years as a foreign correspondent, there is an air of veracity around the characters and their interactions . . . Hanington has a great feel for both his characters and their milieu and this makes *A Dying Breed* both an effective and illuminating thriller. He eschews the usual lone wolf action hero style for a more intelligent, considered plot which manages to impart a lot of information and opinion in a manner that is on the whole both engaging and entertaining'

Austcrimefiction.org

'*A Dying Breed* is the first book by Peter Hanington; I hope it won't be his last . . . This book is fast-paced and extremely well-written . . . hard to put down and leaves no questions unasked. Just like a good news story really' *Booksellers New Zealand Blog*

'This has the old-fashioned phrasing and style of a John Le Carré thriller. But once you overcome that anachronism, it settles into a modern, fast-paced thriller set in a post-conflict Afghanistan'

Stuff.co.nz

'Hanington perfectly illustrates the hierarchy of a news organisation and uses humour in describing the daily struggle for ratings while balancing ethics and pressure from agenda-driven authorities . . . It's adventurous and entertaining' *Otago Daily Times*

PETER HANINGTON

A

DYING

BREED

TWO
ROADS

www.tworoadsbooks.com

First published in Great Britain in 2016 by Two Roads
An imprint of John Murray Press
An Hachette UK company

First published in paperback in 2016

1

ISBN 9781473625433
Ebook ISBN 9781473625440
Audio Digital Download ISBN 9781473631373

Printed and bound by CPI Group (UK) Ltd, Croydon, CR0 4YY

Hodder & Stoughton Ltd
Carmelite House
50 Victoria Embankment
London EC4Y 0DZ

www.hodder.co.uk

For my mother, my father and for Vic. Obviously.

CONTENTS

Prologue

DATELINE: All Souls Church, Langham Place, London, W1, June 14th

Crossing the threshold of All Souls Church, Carver raised a hand to cross himself, then stopped. He muttered something that was not a prayer and jammed the offending hand back into his blazer pocket. He looked around. Tall Corinthian columns and sun-washed Bath stone were at his back, but inside it was a rather uninspiring 1970s sort of arrangement, designed to accommodate the maximum number of worshippers with the minimum fuss. Up in the balcony, the church rector stopped what he was doing and watched the visitor. He saw a bespectacled man somewhere around sixty, thinning on top and heavy in the middle; in his right hand he held a well-worn yellow plastic carrier bag. Not a church regular, nor a tourist by the looks of him. The rector went back to work, checking the hymnals for blasphemous graffiti and general wear and tear.

William Carver wandered down the central aisle. He took a look at the old Hunter church organ, in its fine mahogany case, and at a stained-glass tableau featuring an earnest-looking

1

shepherd and several cross-eyed sheep. Carver checked his watch and turned to leave; he was really only killing time. On the way back out, his eye caught sight of a single flickering light in an otherwise inky corner of All Souls. William sighed and walked in that direction. The pound coin he dropped into the empty black tin collection box hit the bottom with a loud rattle. He took a votive candle from the cardboard box, unpicked the wick, and, using the flame of the only other slim white candle in the sand-filled tray, lit his offering. He held it for a moment, staring into the flame and enjoying the sweet smell of burning wax, before planting it front and centre in the sand. He remembered how his mother would always congratulate him on picking the best spot for his candle and how, after the seemingly endless Sunday service, as they filed out, she would observe that his flame appeared to be burning a little brighter than all the others. Ridiculous, of course – all the candles burnt more or less the same.

He thought about his mother and then, inevitably, about his father. But there would be no one pound candle for him.

Outside the church, Carver's eyes took time to adjust to the bright morning light; once they did, he checked his watch again. He had a meeting with the head of BBC personnel at ten. It was not quite quarter to, he was still early, but then he was always early, even for appointments that he had no interest in keeping, like this one. His editor had described it as a formality, a ten-minute sit-down with one of the big BBC bosses, something that all the veteran journalists were having to endure. He ambled across the part-pedestrianised road and in through the high, handsome doors of Broadcasting House. How many times had he walked into this building? Thousands or maybe even tens of thousands of times, he guessed. Nevertheless William found it impossible not to feel a swell of pride, glancing up at the sculptures of Prospero and Ariel in all their art deco glory. Inside, he sat down on a worn leather bench in the corner of reception and watched as a tour party assembled. The guide was an enthusiastic young woman with a south London accent and an infectious laugh. She had a group of sweatshirt-wearing schoolchildren rapt.

'*Nation shall speak peace unto nation.* Give me a better motto than that and I'll give you a fiver. Go on!' The children laughed. William had always meant to take the tour and he was tempted to attach himself to the back of the group now, but the receptionist was waving him over.

'Mr Drice is ready for you now, sir. He's up on the sixth floor. Do you know it?'

He knew it. The sixth was where the bosses lived and the story was that BBC management had recently had the old oak panelling, which had been stripped out twenty years ago, reinstated at considerable cost. William was interested to see it. He rode the juddery antique lift to the sixth floor and when the doors opened, there was Drice, standing, waiting for him with a thin smile and an outstretched hand. The management man wore a tailored blue suit and steel-rimmed glasses. He gave William a hot and overly firm handshake before leading him into the refurbished office. The oak did look good, William thought, gave the place an air of authority. The desk was top quality too, an old antique affair, leather-topped, broad and deep; a little too big, in fact, for the number of items Drice had to place upon it. He had a phone, a small pile of papers and an expensive fountain pen, but that was it. William wondered where his computer was. Stowed away in one of the drawers, he guessed, so as not to spoil the look, although that was already slightly spoilt by the strange black moulded chair the man was now bobbing backwards and forwards in.

'Thanks so much for coming to see me, William.'

'I wasn't given much choice.'

Carver sat in the high-backed wooden seat opposite Drice and glanced around. The office was at the very front of Broadcasting

House, with windows on all sides, and as a result, sitting there felt rather like sitting in the prow of a ship.

'You've a good view up here.'

Drice nodded. 'Yes, it's terrific on a clear day. Not so good on a dreary day, a bit—'

William waited while the man tried to locate an adjective.

'—well, dreary.'

Carver placed his plastic bag down at the side of his chair and pointed at the wall. 'How much did the oak panelling cost?'

Drice hoisted both eyebrows in a look of mock horror. 'Ha. That's what I love about you old hacks, no messing about. Straight to the nub, right to the tricky question.'

Carver said nothing. He just waited.

'Well, let's see. I think I can safely say that it didn't cost half as much as you think it did.'

'A hundred quid?'

'Ha. Good one. No, no, a bit more than that.' Drice paused. 'I would tell you, William, but you wouldn't believe how quickly a thing like that can end up in the newspapers. I tell you in confidence, you tell someone else in confidence, the next thing you know, I'm reading about it in the *Daily Wotsit*.'

He waved a hand above his head and smiled. 'This place leaks like a sieve.'

William nodded but did not smile back. 'It might have something to do with that big antenna on the roof.'

'Ha. It might do, might well do. So, can I get you anything? A tea, coffee, mineral water? Something like that, before we get down to business?'

'I'm fine.'

'Good. Good, you're busy, I'm busy . . .' Drice put his hands down flat either side of the pile of papers. 'So William, tell me, what are your plans?'

'My plans?'

4

'Yes. Medium term, I mean?'

Carver shrugged, uncertain what 'medium term' might mean. 'Well, I've got a couple of stories I'm working on here, investigative stuff, domestic, but I'm heading back to Afghanistan the day after tomorrow.'

Drice nodded. He glanced briefly out of one of the many windows and then back at Carver. 'Afghanistan, yes, of course. Excellent.'

William shifted in his seat. It seemed this conversation was going to be an even bigger waste of time than he had feared. He broke eye contact with Drice and looked past him, out towards the Langham Hotel across the road. The wind was getting up and a bright Union flag on the hotel roof had unfurled itself from its pole and was fluttering keenly in the breeze. William watched it and his mind was beginning to wander when a tight little cough summoned him back to the room.

'I wonder, have you thought about VR?'

William was confused. He frowned. 'Via? I'm flying via Delhi. British Airways: Heathrow, Delhi, Kabul. That's the cheapest decent flight I could get.'

Drice smiled. 'Sorry. My fault, talking in jargon. Not *via*; VR, voluntary redundancy. I wondered whether you'd given that some thought recently?'

Now Carver laughed. 'Redundancy? You want rid of me? Is that what this meeting's about?' He sat and waited for the denial, the embarrassed apology. Neither came.

Instead Drice leant back in his ergonomic chair. 'Well, as you know, things are pretty tough for the Beeb right now. Licence fee settlements not what they used to be, Foreign Office funding for the World Service gone, free licences for the oldies and all that. We're having to tighten our belts . . .'

William glanced again at the oak panelling.

'Explore all the possibilities. And what this meeting is about, part of my job, is to look at the wage bill and talk to the senior fellows – veterans like you – see whether they've considered all the options.'

'Option one being that I sack myself and save you the trouble?'

'Not at all. There are lots of options, I'm sure.' Drice did not look sure. 'But, as you know, times are changing. The chaps running news, your bosses, they want their people multi-platform these days. You know, versatile, radio-friendly but telegenic too. Journalists who can write the online piece, file the radio bulletin, do the TV two-way and be Tweeting and Facebooking as they go. Makes a lot of sense, given that's how the commentariat are getting their news these days.'

William looked at the man; he had understood about half of what Drice had just said.

'An example for you . . . Last week, John Brandon. You know? The *Ten O'Clock News* man?'

William conceded that he knew him.

'John wrote this piece . . . Pretty personal it was, rather controversial. All about the price you pay for being a war corr. That piece set the Twittersphere alight.'

Drice beamed with happiness at the very memory of it.

William hadn't seen it. He glanced down at the plastic bag by his feet; inside were his tape recorder and notepads. 'I'm good at what I do.'

But as he said this, his face shaped itself into a scowl; he hated how weak it sounded, how apologetic.

Drice moved in, leaning across the large desk. 'Of course you are, William, of course. But you've been doing it a long time and—'

'And that's why I'm good at it.'

This was said with more confidence, but having said it, William stopped, suddenly filled with doubt. Was the statement still true? Was he still good at what he did? What if Drice was right? That things had changed and he had not. The management man pressed his advantage.

'All we're asking is that you have a think about it. I had my team do a few sums and they've come back with this . . .' Drice pulled a letter with Carver's name and staff number on it from the foot of his pile of papers and pushed it slowly, ceremonially across the desk. 'That's what you could expect to get if you took redundancy any time in the next few months.'

William ignored the piece of paper and looked out over Drice's shoulder. The flag was struggling to find its rhythm, snapping backwards and forwards in the wind.

'Take a look, it's a tidy sum.'

The management man licked his lips. Eventually Carver retrieved the letter, folded it in half and placed it in his jacket pocket, unread. This unsettled Drice, and he shuffled awkwardly in his seat and stared at the man opposite him. He'd conducted dozens of these sorts of conversations and this hadn't happened before. Usually the person he was talking to looked carefully at the numbers on the piece of paper, was pleasantly surprised, said thank you and so on. But not this man. He stumbled on:

'Good. Well then, yes, take it with you, read it later, give it some thought.'

Drice picked up his neat pile of papers, tapped it together once more, then put it back down.

'So, you're off to Afghanistan, you said? Part of the big election jamboree, I suppose?'

William was still lost in thought. 'What? No, no, I was going back anyway.'

'Oh. Well, good timing I suppose . . . an exciting time? What do you think's going to happen?'

'What?'

'In Afghanistan. With the election. What do you think will happen?'

William picked up his plastic bag. 'Dying. Dying is going to happen.'

PART ONE

1 The Wedding Party

DATELINE: Central Kabul, Afghanistan, June 21st

If Baba had been asked to count his blessings, then number one, ahead of his wife, four children and robust health, would be the stone fountain in his front garden. He fussed over it the way other men in Kabul attended to their cars or their mistresses and he fussed most on the day of a wedding, which was why he was up early this morning, preparing to coax the most he could from the fountain's fickle pump. The night before, while climbing into bed, he had slowly and deliberately knocked his head five times against the wooden headboard, thereby informing his famous body clock that he needed to rise at five sharp. At ten past five his wife, Soraya, had gently pinched his nose to stifle the snores and, when that failed, pulled her husband's share of the sheets and blankets over to her side of the bed. Before long, Baba woke, checked his watch and rose to a sitting position with a satisfied growl. He pushed himself up from the bed, stretched and began to dress as quietly as he knew how. Soraya watched in silence as he struggled out of his vest and long johns and into his work clothes: a grease-stained white T-shirt, jeans and flip-flops. Baba tiptoed from the room but quickly came back again and went over to his bedside table. Groping around, he found the American-made workman's torch that his son had given him for his last birthday. He pulled the elastic strap over his bald head and positioned the torch front and centre before departing again, his flip-flops slapping on the ceramic tiles. Still Soraya lay motionless, her dark eyes open, and a minute later she was rewarded as her husband returned, standing in the doorway, the torch switched on – a huge human lighthouse. The yellow beam swept the room, carefully avoiding Soraya's side of the bed, before settling on a tool belt that was hanging over the back of her dressing chair. Baba took the belt, strapped it beneath his large stomach and left again, closing the door gently behind him. Only now did Soraya move, shuffling over to her husband's side of the bed. She slid easily into the indentation he had left in the old mattress, sighed deeply and closed her eyes.

Baba made himself a strong black coffee, slipped the steel bolt on the front door and stepped outside into the still sleeping city. There was a little moisture in the Kabul air and the sky was iron grey; a touch of yellow on the horizon, the only hint of the heat to come. He strode down the garden and circled the fountain before setting to work, unlocking the small door at the base of the beloved water feature and shining his head-torch inside. The fountain was a three-tiered Italianate affair comprising three ornate stone basins separated and supported by a thick central column. A rubber pipe inside the column pushed the water up and out of the fountainhead, from where it worked its way back down, ending up back at the lowest bowl before being pumped up again. The water went nowhere but it made a pretty noise and a pleasing cascade, and when it was working well it could look quite dramatic. Baba knew that his fountain and the well-tended front garden were the reason why so many wedding parties chose his modest guesthouse over the many more prestigious venues in Kabul. This little patch of green in a dirty, dusty city was a good place for a party but – more importantly – it was the perfect place for a picture. If you arranged your wedding group correctly and framed the photograph carefully, you might imagine your reception had taken place in the grounds of an English country house or even a small French chateau. Baba's cousin, Ali, was expert in creating this impression, and he was the photographer who most couples opted for, after a little cajoling from their host. In return for this recommendation, Ali was required to give Baba ten per cent of the fee and one seven-by-five group shot of each wedding party. These photos were kept in a scrapbook that Baba would flick through with Soraya. She would comment on the cut of a certain dress or the haughty manner of a particular mother. But Baba had no interest in how beautiful the bride was, or how distinguished the family. His eye went straight to the fountain and the plume of water being pushed skywards. As far as he was concerned, the success of a wedding was determined solely by the height the spout achieved. Baba's eye often came to rest on a picture of a particular wedding party that had ended early and acrimoniously after an argument over the size of the dowry. Looking at the picture, anyone could have guessed at the trouble to come; the stormy countenances of the parents were unmissable. Baba didn't see these warnings signs, however; he saw a fountain spouting water a full metre into the air.

'Ah yes, an excellent wedding! A great success.' A metre was an unattainable dream these days. After two hours of hard labour, Baba had cleaned the filtration system with a toothbrush, he'd run boiling water through the pipes a dozen times and now he was hitting the nearby generator with a spanner. If he saw the dark blue Toyota crawling along his side of Passport Street and back down the other side, it wasn't fixed enough in his memory for him to mention it later.

The rubber tubing was clogged with years of dirt and detritus that no amount of boiled water could clear, and his attempts at solving the problem by making the pump push harder had simply made the fountain noisy. Without new parts it was a losing battle, and there were no new parts to be had in a country at war. Baba sweated and tinkered with the guts of the fountain for another hour before giving up. Slamming the small door shut, he hauled himself to his feet and scowled. He unbuckled his tool belt, let it fall to the ground with a clatter and stormed back inside, returning with an old wooden school ruler. He measured the plume of water.

'Six centimetres only!' He shook his head in defeat.

Baba glanced at his watch and considered taking another tilt at it, but at that moment Soraya called his name. He looked again at the time. There were too many other chores to do: he needed to collect the mirror, buy the henna and find an amplifier for the band. Baba took a fistful of lavender, crushed it in his hand and sprinkled it into the water – an old chef garnishing his soup. As soon as he left the house, Soraya would remove the lavender with a tea strainer and pour a splash of her own lily-of-the-valley perfume into the highest bowl. The perfume would splash from one bowl to the next for several hours, and would remain forever in the minds of hundreds of Afghan women who would always associate the scent with their wedding day.

Soraya waged a one-woman campaign against the increasingly popular western-style wedding and the secret of her success was planning. No detail was too small not to merit her fullest attention, and an evening wedding meant a day's work. Baba's three jobs would force him out of the house and out of the way until five in the afternoon, an hour or so before the guests would begin to arrive. In this time Soraya and her two daughters prepared all the food and decorated two high-backed chairs where bride and groom would receive their guests with fresh flowers from the garden. They set and decorated the six round tables which Soraya had squeezed into the main dining room, and assembled a raised stage for the band in the hall. Finally, Soraya would attach her feather duster to a broomstick and carefully polish the old French chandelier that hung from the centre of the dining room ceiling.

Baba's tasks took even longer than his wife had estimated, and by the time he got home there was already a short line of taxis and private cars idling in the road outside the guesthouse. Soraya was organising the close relatives of the bride and groom into a receiving line at the gate and cousin Ali had attached his tiny DV camera to a tripod that looked far too large for it. He crouched behind, ready to film the early arrivals.

The ceremony started well. The married couple made an attractive pair and seemed enchanted both with each other and with the day. The groom endeared himself to Baba by commenting favourably on the quality of the garden and the fountain, and Baba reciprocated by being more generous than usual with the complimentary drinks. When the band played the opening bars of the *Ahesta Boro*, the slow wedding march marking the bride and groom's arrival, the guests stood and Soraya pulled herself up against the door frame and stood on tiptoes to take in the scene. It seemed to her that everyone invited had gone to the greatest trouble. Neither family was wealthy, but whatever good jewels the women had, they were wearing, and it was obvious many women had come straight from the beauty salon to the wedding reception. Soraya admired their finely embroidered kameezes and colourful silk headscarves. In her experience, you could usually count on the women to make an effort, only to be let down by their men. But not so today. The young men in the room wore what she recognised from magazines to be the latest in western-style suits with gaudy patterned ties. The older men were more soberly dressed but every suit was pressed, many wore buttonholes and there were even a couple of old Tajiks with dyed beards and embroidered pillbox hats. She went to find her husband, to remind him to tell Ali that he mustn't only film the pretty young women, but also to try and persuade him to come and watch some of the wedding. Baba was in the garden smoking a Turkish cigarette.

'I keep getting ambushed by aunties. They talk at me for an hour but it seems they still have more talk left.'

Baba reluctantly allowed himself to be dragged back inside. Soraya gave him a large glass of punch and stood between him and the exit. Slowly the mood in the room, the joy, percolated through Baba too. The Nikah ceremony, which he usually tried hard to miss, finding it old-fashioned and fake, on this occasion almost moved him to tears. He watched, beaming, as close relatives covered the bride and groom in a richly decorated shawl and then, reaching beneath the cloth, passed them the large silver-framed mirror he had collected earlier from the antique dealer. The pair giggled as they looked at each other in the mirror, and then he and all the other guests craned their necks closer to hear the groom's shy but certain voice as he recited an extract from the Koran:

'And one of His signs is that He created mates for you from yourselves that you may find rest in them and He put between you love and compassion; most surely there are signs in this for a people who reflect.'

Baba reached instinctively for Soraya's plump hand and held it firm. The music started again and the guests nearest to the door parted to allow a small girl, no more than seven years old, wearing a white dress and in bare feet, to come twirling through the crowd. She was carrying a silver tray of candles, flowers and small clay dishes containing henna. She danced her way round the room and up to the bride and groom, passing them the tray with a modest curtsey.

The wedding party was dancing its second and final Attan when the bomb exploded. Baba felt the blast before he heard it: all the guests were inside the house but the front door had been left open against the heat and the bomb sucked the air suddenly from the room. Then the large window in the front room seemed to bow

16

and bend before cracking neatly down the centre. Baba would remember this cracking sound more clearly than the deafening bang that followed. The explosion smashed the window and a hail of shattered glass filled the room. Next there was silence before the sound of a small child sobbing was drowned out by Baba's loud voice, shouting for everyone to stay low and remain where they were, in case of a second blast. Soraya's chandelier swung from side to side, shedding glass like tears.

Baba waited for as long as his instincts would allow – half a minute, which felt to him like half an hour. Then he caught Ali's eye, stood and headed for the door, his cousin following him, camera in hand. The blast had come from the direction of Savi's tailor's shop, just down the street from the guesthouse, and Baba strode through the garden and into the road expecting to see the shop destroyed. In fact the building was still standing although it was burning furiously, flames pushing outwards from a huge hole where the front door used to be. The signage, windows and decorative coping were all gone. Baba moved closer but then paused. He doubted whether anyone could have survived such a blast. He saw a bloodied limb lying on the step in front of the shop, like a leg of lamb on a butcher's slab. Then the screaming started.

What little passing traffic there was at that time of night had stopped and people were getting out of their cars to help or take a look. But one car kept moving, weaving through the stationary vehicles and away from the explosion. The dark blue Toyota travelled slowly up Passport Street, signalled right, and turned on to the main road.

The blast moved the pane of glass in Vivian's window enough to dislodge some of the dried putty from one side of the frame. She threw down her book, rolled off the single bed and peered out. It was hard to see much. The windows were filthy and had thick gaffer-tape crosses stuck on them corner to corner. She carefully lifted a window and leant out. Her eyes swept the horizon, pausing when she saw a pall of dark smoke and dust billowing from somewhere to the east. It was close. Maybe four or five kilometres. The cloud rose and spread as she watched, blossoming grey and white against a red sky. Vivian Fox pulled on her boots and grabbed her shoulder bag from a plastic coat hook on the back of the door. She carried this shoulder bag everywhere; inside were two digital Marantz sound recorders, half a dozen sound cards, two mics, leads and spare leads, an instruction manual and enough batteries to record several days' worth of audio if that were required. She checked the equipment every morning and evening, in case sand or dust had somehow fouled the mechanism. But on this assignment that was unlikely. So far the man she was meant to be working with hadn't allowed her to open the bag, preferring instead to use his old MiniDisc recorder, which he kept in his jacket pocket wrapped in a plastic carrier bag. Vivian opened the door to her clothes cupboard and looked herself up and down in the three-quarter-length mirror: beige cargo pants with a white linen shirt tucked in and buttoned almost to the neck; on her feet, a pair of new Bata boots; no jewellery, no make-up; black hair pulled into a neat ponytail. She checked her trouser pocket for the plain navy-blue headscarf she wore everywhere outside of the BBC house or the several hotels where the rest of the western media had set up shop.

'Okay,' she muttered to herself, 'let's try again.'

She walked down the corridor and knocked gingerly on William Carver's door. She hadn't spoken to her colleague since the early hours of the morning and was uncertain how much of the awkward evening the reporter would remember. William had made a drunken pass at her in a hotel bar in front of fellow journalists and then again in the taxi on the way back to the BBC house. The polite goodnight peck on the cheek had not felt like the full stop she was hoping for, and sure enough, ten minutes later, Carver had rapped on her door waving a bottle of cheap vodka and a couple of plastic glasses.

'How do you fancy a nightcap?' The lenses of his gold-rimmed spectacles were smudged and sweat had plastered strands of thinning black hair to his freckled scalp.

Vivian had tugged her oversized white T-shirt down to cover a little more thigh. 'William. It's a really sweet idea but it's been such a long day. I want to be up in time to listen to your programme online. We're three and a half hours ahead here so . . .'

Carver had scowled and shoved the plastic glasses into the pocket of his blazer jacket, but had kept hold of the bottle. 'I know what the bloody time difference is between London and Kabul.'

'I'm sorry. But, hey listen—'

Vivian had been about to offer an olive branch: breakfast or a drink tomorrow. Carver didn't let her. He had leant in closer, his breath sour, flecks of white spittle at the corners of his mouth. 'No, you listen. I find my own stories, I do my own interviews and I mix my own bloody packages. So if you aren't here for fun, Viv, what are you here for?' He had turned away, and as she closed her bedroom door, Vivian heard angry mumbling and the metallic snap of the vodka bottle top being twisted open.

The question Carver posed was the same one she'd been asking herself for the last five days, as she traipsed around after the reporter while he did his best to ignore her. She'd been warned that William Carver could be hard work, that he was set in his ways, but she'd never known a journalist so suspicious. And suspicious not of a source or a story, but of his own producer.

Vivian checked her watch. Nearly thirteen hours had passed since she'd snubbed his invitation and she hadn't seen hide nor hair of Carver since. She knocked again, this time a little harder. Nothing. She tried the handle, the door was unlocked and swung open easily, knocking against the empty vodka bottle and sending it rolling slowly across the carpeted floor. Vivian's eye followed its lazy arc past wall, bathroom door, window and . . . William. He was lying naked, stomach up and waxy white in the middle of his double bed. The arm nearest to Vivian hung over the side, hand nearly touching the floor but still holding a plastic glass. She swallowed a gasp and reversed quickly out the room, closing the door gently behind her. She took a few breaths and then banged her fist hard on the door frame while shouting his name.

'William, William. It's Viv.' She heard some muttering and, finally, footsteps. William wrenched open the door and squinted at her. He was wrapped in a thin blue bathrobe several sizes too small. He struggled a moment with his spectacles, the arms twisted like ballerina's legs. Unwrapping them carefully, he planted them across his nose and focused.

'What d'you want? You changed your mind?' He looked down at the empty bottle on the floor. 'The vodka's all gone.'

'It's Thursday night, William. You've slept all day.' Vivian pointed over William's shoulder at the window behind him, grimy and gaffer-taped like her own. 'There's been an explosion, a bomb blast, I think. It's nearby. I thought you might want to check it out?'

William nodded. 'Yeah? Yeah, okay. I thought I heard something. I'll get my stuff together. Come in and wait. Won't take me a minute.'

He turned back towards the bathroom leaving the door ajar. Vivian walked in slowly and stood by the bed. From the other side of the bathroom door, she heard the buzz of an electric shaver and then what sounded like the noise of a dog being choked – this became a slightly softer hacking and hawking while Carver cleared his sinuses. She heard the flush of a toilet but no shower or running water, and in moments William was back, dressed in the same clothes he'd been wearing the night before.

You can hang a lot of weight on a six-foot frame but you can't hang sixteen stone without it showing here and there. Carver was wearing faded, ill-fitting jeans, which were held up around where his waist should have been by a thick brown belt. His white shirt was half tucked in, half hanging out, with at least one button missing in action, and his blue blazer jacket was in need of a wash and press. He wore black trainers over white socks, and in his hand he carried a yellow plastic carrier bag.

'No time for a shower, I guess,' he coughed. 'A tart's bath will have to do.' He caught a disapproving look cross his colleague's face. 'My mum used to call it that. Can you chuck us the aftershave?'

He nodded in the direction of a dark green bottle with a picture of a camel on it. Vivian fetched it from the bedside table, handed it to him and watched as he splashed it around his neck, chest and armpits. A strong smell of sandalwood filled the room. 'I need to make a phone call. How about you go get me some food and I'll see you downstairs.'

'I beg your pardon?' Vivian had accepted that Carver was unlikely to treat her as an equal but she was still not ready to be treated like a servant. She stared at the reporter and he glared back. He obviously saw nothing unusual in the request.

'What? You're my producer, aren't you? Kind of. Well then, go produce me some dinner. Just a cheese sandwich. And a sweet tea – milk and three.'

The BBC house in Kabul was an anonymous whitewashed apartment building not far from the several big hotels where the other media lived. It was remarkable only in that it was one storey taller than most of the surrounding properties and its main selling point was it overlooked a particularly ruined part of Kabul. The television people who made the decisions about where to be based knew a good location for a piece-to-camera when they saw one. Vivian walked down the five stone-floored flights to the ground-floor lobby where there was a glass coffee table strewn with recent copies of the *Herald Tribune*, a brown three-seater sofa and a white Formica reception desk, empty save for a cream-coloured finger-dial phone *circa* 1980, wired to the wall and working but which no one had ever heard ring or had reason to use. Behind this makeshift reception was a basic kitchen.

A handsome man somewhere in his indefinable fifties stalked the lobby. He was suntanned, wore a white tailored suit, had a long nose and a plume of greying hair, and resembled a rare and rather valuable tropical bird. Vivian nodded at him and he nodded back, eyeing her up and down. They had been introduced the night before and the night before that, but it was clear to Vivian that he still couldn't place her.

'Morning Mr Brandon,' she offered, cheerily. He mumbled a response. John Brandon was not just another reporter. He was a presenter, the face of the *Ten O'Clock News*; live every evening from the cavernous Studio One in New Broadcasting House. He was in Kabul because the BBC had decided the forthcoming Afghan election was a major world news event requiring blanket coverage including a jewel in the crown: an outside broadcast, anchored by Brandon, live into the *Ten*. Vivian skirted past him and went into the kitchen. She filled the electric kettle from the tap marked 'drinkable' and planted it on its base; when she flicked the switch to turn it on, the kitchen and lobby lights dimmed a little – electricity was an unreliable commodity and the expensive petrol generator the BBC had bought was only to be used when it was broadcast-critical. Vivian buttered two slices of white bread and placed several slices of orange American cheese in between before pressing the whole thing together with the palm of her hand. From where she was she could see Brandon pacing up and down, increasingly agitated, waiting for someone else to find a solution to his problem. When William eventually puffed his way to the foot of the stairs, Brandon brightened. Ignoring the reporter's obvious attempt to avoid him, he boldly walked up and clapped him heavily on the back.

'Carver, how are you doing?' His voice was unnecessarily loud and didn't wait on a reply. 'Look. Can you give me a lift to this bombing? I've done a quick piece to camera on the roof but I need to get there while it's still smoking and some tosser's parked in front of the garage. Help a buddy out?'

The slap on the back had become a friendly arm around the shoulder which William was trying to shuffle free from. But to Vivian's surprise, Carver nodded. 'Sure, John. I can help. Why don't you meet us outside in ten minutes? I'm going to fetch my fixer from the hotel. We can pick you up on the way back round.'

'Good man. I'll go and find my shoot-edit.'

Vivian let Brandon leave before handing William a paper bag with the cheese sandwich inside and a polystyrene cup of tea.

'Cheers.'

He took a gulp of tea, and Vivian noticed a slight tremor in his hand as he lifted the drink to his mouth and looked away.

'You said we're going to get your fixer. So am I finally going to meet the mysterious Karim?'

'I guess so.' Carver dropped the sandwich into his plastic carrier bag and headed for the door.

It was only a ten-minute walk from the BBC house to the hotel, but by the time they got there Carver was already sweating heavily. The back of his neck was glazed and there was a tidemark on his shirt, up around his navel. Whenever possible, he tried to avoid meeting Karim in places like this. He didn't encourage contact with other journalists, fearing they might take Karim from him, offering him a contract, a pay rise and a general improvement on his current terms and conditions with Carver. But sometimes there was no choice. The two garages at the BBC house were reserved for TV transport and so the hotel car park was the easiest and safest place to keep the red Honda that William had bought and Karim drove.

Karim Mumtaz was William's best-kept secret and most valuable asset. Orphaned by the Taliban and educated in a missionary school, Karim met Carver in the first few days of the American operation in Afghanistan. He was a driver then, ferrying hacks from hotel to hotel, press conference to press conference. But William had quickly realised he was capable of far more. Karim had a journalist's nose and a gift for languages. He spoke Pashto, Dari, French and some Russian as well as a smattering of English. William had made him a deal. Whenever he was in Kabul, Karim would work exclusively for him. In return, Carver made a number of promises, most of which he'd already kept. He had promised and delivered a textbook and audiotape Teach Yourself English course, which Karim had completed in a fortnight. He'd promised to help Karim learn shorthand and other basic journalistic skills. Finally, he'd promised to speak to a charity in London, which he hoped might be able to help Karim with his most obvious problem.

Two dusty potted palms stood sentry either side of the dark glass sliding doors of the Intercontinental. There is a particular atmosphere in a press hotel; beneath the fragile bonhomie lies a thick layer of rumour and paranoia. In the lobby and the bar, journalists sat around trying to look confident and casual but feeling the very opposite. Every new arrival and departure was carefully observed. Big-name TV correspondents peacocked around, arriving and departing with great purpose and at speed, their producers, soundmen, cameras and translators running alongside. William spotted Karim standing off to one side, watching it all from a safe distance. He walked over, put a sweaty hand on his fixer's wrist and pulled him towards the exit.

'Come on, let's go. The story'll be cold before we get there. Where've you parked?'

'A good place, right by the barrier.'

Karim led the way and they were at the car before he realised that Vivian was with them, half-jogging to keep up. He unlocked the Honda with a click of the key fob and held the back door open for her. 'Hello, I'm Karim. Mr Carver's translator.'

Vivian nodded. The young Afghan was wearing a black leather-look jacket and freshly ironed shirt with a ballpoint pen poking out of the breast pocket. He had combed hair and deep-set, dark eyes. When Vivian smiled and extended a hand, he smiled back and only then did she see the extent of his cleft lip. The top half of Karim's mouth broke open to reveal a curl of bright pink flesh just beneath his nose. She widened her smile in response and held his hand warmly. 'Pleased to meet you, Karim. William's always talking about you. I'm Vivian, Mr Carver's producer.'

Karim climbed into the front seat and, adjusting the rear-view mirror, he caught her eye again. 'A pleasure to meet you, Vivian. Please forgive my ignorance, I did not know Mr Carver had a producer.' He spoke a careful, formal English.

William shifted in his seat. 'I don't. Not really. Now can we get going?' He pulled at a lever beneath him and pushed his seat back as far as it would go, narrowly missing Vivian's legs.

Karim slipped the car into gear and edged out of the car park. William was busy patting at his various trouser and blazer pockets. Eventually he found a small brown plastic bottle, fumbled with the child-proof seal, tipped three pills on to his palm and swallowed them while Vivian watched.

'What are the pills for, William?'

'For fun. You want one?'

'No thanks.'

'Didn't think so.'

Almost as soon as they left the press hotel car park they found themselves in heavy traffic. They lapsed into an awkward silence until William slapped a hand on the dashboard. 'Oh, yeah, I forgot. Karim, can we make a quick stop back at the BBC house? We gotta get something.'

'Right away.'

Karim waited for a gap in the oncoming cars, made a neat U-turn and worked his way back to the BBC's building. A battered van was still blocking the entrance to the garage.

'Viv, can you do us a favour? Jump out and get Brandon, will you?' It was the most civil request Carver had made yet. She smiled and slid across the back seat, jumping out on to the pavement and disappearing into the house.

When she got back to the street with Brandon and his cameraman in tow, the car was gone.

2 London Calling

DATELINE: New Broadcasting House, Portland Place, London, W1, June 21st

The *Today* programme office on the third floor of New Broadcasting House was a mess during daylight and even worse at night. Patrick could pick out the distinct smells of supermarket korma, photocopier toner, industrial carpet shampoo and milk on the turn. Grey desks were arranged in three rows, each lit by a harsh tungsten glare; one for the planning team, one for the duty editor and producers and one for the reporters.

Patrick Reid had first been asked to night-edit a month earlier. It seemed to him a huge responsibility and he was still on probation – or, as the editor Rob Mariscal had put it, 'there till he fucked up or fell off air'. Tonight would be his sixth programme and only the third that was the full three hours long (the others had all been shorter Saturday editions). It would comprise three hours of six news bulletins, five major lead slots and at least twenty-six different stories in total. A fourteen-hour shift, seven million listeners, two highly paid, highly strung presenters and one person in charge: him.

His previous programmes had been patchy at best. He had been nervous and the nervousness had infected the rest of his team and eventually the presenters as well. After the last post-programme meeting, Mariscal had taken Patrick to one side. 'This is one of the toughest jobs in journalism. You need to make quick, clear decisions and hold to them. Your story selection ain't bad but it needs to be broader, not just the boring, worthy stuff. You need to get the presenters and your team to listen to you and respect you. How 'bout you start by trying not to look so fucking terrified all the time? You understand?'

Patrick understood and had tried to take this advice on board, particularly the part about appearing confident. After consultations with his girlfriend and a long look at his bank balance, they'd spent what felt like a small fortune in Paul Smith on a new shirt and a pair of trousers. Patrick initially balked at the price tag and enquired about a sale rail, but Rebecca was insistent: 'It's not an indulgence, Patrick, it's an investment. Grown-up clothes for a grown-up job.' As he performed a self-conscious twirl in the otherwise empty changing room, even Patrick could see that the new clothes did something different to his skinny six-foot two frame. Rebecca confirmed the suspicion: 'They work. It's the high waistline I reckon, and the cut. The trousers make you look tall instead of just gangly and the blue in the shirt brings out the blue in your eyes.'

The Turkish barber that had been cutting Rebecca's father's hair for thirty years performed a similar conjuring trick on Patrick's mop of brown hair and the final touch came in the form of a second-hand brown leather belt which Rebecca found for him in Brick Lane market, well-worn but obviously well loved. Rebecca threaded it through the belt loops on the new trousers and tightened it at the highest hole. 'There you go. So every time you fasten that belt, you straighten your back. No more stooping, got it?'

The evening rush hour had delayed Patrick but he still arrived in the office at half past seven, thirty minutes ahead of a handover meeting when the team which had been working on the programme all day would deliver an à la carte menu of news stories, correspondents' names, political heavyweights, features and fillers from which Patrick must construct his programme. These were the 'prospects'. He arrived early in order to read himself in, check his emails and see what the other parts of the BBC and rival news organisations were planning for the next morning. The four people who made up the day team were hunched over computers, tying down the final details of the stories they had been working on before the prospects were printed. Overseeing them was a wiry woman dressed in a black trouser suit. The duty day editor: Amanda Lake. On the other island of desks a couple of reporters were shutting down their computers, packing up and getting ready to leave. The only unexpected presence was a member of the night team who had arrived even earlier than Patrick and now had his feet up on the desk, reading the late edition of the *Evening Standard*, a half-finished curry at his elbow. Martin Mainwaring wore a white button-down shirt with silver cufflinks and the bottom half of a pinstriped suit; a strange choice for an all-nighter but Martin's regular uniform nevertheless. His short back and sides was combed and, by the look of it, Brylcreemed too. He glanced at Patrick in feigned surprise. He had small green eyes and the beginnings of a boozer's nose.

'All right, Paddy? It's not you in the big chair tonight, is it?'

The enquiry sounded friendly enough but something about Martin's tone betrayed him. He knew full well that Patrick was in charge tonight and, more importantly, that he was not. He was one of two back-up producers despite the fact that he'd been at the programme for three years, as opposed to Patrick's few months. The story went that about a year ago, after much pleading, Martin had been given his first shot at night editing but it had gone very badly. He had frozen. The programme had almost fallen off air and the presenters had rebelled. Under Rob Mariscal you seldom got a second chance. But no one had told Martin.

'Evening Martin. I'm afraid it is me, so prepare for a bumpy night.' Patrick smiled apologetically. He received the thinnest possible smile in return.

'You're not kidding, mate.' Martin lowered his voice to a stage whisper. 'I've had a look at the prospects. Biggest pile of shit I've ever seen.'

Patrick's stomach lurched slightly.

Martin returned to his newspaper, turning the pages noisily. Each desk had a computer screen and keyboard, an eight-inch television monitor and a digital receiver with headphones which allowed you to listen to radio stations, TV channels and feeds from all over the world. Patrick chose a desk as far from his colleague as possible. Many of the TV monitors had been left on and were switched to quad-screen mode, allowing four different channels to be viewed simultaneously: BBC World alongside Al Jazeera above CNN and Sky. A few of the journalists had also left their computer monitors on with the newswire services ticking over. The newswires still had the power to hold Patrick, and instead of logging on, he found himself staring at a neighbouring screen as the stories tumbled in. They came from Reuters, AFP, AP, PA, TASS and others. Any dispatch that an agency considered important was flashed at the top of the page: *TASS, Caucasus Two Police Dead*.

If a wire was considered urgent, then a bolt of lightning symbol appeared alongside it. The headlines piled in upon each other, each new one pushing its predecessor down the screen until eventually it fell off the bottom. Patrick read a few of the recent arrivals:

BC US Ohio failed Execution, 5th lead Writethru. Judges halt second attempt at lethal injection after a 2-and-a-half-hour attempt fails to kill man.

BC Iraq Crime Wave. Kidnappers holding a teacher's 10-year-old son gave him two days to find $90,000. When he could not pay they chopped off the boy's head and hands and left the body parts at a city dump.

US Casino Tattoo. An American mother has had the name of a casino permanently tattooed on her forehead after selling advertising space to pay her child's school fees.

There were more stories than you knew what to do with, more stories than you could ever tell. As he watched, a new wire dropped. A flashed story from AP in Afghanistan, slugged *BOMB BLAST KABUL*. A suspected Taliban attack had killed several people in central Kabul. There was very little detail but Patrick read what there was: small death toll, no westerners, no Allied forces. He clicked the cursor and closed the story down.

Patrick pulled himself away from the wires and tried to focus on his own programme. He logged in and checked his messages and then the night schedule: a daily PA wire which ran through the domestic and international stories expected to make news overnight and in the following day's papers. Patrick printed a copy of this off and was making notes when his second producer turned up. Hilary Gore was just twenty-five but she wore clothes Patrick's mum would consider frumpy. He had taken against her early on, alienated by her strident Home Counties accent and overheard conversations with 'mummy'. But, slowly, he had come to realise that she was one of the hardest-working and most diligent journalists the programme had. Rob had destroyed her confidence in one brutal morning meeting six months before, and ever since, Hilary had preferred to work the night shift. Patrick considered this his good fortune. She had identified him as a fellow struggler and adopted him. As he watched, Hilary pulled a bundle of old newspaper from her tote bag and placed it on his desk.

'What's this?'

'Open it, you wazzock.'

Patrick unwrapped the parcel tentatively. Inside was a slightly faded, second-hand coffee mug with a chip on the lip. He held the mug up and turned it round: 'Happy Birthday Patrick,' it read.

'I saw it at our village jumble sale and I thought: I know the very man. Twenty pence!'

'Thanks, Hilary, that's really kind.'

A slight blush coloured Hilary's neck. She shook her head. 'It's not a token of affection, Patrick; it's an environmental intervention. I've counted how many paper cups you go through in a night shift and it's an outrage. Now you've no excuse. You have to use your mug for tea, coffee and water, no excuses. You and me together, Patrick, saving the planet one paper cup at a time.' She planted her bottom on a revolving chair and struggled with her Hunter wellies, their tread filled with rich, dark soil, until inching them off to reveal a pair of firm calves and thick red hiking socks. Amanda was standing watching, unsmiling, at the door to Rob's empty office. She waved a sheath of papers in his direction.

'I've got the prospects and a life to get on with. Can we do this?'

The handover meeting was brief and business-like. Amanda ran swiftly through the stories, first home news, then foreign, providing only the minimum information required. Patrick got the same feeling he always did from Amanda; that she disliked him but not strongly and for no particular reason. She raced through the prospects and a meeting that often took an hour lasted half that, which was fine by Patrick. He flicked through the four pages one more time, Rob's advice about appearing confident rattling around his head.

'What about that failed execution in Ohio? It sounded pretty nasty.'

Amanda pushed her glasses a little further up her thin nose. 'You can fix a two-way on that if you like. I didn't think it was a big deal.'

Patrick nodded. 'And did you see that wire that just dropped? A bomb blast in Kabul?'

Amanda shifted in her seat. 'I saw it. It doesn't look like there's much in it. It's the election next week and the whole BBC News machine's going huge on that, so unless we can't avoid it, we're meant to leave Afghanistan alone.'

'Okay. Who told you that? Rob?'

'No, it came from higher than Rob. I don't know who made the call, but it was well above my pay grade, Patrick, which means it was way, way above yours.'

3 The Leather-bound Book

DATELINE: Passport Street, central Kabul, June 21st

Karim steered the Honda expertly through the dusty back streets, circumventing several roadblocks, and eventually parking just one street away from the tailor's shop. Both men remained silent throughout the journey. William was waiting for the painkillers to work and trying to forget about having ditched Vivian back at the BBC house. This wasn't easy; Karim's disapproval, while not verbal, was palpable.

As his translator locked the car, William snapped: 'I had my reasons, all right, Karim? Good reasons, so can we just leave it at that?'

Karim's nod was cold comfort and as they walked in the direction of the police sirens Carver considered his good reasons. He hadn't had a producer in years, hadn't needed one, so why would the BBC insist on assigning someone now, unless they had an ulterior motive? It seemed to William that the motive was blindingly obvious: they wanted rid of him, he'd been told as much by the head of personnel, and Vivian's job was to help build a case against him. What other explanation was there?

Carver and Karim had reported on enough firefights, bombings and Taliban attacks to have settled into a familiar pattern; a division of labour that played to both men's strengths and which accommodated William's weaknesses. William would approach any English-speaking witnesses and get what he could on tape, while Karim would attempt to talk or bribe his way round the police cordon. Carver started at the guesthouse. The wedding reception had broken up and the guests were gone but the owner was more than happy to sit down with him. He offered William a green tea, which was refused, then a whisky with ice, which the reporter accepted with muttered thanks. Hair of the dog. He took out his recorder, notepad and pen — the shake in his right hand still there but not so noticeable — the pills would start to work soon and the scotch would surely help.

'Okay, sir, so is it Mr Baba or Baba something?' he asked.

'Just Baba. Everybody knows Baba.'

William doubted whether everyone back in Britain was familiar with Baba, but he let it pass. The big man had what looked like small shaving cuts around his face, neck and hands but seemed otherwise unhurt.

'Was anyone at the wedding party among the dead or injured?'

Baba answered in the negative. There were a few people with small cuts like him but thankfully no women or children had been hurt. Then he went off on a confusing tangent, talking about a fountain which had been damaged and a ceremonial mirror that had been smashed and would have to be replaced. Carver listened patiently and when Baba had finished he pressed the stop button on the MiniDisc and deleted the file. None of it was of any use. He tried again.

'Okay. So, Mr Baba. Let's go back to the beginning, can we? In your own words, can you tell me exactly what happened?' Carver laid the foam-headed microphone back on the table and pressed record. The green lights on the machine danced up to red and then found their level. When Baba coughed they bounced up again, too high for William's liking. He tweaked a dial, then sat back in the chair, pen in one hand, whisky in the other.

William was getting the feeling that Baba had told this story a couple of times already and that it was being lightly polished with each new telling. He didn't mind that. His job had taught him to wait, to let people say what they wanted to say in their own time. As Baba told his tale, William's hand steadied and his head cleared. He made the occasional shorthand note and nodded and shook his head at the appropriate moments, reassuring his interviewee, asking the right questions at the right time, drawing out the details. Whatever else he had lost, whatever other people thought of him, he was still a good listener.

'I ran over the road, very fast.' Baba moved his arms at his side, miming. 'I was about to run into the shop, into the flames, when my cousin stopped me. "It is suicide," he said and I think he was definitely correct and anyway the first emergency vehicle arrived very soon then.'

'I see, so what are we talking about? Twenty minutes after the blast? Thirty?'

'No. Five or ten minutes maximum. Ambulance. Ali, my cousin, he said they must have been passing because usually you wait and wait and wait. Long time.'

'Yes. That is unusual . . . Lucky.'

At first Baba nodded, but then stopped and shook his head. 'Not lucky, not really. Everybody inside was already dead. The police and army closed up the street and started taking the bodies away, straight away. A great tragedy.'

Carver gave a sympathetic nod. 'Yes. I hear an important local politician is among the dead. Do you know anything about him?'

Baba looked up and wiped his nose on the sleeve of his black chapan. He had changed out of his wedding outfit into this more sombre loose shirt with wide sleeves.

'No. But I heard this too. I do not know who he is.' He paused and lowered his eyes. 'It is not the politician I am upset for. We have plenty of politicians, but Mr Savi was one of the last good tailors left in Kabul. This shirt' – Baba pulled at the front of his chapan – 'he made this shirt. Mr Make-to-Measure, we called him. He was a good man.'

Baba choked a little and William looked away as the man's brown eyes filled with tears. He pressed a button on his recorder, stopped the recording and saved the sound file. In time Baba gathered himself, pulled a large white handkerchief from somewhere inside the folds of his shirt and blew his nose loudly.

'Mr Carver?'

'Yes, sir?'

'I would like to try and tell the story again. I missed some things, I think, and I owe it to my friend to say it well.' William nodded.

He pressed the record button and waited, holding the notepad and pen out in front of him now and at a different angle. Baba retold his story, this time with more detail and less emotion. William knew it would be the first account he would use but he let the man talk and as he did, he studied his face and doodled. When Baba had finished, he put the notepad down on the table next to his empty glass. He was checking the tape recorder when he saw his interviewee stretch out a large hand and pick up the notepad.

'What were you writing there, can I see it?' He gave William no time to answer but started flicking through the pages until he found what he was looking for. On the left-hand page of the book was the day's date and a spidery scribble which looked more like Arabic than English but made no sense to Baba; on the right-hand page, spilling out from the margin, was a sketch of Baba.

Carver flushed. 'I'm sorry, it's just a doodle. A bad habit.'

Baba shook his head. 'Why are you sorry? It is good, it looks like me.'

Sure enough, with a few biro lines and some subtle shading, Carver had managed to capture the man sitting opposite him.

'Just like me. But I look sad.'

Carver shrugged. 'Well, yes.'

'It is correct, I am sad. When you draw me again, I will be happy.'

'Okay.'

'And you will do my better side. In this one' – he held the picture up for Carver to see – 'you have my bad side. Soraya, my wife, always tells me that my other side has a smaller nose and not so many chins. Next time you can draw that side. I will put it in a frame, it is her birthday in a month. Agreed?'

Carver smiled. 'Agreed. I should go and speak to my colleague now, Baba. Thank you for your time.' He raised his empty glass: 'And for the whisky. This is my card.' He handed over a BBC business card with all the phone numbers and email addresses crossed out and an Afghan mobile number written just beneath his name in biro. 'If you think of anything else, or if you just want to talk, give me a call.'

Baba put a meaty hand over his heart. 'You have my word.'

Karim had found a way through the police line and when William saw him he was standing talking to an Afghan officer guarding the scene. Carver waved him over.

'How's it going? Who's the dead politician? Anyone who's anyone?'

Karim took the red reporter pad that William had bought him out from his jacket pocket and flicked through the pages until he found his most recent notes. 'Four dead, the policeman says. The target was the new district chief, Fazil Jabar. You have heard of him?'

William nodded vaguely; it rang a distant bell.

Karim was happy to jog his boss's memory. 'Jabar signed up to the NATO counterinsurgency programme last month. He is – he was – very important. The Allies were very pleased.'

'Right. And it looks like he was spending some of the dollars they gave him on a few new suits . . .'

Karim nodded and continued. 'Three others passed away as well.'

Carver tutted. 'Don't use euphemisms.'

'I beg your pardon?'

'I don't want to hear you using euphemisms, weasel words like "passed away", "passed on", stuff like that. The dead haven't got much to look forward to, the least you can give them is the plain-spoken truth.'

Karim gave a shame-faced nod. 'I understand. So the other dead are his son, thirteen years old, his bodyguard – an old man who has worked for Jabar for years. They are both inside, all burnt up.'

William pointed a finger at Karim's notes. 'Charred. You'd say charred if you were writing this for broadcast. Not burnt up.'

'Charred. Okay. Yes.' Karim wrote this new word in his notebook in a slow and careful hand.

'So that's two bodies inside. What about Jabar and the other bloke, that's the tailor himself we're talking about, is it?'

'Yes, Jabar and Mr Savi, that's the tailor; they were taken away in a military ambulance. Very soon after the bomb, the police say.'

'I heard that too. Ten minutes, my witness said. Most Afghans have to call a cab to get themselves to the morgue. What made this guy so special?'

Karim shrugged. 'He was a big man. VIP.'

Carver nodded. 'Must've been. And did the police say how he and the tailor died? Blast? Burns?'

'Jabar was blown into pieces, died straight away, they say. The tailor was all burnt up – charred. The policeman told me he died in the ambulance.'

William stared into the distance, down towards the far end of Passport Street, weighing all this information up. 'How about the bomb? Did you get anything on that? Four bodies, not five, so not a suicide job. Remote control?'

'Might be. I had a look inside. There are some parts of broken suitcase, I think. They haven't cleaned up yet.'

'Can you get me in there before they do?'

Karim looked back over his shoulder; the Afghan policeman was watching them keenly. 'Maybe. The officer in charge, he's not friendly but he likes money. I gave him some Afghani but I think he would like American dollars even more.'

William reached for his wallet, pulled out a twenty-dollar bill and handed it to Karim. 'Try him on that for starters.'

Inside the shop was devastation. What hadn't been damaged by the blast or the flames had been drenched by the firemen. A string of bare light bulbs in wire mesh covers lit the scene. There were two bodies on the floor; both were covered with blue hospital sheets stained a deep bloody red in various places. The outlines of the bodies were clear and it was obvious which corpse was which: one was William's height and a similar build, the other that of a child. The policeman had told Karim that they were going to be removed soon and warned him not to touch; the deal was, they could look around but stay clear of the two dead bodies. William kicked at the rolls of linen and tweed scattered about the floor. Almost all were burnt and smoke-damaged beyond use. Karim found and pocketed a scrap of scorched circuit board, slipping it inside his jacket while the policeman was distracted by

William, who was stalking around like a black crow picking at carrion. The journalist was examining one of the tailor's shop dummies, still somehow standing upright and wearing a chalked-up suit in a Prince of Wales check. He noticed something interesting at the base of the mannequin and bent into a low crouch. Poking out from underneath a roll of white linen was a navy-blue, leather-bound appointments book. William picked it up and flicked through it quickly before stuffing it into his plastic bag. Both Karim and the policeman watched this unsubtle operation, and when William made to leave the shop, the officer held out an arm. Carver reached again for his wallet, removed three more American twenties and pressed them into the policeman's hand. Once outside the shop, the two men compared notes.

'I'll take a look through the tailor's appointments book in case there's anything interesting, but it looks pretty straight up and down to me.'

'Okay. But the circuit board is unusual. I will take it to Staff Sergeant Chaundy, yes?'

'Sure, check it out and I'll have a listen back to my interview, see if I can get some human interest out of it. If not, I reckon it's a short bulletins piece at best.'

Karim was disappointed.

'Are you sure? Fazil Jabar, he was a big man.'

'For us maybe. Not for London. *Taliban blows up American ally*. About as easy to sell as a Catholic Pope.'

In the car on the way back to the BBC house, William flicked idly through the leather-bound book, then a second time more slowly, and then a third. When Karim glanced over, he saw that the journalist was carefully turning down the top corners of several pages.

'You have found something?'

Carver looked up from the book, slightly startled. 'What? Oh, I don't know. It's probably nothing.'

*

Patrick had spent three hours considering his list, resolving to move things around and then changing his mind. He compared his programme with what other news outlets were planning and could see no significant omissions. Amanda had constructed a solid enough show, despite Martin's misgivings, and now he just had to steer it through the night. He typed *Kabul* into the newswire's search box again, the third time he had done this. The most recent update had a little more detail, but not much. The death toll had remained small and the name of the man who had been killed meant nothing to him. His team was settling in for a long and uneventful shift when the phone rang. Patrick got there first.

'Hello, *Today* programme?' He heard a stifled giggle at the other end of the line and then his girlfriend's clipped impression of what she called his posh work voice.

'Hello *Today* programme. Rebecca Black speaking.'

At the sound of her voice, Patrick relaxed. He felt his shoulders loosen. 'Hey. How are you?'

'I'm in bed, snug as a bug. I have Ovaltine and gossip magazines; I'm in seventh heaven. How are you? How's your list?'

Patrick sighed. 'Oh. It's all right. It's not going to pull up any trees.'

'Good. We like trees, don't we?' She took a sip of her drink. '*Ouch*! Hot. So anything I should be getting up early to listen out for?'

Patrick looked at his list again. It included interviews with a four-star general, a bishop, five politicians and a Harvard economist. His programme would make some news, it would generate stories that could be picked over through the day, but was there anything that Rebecca should set her alarm for? He opened three portrait-shaped windows on his computer screen, each containing one hour of the programme, and ran his eye over the rough running order Amanda had left for him.

'Nah, not really, baby, better you sleep.' He clicked the pages closed. 'I should get on with the programme, start reading the briefs. Sleep well.'

'Okay. And you stay awake well. Don't touch the salad till after two. I put a load of slow release carbohydrates in there, help keep you perky during the show.'

'Thanks, doll. See you tomorrow.'

Patrick stuck his mobile back in the front pocket of his rucksack and pulled out the Tupperware bowl of chicken salad that Rebecca had made for him. He peeled off the lid, gave it a sniff and tucked in. It was two hours too early but he was hungry and it was good. Maybe a little heavy on the dressing, which tasted like three parts garlic one part oil. Patrick had noticed that ever since he'd told Rebecca some of the stories he'd heard of night shift trysts in stationery storerooms and empty studios, his girlfriend had made food for him more often, and had upped the garlic content: 'To keep vampires at bay. And anyone who might want to snog you in the dead of night,' she'd explained.

He looked around. There was no one who wanted to snog him, in fact there was no one at all. He wondered where his team had gone. The phone rang again; the shrill sound made Patrick jump and he checked the clock. Midnight.

'*Today* programme.'

'Are you in charge?' It was Rob Mariscal.

'Hi Rob. Yeah it's me, Patrick. How are you?'

Mariscal ignored the pointless question. ''Ave you been interfered with yet?'

Patrick found himself slipping into a version of Rob's odd cockney. 'I got a quick call from Jamie just after the *Ten*.'

'All right. So what've you got?'

Patrick ran through the main stories he was planning to cover in the morning, the lead slots and a couple of other things he hoped might impress, including the failed execution in Ohio. There was a long pause at the other end of the line, the sound of a cigarette lighter failing to light, then another pause. 'Is that it?'

Patrick looked again at the running order on the screen in front of him. 'Er—yeah, that's about it.'

He heard Rob smack the lighter hard against his palm, light the cigarette and take a long pull. His editor was somewhere very quiet, very still. Something about the acoustics led Patrick to think he was outdoors, maybe at his place in the country, where he had a wife who no one had ever met and two or three children.

'Right. Well, it's not much good, is it? It's boring. You're going to have to change it.'

'Change what?'

'Change most of it, I reckon.'

'But, Rob, that's the stuff I was left.' Patrick realised his mistake the second he said it.

'What? I don't give a shit what you were left. You've been in charge for—for how long? Four hours? More than four hours and as far as I can see, you've done fuck all. So change it. Change it now. Make it better. Make it interesting. Make it *good*. That's your job.'

The phone line went dead. Patrick replaced the receiver slowly. He felt nauseous, his neck and face hot. His two colleagues had drifted back in during the call and now Martin was at his side, standing a little too close. He made no attempt to keep the glee from his voice. 'Rob not happy?'

'No. He wants some changes.' Patrick stared at his hands. They were shaking. Mariscal was famous for his temper, squalls of fury that would blow up in an instant and blow away just as quickly, but rarely without damage. Sometimes the temper would break someone's confidence the way a tornado breaks a house. And without confidence it was impossible to work at *Today*.

Patrick had seen it happen to other people but this was the first time he'd experienced it himself. Hilary and Martin looked at him expectantly. This was it then; this was what it was all about. Take charge, find stories, be decisive. He stood and stretched, unfastened and then refastened his new belt. He wasn't sure he could do it.

BBC house, central Kabul, Afghanistan, June 21st

Vivian had looked in Carver's room, in the kitchen, television room and various toilets before she'd thought to look for him up on the roof of the BBC house. She had spent the evening cursing the correspondent and considering her options. Taking the Kabul producer's job had come at a significant cost, both to her ageing parents' peace of mind and to her personal life. In the most recent round of BBC Newsgathering appointments, she was offered her pick of field producer jobs, including everyone else's favourite: Washington. But Vivian hadn't wanted the White House, she'd wanted this.

Her boyfriend of some two years standing, Donald, had been in the running for the same set of jobs, but while she had been offered her pick of foreign postings, he was offered nothing. Vivian's best friend had sounded the first alarm: 'How's Donald dealing with this?' 'Oh, don't worry. I've spoken to him, he's good, great in fact. He's taken it like a man.' 'That's what I'm worried about.'

Sure enough, Donald's mask slipped less than seventy-two hours later. The late-night text message he sent was long and rambling but once she subbed it down it amounted to the pretty straightforward accusation that she must have fucked someone in order to be offered the job she'd been offered. Looking back on it, Vivian wished Donald had written his bile-filled nonsense in an actual letter so that she could have burnt or shredded it – pressing *delete* seemed insufficient. So instead she kept it, returning to it now and again: 'It's like reading a cautionary tale,' she told friends, but sometimes she worried that rereading it, as she had done again earlier this evening, was more like an intellectual form of self-harm.

At the foot of the staircase that led from the top floor bedrooms to the roof, a hack with a grudge and a sense of humour had drawn a thick line in red marker and written above it the message: *WARNING! Beyond this point, journalism ends and television begins.*

Carver liked to spend time up on the roof, but only when the TV people were elsewhere. Given the number of different programmes and audiences the correspondents were serving, finding such quiet moments wasn't easy, but William had found that between three and four in the morning he could have the roof to himself. The air was cleaner there than on the street and the view was impressive. William had picked his way through the black spaghetti of TV cabling, past the arc lights and satellite dishes, to his favourite spot. He sat on a wooden folding chair watching the broken city sleep. When he heard movement, he looked back over his shoulder and saw Vivian approaching. He gave a half-hearted wave; there was no avoiding her now. She stopped directly in front of him and switched on an arc light. William winced and shielded his eyes. 'Hello.'

'What you did to me earlier was unforgivable, William. I've worked with some wankers in this job, but you take the biscuit, you really do.'

'Thanks.'

'I didn't ask for this job. Newsgathering assigned me to you and despite your reputation I agreed. Rob Mariscal approved it, you know that? In fact, he requested it.'

Carver looked up sharply, squinting against the glare. 'Mariscal asked that you were assigned to me?'

'Yeah. He probably wasn't given much choice. You haven't been on air in weeks, maybe months.'

Carver shrugged. This was technically true. He told anyone who asked that he was working on a long-form piece, something investigative, but that was as much detail as he would give. During his last few terms in Afghanistan, repeated requests from London for packages on a range of subjects – army recruitment, sniffer dogs, heroin reduction – were all met with the same surly silence. Hence Vivian, he supposed. A radio producer to help him produce some radio. 'I've filed bulletin pieces. And some other stuff.'

'All unusable, apparently.'

'Unused, not unusable.' William had heard that the intake desk in London referred to his occasional bulletin pieces as *grimgrams* – tales of everyday Afghan death and despair which no longer surprised anyone and were therefore, by definition, not news. 'Anyway, I'm going to file something tonight, on this tailor's shop bombing.'

Vivian looked around. She could see a half-empty bottle of red wine and one of the two sandwiches that she had made for him a few hours ago, curled at the corners. A large leather bound book, a photo album perhaps, stood propped against his chair leg, but there was no sign that William was working on anything. 'I don't believe you. And even if you were, I wouldn't bother. I spoke to London, they're not interested. Brandon's going to use some of the bombing to colour his telly piece tomorrow night. But they've already said they don't want anything from us . . . from you.'

William stretched. 'That's a bad call, Viv. You should've sold the story harder. Fazil—' he dredged his memory for the name, finding it in the nick of time '—Fazil Jabar was a big deal. A key NATO ally. This is an important story. The *Today* programme will take it if I give it a push. I'm going downstairs to put it together right now.'

Vivian hesitated, her anger now rather dissipated, replaced by uncertainty. 'Won't that kind of screw John Brandon's telly thing?'

'Then it's a win win,' muttered Carver, hauling himself up from the wooden chair.

4 A Little Story

DATELINE: *Today* programme offices, BBC News Centre, Portland Place, London, W1, June 22nd

Patrick wondered whether he was about to make a career-ending decision. How late was too late to disturb the man that had recently hired you and could easily fire you?

It was past two in the morning and Patrick had just put the phone down on Carver. He had a story, a decent story, worth a lead slot, he said. It was the sort of story Patrick hoped might just save his programme from a mauling. Mariscal's phone rang six times. Seven. Eight. Patrick was about to hang up when a tired voice answered:

'This better be *fucking* good.'

Patrick had a single sentence ready to go. 'Rob, it's Patrick—'

'I mean really fucking good. Like Lady Diana meets O. J. Simpson in Tiananmen fucking Square . . .'

'Er, yes. So Rob, this Afghan politician's been blown up in Kabul, a district chief, big player, he—'

'Wait, wait. You've called me at two in the morning to tell me there's trouble in Afghanistan?'

'No, no. Well, yes, but this is significant. Four dead and—'

'Four? Fucking four?'

'Yes.'

'Any Brits?'

'No.'

'Women, babies, bunny rabbits?'

'No, but—'

'Then tell me why I should give a shit?'

'Well, Carver says this guy is significant. Not a household name, at least not here, but important.'

There was a pause. Patrick heard Mariscal shuffling out of bed and standing up. There were footsteps as he left one room and entered another. A door closed.

'Did you say Carver? As in William Carver?'

'Yes. He rang and—'

'Wait, hold up. So Carver phoned you? What did he say, exactly?'

Patrick tried to remember the exact words. 'Well, he didn't introduce himself, but I knew the voice. I think he just said "I've got a little story."'

Mariscal's throaty laugh triggered a short smoker's coughing fit. 'Great. The five most dangerous words in journalism.'

Patrick was confused but ploughed on: 'The piece seems straightforward enough and I need another story. My problem is that Amanda warned me to leave Afghanistan alone because of the election. She said—'

'Forget that. Forget all that. That's just what the bosses want; it's what telly wants. A nice slow build-up to the election jamboree. They plotted the news trajectory on some grid weeks ago. That's not what we do, though, is it? If Carver says it's a story, then it's probably a story.'

Patrick could hear Mariscal weighing something up. A few seconds of silence. 'Okay, so listen. It's up to you, your call. You need something, a decent tale, and maybe this is it. I wouldn't mind hearing a bit of something from Afghanistan tomorrow, but it's your decision. Understand?'

'Sure. Great. Thanks. I'm sorry to—'

'And Patrick, when you speak to Carver, make sure to let him know it was your decision. Got that?'

'Yes, boss.'

'And remind him I need him back in London next week. I want to see his fat face at the summer party and if I don't, I'll cancel his credit cards and set fire to his flat. Tell him that. I'm serious.'

Even before he had had to endure it himself, Patrick considered the programme post-mortem a cruel ordeal. After every show, before they were allowed to head home, the night editor and his or her team had to sit and listen as Rob Mariscal, the presenters and anyone else who was in the office at ten past nine picked over their programme.

Patrick took the only empty seat left, on a purple three-seater sofa between Hilary and Martin. Both were the colour of dead coral; they were red-eyed and dog-tired and he was sure he looked no better. It had been a grim fourteen hours, it always was, and he was desperate for bed. The room waited in silence for Mariscal to speak. He was stretched out on the floor, back to the glass partition, wearing his usual black shirt, black shoes, black trousers, and reading a red top.

'So Patrick, how was that?'

Patrick looked at the running order on his lap, searching for highlights, redemption, and finding none. 'Well, I thought it went okay. We made a few changes overnight, added some stuff. Did what we could, you know . . .' He was mumbling. He was so exhausted he could barely formulate sentences. As he glanced up from his papers his eyes met Amanda's. The hostility in her face was alarming. 'So, yeah, anyway. I thought it was okay.'

Rob waited to see whether Patrick had anything more eloquent or interesting to say, and when it became clear he hadn't, he opened the discussion up to the room. 'Right then. So our battle-scarred night editor makes a heady claim. He says his programme was "okay". Do we concur?'

Compared to his previous programmes, the show got a fairly positive reception. William's Kabul story, which Patrick had decided to place prominently at half past seven, was popular, as was a moving interview about the failed Ohio execution. But somehow he got little credit for either. The only direct comment concerning Patrick came from Amanda, who questioned his decision to stick with the electoral reform story, which she herself had fixed for him at ten past eight, in the lead slot.

'It's easy in retrospect, I know' – she looked at Patrick – 'but I wonder whether it might have been, well, braver to go with the Afghan stuff at ten past eight? That was the breaking story, after all, and we don't often hear that kind of on-the-ground actuality that Carver gathered, do we?'

There were plenty of free seats on the Tube home to Highbury, but Patrick chose to stand. Twice that month he had fallen asleep on the Victoria Line and ended up in parts of north-east London he'd never seen before and never wanted to see again. By the time he reached the door to their top-floor flat his breath was quick and shallow and he felt like he'd run a long race. He dropped his rucksack in the hall, walked into the bedroom and pulled the curtains closed. He kicked off his shoes and fell face down on the bed. He was asleep in seconds, still fully dressed.

Rebecca got back from work just after five. The novelty of their newly rented flat had not yet worn off, and when she turned the Yale and saw her boyfriend's bag in the middle of the hall, it was affection, not irritation she felt. Peering round the bedroom door she saw Patrick sprawled on the duvet. He looked like he'd fallen from the sky, through the roof, landed on the bed, and somehow survived. She got a blanket from the airing cupboard and tucked it in around him.

He opened one eye and smiled. 'Hey.'

'Hey. I heard some of the show, sounded good.'

'Nah. I'm a disaster.'

'Shh. No you're not, you're a genius. Award-winning journalist. Remember?' Rebecca gestured at the opposite wall and a picture hanging there. She brushed a few strands of hair away from his eyes and placed her cold hand on his forehead. 'Sleep another hour. We'll talk later.'

Patrick squinted. From where he lay he could only see the outline and colours of the framed newspaper front page. It was the first thing they had hung on the wall when they moved in. Under the sky-blue *South London Press* banner, in 96 point Helvetica, it read: *INNOCENT: SAVED BY THE SLP*. They had forgotten his byline but it was his story nonetheless. His and Rebecca's.

Before his break at the BBC, Patrick had spent four years working at south London's finest local newspaper. He was the most junior of junior reporters but he had completed his training, got his qualifications and was writing his own stuff. He got a huge thrill from every byline, no matter how insignificant the story and whatever the assignment. He tried to be distinctive and to write well, clear and simple. Now and again he tried to get the odd rhetorical flourish past the subs. Most of the time he failed. He received regular lectures from the news editor, Keith Rockham, about respecting the house style and once or twice argued back, wondering out loud whether the house couldn't use a lick of paint or some geraniums in the window. Keith would hear him out patiently before batting him away.

'Listen, sunshine. The *South London Press* house style was working just fine before you arrived and it'll be going strong long after you fuck off to some gay broadsheet. So do what you're told.'

The week of the award-winning story and the life-changing meeting had been a slow one. South London's criminal underclass had failed to shoot, stab or molest enough people to fill all six news pages, and Keith was getting desperate. The day before the print deadline he was raking through the all but redundant fax tray when a previously unnoticed press release caught his eye. It had a childish drawing at the top, a sad-looking kid staring out of the window of a cartoon plane. Beneath, a handwritten headline proclaimed: *Innocent until proven guilty! Community rallies behind threatened family*. The amateur hack continued:

> *A Peckham mother and her two children are fighting deportation to the Congo. Piti Nollom, 38, and one of her two boys, five-year-old Jacob, are being held at Yarl's Wood detention centre after authorities took them from their home in Leighton Street at 5.30 a.m. on Monday of last week. Her eldest son, nine-year-old Innocent, is being allowed to continue with his schooling and is staying with a family friend but he too faces deportation! Rebecca Black of Peckham Green Primary School teaches the eldest child and is organising the campaign to stop the deportation and secure asylum for the family.*
>
> *'This family arrived in south London four years ago. They have settled in well and are valued members of our school and community. Piti is a Parent Representative and her son, Innocent, is a clever and kind young boy who deserves a chance. Piti believes she will be arrested and possibly killed if she is forced to return to the Congo. We are talking to lawyers who suggest there is strong evidence that could lead to a fresh appeal.'*

Dear South London Press, it concluded, *please help bring this story to the public's attention. YOU can make a difference!*

Keith dropped the other press releases in the bin and walked up to Patrick's desk. 'Paddy. Take a look at this one, will you? I need something and this lot have practically written the story for you. Go down and check it's not bullshit, make sure the family aren't a bunch of terrorists, get some photos, and Bob's your mother's brother, yeah?' He looked again at the press release and laughed. 'YOU can make a difference, Paddy, *YOU*! And even if you can't, you can fill a few inches on page 5. Go on, get busy.'

Patrick had phoned the school and arranged to meet the campaign organiser and the headmaster who was supporting them on the quiet. If he arrived just after school pick-up, the headmaster's secretary said, they'd keep some kids back, including Innocent. They would get permission from parents for a group photograph.

Rebecca Black met Patrick in the foyer. She stood five feet four in sensible shoes, had a neat blonde bob, blue eyes and bright red lipstick. She knocked Patrick sideways from the start. He spoke to her first and for significantly longer than was necessary. He had to ask more or less the same question several times before he remembered to make proper notes. He was trying to think of other, more interesting questions when she brought the interview to a close, insisting she introduce him to the headmaster, a couple of other teachers and some parents. She stayed with him while he quizzed them all, making copious notes in his best shorthand. Interviews over, he asked Rebecca to arrange Innocent and a few of the other children into a group so he could take pictures. Rebecca put Innocent at the centre of the group and placed herself on the fringe. It took Patrick a while to persuade her that she should be in the middle of the shot, alongside Innocent.

'Why do you need me in the middle?'

'Well, because you're the campaign organiser. At the *South London Press*, we always like to put the campaign organiser in the middle of the photo.'

'Really? That's a strange rule.'

'Well, maybe. But we always do it that way.'

When the photo-shoot was over, the children drifted home while

Rebecca waited patiently for Patrick to pack the camera and notebooks away inside his bag.

'So, do you know when the story might go in? The lawyers say a bit of publicity would really help right now. It'd be great if you could get it in this week's paper.'

'Well, it's up to my news editor, really.'

'Right. But maybe you could put in a good word?'

Patrick nodded. 'Yeah, I can try. In fact, you know what? I was just thinking. Or rather wondering. Maybe we could go get a drink and you could tell me a bit more about Innocent. Then I'd be able to make a stronger case, you know, to Keith, the news editor.'

Rebecca examined Patrick's face, her own softening a little. 'Are you suggesting, Mr Reid, that there's a better chance of your paper running this story if I buy you a drink?'

'Yes.'

'Surely I could report you for that.'

'Who to?'

'Your editor.'

'He'd be on my side. He's a monster.' Patrick grinned.

'The National Union of Journalists, then, or the Guild of Newspaper-people or something?'

'Nah. No hope.'

'Really? What kind of dreadful profession is it you work in?'

'A really dreadful, completely unethical one. If we went for a drink, I could tell you about it. It'll make your hair curl.' Patrick glanced at Rebecca's hair again. It didn't need to curl, it was perfect.

He woke an hour later to the sound of saucepans clanking and the smell of soy sauce. Rebecca crept into their bedroom in stockinged feet, a cup of coffee in her hand, and Patrick watched through half-closed eyes, feigning sleep. She had changed out of her work clothes and into a shift dress; sky blue with white polka dots. Rebecca saw a smile crease the corner of Patrick's mouth.

'Stop faking. I know you're awake. You have to lay the table. I've done everything else.'

Patrick went for a shower, changed into some clean clothes, and by the time he returned to the sitting room that doubled as a dining room; the table was laid and the candles lit. Rebecca had made his second favourite supper, her own-recipe Chinese stir fry, and had bought a bottle of good red wine – good meaning a bottle that cost six pounds rather than the usual four. They ate hungrily, talked little. He was about to pour them both a second glass when she cleared the small table and led him next door to the double bed. They made awkward love. Patrick still felt uncomfortable having Rebecca look at his naked frame and slightly guilty when allowed to look at hers. Afterwards she lay smiling up at him from the crook of his arm, and a watery spring sunlight was fading away outside.

'Okay, so how bad was work?'

'Well, we didn't fall off air.'

'That's good.'

'But I don't know how much longer I can do this for, Becs. I'm out of my depth.' His girlfriend shook her head. 'I really am. They all seem so sure, so certain. About everything.'

'I hate certainty.'

'Me too. But unfortunately in this job it seems to be more highly prized than chronic indecision, which is what I bring to the party.'

'It's not a party without chronic indecision.'

'Yeah.' He laughed quietly.

'How was the post-mortem? How did that go?'

Patrick shrugged and shuffled his arm out from underneath Rebecca's shoulder. He knew what was coming.

'Go on, tell me. Was Amanda Lake there? Did she say anything?'

Having heard Patrick recount a couple of Amanda's catty comments, Rebecca had formed a firm and entirely negative opinion of his colleague. She had become Rebecca's public enemy number one, in her mind the obstacle that was stopping Patrick from getting the recognition and respect she knew he deserved. She only ever referred to her using her full name. Patrick reluctantly recounted Amanda's contribution to the programme post-mortem, and Rebecca gasped.

'She did not! Braver? She said that? I swear, if I ever meet Amanda Lake, I will punch her in the face!'

Patrick believed her and made a mental note never to allow such a meeting to take place. He reached back under his girlfriend's pillow and pulled her a little closer. He could feel the room darkening around them as they lay in the warm bed. The only light making its way through the thin curtains now came from a sodium streetlight, brightening pale pink to yellow as Patrick watched. Rebecca's breathing was slow and even. He thought she had fallen asleep. When she suddenly opened her eyes and spoke, he jumped.

Her voice was calm and considered. 'So how about this? You go and talk to Rob Mariscal. You ask for a meeting. Or even better, go for a drink. You find out from him, from the horse's mouth, what's wrong, and then we work out how to fix it.'

Patrick nodded. It was the right and obvious thing to do. If he had made a connection with anyone at the programme, if he had an ally there, then it was Mariscal.

5   Arses and Elbows

DATELINE: British Army barracks, Kabul International Airport, June 22nd

Chaundy took a ballpoint pen from behind his ear and poked at the debris; bored at first, he quickly got interested and then engrossed. He pulled a pair of latex gloves and then a black eyepiece, similar to the ones Karim had seen the Kabul diamond merchants use, from his trouser pocket. The staff sergeant was Carver's contact but when Karim had got in touch, explained who he was and offered a bottle of French brandy in return for a five-minute chat, Chaundy had agreed immediately.

'Where did you get this thing?'

Karim explained that it had been found at the scene of a recent Taliban attack.

'Someone's pulling your plonker, mate.' Chaundy picked up the blackened scrap of circuit board and waved it under Karim's nose. 'Look at that. That's quality. I'll have to check the numbers on that chip—' he flicked the scrap of green and black plastic over and looked closely through the eyeglass '—if I can find any, but it looks European. I'll bet you a tenner that's European. If

I was blowing you up, this is what I'd use. It's not what your lot use on us.'

Karim bridled. 'They're not "my lot", sir.'

Chaundy looked up, momentarily confused. 'What? Oh, yeah. Sorry. All I'm saying is the Afghan nut-jobs who make bombs don't have access to this stuff, fancy circuit boards and Semtex. They make their shitty little bombs out of drain cleaner and solvent and acetone, a bit of hydrochloric acid to get it all going. Their bombs are cheap and nasty and very fucking unstable. They go off when you don't want them to, like when you're making them. That's why all the bomb-makers we bring in are covered in burn marks . . . Missing fingers or hands. Half an arm gone, you know?'

Karim looked up from his notepad and nodded. He found himself staring at the sergeant's right arm, scarred and twisted, almost bone thin at the elbow but thick at the forearm with a patchwork of skin grafts.

Chaundy saw him staring. 'Yeah, I got that trying to snuff out a Taliban bomb. They had to cut a load of skin off me thigh and bum to patch it up.' He pointed in the direction of his groin and backside.

Karim shook his head. 'I am sorry.'

'Oh, ta, but don't be, not even Mrs Chaundy goes down there anymore. And if anyone tells you that I don't know my arse from my elbow, then at least you know I've got an excuse!'

Karim didn't entirely understand the joke but he gave what he hoped was a sympathetic smile.

'Anyway. Back to the job in hand. This thing didn't come out of any Kabul cellar. Whoever made this knew what they were doing, they had their pick of electronics and explosives. And whoever paid for it paid top dollar.'

*

After their angry encounter on the roof, Vivian had drafted an email to the head of Newsgathering and to Rob Mariscal, explaining that Carver was impossible to work with. She wanted a transfer, a new assignment. Her finger had hovered over the send button but for the moment the letter remained in drafts. She had never turned down or bailed out of a job before, and she was unwilling to let William Carver spoil her perfect record. She felt a little guilty, too. The package on the tailor's shop bombing had gone down well in London, very well, and her various bosses had assumed they had her to thank for getting William back on the radio. There were half a dozen congratulatory messages in her inbox from different parts of BBC News. Her replies had been modest but not entirely honest; she made no attempt to correct the impression that she and Carver were a team, a team that was working rather well. So she would stick with Carver a while longer, she would try harder and she would make it work. The surge of interest in the Kabul bombing would generate more business, too much for Carver to manage alone. He would have to make use of her, even if it was just to deal with the news desk in London.

The British and Americans had called a joint press conference to make a statement about the dead district chief and to give the names of four British soldiers killed a few days previously in an IED attack. The names and details always emerged a day or so after the deaths; it gave the MoD time to break the news to bereaved families.

William ambled into the Intercontinental Hotel with Vivian close behind, her ponytail moving with a metronomic swing. The doors to the conference room were still closed and a dozen or so journalists were hanging around outside, fiddling with mobile phones and trying to look busy. Carver prowled impatiently, nodding at some people, ignoring others and talking to no one until he noticed a stocky man in his late sixties, tanned and with a face like an old boxer. He was standing close to the corridor wall, staring intently at a gold-framed photograph of old Kabul. He wore beige slacks and a faded denim shirt with pearl poppers, and had an ancient-looking 35 mm camera slung over his left shoulder. When he finished examining the photo, he turned and saw William. He smiled broadly. 'Hey Carver! I can't believe you fell for it too. We're on time. I forgot that military press conferences are always at least half an hour late on principle.'

William held out his right hand and the American took it with both of his. 'Riley. What are you doing here? I thought you'd retired?'

Riley nodded. 'I did. Five years and maybe half a dozen wars ago. But get this: a few months back the *New York Times* found out I wasn't dead, tracked me down at my Miami duplex and did a feature on me. Turns out, according to them I'm a legend! Which is just as well, because I'm a God-awful photographer these days. Cataracts left and right.' He pointed at his milky-blue eyes.

'But you're here working?'

'Kinda. Couldn't say no. They offered me big bucks. A truckload of money. And they bought me a bunch of new kit, digital crap.'

'You still remember what to do with a camera?'

'Ha. I do remember that. Just get close, keep clicking and don't die.'

Riley turned to acknowledge Vivian, who was watching with interest. William kept them waiting a moment, before realising he was expected to make an introduction.

'Sorry. Daniel Riley, Viv.'

The photographer swept down on Vivian's hand and kissed it.

Carver ignored this and continued with his questions. 'So what kind of thing have they got you doing?'

The old man's eyes fell and an embarrassed look flickered briefly across his face. 'Well. I'm goin' on a US Army embed, access all areas, God forgive me. Lots of action shots and Marlboro man bullshit for a Sunday supplement.' He turned to Vivian. 'Excuse my language, miss. So anyways, here I am, killing time in the hotel before they come for me. I thought I'd drop by the presser in case you showed up, Billy-boy. I gather we have *you* to thank for this one. I always enjoy a military press briefing; love watching them put a little lipstick on the pig, reminds me of Vietnam, back when both my knees worked and I believed in something. So are you just here for the conference or have you got a one-to-one with someone?'

'Nothing fixed up but I'm hoping. There's a new British Army PR guy I need to see. Remora, I think he's called.'

Riley straightened. 'I know the one. Captain Remora. I had to take a grip-and-grin picture of him and his American opposite number. He won't talk to you until after the presser and he doesn't like being called the PR guy. He prefers Head of Strategic Communications. You'll know him when you see him – very British, very up his own bony ass. Little silvery teeth. When he smiles he looks like a bust zipper.'

William smiled and turned away from his old colleague, scanning the lobby.

'You've probably noticed already, nothing much has changed.'

'Can say that again; I can't believe how many of the old faces are still knocking around. I'd have thought after all the horseshit we swallowed and spouted over Iraq, a few more might've fallen on their pens.' He turned towards Vivian again. 'Excuse my French.'

Riley stood up from the wall. It was clear he was warming to his theme. 'And afterwards, the weapons that weren't. No weapons but no apologies. A couple of mealy-mouthed mea culpas in the big papers but that's it?'

It was William's turn to look embarrassed. 'The caravan moves on, I guess.'

'I guess it does. I believe you swallowed a little of that horseshit yourself, didn't you, buddy? I listened to some of your pieces, my local public radio station takes BBC World Service in the small hours.'

Carver met Riley's eye. 'I made some mistakes. Trusted some people I shouldn't have.'

There was a silence. It seemed to Vivian that the temperature in the room had suddenly dropped a couple of degrees.

'Those Iraqi exiles you got. That got a lot of play our side of the Pond. Guess you knew that already? Talking 'bout missiles that can hit London in forty-five freakin' minutes. Ridiculous.'

William folded his arms tightly across his chest and stared at the American. 'Is that why you're really here, Daniel? The old cowboy, riding back into town on your high-horse to give us all a lecture on truth?'

'No. I'm just sayin' maybe we shoulda all sniffed the snake oil a bit harder, that's all.'

'Maybe. But I'll be damned if I'm going to take a lecture from you. A sentimental old man who's making some money doing a puff piece for the US Army. I thought you'd *got out* before you *sold out*. Clearly I was wrong.'

Riley's smile slipped from his face. He reached out and steadied himself against the wall. Vivian moved to help him but he waved her away. 'Don't worry, darlin'. I'm fine, just fine. Me and William, we're old friends. This is how old friends talk. Some of the time.'

Carver listened to this, his eyes firmly on his feet. Vivian watched him open his mouth to say something, then change his mind. 'I need to—I need to be somewhere else.'

He picked up his plastic bag and left, leaving Vivian to make awkward small talk with Dan Riley.

'Shall we find some water or a coffee while we wait for the press conference to start?'

'Good idea, young lady. A sit down and a coffee would be great.'

Vivian found two armchairs and flagged down a reluctant member of the hotel staff carrying coffee. Riley lowered himself to a crouch and then dropped the last half-foot into the chair, exhaling sharply.

'Ah, that's better. Not much left in the knees, you see.'

'I'm sure William didn't mean what he said.'

'I'm pretty sure he did. And you know what? He's right. This is a shitty assignment I'm on but it'll keep my creditors at bay for another year or two. It was my fault, shouldn't have dragged up Iraq like that. He's a proud son of a bitch.'

The American heaved a sigh and took a noisy slurp of his drink. 'They make a good cup of coffee in here. No luck introducing democracy, but we do seem to have successfully introduced the latte.'

It was another twenty minutes before the conference doors were flung open and the film crews and soundmen started to pile in. William followed them and took a seat near the back, as far away from Vivian and Riley as possible. The warm-up act was an American officer with thin hair and a little blond moustache, which was worse than no moustache at all. He welcomed 'the gentlemen and ladies of the press', ran through the ground rules and informed the room that the conference proper would start in five minutes sharp, in case anyone wanted to feed it live to 'London, Washington or someplace else'. Vivian saw Captain Remora first. He had entered the conference room from a side door near the back, and had a long stride and a tailored look about him. His dark curly hair was cut short and looked a little too well conditioned for a proper soldier, she thought. He talked with fellow officers at the side of the stage and smiled and nodded in the direction of some of the better-known TV journalists, for whom the front two rows had been reserved. The Captain looked confident but not entirely comfortable until the moment he reached the podium. Once there, he put some papers down in front of him, placed one hand on either side of the lectern, and gazed imperiously across the floor. He had their attention but he cleared his throat anyway. The room fell silent.

'Let's get started, please. I'm Captain J. G. Remora, British Army. I'd first like to make an announcement about the four British soldiers who died three days ago. I'll give you their full names and some relevant personal details. All the families have been informed so you're free to use those details as soon as I give them. Then I'll make some general points about the operation in the south, and finally I'll issue a short statement about the Taliban assassination of District Chief Fazil Jabar. After that, if there's time, I'll take questions from the floor.'

The four men, all from 40 Commando, Royal Marines, had been killed by a roadside bomb while taking part in an operation alongside the Afghan National Army in central Helmand, north of the town of Gereshk. Remora read and then slowly spelt out four ordinary English names. The journalists scribbled them down in shorthand. Within the hour they would be read out solemnly on TV and radio and the next day they would appear in every national newspaper. Within a few days they would be carved on headstones for graveyards in Warrington and Plymouth and Burnley, and a week later on thick Portland stone panels, part of an ever-growing grey memorial wall in Staffordshire. Remora read the names again, more quickly this time, and after each name he gave the dead man's age, family situation, and a brief quote from their commanding officer, a thumbnail sketch of a military career cut short.

Vivian listened to the adjectives used to describe the men. She was struck by the lack of variety. The men had all been 'popular', 'dedicated', 'the best of their generation' and, inevitably, they had been 'brave'. She noted down their ages: twenty-one, twenty, twenty-four and twenty-five. Kids, she thought, all younger than she was. And yet three of the four had been fathers. She underlined the dead men's ages, and as she did so, Remora indicated with a clipped 'right then' that he was moving on.

'Despite this recent tragedy, there has been a marked fall in the number of attacks on NATO forces; a fifteen per cent fall, in fact, which tells us, surely, that our current strategy is working.'

The journalists in the room nodded and scribbled. Remora watched and waited, judging the impact of his words.

'We are regaining the initiative in and around Kandahar and Helmand, the insurgency is losing momentum and both human intelligence and aerial recon tell us the enemy is suffering serious reversals and a significant reduction in their operational capacity. The momentum is firmly on our side. We are, ladies and gentlemen, winning this war.'

Vivian saw an American network producer raise a thumb in the direction of his camera team. That was their soundbite. Cut and print.

Remora looked down at his notes, paused to allow the print hacks time to note what he hoped would be their top line, and then moved on to the killing of Fazil Jabar. He said how sorry the Allied forces and the Afghan government were to have lost such an important supporter and 'partner for peace'. He assured the audience that the NATO counterinsurgency programme would continue as planned and that Jabar's closest colleagues, including those most likely to replace him as district chief, had already pledged their support. The best way to honour the man, he said, was to continue to put pressure on the terrorists who had murdered him. He gave no further details and did not mention Jabar's son, his bodyguard or Mr Savi the tailor. Remora then took four questions, at least two of which appeared to have been planted, as far as Vivian could see. There was one from an American network, one from John Brandon on behalf of the *Ten O'Clock News*, one from Al Jazeera and one from the *International Herald Tribune*. The British officer politely but firmly dead-batted them all. Each answer included a slightly different ten-second soundbite containing his main message: this was a sad loss but the Taliban were fighting a losing battle. William Carver had his hand up throughout the Q&A, but he was not called.

Dan Riley paused as he walked past William on his way out of the room. 'Impressive, huh? I tell you, if they'd had that guy in Vietnam maybe we'd all still be there.' Riley grinned but received nothing from Carver in return. 'Fine, well maybe I'll see you later?'

'Maybe.'

'I hope so, I'm off the booze these days but I'll happily watch you drink.'

Carver hung around as the other hacks and crews drifted from the room, keeping a close eye on Remora. He stopped the Captain together with two of his colleagues as they made their way towards the exit. William proffered his hand and after a moment's pause, Remora took it. You can tell a lot from a handshake and this one came with a good measure of disdain.

'Captain Remora. William Carver from BBC Radio. I hoped to ask a question today but you obviously didn't see me. It was my story that got this Fazil Jabar killing a bit of play, so I was hoping you could spare me two minutes? Off the record, if you prefer?'

Remora leant in towards William. His reply was a tight whisper. 'We haven't worked together before, Mr Carver. But I know of you. I think it's only fair to tell you right now that you and I will *never* have an off-the-record conversation.'

Carver shrugged. 'Fine. On the record, then. Even better. Just a couple of quick questions.'

Remora indicated to his colleagues that they should go ahead without him, and walked William to the far corner of the now near empty room. 'Be quick, if you would, I'm afraid I'm rather busy.'

Carver nodded. 'So am I. This shouldn't take long.' He reached into his plastic bag and pulled out the MiniDisc.

Remora held up a hand and shook his head. 'On the record but not for broadcast. You'll have to use shorthand.'

Carver smiled. He swapped the recorder for a notepad and turned to a clean page. 'Right. Just for background, then. So, I wanted to ask you, approximately how much of that bullshit briefing you just gave do you actually believe? Ten per cent? Fifteen?'

Remora sighed. 'We've lost four brave British service personnel and a valuable ally but you don't want to talk about that, Mr Carver. You want to play silly buggers? I was warned you were anti this war and anti-army, but I thought you BBC boys were at least supposed to pretend to practise objective journalism.'

Carver scribbled a tight spiral in the margin of his notebook. 'For the record, I'm absolutely not anti-army. Some of the best people I've met are military people. As for objectivity, well, you've got me there. I never really bought the idea of objective journalism. There is no objective truth, Captain Remora, as I suspect you know better than most.'

'I know nothing of the sort. I supply simple facts, Mr Carver, that's my job. Your job is to relay them. Everything else is speculation and spin. If that's the game you're in, I'm not sure we have much left to say to one another.'

'Whose facts are we talking about, Captain? Your facts?'

'The facts.'

William flicked backwards a few pages in his notebook and found his shorthand summary of the press conference. 'You have to choose which facts to supply, though, don't you? This is what you said in your briefing: "The number of attacks against NATO forces has fallen by fifteen per cent." That's a fact. But the figure you chose to use is month on month. You might have chosen quarter on quarter, but then your fifteen per cent fall would have been a thirty per cent rise, wouldn't it? Or this month compared to this time last year? Even worse. And that's "winning the war"?'

Captain Remora's face had reddened and a thick vein at his temple was now quite prominent. William wasn't sure whether he'd managed to unsettle the Captain enough to get a straight answer to his next question but he had to try it; the Captain was leaving.

'One last question, Captain,' he said, a little more gently, 'one more fact I'd like to check. I have a name I'd like to run by you.'

'A name?'

'Yes.'

Remora looked at his watch. 'What name?'

Carver knew the name by heart; it was the name that he'd found leafing through Mr Savi's appointments book, the name that had given him that flutter in the stomach that he hadn't felt in months, maybe years. He knew the name but he wanted to take his time, he referred again to his notebook. 'Let's see . . . Richard Roydon.'

As he said this, he studied Remora's face looking for something – surprise, maybe, or irritation. Remora was too polished to exhibit either, but William was sure he saw something, a flicker of recognition perhaps.

'Richard Roydon. No. That name means nothing to me, I'm afraid. Now I do have to go.'

Remora began to walk but set off in the wrong direction. Sure enough, William thought, he's a bit rattled. The Captain tutted furiously to himself and turned. Carver followed, talking more quickly this time.

'He was in the Marines a few years back. After that he worked for Rook Security. I was Googling them and it looks like they did some work for our embassy, here in Kabul, close security work, bodyguarding, stuff like that. No bells?'

'No. Why are you asking me this, Mr Carver?'

'Roydon was having a suit made at the Passport Street tailor's.'

Remora slowed and turned to William. 'Was he? And can I ask how you came across that piece of information?'

'Basic journalism. It doesn't matter how I know it. The question is, did you know it?'

'No, I've told you, I've never heard of the man. And I don't wish to appear dim, but I can't see why it's in the least bit interesting. I'm sure the tailor in question makes suits for all sorts of people. That's his job, after all.'

'That *was* his job.'

'Was his job. Yes.'

'Roydon had the appointment just before Mr Jabar's on the evening of the bombing. In fact, it seems he had appointments around the same time as Fazil Jabar on a number of occasions. So I wanted to talk to him, that's all, see if he could help fill in the gaps a little. You'll probably want to talk to him too, won't you? You or the Military Police. Perhaps he saw something?'

Remora looked William directly in the eye. 'Mr Carver, if you want to talk about Embassy employees, full-time, part-time, freelance or whatever, you need to speak to the Embassy. I really can't help.'

'Fair enough. I'll take it up with the Ambassador. That's a good idea. Thanks for all your help, Captain.'

Remora nodded uncertainly and left the room.

Vivian was pacing up and down, waiting for William at the hotel entrance. It was clear she wanted to talk.

'Something on your mind?'

'William, you can't keep ditching me. I'm your producer, not Dan Riley's.'

'How is he?'

'He was a little shaken up. He's an old man, you didn't need to be so tough on him. Maybe you could apologise?'

Carver shrugged. 'Anything else?'

'Well, I've got a clean feed recording of the press conference and I made a lot of notes. I thought we could go back to the house and—'

'There was nothing worth reporting in that presser.'

'Okay. How about Remora? Can you fill me in on that chat you just had with the Captain?'

'No.'

'Why not?'

Carver was still running on the adrenaline generated by his encounter with Remora. 'Listen, Vivian. I don't need a note-taker or someone to give me lectures on etiquette. You don't speak Dari, Pashto or any other useful language and you know nothing about this country apart from what you've read on Wikipedia. I've got Karim, who quite frankly is worth five of you, so why don't you do us both a favour and bugger off home.'

Vivian's resignation letter was still at the top of her drafts file. When she got back to her room she reread it and pressed send.

Karim brought the Honda to a gentle halt at the back of a dozen other cars. A pair of Afghan policemen in worn grey uniforms stood in front of the roadblock smoking. They seemed in no hurry to let anyone through and had no plans to tell any of the waiting motorists what was going on. Karim cut the engine and stepped into the road. He could feel its heat through the soles of his shoes. The smell of petrol hung on the yellow haze. He stretched and took in his surroundings. He hadn't been stopped on this road before. On one side of the two-lane highway ran a dry river bed and behind that low scrub; on the other, a thirsty-looking cornfield and in the distance a village of eight or nine decaying mud houses. Behind the village the land rose gently and the colours were yellow and grey and dusty green. He turned back and called an inquisitive greeting to the owner of the car in front, who was sitting on his bonnet eating flatbread with his fingers. 'VIP car coming' was the rumour. Why would a VIP need both sides of the road? The answer arrived soon enough, heralded by a growing cloud of dust some half a mile up the road. Karim watched it get closer and soon heard the distinctive rumble of a convoy. The two policemen pinched out their cigarettes, pocketed them and got busy raising the roadblock and ordering the waiting Afghans to get back into their cars.

'For your safety, friend, for your safety.'

The convoy was big: twenty trucks escorted front, back and centre by five black SUVs. The windows were all rolled down and Karim could see that each SUV carried at least four men, all holding automatic weapons and wearing dark sunglasses cut at sharp angles. Private security guards like these had a reputation for being trigger-happy, and the men and women in the queuing cars avoided eye contact. Mothers pushed their children down into the footwells of their vehicles until the convoy had passed, draping the scene in a thick shroud of dust. Karim had worked with William on a story about the convoys. They had spoken to Afghans who had been shot at, sometimes for trying to overtake a slow-moving convoy, sometimes for doing nothing at all, just for being on the same stretch of road. The security men got edgy when confronted with what they considered to be a suspicious vehicle; they were scared of car bombs and when they got scared they were dangerous. Boredom made them dangerous, too. Karim had spoken to dozens of farmers who had lost cattle, shot in the head or sometimes peppered with bullets from more than one gun. They had interviewed the CEO of one of the security companies involved. The softly spoken Dutchman had denied firing at other vehicles but admitted that his men sometimes shot cows. The Taliban hide IEDs in the carcasses of dead animals, he had said, 'My guys are under a lot of pressure.' When William pointed out that the cows were alive and well until the men had shot them, the answer had been 'Better safe than sorry.'

Karim was climbing back into his car when he felt his phone vibrate in the pocket of his jeans. It was a new text message: *Change of plan again. Let's make it 11.* The message was from Rashid. Haroun Rashid was an Afghan businessman who had, he liked to tell anyone he met, 'feet in many pies'. Rashid paid Karim to help him with his conversational English for an hour a week and gave him basic translation jobs when he needed to deal with westerners. Lately he'd also involved the young Afghan in some small currency deals, making sure some of the money would stick to Karim's fingers. Karim was grateful for the work and for the money but his main reason for maintaining a relationship with Rashid was William Carver. Kabul was a mystery to most people; a senseless, dangerous, lawless chaos. Karim understood it better than most, but Rashid understood it completely. He saw the patterns and processes and knew a lot of people and a lot of secrets, some of which he would tell Karim during their regular get-togethers.

But this wasn't a regular get-together. This time Karim had asked to see Rashid – something which had rather thrown the businessman – and now he was getting his own back by repeatedly changing the time of the meeting. It had been ten, then eleven thirty and now it was eleven.

Karim willed the waiting traffic to move. The bombing at the tailor's shop was no longer just another story; it had become an obsession. He realised he was chasing it harder than William wanted him to – or would pay for – and he wasn't entirely sure why he was so gripped by it. But instinct told him there was more to discover. His consultation with Staff Sergeant Chaundy had confirmed him in this opinion, but the circuit board seemed to raise more questions than it answered. His hope was that Rashid could suggest where to go next.

The two men always met at the same place, a dingy back-street café that Rashid said served the best green tea, cake and sugared almonds in Kabul. Karim sat and watched as Rashid posted forkfuls of cake and handfuls of almonds into his hungry mouth while being noisily indiscreet about everyone he knew and quite a few people he didn't.

'A man I buy watches from, you don't know him; last week he hired a mini-van to take his whole family to a wedding, fourteen of them. On the way, they hit a big mine. *Bang*! Blown to bits. Every person dead, wife and children, every person apart from the man and his mother-in-law!'

Rashid took a long swig of tea while watching Karim over the edge of the cup. 'His mother-in-law! Can you imagine it? What sort of luck is that? Poor bastard.'

Poor bastard was Rashid's favourite English phrase. Karim gave a convincing-enough laugh.

'So what's so important that you need to talk to Rashid so urgently? You got a girl into trouble? Is that it?'

Karim blushed. 'No, no. It's nothing like that. I'm working with my English journalist on the bombing at the Passport Street tailor's shop, you heard about it, I'm sure? The Taliban attack that killed Fazil Jabar?'

Rashid nodded somewhat warily. 'Poor bastard.'

'Yes. Poor bastard. But I wondered if you'd heard anything. I know you hear everything so I wondered if anyone had said anything to you about the bombing.'

Rashid fidgeted in his seat. He was a man visibly torn between a desperate need to show off and an instinct for self-preservation.

Karim could always tell when he knew something. It was

unmistakable. 'I have talked to everyone I thought might know something. Police, politicians, journalists. Important people. But nothing. So I say to myself, if anyone knows about this, it will be Rashid.'

This was too much. Rashid looked around the café. There was no one in the place apart from them and the old husband and wife who owned the shop. They were busy dismantling the till which, as far as Karim could recall, had never worked. 'Okay. Now, I know a thing. Maybe it will help you, maybe not. Listening?'

'Yes, sir.'

'Okay. So Rashid is the most popular man in Afghanistan, yes?'

'Right.'

'And Pakistan if we are being truthful. No enemies. Everyone loves Rashid, yes?'

'Yes,' said Karim uncertainly, unsure of what Rashid was getting at.

'So everyone loves Rashid but even I have more security than Fazil Jabar.' He waved his hand in the direction of the street and a large Lexus containing a driver and a thickset bodyguard in a pillbox hat. 'Fazil Jabar is out in the night, in a public place with just one old bodyguard and his only – his only – son? Walking around in his underpants getting measured for a suit? Does that seem to you like a man who fears the Taliban?'

'No, no it does not,' Karim said keenly, immediately seeing that Rashid was on to something.

'No. That's right. Sure, he signed the NATO nonsense. But he didn't believe it. He was a politician *and* a businessman. He signed whatever he needed to sign to remain friends with everyone. He wasn't scared of the Taliban because he was close to the Taliban. Very close.'

'Working with them? That is your suspicion?'

'It is more than a suspicion, Karim. People who know these things tell me the Taliban would never kill Jabar because he is their man. Their man in business, their man in politics, their man full stop.'

'So if the Taliban didn't kill him, who did?'

'I do not know.' Rashid finished his tea and leant closer to Karim. 'But if you find out, my friend, I don't want to know. Do you understand? Usually Rashid wants to know everything, but if you find out who killed Jabar, tell someone else. I do not want to know something which might get me killed.'

Karim nodded vaguely. He was thinking about the implications of Rashid's intelligence. The more he found out about the killing of Fazil Jabar, the more mysterious it seemed. He barely heard Rashid's next instruction.

'Take some advice from an old friend, Karim: find a different story. This one does not need to be told.'

6 The Prawn Curry Contract

DATELINE: New Broadcasting House, Portland Place, London, W1, June 24th

Rob gobbed a grey oyster of phlegm into the bowl of the urinal and washed it away with a stream of pale urine. Patrick had taken the place next to him and was trying hard to pee. He had wanted to get a moment with Mariscal all morning but his boss was never alone or standing still long enough. In desperation, Patrick had followed him into the gents.

Rob looked up. 'All right, Patrick?'

'Yeah, good, thanks Rob.' Patrick paused, suddenly unsure of whether Rebecca's plan was such a good one. 'Er, Rob, I wondered if we could have a private chat, later on today, or after work?'

'More private than this, Patrick?'

'Er, yeah.'

'Sure. In fact you read my mind. I need to talk to you about a couple of things. How about we head off after Monday night drinks, just you and me go for a beer and a quiet chat?'

'Great, thanks Rob.'

'No problem.' Mariscal gave his employee a questioning glance. 'Are you planning on taking a piss, Patrick, or are you just going to stand there looking at my penis?'

'What? Oh yeah, sorry, no, I'm just, you know, nervous.'

Rob zipped up, clapped Patrick on the back with an unwashed hand, and left.

Monday night drinks was an institution Mariscal had introduced the first week he had arrived as editor. 'Team building,' he had explained. 'Everyone welcome.' In truth, you found out pretty quickly how welcome you were.

Rob set off for the pub straight after the four o'clock meeting – 'early bird gets the corner table' – taking a couple of his favourite reporters with him. As others arrived, he indicated where the newcomers should sit. Proximity indicated preference, and this Monday, Patrick found himself sitting next to Hilary, at least half a dozen people away. Others, less favoured or less fortunate, were encouraged to drag a few of the small round tables closer and set up satellite stations on the fringes of the main event. When Rob stood to make one of a series of announcements, Hilary explained the topography of the pub.

'Do you see how it works? He's like some big black hole, sucking us all in.'

Patrick was about to whisper a response when he became aware that Rob was scowling at him.

'Christ on a bike, I'm talking here, new boy. Shut the fuck up.' Mariscal grinned broadly at the expectant faces. 'I would like to say a few words about journalism,' he proclaimed to a smattering of laughter and some mock groans. 'For those of you who are new to the programme, or new to Monday night drinking, I want you to understand that all that stuff you've been told about journalism being the first draft of history, a ringside seat as the world changes, all of that is bollocks.'

Mariscal took a long sip of beer and continued. 'Real journalism is the dirty stuff. The boring stuff . . .'

Patrick looked around the room. All eyes were on Rob, even Hilary's.

'Can I tell you what the best piece of journalism we've done this year is?' This was rhetorical, but Rob required encouragement. Heads duly nodded enthusiastically. 'It wasn't some piece of war reportage or a coup or anything complicated. It was done by that ugly fucker down the end there.' Rob waved his beer glass in the direction of Emmanuel Papadopoulos, a prematurely bald thirty-something reporter who he'd poached from the *Daily Mirror*. Manny was sitting at the edge of the outermost table with just enough room to perch a beer mat and his drink, orange juice and ice by the looks of it. The reporter smiled sheepishly but pulled himself up a little straighter in his seat. Mariscal's praise was rare and his respect a prize worth winning. With most BBC managers, thought Patrick, everything was always 'great'. Not so with Mariscal. The majority of what Rob saw or heard was 'shit'. What was left was 'all right'. Just occasionally, maybe a few times a year, something would come along which was deserving of the only other adjectives Rob ever applied to radio: 'Fucking brilliant. That report from Slough, Manny. That piece was brilliant. The idea was all right, well it was my idea, but the way Manny put that piece together was inspired.'

Rob Mariscal had grown increasingly frustrated with the contradictory immigration figures being issued by central and local government, numbers that varied hugely from one month to the next. No one seemed to know the true scale of immigration, particularly the numbers of people coming from Eastern Europe after the lifting of border restrictions. It mattered to Rob because he liked certainty. It mattered to Slough Borough Council because they were sure they had a much larger immigrant population than Whitehall said they had – which meant they were being short-changed when it came to central government funding. The problem was that no one knew how to count the new arrivals. They moved house and changed jobs too frequently and few registered at doctors' surgeries or job centres. They were slipping through the net. Slough might have had a thousand Poles, or it might have had one hundred thousand. No one knew. Then a young statistician at Thames Valley University came up with an interesting idea: if you couldn't count people because they moved around too much, perhaps you could count something they left behind regardless of where they went, their waste. Rob read about the idea in the *Local Government Chronicle* and was on it straight away.

He called Manny into his office and briefed him. 'Manny, this nutter is going to calculate how many Poles there are in Slough by weighing their shit. Forget everything else, I want you on this. Just this. All day and all night until you've got it on air.' Manny did exactly as he was told. For three months he worked with the statistician, hanging out at sewage works, installing equipment to measure the amount of traffic coming down the pipes. The moment of real genius came, as far as Rob was concerned, when Manny decided to record the whole piece underground, capturing the sound of faeces swilling past him down the old Victorian pipes and drains.

'A hundred feet underground, wader-deep in Slough's stinking gravy . . . brilliant! I didn't just hear that package, I could smell it.'

Rob ran the piece at ten past eight – front and centre in the programme's shop window. Complaints outnumbered plaudits by twenty to one. Listeners called the Slough report racist, sensationalist and tabloid. But most simply called it disgusting. Rob revelled in the reaction.

'That was journalism, Manny, real journalism! Something like that was never going to win a Sony Award, but who wants a Sony Award?'

For a moment Patrick thought Manny was raising his hand, but he was simply reaching for his drink.

'Sony Awards mean nothing. Everyone wins one eventually. What you did was more important. Anyway, that's all I wanted to say. It's my round, who wants what? Manny, I'm getting you two of whatever it is you want. Do you want the barmaid? If you want the barmaid, I'm getting you two fucking barmaids.'

Rob was buzzing and it was infectious. The party had grown in number and there were now more than two dozen producers and reporters crammed around the corner table, every one of them besotted with their editor. Looking on, Patrick saw that Rob Mariscal had that rare gift; he could make people believe in him, march with him, explain and finally justify him.

'You're losing this game a little easily, Patrick. Am I boring you?'

Patrick roused himself, stopped picking at the label on his beer bottle and focused on the chessboard. 'Sorry Rob. A bit tired, that's all.'

Monday drinks had gone on later than Rob had predicted. It had been nine-thirty before they got to his favourite Indian restaurant in the Strand, and past eleven by the time they reached Soho and the private drinking club where Mariscal was a member. Scott House had a small dining room at the front of the building and a bar at the back. The carpet was sticky and the springs had gone on most of the chairs and sofas, but they were comfortable. The walls were barely visible behind dozens of poorly framed oils and watercolours. Most of these pictures had been taken as payment in kind, explained Rob, from Royal Academy artists and piss artists for the last forty-odd years.

Rob was the club's most regular regular. He had a tab and a tacit agreement with the management that he could smoke in the back bar if no one complained. The management was Maggie, a well-maintained woman in her middle fifties who would always greet Mariscal as though he'd been away for a very long time even though he rarely had. She would shoo away her staff and serve Rob herself, sitting him in his favourite corner before fetching him a large tumbler of whisky and ice, placing it in his hand and closing his fingers around it, like a secret.

Rob's promised private chat had begun over a large plate of prawn madras.

'Lemme guess. You're not happy. Not sure you can hack it and you want me to tell you that it's all going to be all right?'

Patrick had turned his fork in the pilau rice and nodded. 'Ha. That's pretty much it. It looks like this won't have to be a very long talk, boss. I'll finish my curry, then go clear my desk.' He smiled at Rob until he saw that Rob wasn't smiling back. A creeping dread took over his stomach.

'No need to do that, not just yet . But I'd be lying if I told you it was all going fine, because it obviously isn't, is it? Listen. I've got a lot of very clever people working for me, extremely fucking erudite, confident. First class honours in all kinds of bollocks, PPEs from Oxford or Cambridge or Harvard or wherever you get a PPE from. Brains that can boil water.'

'Right.'

'But that's not what I need from you.'

'Just as well,' Patrick muttered, attempting a half-hearted joke.

'Do yourself a favour and just listen and eat while I do the talking, yeah?'

Patrick had scooped a pile of prawns on to his fork and nodded. 'The reason I liked the look of you, the reason I gave you the job, was I had an idea that you might make a decent field producer.'

Patrick worked hard not to choke on his mouthful of food; a BBC field producer post was his dream.

'But you have to put a bit of time in on the desk first, so you get to know what makes the programme tick, how the cogs turn, become one of us.'

Patrick nodded. 'Right, I see.'

'But this is the important part, Patrick. I didn't have you marked down for just any old field job. I was thinking of one particular field. One particular piece of livestock, in fact. You've come across William Carver, now.'

''Course, yes.'

'You dealt with him well the other night, ran his story in a good slot too, which is helpful.'

'It was no problem.' Patrick was unsure where this was heading.

'Well, right now, William Carver is my biggest problem and I'm hoping that you might be part of the solution.'

Patrick nodded eagerly.

'Until recently, Carver was the best reporter I had, the best thing the whole programme had. He was a machine. Wind him up, send him off and you could pretty much count on him for regular scoops. I'm talking one or more a month, which is pretty incredible given how complex some of these stories were. And headline-making stuff, all the newspapers were chasing our tail, which is how I like it. His stuff won prizes too, all sorts of weird foreign prizes I didn't even know existed until Carver went and won them. Basically, Carver was my big fat golden egg-laying goose. The best appointment I ever made, until he went strange.'

'When?'

'It started going wrong after Iraq. It's hard to be precise because William was always a bit elusive, borderline nocturnal. But the stream of stories turned into a trickle, and he started staying away longer.'

'Whereabouts?'

'Shitty bits of Africa, the Middle East, Iraq naturally, now Afghanistan. He's been in Afghanistan for months, on and off, but filed almost nothing. I had to get him turfed out of the press hotel – his minibar bill was starting to resemble the US defence budget – and I had fuck all to show for it. He's in the BBC house in Kabul now, but that doesn't seem to have made much difference. He's still off the leash. Newsgathering tried to help out. They gave me their best field producer, Vivian Fox. She's good, smart and very tolerant of arseholes . . . But now she's chucked in the towel. From what I hear we're lucky she just asked for a new assignment, by the sounds of it she could have hit us with a bullying or sexual harassment case. So she wasn't quite right. She couldn't make a connection. But I'm thinking maybe you can.'

Mariscal had fixed Patrick with an even stare. 'You've got bugger all experience but you've done your hostile environment training so the insurance is covered and I figure it's worth a shot.'

'Why me?' Patrick couldn't think of a single reason.

'Well, Carver comes from the same background as you do, bog-standard school, average A levels, ordinary degree, then local newspapers.'

Patrick wasn't sure he liked this summary of his CV but he kept eating and said nothing.

'And all that stuff you talked about at your interview – comforting the afflicted, afflicting the comfortable, speaking truth to power, all that bollocks – when I first knew Carver, long time ago, he used to talk all that corny crap too.'

'He doesn't believe in it anymore?'

'God knows what he believes. He speaks to no one, upsets everyone, doesn't trust a soul. Not even me anymore. He was always a loose cannon, a liability, but we went back a little way and I used to know how to manage him. Now I'm on the outside too. I have no idea why, no idea at all.'

Rob's tone had slowly changed, frustration shading into regret, and Patrick had begun to feel like he was listening to someone telling the story of a love affair gone sour, not a boss describing an unreliable employee. Mariscal had stopped talking and was spooning all the remaining mango chutney and lime pickle into a hole he'd dug in the top of his prawn curry.

'Funnily enough, the last proper story we worked on was out in India. Hand in glove we worked on that. We nailed it, got it on air before anyone else had a sniff of it, screwed them all. Completely.'

It had taken Rob one more round of Kingfishers to tell the story. A large and well-known drinks company, a household name, had opened a plant in a rural part of southern India. In the beginning, the company was welcomed with open arms as a big employer and benefactor, but within a year local farmers began to notice that the water table was falling, wells were drying up and it was getting increasingly hard for them to irrigate their land. The company had always made it clear that they would have to use local water but said they would take no more than one hundred thousand litres a day. The farmers claimed they were taking ten times that. A delegation went to talk to the company about the problem and ask for a solution and compensation of some sort. The company responded by saying they would use less water and even better than that, they'd start providing fertiliser to help improve the quality and yield of the farmers' land.

'So far, so what? Yeah? But what happened next was a lot more interesting and legally difficult. The fertiliser that this company gave or sometimes sold to local farmers to spread across their land wasn't what it seemed. It wasn't some revolutionary new fertiliser developed just for the little farmers. It was actually a sludge, a by-product of their manufacturing process. "Old shit in new bottles" is how William put it.'

The story had continued that the farmers who used the fertiliser said that their crops were growing more slowly and what did grow was bad. There were dozens of stories of children suffering from diarrhoea and assorted illnesses after eating food grown using the new product, and until Carver and Mariscal showed up, this part of the story had gone largely unreported. William had found one piece in the *New Internationalist* and there were a few Indian blogs, but apart from that there was nothing. The obvious reason for the lack of coverage was the absence of proof; it was the word of a few illiterate Indian farmers versus a large, rich and well-respected company. No contest. But what William found changed that. He'd got hold of toxicology reports from a respected Scottish university: a postgraduate who liked India and distrusted big business had spent time carefully collecting and labelling soil samples from dozens of farms that used the sludge, then brought them home to be studied. The results made worrying reading: it was true there were elements in the sludge which could be found in some fertilisers, but there were also very high levels of lead and mercury. The sludge that the company was flogging to farmers was more poison than fertiliser.

Rob had finished his meal and was wiping his plate clean with a garlic naan. 'These farmers were basically paying to poison their own land! Incredible. That won prizes. Lots of prizes. Not that that's any indication of quality, but this was a cracking piece of journalism. Story ended up all over the telly, all over the world, a smooth-looking PR guy apologising live to a few illiterate farmers on CNN, Sky, BBC, everywhere. Brilliant!'

He had swilled the dregs of his lager round the glass and drained it. 'Right. We're all done here. You'll need a whisky to hold that curry down. I know a place in Soho; we'll cab it.'

The five-minute cab ride had been all Rob needed to complete his pitch. 'The Head of News asked me what Carver was working on the other day and I had no idea, I had to make something up. It's embarrassing. So here's the deal. Next time he travels, he travels with you. You're William's last chance at the BBC. And if I'm honest, Paddy, I think he's probably your best chance too. If you get this right, all sorts of doors will open, interesting opportunities. And you'll obviously get all the boring stuff too.

You know? A staff job, bit of security, better money, a pension. It probably means nothing to you right now but trust me, it gets important as you get older.'

On the contrary, Patrick had thought, it meant everything to him. The prospect of a future which featured Rebecca, their shared flat and a steady career with a decent salary seemed almost too good to be true. He would do whatever was necessary.

'William's flying back in for the summer party. I've told him if he doesn't show then he's fired and I think he got that. So I'll introduce you properly there, and after that you stick to him like glue. You'll be his producer but you'll report to me. Directly to me, and I'll need regular updates. Whether it's going well, badly or not going at all, you tell me what he's up to, day and night.'

The cab was pulling up. 'Here we are, Scott's.'

Rob posted a crumpled fiver through the gap in the cabbie's window and jumped from the taxi. Standing on the pavement, he had lit a cigarette and then put another in his mouth and lit that too. He pulled on the second cigarette once or twice, then held it out for Patrick to take.

'You can bring that in, Maggie lets me smoke. But she gets upset if I talk shop too much, so have we got a deal?' Mariscal offered up his hand and Patrick took it and shook it enthusiastically. He had a deal.

Inside the club, they had had the one whisky to hold the curry down and then another before Patrick bought a round of beer chasers and Rob found the chessboard and ordered more drinks. It was clear Mariscal was in no hurry to go anywhere. During their second game, Patrick had moved a bishop to protect his queen, and while he studied the board, Rob checked his watch: twelve thirty. He needed to sleep.

'Check. In fact, checkmate.' Mariscal emptied his whisky, letting the ice rattle against his teeth. He gave a little shiver. 'Maybe you should head home, Paddy. It's been a long day.' From his trouser pocket he dug out a dirty blue twenty-pound note and pressed it into Patrick's hand. 'Get a cab.'

Patrick considered refusing, but the thought of twenty minutes' extra sleep in the back of a taxi and being in his own bed by one was too tempting. He pulled himself up out of the sofa and raised an empty bottle. 'Thanks, boss. Great evening, really great.' He was aware his words were slurring and sliding into each other, but kept going:

'And thanks for the chat, good chat. I am your man.'

Rob smiled back. 'Glad to hear it. Go home.'

When Patrick turned to go he saw that the club was empty. Even Maggie had disappeared. He turned back. 'Rob, you know there's a pull-down sofa at my place, if you want to come back? Kip there?'

Mariscal studied him. 'Listen. Just 'cos you bought me a couple of beers doesn't mean you get to sodomise me. Clear off home. It's early yet, I'm sure something will come along.'

Patrick looked at Rob. He was sure nothing would come along. Mariscal's white belly was peeking through a gap in the buttons of his black shirt, there was a flurry of ash in the folds of his trousers, dandruff on his shoulders, and as he bent forward to reset the chessboard, Patrick could see an inch of grey at the roots of his dark-dyed hair.

Maggie came out of the kitchen just as Patrick was leaving. Her make-up had been carefully reapplied and Rob vaguely recognised the perfume. It was a warming smell, reassuring, and it opened a window on childhood, reminding him of aunties at Christmas.

She came and stood over Rob and looked at the array of framed pictures on the wall above his head. 'There's a Hockney in here somewhere,' she said, almost to herself.

'The fuck there is,' Rob snorted. 'Who told you that?'

'Hockney.' She put a hand on his shoulder and craned her neck to look a little higher, but she couldn't see the picture and she couldn't be bothered to search for it. It was too dark to see very much anyway. 'And a Blake too, somewhere. Peter, not William. One Blake, one Hockney and apart from that, a load of old cock that probably wasn't worth the booze I paid for it. Never mind, eh?'

Rob stood up and found his phone; he selected contacts and found Driver.

'All right, chief. Five fifty pick-up. Can you make sure there's twenty Bensons in the car? And the papers? I'm at the club.'

He considered phoning home, then checked his watch and decided against it. He switched the phone off. 'So Maggie, where to?'

'Bed, my darling. Off to bed. The night is young and neither are we.'

7 Administrators and Adventurers

DATELINE: Central Kabul, Afghanistan, June 26th

Baba had gone overboard. William and Karim sat down at a long trestle table sagging with food and set with the crockery and glassware their host usually reserved for weddings. Baba and his children buzzed around their guests, refilling glasses, bowls and dinner plates as each sip or mouthful was consumed.

'Eat, eat. It is good to eat. You are my honoured guests.'

They ate.

'Mr Baba, this meat! I didn't know you could cook so well,' said Karim.

Baba beamed and patted at his belly. 'Am I not a fat man?'

Soraya stood at the kitchen door and smiled. She had been pleased to cook a meal for the men who had made Baba so happy. William's package about the killing of Fazil Jabar had been played three times on the World Service. Baba, who appeared in the report for a full nineteen seconds, had listened carefully each time, just in case his contribution differed. It didn't. But that didn't stop him listening again and then sending links to all three versions to relatives and friends across Afghanistan and Pakistan. He monopolised the children's computer for an entire day doing it, and then, the following day, after waking in the night with the idea fully formed in his head, he had gone to the print shop to order two thousand new publicity leaflets for the guesthouse with the words *As seen on BBC radio!* splashed across the cover. Baba had been leaving increasingly strange and somewhat surreal messages on William's mobile phone asking when he could make a return visit. So the reporter had arranged to meet Karim at the guesthouse, they could catch up properly and he could find out whether Baba had remembered anything more. It quickly became obvious that he hadn't, he simply wanted to express his thanks. But Baba was right: it was good to eat, and between noisy mouthfuls, William asked Karim to summarise what they knew.

A district chief, Fazil Jabar, and three others were dead. The Kabul government had yet to comment, but the NATO coalition had put on the record that Jabar had been the victim of a Taliban assassination. Against this, one of the best-informed men in Kabul said Jabar was in fact a friend of, possibly even a front for, the Taliban. They had a scrap of circuit board which seemed to suggest that whoever had killed Jabar was well equipped and had money. And they had the name of a man who might or might not have been at the scene of the explosion, the mysterious Richard Roydon.

As Karim went through his notes, Carver realised that his translator had been making most, if not all, of the running. He opened his wallet and forced two fifty-dollar bills into Karim's hand. 'A bonus, for all the extra work'.

Karim protested, but William was insistent: 'Take it, you deserve it, but there's a load more still to do and you're going to have to do a lot of it. I've got a sit-down with the British Ambassador later today, but then I have to get back to London.'

'Why?'

'My boss wants me back for his stupid bloody summer party

and probably to give me another dressing down, but more importantly, I got an interesting email last night, about Jabar.'

Karim's eyes brightened. 'From who?'

'No idea, no name, the person just signed off *an interested party* and it came from a meaningless-looking gmail account, but they say they have further information about Fazil Jabar, *relevant to our investigation*. The whole thing has an official ring to it; he or she says I should make contact when I'm next in England. I'm not convinced, but I'll give it a go. While I'm gone, I want you to keep trying to chase the story down here. First thing you need to do is check out the morgue.'

They ate and drank as much as their stomachs would allow and listened as politely as they could as Baba regaled them with stories of weddings good and bad. When their host finally took a brief toilet break they saw their opportunity, rose, put on their jackets and took their plates to the kitchen.

'You must go?' Baba was almost running back to his guests. 'Even though you only just arrived? Okay, if you must, but let me walk you to your car.'

He led them through the garden, past the fountain which was pumping away noisily in their honour.

Making an appointment to see the British Ambassador had been more straightforward than William expected. He had left a message on the Embassy's answering machine and an Afghan woman had called him back within the hour, suggesting six the following evening. 'Lounge suit,' she had added before hanging up. William had ignored that part of the message. He wasn't even sure he knew what it meant. He was wearing dark Farah trousers, his least dirty white shirt and a crumpled blazer, which he'd cleaned with a wet cloth. The car dropped him at a security post next to an imposing pair of wrought-iron gates. Two Nepalese private security contractors scanned his plastic bag, patted him down and then pointed him in the direction of the Ambassador's residence. He looked at his watch; it was a quarter to six and still uncomfortably hot. Halfway up the drive he stopped, removed his glasses and mopped his brow with his blazer sleeve. An Afghan woman in her forties was spraying the steps and front path with water from a thick white hose, damping down the dust. As William approached, she turned the hose away and placing her thumb across the end, sent a fine spray in the other direction, creating a rainbow in the evening sunlight. William panted self-consciously as he went up the steps and mumbled an apology in the woman's direction. He wasn't expecting a response and was slightly startled when she spoke. It was the same voice he had spoken to on the phone . . .

'Don't worry. Go straight inside. Ambassador Lever is waiting for you in the library, Mr Carver.'

William looked at the woman more closely now. She was beautiful; dark-eyed and with fine features, her black hair was framed by a bright white headscarf. The rest of her clothes were western: jeans and a baggy blue shirt, untucked. Gardening clothes, he guessed. William looked away. He was aware she was watching him, so he wiped his feet rather theatrically on the mat before stepping into the hall.

'Library. Turn third right,' she called after him.

Sure enough, three doors down, by a turn in the stairs, William found the library. Ambassador David Lever was nowhere to be seen, so Carver stood and scanned the bookshelves. They contained all the correct classics and a handful of well-reviewed recent titles. No trash and no surprises save for a couple of books on religious philosophy and the King James Bible and an English-language Koran sitting side by side.

He took both books out and examined them; both had broken spines, the tell-tale sign of regular use.

'Good evening, Mr Carver.'

William pushed the books hastily back in. The Ambassador was dressed exactly as one might expect a British ambassador in Kabul to be dressed: light linen suit, striped shirt and a club tie of some sort. It was only the hat that seemed a touch over the top. William couldn't help but linger on it.

'Ah, my Panama! I know it makes me look like something of a museum piece, but it's the right headgear for this country, and it hides my bald spot.' The Ambassador removed the hat with both hands and dropped it on an armchair before joining William at the bookcase.

'This is an interesting book.' He pulled out a green leather-bound volume from among its neighbours and opened it. 'It's one of those nineteenth-century gazetteers from British East India. Still the best thing I've found if you want to know about the tribes of Afghanistan, or Pakistan for that matter.'

'I'd heard those books were useful, yes,' said William, more than a little impressed.

'I tell you, if a few more of the silly sods in charge of this war had read books like this back at the beginning, things might've turned out a little better, don't you think?'

Such candour, so early in their acquaintance, took William by surprise.

Lever turned the thick pages of the book until he found a faded full-colour plate showing what looked to William like an Afghan tribesman in some sort of battle-dress. 'Here we go. This fellow is a Zadran, real savages by all accounts. A great-great uncle of mine made that engraving. I come from a long line of colonial administrators and adventurers, you see. Some extremely respectable, others completely bonkers. Do you know the type? The kind who used to dye their faces with caustic soda and walnut juice and wander off into the mountains to try and get to know the natives, that sort of thing.'

'Which side of the family are you from, Ambassador? Extremely respectable or completely bonkers?'

'Oh, I'm as respectable as it gets, I'm afraid, Mr Carver. Very boring, I'm sorry to say. My great-great-whatever uncle would be extremely disappointed with me, he really would.' He shut the book and put it back in its place on the shelf. 'What shall we drink?'

Lever took a small silver dinner bell from a nearby coffee table and rang it softly. The same Afghan woman William had met outside appeared in the doorway. She had changed into a smart but simple white shameez. The headscarf was also gone, revealing thick black hair that fell well past her shoulders.

'Good evening, Mrs Ansari. Mr Carver, this is my housekeeper, Mrs Ansari.'

William nodded at the woman and smiled. He'd heard that Lever had trimmed the residence staff dramatically; gardener, cook, secretary and cleaner all given the heave-ho, to be replaced, it seemed, by this one woman.

Both men opted for whisky with water and ice. William fancied that the glass Mrs Ansari handed to the Ambassador was a little darker in colour than his own, but perhaps it was the light.

'So,' said Lever when Mrs Ansari had left the room, 'Captain Remora told me you might be in touch. He doesn't seem to be your biggest fan, I'm afraid.'

'Really? Well I don't like him much either. '

'No, I can understand that. He's not to everyone's taste.' Lever took a long drink of his whisky. 'The Americans love him. They'd bottle him if they could. We had a visit from a four-star general recently and after the press conference he asked whether he could adopt him or naturalise him or some such. They think the sun shines out of his you-know-what.'

William swilled the whisky around his glass. 'They're welcome to him. I don't like the way he works.'

'How so?'

'From what I hear, he attaches strings and makes stipulations in return for Army access, for one thing.'

The Ambassador shrugged. 'That's pretty standard, isn't it?'

'It didn't use to be, and Remora goes further. Demanding copy approval before he'll give any access at all. That's like agreeing to have your bollocks cut off, as far as I'm concerned.'

Lever laughed. 'Indeed? Well many journalists appear not to object.'

There was a brief silence and the Ambassador gave a nervous cough. 'I'm afraid I do have to ask a rather awkward question, Mr Carver – at Remora's behest, I should add.'

William nodded. 'Go ahead.'

'Well, he seems to think you might know the whereabouts of an appointments book. A large ledger which the tailor used. The Afghan investigations team were supposed to have secured it, but it seems it's been mislaid.'

William raised his eyebrows. 'That's careless.'

'Indeed. I don't suppose you've come across it?'

William reached down into his plastic bag and retrieved the book. 'Here you go. For the record, I was going to give it to you whether you asked or not.'

Ambassador Lever's jaw dropped but he swiftly regained his composure, walking over and receiving the book from William with a smile. 'Thank you. Remora will be pleased.'

'I doubt it. Would you be kind enough to tell the Captain I have photocopied every page in front of witnesses who will testify to its origin and authenticity.'

The Ambassador stifled a laugh. 'I'll be sure to tell him that. I believe he was worried that you might be obstructing the investigation. Inadvertently, obviously.'

'I'm not obstructing anything, Ambassador. As for his so-called investigation, it seems to me that my translator and I are the only people doing any investigating.'

'I'll pass that thought on to him as well. You know, Mr Carver, I've been rather looking forward to meeting you. You're an interesting man.'

William frowned. He didn't agree, but nor could he be bothered to challenge the accusation. 'You attended Saint Praxted's school, I hear? Best state school in the country in its time. I know it a little, you see, the current head's an old chum. I understand you won a prize, for piety.' Lever gave his guest an amused look.

William lifted his drink and drained it. 'Where did you hear that?'

'Oh, I asked my people in London to put together a little pen portrait for me. I like to know whom I'm sitting down with. I hope you don't mind?'

It was William's turn to be surprised. He felt unsettled at the thought of a file, but also rather impressed. 'Of course not. I'm flattered. Maybe you'll let me have a look at the file sometime?'

'Maybe. I'd like to ask a personal question. Do you mind?'

William shrugged.

'I'm interested, what happened to the prize-winning piety? How did you lose your faith?'

Carver lifted his drink only to find that he'd already finished it. 'How do you know I've lost my faith?'

'You haven't?'

'Maybe I never had it. My father sent me to Saint Praxted's, I didn't ask to be sent there, I had no choice. I suppose I just tried to fit in, be the good schoolboy. I tried so hard I won a silly prize.' William stopped. This was the most he'd spoken about his childhood in forty years. The Ambassador observed him closely.

'Maybe. But that wouldn't square with the rest of your file. My chaps have you down as a dyed-in-the-wool rebel, very anti-authority.'

'If that means that I object to being told what to do by idiots, then yes, they got that one spot on.' William shifted in his seat.

'Ambassador, I don't want to be difficult, but I'd rather not discuss my religious beliefs or lack thereof right now. That's not why I'm here.'

'I'm sorry, I was being nosy. I'm always fascinated by how and why people lose their faith. I've been trying to lose mine for years, you see.' The Ambassador's smile was sincere.

William nodded then furrowed his brow, reaching for something. '*God is in heaven and you upon the earth; therefore let your words be few*. Isn't that how it goes?'

The Ambassador's smile broadened. 'Ah, so Saint Praxted's did do their work, whether you liked it or not. *Ecclesiastes* still firmly lodged in the old brain box. Once it's in, there's no shifting it.'

Carver rapped a knuckled hand against the side of his head, his face softening a little. 'Maybe another whisky would help dislodge it?'

'Certainly.' Lever beckoned to Mrs Ansari, who refilled their drinks. William watched his host stare appreciatively at the woman as she bent from the waist to hand him the glass. 'Your health. Shall we take these to the table?'

The springs of the sofa gave a sigh of relief as Carver hauled himself upright and followed Lever across the hall into a dimly lit dining room. In the centre was a large polished oak table, set for two. The Ambassador put his whisky down and picked up a large glass of water.

'I always drink half a pint of water before eating a meal. Stops me overeating.'

Mrs Ansari put William's food down in front of him. He had his fork in his hand and was about to dig in when he felt Lever's eyes on him.

'Do you mind if I say grace?'

'Of course not.'

Carver did not join in the prayer but he put his fork back down and kept his head bowed. Then they ate. The food was simple but good. Boned chicken in some sort of cream and herb sauce, a side dish of onions and a perfectly cooked rice dish flavoured with something William couldn't quite place. He was a messy eater. He kept his head low so the fork had only a short distance to travel between plate and mouth and he had his napkin tucked into his shirt collar just in case. He could sense Lever watching him.

'This rice is excellent,' he mumbled, mouth still full.

Lever winced almost imperceptibly. 'Cardamom. And the chicken is cooked in tarragon. Mrs Ansari grows the herbs right here, in the garden.'

'I'm amazed anything grows out here.'

'I was sceptical too, when I first arrived. I was something of an amateur gardener back in England – just flower borders and a few vegetables – but I never liked the look of the soil here. I thought earth had to be nice and damp and dark. Mrs Ansari has educated me. You can grow a lot in yellow and red soil if you know what you're doing. And if you stick at it.'

There was a silence. Lever rested his knife and fork neatly on the edge of his plate. 'That's my job, Mr Carver, sticking at it. God knows we haven't covered ourselves in glory here in Afghanistan in recent times, but I still think we can do some good, make a difference.'

William had heard this kind of talk countless times. 'What kind of difference are you hoping to make, Ambassador?'

'Creating jobs, building a bit of security, building up the economy. It's all still possible, even now.'

'So we're building? I thought we were just standing in a big bloody hole and digging, digging, digging.'

'We're digging, yes, but only so we can start planting and building. I'd really like to convince you of that, you and your friends in the media. I honestly believe it's true.'

'I'd like to believe it too, Ambassador. But I shan't hold my breath.'

Lever reeled off a number of projects and initiatives which the Embassy was involved in, and William listened politely, asked questions, took some notes and promised he would visit some. If the work they were doing was as significant as Lever believed, if it was newsworthy, then he would do his best to cover it. The two men exchanged stories of their time in Kabul and William's tours of the rest of the region, they got along well enough and ate Mrs Ansari's excellent meal.

As she cleared their plates, William looked at his watch. 'I don't want to keep you up late, Ambassador. I'm sure Captain Remora told you why I wanted to talk to you? I'm interested in the killing of Fazil Jabar.'

'Yes. A tragic business.'

William leant back in his chair and looked directly into Lever's grey eyes. 'Yes. Nasty. Ambassador, I want to ask you about a man called Richard Roydon. Does that name ring a bell?'

The diplomat answered swiftly and his response was far more fluent than anything else he'd said. It didn't just sound fluent, William thought, it sounded rehearsed.

'Yes, of course. I didn't know him terribly well but he did some work for us while he was at Rook Security, just extra shifts on the gate when the threat level was high, and some personal security for visiting VIPs from time to time, select committee MPs, junior FCO people and such like. Why do you ask?'

Carver ignored the question. 'So he's not working for you now?'

'No, no. All a bit unfortunate, actually. He came highly recommended, a former Royal Marine with a decent service record. But he became a little—unreliable, to be perfectly frank. Too fond of a drink, some people said. I gather he missed a few shifts, turned up late or not at all, so we had to tell Rook to send us someone else. I think they let him go in the end, but I'm not sure of that.'

'And you don't know where he is now?'

'No idea. I remember he told me once that he wanted to set up a business selling ice in Nairobi. But who knows? He might just as easily have joined up with another security firm after Rook let him go. There's still a lot of money to be made riding with the convoys, a thousand pounds a day if it's dangerous enough. So he could be doing that. There was always something of the buccaneer about him.'

'Right. The reason I ask is that Roydon was having a suit made at the tailor's in Passport Street. According to Mr Savi's appointments book, he was due to be there just an hour or so before the bomb went off.'

The Ambassador reached up towards his shoulder and massaged away a pain, real or imaginary. 'Really? More a matter for the Afghan authorities than me, I'm afraid, Mr Carver. I really have no idea where he is these days. What else have your enquiries revealed, out of interest?'

Carver paused. 'Not much really. Not much at all. I've taken up enough of your time, Ambassador, I should go. I told the car to wait for me outside from nine, he'll be wondering where I am. Thank you for dinner, it was excellent. Will you thank your housekeeper for me? Perhaps I could offer her a lift home? I'm heading back into town.'

Lever smiled kindly. 'That's very thoughtful, Mr Carver, but I believe she's made her own arrangements.'

8 The Summer Party

DATELINE: Royal Institute of British Architects, Upper Portland Place, London, W1, June 30th

The *Today* programme summer party was a significant fixture in the political calendar. It was previewed in the Court and Social pages of *The Times* and usually provided several items for the next day's gossip columns, depending on the quality of the guests and the quantity of wine consumed.

Rob Mariscal leant against the Portland stone entrance and first ran an approving eye and then the palm of his right hand over the cold, beautifully decorated bronze door. He lit a fresh cigarette with the stub of his last and gave a smoky sigh of satisfaction.

The RIBA building was a good choice of venue: symmetrical, austere, classy. Rob wasn't architecturally literate, but he knew what he liked. The smart-suited PR man who'd been assigned to show him the various reception rooms on offer hadn't needed to go any further than the foyer and the Florence Hall. Rob had fallen for the huge main staircase and its marble columns, the etched glass and panelling. He wasn't particularly interested in the 'deeply splayed piers of Perrycot limestone' but he let the guy finish his spiel: 'art and craft to the highest standard, as you can see, opened by King George V and Queen Mary!' Rob had seen and heard enough. He agreed a date and they haggled over the price, pointing out that a couple of minor royals were expected as well as most of the people who ran the country. 'Loads of snappers, too. Guaranteed.' The price came down five hundred pounds and they shook hands.

Rob considered alcohol the key to any party, and especially this one, so he'd chosen the drinks himself with great care after a long and happy afternoon spent gargling and gobbing at a wine warehouse. The BBC budget was small, but he was creative and had settled on two Spanish wines: a crisp floral Verdejo and a mature red from Catalonia which tasted like good Merlot but was about half the price. He'd ordered a dozen boxes of each and a Crémant that he knew was close enough to champagne to fool four-fifths of his guests: he had the waiters wrap a starched napkin round the labels and kept a twelve-bottle box of Moët in a cooler next to the reception table for show. He'd posted his two prettiest members of staff at the reception table, both dressed, at his request, in 'small black numbers'.

Rob checked his name badge, and after experimenting with it on his shirt and then his tie, decided it looked best pinned to his trouser pocket. He wore his usual uniform of black but the shoes were polished and the shirt was fresh out of the box. His chaotic hair was unbrushed but recently dyed and as dark as his clothes.

Stepping down towards the kerb, he tried to flatten the obvious shirt folds over his paunch with one hand while greeting a couple of early and not very important guests with the other. The *Thought for the Day* contributors always arrived early, left late and ate like animals in between, but he had to invite them; half a dozen top Christians and one each from all the other major world religions, that was the rule.

A summer shower had put a shine on the pavement outside. A

steady stream of guests was now beginning to arrive; some by foot, some in black cabs, and, to Rob's relief, at least half a dozen in ministerial cars. They began to flow in, moving towards the foyer table to collect their badges and glasses of Crémant. Every new arrival loitered at the table a little longer than necessary, pretending to look for their own name while speed-reading other badges to see who else was expected. There was something for everyone. One current and three former prime ministers, several minor royals, cabinet ministers, and their various spads and shadows. There were CEOs, scientists, controversialists, commentators and newspaper editors by the dozen. There were several actors and musicians with political interests, artists, fashion designers and people who, if they were famous at all, were famous for being at parties like this one.

The *Today* programme was a virtual thing, a play in three hour-long parts which floated out from the nation's radios each morning but soon disappeared to wherever radio waves and thoughts and ideas and arguments go. Up into the ether. The summer party was an annual attempt to fix it in time and space. As far as Mariscal was concerned, it wasn't just a party; it was an installation, a physical representation of a virtual thing. He began to work the room, a full bottle of the good champagne in his left hand, his right hand ready to slap backs and grip shoulders. He watched the most senior Catholic in the country break away from a group of high clergy, catch a cocktail waitress by the arm and post half a dozen caviar-covered blinis into his wide mouth like they were communion wafers.

Rob was enjoying himself right up until the moment his eyes settled on William Carver. 'Fuck me, he turned up.'

He hadn't seen William arrive but it seemed obvious that the reporter had come straight from the airport. He had a small suitcase by his chair and was wearing a pair of bright red sky socks. Carver was sitting hunched in a corner while scribbling something in his notepad, his mobile phone sticking out of his mouth like an oversized choc ice. Surrounded on every side by respectable people in lounge suits or evening wear, it looked to Rob like William had sprinted through a charity shop grabbing what he could.

Patrick had noticed Carver too. But seeing in the flesh the unpredictable man whose future was now tied inextricably to his own, he grew nervous; he needed some space and a little quiet before being introduced. He wandered out of the hall, past the bathrooms and up two flights of stairs, eventually finding an unlocked door and an empty room with large picture windows that looked out over Portland Place. After a struggle he managed to hoist one of the windows open. He leant out, switched on his mobile phone and waited for it to establish a signal. A few newspaper photographers were gathered on the pavement below and further down the road he could see a lone protestor camped opposite the Chinese Embassy: Falun Gong. The man had been there so long he'd become a permanent fixture as newsworthy as the lamp post he sat next to. The phone vibrated in his hand. One new message: *Call me?*

When Rebecca picked up, the background noise down the line meant Patrick could place her immediately. She was in the pub just down the road from her school, sitting far too close to the jukebox. Her voice cut through the din. It was a great voice, he thought, always on the edge of laughter. 'Hey, you. Can you hear me? It's loud in here. How's the party?'

'It's good, really packed, lots of drunk and sweaty politicians. The Prime Minister's coming later.'

'Sounds lovely. Any sign of William Carver yet?'

'Yep. He just arrived. I'm hoping Rob's going to introduce us.'

'Okay. Good luck, baby. We'll talk later—oh wait, wait, have you done that thing I asked you to do?'

Rebecca had made Patrick promise that he'd talk to the new Education Secretary. He had to persuade her to drop testing and give all primary school teachers an extra five grand a year.

'I had a word. She said she'll drop the tests but only if you all agree to take shorter summer holidays and stop wearing those nasty cardigans.'

Rebecca sniggered appreciatively and he listened as she passed this news to her drinking pals, all fellow teachers. There was the sound of easy laughter. Patrick wished he were there.

'Okay, I've chatted to my lot. Tell her we can talk about the summer holidays but the cardigans are non-negotiable.'

'Right you are.'

'Good. And don't forget the five grand.'

'Sure. I'll go tell her. But just remind me what I get in return for this little service?'

Rebecca laughed. There was a pause and when his girlfriend next spoke the phone was muffled with half a hand. 'If that was your shot at a little bit of phone-sex, then it was rubbish. Having said that, I am wearing that red dress you like and if you don't come home too drunk, maybe I'll let you help me take it off. Now go and chat to the Prince of Wales, I'm up next on the pool table.'

The line went dead. Now Patrick really wanted to be at the pub. He loved watching Rebecca play. She was terrible, but she played the most unintentionally sexy game of pub pool he'd ever seen.

Patrick leant as far as he could out of the window and took a few gulps of fresh air. He was about to switch the phone off when it vibrated in his hand. A message, sender unknown: *Don't do it!* Patrick turned and saw Anna McCarthy standing in the doorway staring at him. She had taken Rob's request to wear a little black dress extremely seriously and Patrick tried not to stare and then not to blush but didn't do too well at either.

He pointed at his phone. 'Hey, Anna. I didn't know you had my number.'

'Oh yeah, I have your number.' She smiled.

'Right. Who's looking after the reception table?' he asked stupidly. Anna let the unintended insult pass. As a broadcast assistant, she was on the very lowest rung of the ladder – a glorified secretary, used to being underestimated, patronised.

'I've left Hilary in charge.'

'I'm sure Rob would prefer it if you were front of house,' he said, trying lamely to flatter.

'He'll forgive me.'

This was undoubtedly true. Anna reached into a clutch bag and pulled out a tin box. 'Although maybe he won't. He doesn't like the dress, says there's not enough décolletage.'

'How much décolletage does a man need!'

Anna smiled. This was better. 'Your tie is a right mess. Allow me.' She loosened, straightened and tightened the knot of Patrick's tie while he stared fixedly over her head. Her hair was dark brown, a mess of corkscrew curls, and he could smell her shampoo. She stood back and nodded. 'Better. Almost presentable.' She took some makings out of her tin box and within seconds had constructed a neat roll-up; she lit it and took a few draws before holding it out for Patrick to share. 'Want some?'

He eyed the half-smoked cigarette warily.

'Always so suspicious, Patrick. It's just tobacco.'

Patrick shook his head and Anna finished the fag and flicked the roach out of the window in the direction of the newspapermen. 'Come on. Rob wants to see you.'

'Why?'

'How would I know? Maybe he doesn't like your décolletage either?'

They walked downstairs and pushed back into the party. The noise now was immense. Patrick found several of his colleagues bunched together and was being drawn into a conversation when Rob caught sight of him and waved him over. He made his apologies and joined his boss at the back of the room.

'You're supposed to be mingling, you stupid fucker, not talking to those idiots. You can see them any day of the week.'

Patrick apologised and Rob poured an inch of the good champagne into his empty glass. 'Plus you stink of dope.'

Patrick flushed with embarrassment, unsure of how to respond. As it turned out, no response was expected. 'Okay, so here's where it starts. You see Carver?' Rob nodded towards the other side of the hall. 'Over there, talking to the second ugliest man in the room.' Patrick followed Rob's glare and there indeed was William, perched uncomfortably on the edge of a high-backed designer chair, leaning forward and concentrating his attention on a bearded man in a cord jacket. The bearded man was waving a bandaged hand at him and talking with some urgency.

Patrick recognised him. 'That bloke's called Berry. Dr Berry, I think he said. He's something or other at the FCO.'

Mariscal looked vaguely impressed. 'How d'you know that?'

'He wasn't on the guest list. I helped him blag his way in. He said it was important.'

Mariscal led Patrick closer to the two men but the volume of noise in the Florence Hall made it impossible to hear anything of their conversation, and even William was having to lean in.

'This is a ridiculous place to meet, Mr Carver.'

William gave a shrug. 'You asked to see me, you're seeing me.'

'Yes. But why here?'

Carver looked around the room. 'What could be less suspicious than a hack and a Whitehall mandarin shooting the breeze at the *Today* programme summer party? I believe they call it hiding in plain sight.'

'I'm hardly a mandarin, Mr Carver, I'm a middle-ranking civil servant, my boss gets invited to these sorts of occasions, I don't.'

'You managed to get in okay though, didn't you?'

'One of your colleagues was kind enough to help.'

'So here we are.'

The bearded man gave William an exasperated look. 'I understand your scepticism, Mr Carver, I know a little of your recent history, but hopefully the fact that I turned up here will show you I am sincere.'

Carver pushed his glasses higher up his nose and gave a grudging nod. As Rob and Patrick watched, the civil servant took a pen and business card from his breast pocket, scribbled something down and handed the card to William. They exchanged a few more words and then the man left. William pocketed the card.

Mariscal waited until the mysterious Dr Berry had left the room, then gave Patrick's arm a squeeze. 'Okay, Paddy, here we go. First day of the rest of your life. Go introduce yourself.'

'I thought you were going to introduce me?'

'No, it's better you do it. Just remind him it was you in charge the night his Afghan story ran. Then you're up and running.'

Rob had seen someone else he needed to talk to and walked off waving. Patrick worked his way across the room towards William. He told himself the nervous clench in his stomach was irrational.

'Mr Carver? Hello. I'm Patrick Reid.'

William looked up briefly, then looked back at his notebook. 'Do I know you?'

'Yes, well no but we spoke the other night.'

'Yeah?'

'I was editing last Friday. I ran your Afghan piece, as a lead, remember?'

William glanced up again. 'That's your job, isn't it? To run pieces on the radio? What do you want, a medal?'

'No. No, I just wanted to meet you. I know you've just flown in and I'm sure you must be knackered, but Rob's assigned me to work with you for a while, so I thought I'd come over and, you know, introduce myself.'

'Work with me? Like how? Another producer?' Patrick was swaying slightly on the balls of his feet.

'Yeah, I mean, yes, I guess I'm your new producer. If that's all right with you.'

110

'It's not all right with me. First that annoying young woman in Kabul, now' – he looked at Patrick with naked contempt – 'this? Forget it. I'm going to have this out with Rob.'

Carver stood up sharply, picked up his suitcase and pushed past Patrick.

'I'll see you later,' said Patrick weakly.

'I doubt it.'

9 The Missing Man

DATELINE: Zarnegar Hospital morgue, Kabul, June 30th

This was not Karim's first visit to a morgue but it was the first time he'd gone alone. He and William had visited half a dozen hospital morgues when the reporter was trying to get a more accurate picture of the number of civilians being killed each day in Kabul. Most recently and more upsettingly, Karim had escorted his mother's older sister when she was asked to come and identify a man the authorities believed to be her husband. The old man had been killed by a scrap of shrapnel during an abortive Taliban attack on the Afghan National Army. In the confusion he'd been taken to a hospital on the far side of the city. Dead on arrival, he had lain unidentified and missing for two days. It was a common story. While he was missing, there was hope, and Karim was struck by how reluctant his aunt had been to let go of this shred of optimism. He remembered her turning away when the cloth-bound cadaver was pulled smoothly from the refrigerated drawer and when the doctor folded back the shroud to reveal a face, his aunt examined it so closely, so carefully, looking, he realised later, for something which might tell her this was not the man she had known for almost fifty years. Finding no such sign she had collapsed; all the scaffolding which held her upright suddenly gone. Bending down to help her, he had felt the tears on her face and heard her whisper 'Habibi, habibi.' Husband, husband. Karim had had to carry her from the cold room and had been struck by how little she weighed, almost nothing, like he was carrying a bundle of clothes, not a woman, a wife and mother. She had eaten half a plate of food at the reception which followed the funeral, but only for appearances and not again afterwards. The family had buried her a few weeks later, in a child-sized coffin.

By the look of it, this hospital morgue had been recently refitted. It was a wide white-walled room with bright strip lighting. There was a bank of stainless steel fridges, each large enough and long enough to house one cadaver, along one wall. There was a door to a cold storage room in the far wall; it was open and frozen air billowed out between thick vertical strips of orange PVC. There were two steel tables bolted to the floor and on one of these lay a tall-looking corpse covered in a blue cloth. The only living thing in the room was a woman in white plastic scrubs, busily washing down the floor with a yellow hose. Karim watched the water sloosh around the table legs and then pool and eddy at a large steel drain in the centre of the room. The floor sloped slightly from the walls to this central point. The coarse grey concrete was stained a pale pink by regular washings of blood. She caught sight of Karim but did not acknowledge him. Instead, she finished her work, waiting until the last of the water had gurgled and gone before lifting the drain grille with a gloved hand, picking a few pieces of bone and gristle from the metal and dropping them down the dark hole. She took her time folding the hose into neat loops, hung it on the brass standing tap in the corner of the room, then removed her scrubs, thrusting them deep into a pedal bin, followed by her gloves. Only after this procedure was finished did she turn to face Karim. The woman was birdlike, tiny, with bright eyes and a sharp nose. She looked more like one of the new government ministers than a mortician. She wore a black shirt and trousers, a gold wedding band but no other jewellery. The only colour on her was in a bright flowered scarf tied loosely at her collar. Karim guessed that maybe this was intended to cover the most obvious signs of age. In a kinder light, she might have passed for late forties but here, under a tungsten glare, every line showed. Karim put her closer to sixty.

'I assume you are the young man who has bribed my superior for information?'

Karim was taken aback by the directness of her manner. 'Are you the chief mortician?'

'The chief mortician, the junior mortician, the cleaner, the cook and the make-up artist.' She walked away past the bank of steel refrigerators to a desk with a cheap-looking microwave oven on it, opened the door and took out a Tupperware bowl. The woman loosened the lid and put it back in, punching two minutes thirty into the timer. She turned back and stared questioningly at Karim. It was his turn to speak but he could think of nothing to say beyond asking for the information he had paid for. But somehow that seemed unwise.

'I'm sure you do all those jobs very well, Mrs—Mrs—?'

'Raveed. It's Mrs Raveed. And you're right, I do.' Karim nodded. The smell of the room was changing from chemical to curry as Mrs Raveed's lunch warmed in the microwave. The machine emitted a tired ping and she opened it. Karim watched her decant the curry from the Tupperware into a shiny, kidney-shaped silver bowl more often used for holding human offal. Mrs Raveed brought her lunch back and sat down at the reception desk by the door. She gestured that Karim should sit down opposite. In the desk drawer she found a knife and fork wrapped in a paper napkin, and began to eat. Between tiny mouthfuls she spoke.

'I came back to Kabul soon after the Americans drove the Taliban out. I wanted to help rebuild this place, train the next generation of doctors. Instead, here I am, reassembling dead bodies all day long. Applying blusher to the faces of dead children so their parents can look at them long enough to say goodbye.'

Karim looked at the pink-hued concrete floor.

'And as for training the next generation, there aren't any young people to train. There is no money to pay their wages. With so much dying on the streets, why would anyone want to spend their working hours looking at dead people too? I don't blame them.'

Karim nodded, he hoped sympathetically.

Mrs Raveed smiled. 'That's who I am. Now, you. You're here to take a look at the people who were murdered at Passport Street, at the tailor's shop, yes?'

'In the bombing, yes.'

'The bombing, right. And what's your angle? You want to find out something about one of the dead, a distinctive birthmark? So you can extort money from a gullible relative? Persuade them they're still alive?' The woman's tone wasn't judgemental, just inquisitive.

Karim stuttered. 'Wh-what? No! Not at all, Mrs Raveed. I am not a criminal. I am a translator.'

The woman gave a snort of laughter. 'A translator? You are a translator. Okay. Then maybe there has been a mistake. You understand that most of the people I have with me here, they don't talk much anymore.'

Karim reddened. 'What I should say is I am a translator and as part of my job I work for a British journalist. Together we are investigating the bombing, trying to find out what happened.'

'Are you indeed?' The woman stared at Karim for a moment and then went back to eating.

Karim sensed that something was expected of him and reached into his pocket. 'Your supervisor suggested that you might be able to help, to spare me a little time, Mrs Raveed. In return for a small token.' He pushed a fifty-dollar bill across the table. The woman looked at it with interest.

'He suggested that you give me this?' Karim nodded. Mrs Raveed smiled and then pushed the note back across the table. 'He was teasing you, young man. Or testing me. You don't have to bribe me, you just have to be patient. I haven't finished my lunch, that's all.' She ate more quickly now, clearing her bowl and cutlery into one of the sinks before turning to Karim. 'So, two of the tailor's shop victims were what one would expect, typical bomb blast, severe and multiple injuries, burns.'

'Charring?'

'If you like, yes, severe charring, amongst other things. But the politician, what was his name?'

'Jabar. Fazil Jabar.'

'Jabar, that's it. He is rather more unusual. Maybe it will interest you.' Karim nodded in anticipation of some revelation but Mrs Raveed gestured towards the cold curtained room. 'Why don't you take a look?' Karim shook his head. 'Go ahead, be my guest.'

'Couldn't you just tell me what you have noticed, Mrs Raveed?'

'No. I want you to see for yourself and think for yourself; let's see if we agree. Get a gown on. The bodies are through there, all tagged and bagged. Neat and tidy.'

Karim saw that it would be useless to protest. He took a gown down from a set of pegs by the door and put it on. Mrs Raveed pulled the PVC strip curtain aside and pointed to a row of body bags at the rear of the storage room. The first body Karim came to was lying in a bag with one end left unzipped and open just sufficient to allow a clear view of the face. He moved closer and saw it was that of a young boy, eyes closed, peaceful. Karim looked down at the dead child. He had to contain a powerful urge to shake the boy, wake him and get him out of the frozen room. He stared at Jabar's son for a while before moving on to the second corpse. There was a strip of masking tape stuck to this black bag with a name written on it. Karim recognised it as that of Jabar's bodyguard. He glanced down at the old face, then turned quickly away: the man's eyes were frozen open with a look of comic shock, as though death had taken him by surprise. This second body had a smaller see-through plastic bag lying alongside it, sealed with a rip tag. Inside was a foot, burnt black in places and turning blue from the cold.

The masking tape attached to the third body bag read *FAZIL JABAR*. Karim swallowed back a mouthful of saliva and steeled himself, preparing to look at the dead man's face. As it turned out, there wasn't a great deal to look at; a fair amount of the right-hand side of Jabar's face had been burnt or blown away. Karim was beginning to feel nauseous. The interesting thing that Mrs Raveed spoke of was not obvious, and he didn't want to investigate any further. He didn't have the stomach for it. The tailor's corpse didn't seem to be with the other bodies anyway, and he'd had enough. Mrs Raveed was waiting for him just outside the cold store door.

'So what do you think?'

'I think I will be sick.'

'Sniff at this.' She handed him a handkerchief doused in peppermint, and he breathed deeply through his nostrils. 'So, do you see now what puzzles me?'

Karim held the handkerchief hard to his nose and shook his head. Mrs Raveed seemed disappointed. A teacher let down by her newest pupil. 'I know his face looks a mess but if you look a little closer at Jabar, there's something odd. The papers said he was blown up, and he was, but that wasn't his only misfortune.'

Karim removed the handkerchief. 'What else?'

'A shot to the head, point blank range. Just here.' Mrs Raveed pointed to her right temple just around the hairline. Karim swore under his breath and then quickly apologised.

'That's terrible, incredible.' He stared at the mortician, who shrugged.

'Not incredible, unusual, yes.'

'But who could have shot Jabar? How?' Karim asked, almost of himself.

'You're the journalist, young man. Or the translator for the journalist. You'll have to work that one out. If you want my opinion, the explosion didn't do its job, someone saw that and decided to make sure.'

'Who else knows this, Mrs Raveed? Who else have you told?'

The woman shrugged. 'No one. I've told no one else. Nobody has asked. The authorities seem to have very little interest in poor Mr Jabar.' She lowered her voice, as if the dead might hear. 'Or maybe they know already, because someone, somewhere removed the bullet before he arrived here.'

'Maybe the shot passed right through him?'

'It didn't. I may be getting old but I know an exit wound when I see one. There's no exit wound on Jabar. By the time these three arrived, they'd been checked over and packed up. They were already in body bags.'

Karim stood extremely still, staring at his feet, trying to process what he'd been told. Something was nagging at him. 'Three bodies? But there were four people killed at Passport Street, Mrs Raveed. Where's the body of the tailor, Mr Savi?'

The woman shrugged. 'I have no idea, but it didn't come here.'

'You are sure?'

The mortician smiled. 'Are you suggesting that I'm in the habit of mislaying dead people? I must get on now. I think you've had more than your money's worth, if you'll excuse me.'

'Of course. Thank you, Mrs Raveed. Thank you very much.'

Outside, on the street, Karim rested his back against the hospital wall, warm from the sun, going over in his mind the possible consequences of what he'd seen and what Mrs Raveed had just told him. Despite the general hustle and bustle of people entering and exiting the hospital, he became aware of a small-framed

Afghan man with a well-kept moustache observing him from the other side of the road. A plain-clothes policeman, perhaps, although there was something about him that didn't quite add up. Karim was about to get his notebook and pen out to make a list of the newly acquired information when the man crossed the road heading directly for him. Karim's nerves were already ragged; he stepped away from the wall and stood up straight, tense. He was used to seeing policemen pretending to look like something else, but here was something different. Here was someone trying very deliberately to look like a policeman. The man walked up to Karim, smiling broadly and holding out his police ID. Karim was pretty sure it was fake. He had occasionally dealt in counterfeit ID and this one wasn't even particularly convincing. Bought in a hurry, he thought. Karim gave no sign of doubting the man's credentials and nodded a guarded greeting.

'I'm from the National Directorate of Security. We need to talk to you, in private,' the man said.

'About what?'

'I'll tell you in the car, but it's only routine, no need to worry. Please, follow me.' The Moustache took hold of Karim's elbow; he had a surprisingly firm grip for a small man.

The car in question was parked some fifty metres away from the hospital, which also seemed strange. Couldn't a policeman park where he liked?

Karim knew he was in trouble when he realised the vehicle they were heading for was a black SUV that was so new it looked like it had just rolled off the assembly line. Unlike any Afghan police car Karim had ever seen. As he got closer he saw the shadows of two other men sitting inside, one in the front, one behind. They looked even less like Afghan police than the man escorting Karim; they looked like bandits. When Moustache opened the back door, Karim made his move. He brought his heel down hard on the man's foot and slammed the car door shut, trapping the hand of the bandit who'd been reaching out to receive him. He heard a loud yell of pain from inside the car and felt Moustache grab at his jacket, but he was too quick. He broke free from the man's grip and ran.

Karim tried to keep his head down and stay as close as possible to the shop fronts and offices along the main road; the street was not particularly busy at this time of day, but he thought there might be enough people around to make his assailants think twice before chasing after him. He was about to make his first turn, off the main street and up a side road, when he heard a distant cracking sound and immediately felt a powerful pain in his right side – a burning sensation, as though someone had brought a hot iron down hard on his right hip. The young Afghan slowed but didn't stop. He made the turn. Looking down at his side, he saw a tear in his shirt at waist height and a spray of blood down one trouser leg. He had not been shot before. The sound of his heartbeat was loud in his ears and his breathing was shallow and too fast. He was terrified but at the same time he had never felt more alert; as though the cinema reel had slowed, giving him time to look at every part of the frame.

Karim knew a couple of people in this neighbourhood. But did he know any of them well enough to entrust his life to them? There was a local shopkeeper he could get to who would let him hide on his premises, he was sure. But he suspected the man would just as quickly give him up, if threatened or bribed. He decided his best hope was to get back to his own car. He figured he knew these streets as well as anyone. He was halfway up the alley now and still running, not so quickly and with some pain, but still faster than most could manage, and he knew where he was going. From the main street, this side road looked like a dead end. Only once you reached the wall could you see that what looked like a shadow was in fact a narrow passageway to the road that ran parallel to the street he'd parked on. He looked down to see how much blood he was leaking and whether it was leaving any kind of trail. He could see nothing on the floor, although his shirt tail was red now and he could feel a trickle of blood running down his right leg. He jogged down the passageway, past several breezeblock houses and an open sewer, until he reached the road. He took a left and after a couple more dusty shortcuts ended up at a point where he could see his parked car. He waited and watched for a while but there was no sign of the black SUV or the men who'd tried to take him. He wondered what this meant. If they didn't know which car was his or how he'd got there, maybe they'd only become interested in him after he left the morgue. His head was spinning; there was too much to think about. He needed to find somewhere safe, make some proper notes and most importantly get a message to William Carver. William would know what to do. Karim took another good long look up and down the road before quickly walking to his Honda and climbing in. He put the key in the ignition and it started first time. Sitting low in the driver's seat, he put a clean foot to the clutch, his blood-filled shoe to the accelerator, and drove off slowly in the direction of the BBC house.

10 A Fortuitous Killing

DATELINE: Stockwell Road, London, SW9, June 30th

William dropped his suitcase on the floor and felt around for the light switch. He flicked it on. Nothing happened. He flicked it again: still nothing. They had cut off his electricity.

'Bollocks. Not again.'

He swept a pile of mail out of the way with his foot and started digging about in his luggage. At the bottom of the case, wrapped in a woollen jumper, he found what he was looking for. Carver slipped the night vision goggles over his head and turned them on. A strange grey-green version of his flat flickered into focus.

William walked through to the kitchen and checked the hob: thankfully the gas still worked. He made some tea, lit candles and boiled enough water for a tepid bath.

He had spent nearly an hour at the party, trying to grab Rob to tell him where to stick his supposed new producer, but Mariscal kept fobbing him off, introducing him to various members of the great and the good, few of whom William could even identify. Eventually he had tired of the game and left. He would go ahead and book his flight back to Kabul, and if Mariscal wanted to send another pointless producer chasing after him, then that was his call.

After an unsatisfactory attempt at a bath, William filled two hot water bottles and got into bed with as many blankets as he could find. England felt incredibly cold after Kabul. He'd just taken the second of two sleeping pills when his mobile phone buzzed into life and made a little circular dance around the bedside table. Two missed calls and two new messages. He dialled 901. The first was from Mariscal.

'Mate, it's Rob here. Look, sorry I couldn't chat at the party, I didn't want a big scene in front of all those punters. I'm sorry about pushing this producer thing on you but I don't have a choice. Patrick's a decent kid, came up through local papers like someone else I used to know, and I think you might like him if you give him a chance. But the bottom line is: whether you like him or not, he's going with you. This isn't a request, it's an order. I know you'll probably try and head off without him, but do yourself a favour and don't bother. You won't be able to. Anyway. Hope you're okay. Maybe we could get a beer sometime? Chat about the good times? There were some of those, if you remember. How about you give me a call in the morning?'

William listened to Rob hang up and then pressed 3 for delete. The second message kicked straight in. He heard static and then a soft Afghan voice: Karim. He sat up in bed and pressed the phone hard to his ear. His translator sounded nervous, unsure whether he should even be making the call.

'William, it is your friend. I have found something new, something I need to tell you about. I know I must not say anything important on the telephone so I will not speak now, but it would be very good if you could be here again soon so we can talk. I am not in the usual place but I will find you. And I must say another thing, which is to be careful. I was not careful enough. I am fine, do not worry, but you should know that others are interested in the same thing we are. Okay. Goodbye.'

William listened to the message twice and then saved it. He could feel the sleeping pills taking effect and he was pretty sure there was nothing he could do for Karim tonight. He changed the phone's setting to outdoor, in the hope that a louder ring tone would wake him if Karim had reason to call again.

Karim did not call. But he would not have woken William even if he had.

Patrick was hung over. He hadn't left the party until well after one, and thinking back over what he'd drunk he realised he must have had his own and several other people's share of the good champagne as well as quite a bit of the cheap white wine, when cheap white was all that was left. Rebecca's red dress was hanging provocatively over the bedroom door when he got in, but she was fast asleep and he realised now that that was probably just as well. She'd left for work at her usual time and he hadn't heard a thing. He was off shift, at least, so he could nurse himself back to health and then work out where he stood with Carver once his head had cleared. Rob had assured him that when William left the country, Patrick would too, but as far as he knew, that wasn't imminent. He lay in bed until half nine when greed got the better of sloth and he slipped a pair of jeans on over his pyjamas and made for the corner shop, in search of bacon.

Carver was sitting on a park bench directly opposite Patrick's flat, plastic bag at his feet. He was looking at the ice cream van that had just rolled up, ready to serve the mums and toddlers at a nearby play park. When he turned back towards the flat and saw Patrick coming down the steps, he waved.

'You're a late riser,' he called out. 'I've been here bloody hours.'

Patrick was momentarily speechless.

'How do you know where I live?' was all he could think of to say.

'All your details are in the system. Zero one zero eight eighty-seven, two nine seven five four two, nine six two five five eight . . .'

Patrick realised that the sequence of numbers Carver was reeling off were his date of birth, staff and passport numbers. 'Flat four, 128, Highbury Hill, N5 2LA. It's all in there.'

'Including my phone number; why didn't you just ring?'

'I prefer the personal touch. By the way, who was that blonde who came out earlier? Is she your sister?'

Patrick sat down next to Carver. 'What? No, she's my girlfriend.'

'Really? She was carrying some sort of satchel. Is she still at school or something?'

'She's a teacher.'

'A teacher. Really? I would've done a hell of a lot better at school if the teachers looked like that.' William eyed Patrick up and down. 'How does a bloke like you get a girlfriend like that?' He seemed genuinely interested.

Patrick shrugged. 'I don't know. Charm, I guess.'

Carver stifled a laugh. 'Charm. That's a good one.' He looked up at the tall terraced houses that ran the length of Highbury Fields. 'I used to work around here, did Mariscal tell you that?'

Patrick shook his head.

'That was another reason for coming up; I haven't seen the place in a while.'

Patrick gave an encouraging nod.

'It's changed a bit, I guess.'

'Just a bit. Look at all the cars outside those houses.' He pointed at the resident parking bays. 'Audi, Audi, Porsche, Mercedes . . .'

'Gentrification.'

'Yeah, gentrification. Shame, gentrification kills journalism, anything that's good news for estate agents is bad news for journalists. Holloway and Highbury used to be my beat, junior crime reporter. Time was, I could fill six pages just with what went on in this little patch.' William was warming to his theme. 'Your place for instance . . .' He waved a hand in the direction of Patrick's flat. 'There was a double murder and suicide down on the ground floor of your place, back in the seventies. Gory, it was.'

Patrick stared at Carver, who was smiling. 'You want to know the details?'

'I guess.'

'I bet you do. It was this young guy. Your age. He was still living at home – not very happily, it turned out. He killed his mum and dad, poisoned them both with rat poison, and then put his head inside a black plastic sack and cut his own throat.'

'Why the black plastic sack?'

'Good question. He was being nice – didn't want to make a lot of mess for his sister to clear up.'

'Considerate.'

'He was. His sister was very grateful too.'

'You spoke to her?'

''Course, that was my job. I always did the death knock.'

Patrick gave Carver a blank look.

'The death knock; you don't know about the death knock? When something awful's happened to a family, a death or disaster, some poor bastard has to go knock on the door and try and get a quote . . . a quote and photo. I did that.'

Patrick was aware of the practice but had never had to do it. 'That's a shitty job.'

Carver shrugged. 'I guess, but I didn't mind. I was good at it. People seemed to like talking to me and I liked listening. Being young helped, I think, young and green.' He examined Patrick. 'Mariscal said you came up through local papers?'

Patrick nodded enthusiastically. 'That's right, *South London Press*.'

Carver raised an eyebrow. 'Good paper, the *South London Press*. Still in Streatham?'

'Yeah, just off the High Street.'

'They should've got you doing the death knock.'

'I was very junior.'

'I told you already, the younger the better. Maybe they missed a trick. Anyway, I was about to get an ice cream. You want one?'

'Er, not really.'

'Suit yourself.' William walked the few yards to the ice cream van, taking his bag with him.

Patrick watched him wait his turn, order and then start to fumble around in his pockets. He turned round and hurried back. 'I've got no English money on me. Lend us a fiver.' Patrick found a five-pound note in the pocket of his jeans and handed it over.

Clouds moved fast across a bright blue sky and the occasional ray of sunshine shone through the leaves of the London plane trees, casting blurred green shadows on the pavement. The air felt fresh. William returned with a cider ice lolly for himself and a ninety-nine with a chocolate flake for Patrick.

'Here you go.'

'Oh, okay, thanks.' Patrick waited for Carver to speak. He was determined not to repeat the previous evening's humiliation. He wondered, fleetingly, if the reporter had come to apologise.

'Okay, so I called up BBC travel first thing this morning to book my flight back to Kabul and my travel privileges have been removed. They say they can't take a booking from me unless you're booked on the same plane, train, boat, whatever. Mariscal's orders. Did you know about this?'

'No—not exactly.'

'Not exactly. Well, it's a pain in the arse. A big bloody pain, but I don't see any way round it. It looks like it's working with you or not working at all, and right now, I need to work. Have you any idea what this is all about? Has Rob told you what he's playing at?'

Patrick had already considered how a conversation like this might go, and had resolved to be as honest as possible. 'He told me a few things. He's not happy; he says you aren't on air enough, that he doesn't know what you're up to most of the time and you upset everyone you work with. So I think partly he's just pissed off. But also, I think he's worried about you.'

Carver looked up from his ice lolly. 'Worried about me?' He repeated the words as though trying to hear for himself whether the idea was credible. 'I don't buy it. But I don't suppose it matters whether I buy it or not. So Patrick Reid, here's how it's going to go. First, you're going to have to do exactly what I tell you when I tell you, got that?'

'Sure, I'm your producer.'

'Fine, call yourself whatever you want. Second, whenever Mariscal asks you how we're getting on, you say everything is hunky-dory. But you tell him the absolute minimum. If you can get away with telling him nothing, tell him nothing. Yes?'

This was more difficult. Patrick wondered how he was supposed to square the two men's differing expectations, their contradictory demands. 'But Mariscal's—'

'No buts. That's it. That's the deal. We're agreed, then?' Carver's question invited no answer. He stood and finished his lolly in three bites, shivering as he did so. He stared at Patrick's almost untouched ice cream. 'Do you want that chocolate flake?'

'What? Er, yes.'

'Fine. It's just sometimes people don't like the chocolate flake.' Carver picked up his plastic bag. 'So you go ahead and book us on the first available flight back to Kabul, via Delhi or wherever. Get us on something tomorrow if there is something, day after if not. No later than that, right?'

Patrick nodded.

'I'm meeting a contact later tonight.'

'Do you want me to come?'

William looked at Patrick with disbelief. 'No, I don't want you to come. He's my contact.'

'Is it Berry?'

Carver sat back down. He shuffled closer to Patrick and spoke in low whisper. 'How the hell do you know about Berry?'

'I saw you talking last night, at the party . . .'

'Yeah, but how do you—never mind. No, it's not Berry. I'm not going to tell you who it is, but after I've met him, once I know what's going on, I'll give you a call. I've got your mobile, give me your home number.' Patrick dictated his home number and William punched it into his phone. 'What if your girlfriend picks up. Does she know about me?'

'Yes.'

'And she knows you're heading off to Afghanistan to get your bollocks shot off?'

'I didn't put it like that.'

'She can't be that keen if she's all right with you buggering off to the most dangerous country in the world without a second thought.' William didn't give Patrick time to frame a reply. He put his hand on Patrick's shoulder and used it to push himself upright. 'Don't worry; anything happens to you, I'll look after her. What did you say her name was?'

William arrived half an hour early for his appointment at the Charing Cross hotel. It was dusk and the pigeons were quick-stepping across the cobblestones, picking at scraps of discarded food and trying to avoid the waves of office workers rushing for trains that would take them home to the suburbs. Carver held a copy of the *Economist* open in front of him but he wasn't reading it. Instead, he watched the people and the traffic and the sky, which was turning a rich red high above Trafalgar Square. There was an annoying twitch around his left eyelid. He rubbed at it and tried to remember what its cause was: lack of sleep? Not enough vitamin C? A coach crawled slowly down the Strand before turning and parking illegally on a side road not far from where William stood. *Chatham Special*, it said on the front.

'That's a lie,' William muttered. The coach doors opened with a pneumatic hiss and a small army of theatre-goers tumbled out. They formed an orderly line on the pavement. All were older than William, and all were dressed for a big night out: the men wore blazers with polished buttons; the women were dressed like Queen Elizabeth at various stages of her long career.

Dr Berry was late and William was aware that the smartly dressed redhead reading the *Evening Standard* by Boots hadn't moved or, it seemed, turned a page of her paper in at least ten minutes. There was a watchful air to her that William didn't like. He decided to take a walk around the block. By the time he got back the woman had gone but there was still no sign of Berry. He decided to check inside. He looked in the Strand lounge first; it was crowded and he heard several languages being spoken simultaneously. His eyes swept the room in search of a middle-aged civil servant with a beard. He found Berry in the next-door bar. It was quieter in here and his man was sitting with his back to the door staring up at an old print of Charing Cross station, *circa* 1900. William took the chair opposite, smiled and offered his hand, which Berry shook briefly but with a good grip. Berry's other hand was lightly bandaged and held an empty glass. Something about the man's mood and manner told William that this finished drink had not been his first.

'Good evening.'

'I thought you'd stood me up. I was about to head off home.'

'I'm sorry, I thought we were meeting outside.' William wouldn't tell Berry about the woman in the suit; his contact seemed fragile enough already. 'Can I get you another drink?' He nodded at the empty glass.

'Why not? Gin and tonic, lots of ice.'

William went to the bar and returned quickly with a double gin and tonic and a Coke for himself. Berry watched as he fumbled the receipt into his wallet.

'Ah, yes. You can claim for that, I suppose. "Drinks with an informer." Is that what you'll write on the expenses slip?'

William smiled but otherwise ignored the question. Berry looked dreadful, much worse than at the party the previous night. His brown eyes were heavily bagged, his beard unkempt and his hair uncombed.

'I suppose you do this sort of thing a lot, Mr Carver?'

'This sort of thing?'

'Meeting with people in anonymous hotels, hoping they will tell you things they shouldn't?'

'I do it quite a lot, yes. It seems to be part of the job. What happened to your hand?'

Berry looked down at the bandage. 'Sawing logs. The wood was too young, too much sap. Damn saw nearly had me ruddy hand off. I should know better.' He twisted the bandage and took a gulp of his drink. 'Do you know, Mr Carver, I once wanted to be a journalist? I tried my hand at university and I rather liked it. My father talked me out of the idea in the end. He said that journalists were a grubby bunch who were paid not very much money to ask questions about things which were none of their business.'

Carver smiled. 'That about sums it up. Wise man, your dad.'

'Not really. A time-serving, middle-ranking civil servant, just like me. Just exactly like me. How about another drink?'

'Sure. Same again?' Carver still wasn't sure what to make of this man.

'Make it a double.'

William returned with a treble. He tucked the second receipt away next to the first while Berry watched. No point hiding it.

'What shall we talk about, Dr Berry?'

'Right, so I heard your report on the killing of Fazil Jabar.' Berry rubbed at his beard.

'Yes, you told me that, at the party.'

'So I did. Well, your report was straightforward, perfectly good as far as it went, but I just wondered whether you were planning to do any more on Jabar?'

'I don't know. Do you think I should?'

'Was everything that you know about Fazil Jabar in that report?'

'Everything I knew then, not everything I know now.'

'What do you know now?'

Carver set his drink down a little sharply. He took a quick glance around the bar before answering. 'Forgive me, Dr Berry, but I've been shafted by spooks too recently and too thoroughly to just sit here and tell you everything I know with no quid pro quo and no guarantee that you aren't playing me. You asked to meet me, remember? Not the other way round.'

The civil servant held up a placatory hand. 'Quite right. Quite right. Let me start again. I have no intention of shafting you, as you put it. I'm trying to help. Your report on the killing of Fazil Jabar was very straightforward, but Jabar wasn't straightforward; he was a complicated character, and significant. Do you have any idea how fortuitous it was that the Taliban decided to blow him to hell?'

'Fortuitous? For who?'

'For whom. Good question. For us, I suppose. For the UK. For British business.'

'Go on.'

'I work in a department of government that attempts to pursue British commercial interests overseas, using various levers.'

'You're a trade official.'

'Yes, in a manner of speaking. I work at the points where our trading interests overlap with other departmental business. Where trade meets development, or defence, or diplomacy, or all those things. There has been a lot of talk recently about using every means at our disposal to help British industry. That's what my department is for.'

'Promoting UK plc,' said William. Berry winced.

'Exactly. Dreadful phrase, but yes.' He took a sip of his drink and looked around the bar. 'The day Fazil Jabar got himself blown up was a rather good day for UK plc. You see, one of the biggest prizes in Afghanistan at the moment is a licence to run a new telecommunications operation, a mobile network.'

'Really? That's hard to believe. The place is practically in the Stone Age.'

'True. But it will skip the various ages between stone and whatever we are now very quickly. We estimate that the telecoms licence will be worth hundreds of millions, perhaps billions, within a decade. In India, Mr Carver, more people have mobile phones than toothbrushes.'

William nodded, encouraging his man on.

'Fazil Jabar was a district chief. He was a reasonably successful politician, but he was more than that. He was also a lobbyist. The public face for a group of Afghan businesses who had come together to win the telecommunications contract. This wasn't a secret but it wasn't much reported either. Some of the people in this consortium weren't altogether respectable, I fear, but Jabar made the whole thing look rather good, not least because his cousin happens to be the Afghan communications minister. I'm sure you know, Mr Carver, that in Kabul such coincidences can be remarkably important. With Jabar on board, they were well ahead of any other bidders. The Afghan government is due to make the decision in the next few weeks, and no one seriously expected Fazil Jabar's group to fail.'

'I'm with you.'

'A competing bid, a UK-led bid, was running in a very creditable second place. Now, with Jabar gone, it seems we're right out in front.'

'Lucky us. So what are you suggesting, Doctor?'

Berry folded his arms. 'I'm not suggesting anything, Mr Carver, and thus far I'm not telling you anything which you couldn't have heard from several other people or even discovered for yourself, if you were reading the right trade journals. I only contacted you because, so far, no one seems to be looking at the bigger picture and I think that might be—remiss.'

'I see.' William paused. 'So, say you were me, Dr Berry, and you wanted to learn a little more, join up some of these dots which you have been talking about. Where would you be looking?'

'I can't tell you how to do your job, Carver, but I would've thought that basic journalistic practice would point you in the direction of Companies House. A careful look at the company accounts for the UK bidders might be helpful. The lead firm is Aftel, a subsidiary of one of the big boys. Maybe there's something interesting there?' Berry glanced nervously around the bar again and then looked at his watch, which was attached rather loosely to the wrist above his bandaged hand. 'I should go. We've talked long enough. Or rather, I've talked. My wife might wonder where I am.' The civil servant picked up his briefcase and stood a little unsteadily. William got up to help, but Berry waved him away. 'I'm fine. Good luck, goodbye.'

Carver finished his Coke, then ordered a large whisky and drank it down. If he stayed, he knew he would just keep drinking. He considered going back to his flat, but there was nothing for him there. He needed to think, and he did his best thinking on the move. The rush-hour crowd had thinned by the time he left the hotel. He took the stairs down into Charing Cross underground station and followed the signs for the Northern Line; opting for northbound, he walked to the end of the platform and when the next train drew in, he settled himself in the last seat in the last carriage, next to the locked driver's cab. He placed his plastic bag of papers next to him and pulled out the notebook and biro. The journey to the end of the line took forty minutes. At High Barnet he got out, crossed the platform, and took the next train south, back the way he'd come.

11 The Watchers and the Watched

DATELINE: Kilburn High Road, London, NW6, July 1st

She could hear Mariscal wheezing his way up the last flight of stairs. The woman watched through the peephole as he caught his breath, leaning with one hand on the bannister, the other swinging like a dead weight. The fish-eye lens exaggerated the size of his head and made her smile. He took a few deep breaths, ruffled his hair, tucked in his shirt, and knocked twice. She opened straight away, taking him by surprise.

'Oh, all right, love? How're you?'

She stared at him. 'No flowers, Rob? No bottle of wine?'

Rob glanced down at his hands, as if he might have brought something but had somehow forgotten he was holding it. 'I thought I was coming over for a shag. I brought my penis,' he grinned, half-apologetically. He walked past the woman into the flat. 'Nice place you've got here.' It was a decent size, for a bedsit. He'd seen worse. He'd lived in worse. The walls were whitewashed, clean and without decoration apart from a framed Dora Maar print hanging above the single bed. There was a kitchen at one end, an armchair, a wooden folding chair and an expensive-looking armoire with a pile of suitcases stacked on top.

'Planning a big trip?'

'No. It's books. Lots of books.'

Rob nodded, acknowledging that he knew about books and could see that they might be stored in suitcases. He pulled a packet of fags from his front pocket.

'You can't smoke in here,' she said.

'Why not?'

'I don't smoke. My boyfriend will smell it.'

'Oh, right. Can't I just pop my head out there?' He gestured at the window by the bed and she nodded. Rob knelt on the bed, pushed the sash window open and stuck his head through. He smoked two cigarettes in quick succession, flicking the ash on a bird-shit-stained shop awning below. While he smoked, she made two small coffees, each with a shot of brandy. She brought them over and handed him one. He took a slurp.

'God, that's strong. Tastes like rocket fuel.'

'It's Spanish.'

'Ah. *Muy bien.*'

They drank in silence, sitting awkwardly, side-by-side, on the narrow bed, exchanging the odd glance. After a few minutes of this she finished her coffee in a quick gulp, took the half-finished cup from his hand and walked back to the kitchen.

'Take off your clothes,' she ordered from the other side of the room.

Rob did as she asked. He placed his shoes under the folding chair and draped his trousers over it, his Paisley Y-fronts hidden underneath. He kept his black shirt on, unbuttoned to the top of his gut, and climbed into bed. The sheets felt good, clean and cold. When she returned her hands were red from the hot washing-up water and her face was a little pale. She lifted her patterned dress over her head in one movement and draped it over the armchair. Underneath she wore a bright white, new-looking bra and knickers. Rob breathed in quietly. The woman slid under the duvet, pulling it up to her neck, and pushed Rob over to the side closest to the wall. He reached for the blind-pull but she moved one slim leg over his, rolled on top of him and pinned both arms above his head. 'No blinds. I want to look at you.'

'I look a lot better with the lights off.'

'Tough.' She freed his left hand and placed it on her shoulder; while he fumbled with her bra clip she unbuttoned his black shirt and dragged it from under him, tearing it very slightly. He sucked in his belly and held it for as long as he could. The blinds stayed up and the window stayed open. The street noise was louder than their fucking until the moment Rob came with an animal grunt.

Afterwards he moved his arm under and around her, dragging them tightly together, his face in her hair. She closed her eyes. She could smell sweat, work and old smoke. Rob lay very still. He would have liked to stay, but he couldn't. He counted silently in his head to one hundred and then began slowly disentangling himself.

'I'd better get going. Loads of meetings. And the cab's a wait-and-return.' He half dressed and then looked around. 'Where's the bathroom?'

'Downstairs. It's shared.'

'You're joking.'

She watched him consider dashing downstairs in his shirt and socks and then reject the idea. 'Do you mind if I use that?' He nodded at the kitchen. There was the sound of running water. Kneeling up on the bed, she watched as Rob Mariscal washed his prick with Fairy Liquid. When he returned, she was lying back down, wrapped tightly in the stained white sheet. He finished dressing, sitting on the end of the bed to tie his shoes. Then he stood, uncertain.

'So, listen. Er, thanks, that was, you know? Really nice. How about next time we go for dinner? I saw a decent-looking pizza place downstairs.'

She smiled and nodded, certain that this dinner would never happen. 'Sure. Why not? You should go. We'll talk later.'

Rob smiled broadly; he'd been pardoned. He bent and kissed her on the forehead before walking towards the door. She gave him time to work his way down the stairs and then sat up and looked out on to the street. She could still taste him in her mouth – his sour, smoky breath. There he was, a lit fag already hanging from his lower lip, hoiking up his trousers with one hand while waving at his driver with the other. She wondered how it was possible to have feelings for Rob Mariscal.

The armchair was close to the wardrobe. She stepped on to it, found her balance and, stretching, pulled down the top suitcase then the two smaller ones beneath. She reached into the smallest case and retrieved the camera that had been taped inside, its lens wedged into a neat hole cut into the side. She pressed a button and waited while the machine coughed up its contents with a mechanical whirr. She looked at the tape. Sixty minutes. What a joke. The woman wondered where she might find cheaper tapes with a shorter duration.

Five past nine. The visitors' entrance to Companies House was still locked. Patrick watched the receptionist wandering about inside and tried to hide his growing impatience.

Carver had finally returned Patrick's increasingly desperate voicemail messages just before midnight. He'd called on the home number and spoken briefly to Rebecca before she handed the phone over.

'All right Patrick, how you getting along?'

'Fine,' said Patrick, wrong-footed by Carver's friendly tone. 'Did you get my message about Kabul? We're booked on the lunchtime flight, day after tomorrow, via Delhi; that was the first flight I could get us on.'

'That's fine.' William had sounded pleased, 'because we've both got things we need to do tomorrow. I spoke to my contact and there's a little work I need from you. Research work.'

Patrick's spirits lifted further. Research. Some proper journalism at last. 'Great. That's fantastic. What is it?'

'Don't get too excited and don't ask stupid questions over the phone. Just clear your diary for tomorrow and meet me at half eight outside the British Museum.'

'Half eight. I'll be there.'

'Good. See you then. Oh, and Patrick—bring a calculator.'

Rebecca watched Patrick replace the receiver. 'So that was William Carver?'

'Yeah.'

'He was charming.'

'Really? I've never heard him called that before. What'd he say?'

'He said that I shouldn't worry, that he'd look after you. Bring you back in one piece from Afghanistan.' Patrick had nodded. He tried to frame a reassuring sentence or even better a joke that might counter the sudden seriousness that both felt. But he was too slow and Rebecca had turned away.

The polystyrene cup of tea that William had bought Patrick was tepid by the time he got to the British Museum, but he drank it anyway. He'd arrived ten minutes late after getting stuck on the Tube and was kicking himself. Carver wasn't impressed either, but nor was he interested in an apology or an explanation.

'Forget it. Just don't let it happen again. Always arrive early, it gives you the advantage.' William talked Patrick quickly through the assignment. 'Companies House is just round the corner. It opens at nine and I need you to go and find out everything you can about a telecoms company called Aftel. Especially anything you can find on their interests in Afghanistan or Pakistan. Every bit of paperwork you can get: balance sheets, past accounts, list of directors current and previous, everything. Find it, skim-read it and print it out. Got that?'

'Got it, yes. A-F-T-E-L?'

'That's right. Now listen carefully to this next part. I need you to draw as little attention to yourself as possible. You're arriving nice and early so hopefully it'll be quiet. But still, I don't want you to tell anyone else what you're looking for. Don't talk to anyone unless you have to, don't sign in or out with your real name, don't pay for anything with a card. Have you got some cash?'

'Forty quid.'

'Good. And a calculator?' Patrick patted the front pocket of his rucksack. 'Excellent. So anyone asks, you're just a businessman, right? Checking out some accounts before deciding to invest. Understood?'

'I understand, William, it's fine. You can count on me.'

Seven minutes past nine. Patrick watched the receptionist lining up pens on his desk and then lift the phone to check for a dial tone. The receptionist looked at his watch, then through the closed glass doors at Patrick, stood and then sat back down and started reading a graphic novel of some sort. Patrick was going to strangle this kid with his own tie when he eventually got through the door. At nine minutes past nine the receptionist got up, walked across the lobby achingly slowly and unlocked the doors.

'Good morning, sir. You're a keen one.' The boy did not look long out of his teens. He wore a purple shirt with a black bootlace tie. His dark hair was Brylcreemed and carefully combed. There was a smattering of acne around his forehead. Patrick followed him back to his desk and waited while he sat back down.

'Do you want to register a company today, then, sir?' The *sir* was a shade snide this time. Patrick remembered William's instruction about drawing as little attention as possible. He didn't want an argument, just in and out.

'No, thank you. I've just come to look at a few company accounts.'

'Right you are. Then you'll need the reading room and computers. Through the double doors, right down to the end, big room on the left.'

'Thank you.' Patrick picked up his bag.

'Could you sign in here first, please, sir.' The young man pointed at the visitors' book, lying open on the counter in front of him. Patrick bent over the book, picked up a nearby biro and wrote *GEORGE ELIOT* in loose, hopefully hard-to-read capitals. The kid wasn't looking anyway, absorbed, once more, in his comic.

The Companies House reading room reminded Patrick of his old school library; there were four long lines of cheap white desks, one line down each wall and two facing each other down the middle. Every desk had an identical black computer terminal on top. As he surveyed the room he saw there was one other visitor, which was something of a surprise given he knew he had been first through the door. She must have walked by while he was signing in. He looked at the redheaded woman. She was wearing a white blouse and sat hunched over a keyboard exactly halfway down the central line of tables. He sat as far from her as possible and got out his calculator and notebook. A laminated card stuck to the front of each computer explained how to switch it on and conduct a basic search. Patrick followed the instructions carefully and was soon looking at an alphabetised list of UK-registered companies. He picked a few company names at random and opened the details, and was surprised by how many of the businesses he chose seemed already to have been wound up. Almost every company he looked at was dead or dormant. All those high hopes and ruined dreams expressed in a few cold details.

Name and Registered Office:
Company Number:
Status:
Company type:
Last accounts made up to:

He found the basic information on Aftel easily enough, but it was clear he was going to have to pay for the detailed accounts and everything else he needed. The computer gave him the option of paying by credit card, which he rejected, as William had instructed. With a sigh which prompted the redhead to look over in his direction, he pushed back his chair and went to find the receptionist. A straight-faced lie and a straightforward bribe were enough to get the boy to do him the favour he needed. Patrick was surprised at how easy it was. He'd forgotten his wallet, he said, and only had a some notes in his pockets. If the receptionist would log in and print the full Aftel report and accounts, which usually cost twenty-five pounds, Patrick would give him thirty in cash.

Twenty minutes later Patrick was staring at over eighty pages of detailed company information. He pored over the first few pages, trying hard to concentrate on the contents: date of incorporation, previous names, directors' remuneration and other interests, company structure, share offerings, shareholders and the rest. He wrote the details down on his pad and then moved on to the accounts themselves. They were all but meaningless. Numbers were a language Patrick didn't understand. The harder he concentrated on the columns of figures, the more they moved around, drifted and swam around the screen. Within ten minutes he could feel the hard push of a headache setting up home behind his right eyeball. He stopped, massaged the back of his neck and checked his watch. The redhead at the only other occupied desk was making notes on a legal pad and staring hard at her screen.

After another twenty minutes he gave up. He would take this lot home and try to find something interesting in it there. Maybe Rebecca could help. She was good with numbers. He was shutting the machine down when he felt the receptionist at his shoulder.

'Everything's online now, you know. Eighty-three per cent of people setting up companies set them up electronically.'

'I'm not setting up a company.'

'I know, you said. But you could've done that from home, that's all. I thought you might like to know.'

Patrick didn't look up. 'I'll bear it in mind.'

'So what exactly are you?' The boy was clearly getting to the point now: 'Some sort of private investigator?'

Patrick sensed movement or interest from the woman at the other desk. He attempted a patronising little laugh. 'No, nothing so exciting. I'm just a businessman.'

'Yeah? What sort of business?'

'The mind-your-own type.'

Patrick logged out of the computer and stood up sharply, pushing the back leg of his chair into the boy's ankle. 'Sorry,' he said involuntarily. He hurried from the room, down the corridor and back out the front doors of Companies House. 'Hardly bloody inconspicuous,' he scolded himself, but at least he had the information William wanted.

He caught the bus back to Highbury. Sat at the back of the top deck leafing through the Aftel printouts, he still saw nothing that looked very interesting. Once home, he laid everything out on the floor and started going through it chronologically. He'd been reading for a couple of hours when the phone rang: 'Hello, Patrick. I'm outside, on our bench. Fancy an ice cream?' He went to the bedroom and drew the curtains. There was Carver, sitting in the middle of what was apparently now *their* bench, waving a ninety-nine up in the direction of his window. Patrick tidied the papers from the floor, shoved them into a plastic bag, grabbed his keys and ran downstairs.

'How'd you get on?'

'Good. Got a lot of material. Can't make much of it yet. A lot of financials.'

'Don't worry, I'll take care of that.' Carver held out his hand and Patrick somewhat reluctantly passed over the bag. 'So it all went fine? Nothing I need to know about?'

Patrick paused. 'Well. This might sound a bit crazy, but there was this woman there, at Companies House. She must've arrived just after me and I got the feeling she was—well, watching.'

'What did she look like?'

'Smart. Business-suit smart. Thirty, maybe. Quite pretty with long red hair – long but tied back.'

'Good. I've clocked her too. I'm pretty sure she was watching you.'

'What?'

'Don't worry, she didn't follow you home.'

'How do you know?'

'Because I followed you home. I was watching her. And you. I was watching both of you. She tailed me to the British Museum and when you left she broke off and went after you, so I followed. There was probably someone else watching me, and another person watching you and her, who knows . . .'

'But who is she? And why didn't you let me know while I was in there? You could have texted me.' Patrick was amazed; he had assumed Carver's caution to be either paranoia or unnecessary theatrics.

'I've no idea who she is. Could be anyone. A spook? Someone working for the telecoms company? I didn't let you know because I was interested to see whether you noticed her, and whether you'd tell me about her if you did. So, well done. You passed.'

'I passed? So you didn't trust me?'

William laughed. "Course I don't trust you, Patrick. I barely know you. But fair's fair. I don't expect you to trust me either. It's a perfectly equal relationship.'

'Built on total distrust.'

'Yes. But cheer up, the fact that she was there is good news. Well, good news and bad news. Good news for us because it means Berry's almost certainly straight and that he's pointing me at something worth looking at. Bad news for Berry, of course, because it means someone's on to him.'

Patrick nodded, trying to keep up. 'So what do we do now?' he asked, trying to create the impression that they were taking decisions together.

'We take a long, hard look at Aftel. I know a bloke back at the BBC who knows numbers. I'll take him the accounts, see if he can find something interesting in them.'

'Right. Someone in the business unit?'

Carver scoffed. 'No, Patrick, not the business unit. Haven't you noticed yet? There are a lot of interesting people working at the BBC – incredible expertise in all sorts of areas – trouble is, only half of them are journalists. I'm taking these numbers to Donnie. You know him?'

Patrick shook his head.

'Thought not. He won't be around until a lot later. I've got some stuff to do until then.'

'Okay. What should I do?'

'I'm not your mother, Patrick. Do what you like. Go pack a suitcase, say your goodbyes. I'll see you at Heathrow tomorrow morning. Don't be late.'

A sleepy BBC security guard glanced at William's staff pass and ushered him into a steel and glass cylinder where he was slowly rotated. He took the lift three floors up to the *Today* programme production office. He had forgotten how much he disliked the place. The dull hum of a hundred sleeping computers, the cold tungsten light; day or night, the office looked the same. He put his head around the office door. There was no one on the night shift he recognised or wanted to see, so he carried on along the corridor, deep into the bowels of the building. It took him twenty minutes to find who he was looking for.

'Donnie! Hey, Donnie!' The round-shouldered man in dark overalls pulling a red roll-along vacuum cleaner didn't turn around. William broke into an ungainly jog and caught him at the lift, panting. 'Hey Donnie. Hold up.'

The cleaner pulled a pair of battered silver headphones from his ears and draped them around his neck. The red vacuum cleaner had a big smile on its face. Donnie didn't. 'Hello Carver.'

'How are you doing?'

'Same as ever. What do you want?' He stepped into the lift.

William followed. 'I haven't seen you for months. You're looking well. Any news?'

'No news. But I have four miles of corridor left to clean tonight.'

William persisted. 'Right. I was in the building putting a piece together; thought I'd come say hello. Buy you breakfast?'

The lift made its shuddering descent.

'No thanks.' Donnie pulled the vacuum cleaner out of the lift and into a part of the building William had never seen before. The floor was poured concrete and the walls were painted ox-blood red up to waist height. They pushed through four heavy swing doors before Donnie stopped at a black metal door marked *Maintenance*. He unlocked the door, switched on the light and indicated with his head that William should follow him. The maintenance store was crammed with cleaning equipment, leaving room for just one sunken sofa and a row of green lockers. Donnie opened his locker and pulled out a plastic ice cream box fastened with an elastic band. 'I bring my own breakfast. It saves me one thousand seven hundred and fifty pounds a year.' Inside the locker

William could see three thick economics textbooks stacked beneath a change of clothes and a pair of trainers. Donnie sat down on the sofa and began to eat. 'I'm on break for ten minutes, so say what you gotta say.'

'I need a favour. I need someone who knows numbers.'

'Explain.'

William told Donnie what he had: eighty-odd pages of company accounts that he couldn't make head nor tail of. And what he needed: a breakdown of what sort of state this telecoms business was in, whether it was vulnerable, and anything interesting, any signs that something odd might be going on. 'There's something hiding in those numbers, Donnie. I know it but I just can't see it.'

William could tell from Donnie's body language that he was tempted, interested but not yet hooked.

'That all sounds pretty straightforward, man. Why don't you ask your business correspondent to do that for you? She's supposed to be real smart.'

This was a setback. William knew from previous conversations that Donnie didn't like the BBC business correspondent.

'So smart, she called the end of the recession eight months early,' Donnie went on, muttering a little. 'I told her. I saw her in the lift at Christmas and I told her exactly when we'd pull out of recession. She looked at me like I was shit on her shoes.' He was standing now, pacing up and down the small room. William nodded sympathetically. 'I called it right, she called it wrong. Yes?'

'Yes.'

'So how come she's on a hundred and sixty grand and I'm pulling Henry the fucking hoover around? Answer me that.'

William looked at him. 'It's because you're black, Donnie.'

'Damn right.'

'And maybe also 'cos she's got a first from Cambridge, a masters from Harvard, a few years in academia, and one in Downing Street. Whereas you, Donnie, are just off the banana boat from

Ghana with an asylum claim pending.' William smiled as he spoke.

'It's Guyana, you ignorant racist shitbag.' Donnie crashed back down into the wrecked sofa and bellowed with laughter. He slapped his knee and then looked at William. 'Go on then, fat boy. Give me the accounts, I'll do it. I'll go through the accounts and write it all up for you. You got me, again.'

Carver looked nervous. 'In layman's language, though, yeah? Stuff real people can read.'

'I'll give you an executive summary, one that'll work for very stupid executives and it will cost you three hundred pounds.'

'What! No way. Two hundred and I need it tomorrow.'

'Tomorrow! As in later today? I'll take it to the canteen now and go through it all there, but that'll be two fifty. And I'll take the cheque right now; I know you always carry that little cheque book of yours around.'

William took the Aftel accounts from his plastic bag and handed them over; then he dug deeper till he found a dog-eared cheque book. He bent down and wrote the cheque out on the arm of the sofa before handing it to Donnie, who examined it carefully before pocketing it and waving William away.

Carver was at the door before he turned and glanced back over his shoulder. 'Do me a favour, will you, Donnie? Remember me when you're incredibly rich.'

Donnie looked William up and down. 'I forgot you already.'

12   Crippled but Unconquered

DATELINE: Hyde Park Corner, London, W2, July 2nd

Rob Mariscal sat low on the back seat of the black cab, his feet on the flip-down chair in front of him. He had a thick blanket of newspapers on his lap but he wasn't reading them and they were left behind when the taxi dropped him at his Piccadilly destination. The prestigious address, with curtained windows and high vaulting doorway, looked to Rob more like a Victorian engraving than an actual building. On cloud-covered days like this it was particularly cheerless – grey and almost completely anonymous – but Rob guessed this was how the inhabitants liked it. He walked through the doorway, which led on to a huge marble hall, and was about to engage the formidable-looking moustachioed doorman in conversation when his lunch companion appeared.

'It's all right, Arthur, Mr Mariscal is with me.'

The legend in club land was that Arthur never forgot a name, but Rob had been here several times and Arthur had never remembered his. The man meeting Rob smiled broadly. He was in his thirties but looked younger, with lively brown eyes, a chubby face and neat dark hair that looked like it had been recently

Brylcreemed or oiled. 'Good to see you again, Rob. I thought I'd treat you to lunch, but looking at you, I think we'll have to sit down the dirty end.'

'What?'

'It's the rule. No tails or dinner jacket, then you have to eat down at the dirty end of the dining room.'

'Right.'

The man led Rob across the marble hall and into a part of the building previously unknown to him. They wandered past bronze busts, terracotta statues, Grecian pillars. Occasionally Rob's lunch companion would give a nod of acknowledgement to a fellow clubman heading in the opposite direction. They eventually arrived outside the dining room. A huge oil painting of a stricken ship was hanging on a wall.

'*Crippled but Unconquered.*'

'What?'

'That's the name of the picture. *Crippled but Unconquered.* W. L. Wyllie. Beautiful, isn't it?'

'Not really.'

'Oh, right. Maybe horses are more your thing? There are a couple of Stubbs next door. I'll show you later.'

Rob shrugged. They were shown to a table in the furthermost corner of the room. Mariscal sniffed at the air. The place smelt of furniture polish and boiled cabbage, though he could see no sign of that vegetable on the menu. He ran his eye down the à la carte. Just about every dish on it was an old public school favourite that the members of this club had obviously never outgrown.

'I'd steer clear of the meatloaf if I were you, very dubious. The best-case scenario is it's yesterday's roast beef in disguise, but I wouldn't bet on it. The veal is usually pretty reliable.'

Rob nodded. 'I'll just have the pasta. No starter. I can't be away long.'

His companion gave an understanding smile. 'A busy time, I'm sure.'

Rob nodded again, more slowly. 'So what's this all about then, Graham?'

Mariscal knew very little about the man sitting opposite him but he was pretty sure his name wasn't Graham. 'What makes you so anxious to renew our acquaintance?'

The man who wasn't Graham took a sip of water. 'Well, Rob, we hadn't heard from you for a while and we were wondering how you were and, to be frank, whether you were still willing to be helpful, from time to time?'

'Who's *we*, Graham?'

The man sighed. It seemed this wouldn't be as straightforward as he'd hoped. 'That's rather a stupid beginning for an intelligent man, if you don't mind me saying, Robert.'

'This isn't the beginning though, Graham. This is the end. I don't want to play anymore. Do you understand?'

The man leant back in his chair and took a long look at Mariscal. He appeared genuinely saddened. 'Ah, I see. But I'm afraid you don't get to decide that, Rob. That's a decision for others.' He glanced down at the menu. 'How about we get our lunch order in?'

A waiter appeared suddenly at Rob's shoulder, as if Graham had conjured him up.

'Pasta and a large glass of Merlot,' Rob snapped angrily.

Graham took longer, eventually ordering a plate of the reliable veal and a glass of house white. '*Cartes sur table*, Rob, the way we used to play. One of your journalists is causing us some concern, our old friend Carver.'

Rob smiled. He might have known this would be about William. 'I see. But William Carver isn't your friend any more, Graham. Quite the opposite, in fact. You screwed that one up good and proper.'

'We did?'

'Yes, you did.'

'How so?'

'Unlike most hacks, Carver took all that bollocks over Iraq rather personally. Seems he didn't like being lied to. Those Iraqi exiles you sold him? Saddam's scary weapons? He hasn't forgiven you for lying to him or himself for believing you. As far as Carver's concerned, you lot are incapable of truth.'

Graham shrugged. 'Well if that's how he feels, then that's how he feels. But I must say, it's a little childish. We made a few mistakes, no doubt about it, but no one lied to anyone, Rob. We believed in the threat, the exiles, the weapons.'

'Really?'

'Absolutely. Intelligence is guesswork, Rob, it's riddled with error, bound to be. But life goes on.'

The food arrived and was placed in front of the two men. Rob waited till the waiter was out of earshot before continuing.

'I think your reaction to being made a fool of is a little more philosophical than Carver's. As far as he's concerned, he put his reputation on the line. And he lost it.'

'Oh, what rubbish. And anyway, all that Iraqi business is ancient history now. No one remembers, no one cares.'

'Carver remembers very well and he cares—deeply.'

'Well I'm sorry he feels that way but the fact is, a war was coming whatever happened. Carver needs to put his ego to one side.'

'That's not how I remember it, Graham. I remember it all being very tense, very in the balance. What Carver put on the radio, what I put on the radio, *mattered*. Close votes in the House of Commons, remember that? Millions of people marching in London, all manner of pissing about at the UN. The pieces we did helped you out and you know it. A convincing lie can be extremely effective, particularly when it comes from someone who people trust, like Carver. And when you put it on our programme, right there between the God slot and the good old English weather, it's like carving it in granite, Graham.'

The man laughed. 'Get over yourself, Rob; really, you should hear how you sound.'

Mariscal took a mouthful of his pasta. It was horrible. He put his fork down and pushed his chair back to leave. Before he could move, Graham had reached across the table and had his forearm in a tight grip. He raised his voice loud enough that the other diners looked in their direction.

'Sit down and listen. I need one more minute and then you can go, understand?' There was steel in Graham's voice, and Rob remembered why, in the old days, this man unnerved him. He pulled his chair back towards the table and took a gulp of wine.

'One minute.'

'We've been keeping an eye on what Carver is up to in Kabul.'

'And?'

'He's digging in the wrong place and he's putting the spade in too deep. You won't get anything out of it, you have to trust me on that one, but he might screw up some important work we're doing. And he might get into a lot of trouble.'

'You in the business of threatening journalists now, Graham?'

'I'm not talking about trouble from us, Rob; I'm talking about trouble from the kind of people who dump your headless body by the side of the Kandahar road. He's your reporter, we consider him your responsibility and we need to see a little control, for his sake and ours.'

'Meaning what?'

'We know he's on his way back to Afghanistan and that you're trying to put him back on the leash, and that's all good. Just get him out of Kabul for a spell. We might be able to help. There's a big poppy eradication operation due to kick off in the next few days, American-led, lots of planes spraying poison, pissed off farmers and all that. Lots of noise, colour. He can be the only guy who gets to go. Good news story for us, decent exclusive for you.'

Rob nodded. 'And if he won't agree?'

'You're his manager, aren't you? So *manage* him. But—' Graham took a silvery DVD in a clear plastic wallet from his jacket pocket and handed it to Rob. 'But if you need another reason to do the right thing, then this might persuade you.'

'What is it?'

'Think of it as a motivational video, of sorts.'

Rob pocketed the disc, took one more swig of wine and left.

In the cab on the way back to Broadcasting House, he tried to remember how it had started. The friendly late-night briefing call so he had a handle on where the government thought a particular story was going, first-name terms, harmless, flattering even. Then a tidbit of information no one else knew, a quiet conversation about a minister who was on the skids and being gently pushed in the direction of the trapdoor. After that, the occasional face-to-face security briefing from Graham and someone else so important that he didn't have a fake name, he had no name at all. Further briefings for Mariscal and Carver 'across the river' at that monstrosity on the Thames. Drinks at Downing Street, tea at Downing Street, a quiet chat with the Prime Minister, if Rob wouldn't mind, the PM would appreciate his advice on such-and-such. A seat near the front of the plane, when the PM was on his way to Washington. He knew how it had started, all right. He just didn't know how it would end.

PART TWO

13 A Long Way from Home

DATELINE: Terminal 5, Heathrow Airport, London, July 3rd

The journey from London to Kabul would be a long one: two seven-hour flights punctuated by a four-hour stop-over in Delhi. Patrick got to the airport in good time but Carver had arrived even earlier, checking himself in and ensuring he would be sitting on his own on both flights.

'I need the bulkhead seat,' he offered, 'and you're better off by yourself anyway, aren't you? You can do some reading.'

Patrick was more relieved than offended; he had been secretly dreading a seven-hour stretch of enforced intimacy. He selected the check-in desk manned by the most sympathetic-looking staff member and silently rehearsed his speech about how, as a BBC journalist en route to a war zone, he was carrying fragile recording kit and would need to take extra bags into the cabin. He took two calls while they waited to board the plane and let two more go to voicemail. The messages were both from his father, who, between nervous coughs, wished him good luck, warned him to keep his head down, and promised to buy him a pint when he got back. 'Well, okay then, son. That's all I had to say really. I don't want

159

to take up more space on your tape, so I'll sign off. Take care. Dad.' It was a running family joke that Patrick's father ended answerphone messages as though he were signing a letter. Sometimes he even finished with *Yours*.

His father's second message was to reassure Patrick that he would call Rebecca every day. This was hardly surprising; Patrick's father found an excuse to call Rebecca most days anyway. If he had done nothing else to please his father – and sometimes Patrick suspected he hadn't – the fact that he had brought Rebecca into the family more than made up for it. 'The only half-crown article in a sixpenny bazaar,' as his father liked to say. Of course he'll phone her, thought Patrick. If I stay away longer than a fortnight he'll probably move in. He deleted the second message but kept the first.

The calls he took were from Rebecca herself and Rob Mariscal. Neither went particularly well. Rebecca was between classes and the line was poor. They both had too much and too little to say to each other. After wading through some small talk – the journey to the airport, which books he had for the plane, her journey to work – Patrick made a joke at his dad's expense and immediately regretted it. She talked about the friends she would be seeing that night. Then there was a pause, and Patrick said he would call as soon as he arrived, as long as the mobile worked, or even if it didn't he'd find a phone. Rebecca said she should go and he told her that he loved her. He was surprised that he'd said it, and even more surprised at how it sounded: absolutely true. There was a mumbled noise from the other end of the line, but before Patrick could ask her to repeat it, the phone went dead.

Rob had rung immediately afterwards. No niceties. 'You've been engaged for fucking ages. What's going on? You with Carver?'

'Yeah Rob, 'course.' Patrick glanced over at his colleague, who was sitting as far from him as the narrow and overheated departure lounge allowed. 'It's all good. We're just about to jump on the plane.' He tried to sound bright.

'Okay. So what sort of stories are you planning to get me?'

'Well,' Patrick faltered, 'William wants to get back to the Fazil Jabar story as soon as we can.'

'I don't give a fuck what William wants,' snapped Mariscal. 'What about the election?'

Patrick was surprised. Rob had told him several times how bored he was by the prospect of the Afghan election. 'You want an election piece?' He could hear Rob taking a slow drag on his cigarette.

'Not really. The fact that we all know the result before the polls have even opened takes some of the fun out of it, don't you think?'

'How about corruption?'

'Fuck no.'

Patrick felt a flash of irritation. You're sending me there, he thought, why don't you just tell me what you want? But he persevered. 'How about a post-election piece, then? You know, the horse-trading and all that. We could get something ready to go, as soon as the results are in.'

Rob sniffed. 'Horse-trading? I suppose in that shithole it *will* involve the actual trading of horses?'

Patrick laughed, relieved that the idea hadn't been immediately rejected. 'Probably.'

'Fine. Do that. But there's something else I need you to do first. I want Carver to do a poppy piece. There's a trip out of Kabul the day after you arrive; you get to go see the NATO poppy eradication programme: spraying fields, fucking up little farmers, that kind of thing. It's all William's, no one else is going. He'll love it.'

'So it's an embed?'

'Not really. An overnight thing. Quick trip out and back.'

'But it's a facility?'

161

'Yeah, kind of. But listen, Patrick. Don't sell it to William that way. This is a decent, legitimate story. You're the only media on it. The press liaison guy for the Brits in Kabul is called Captain Remora. Get in touch with him when you get there. This isn't optional, Patrick, you understand? I'm telling you I want Carver on that trip.'

'Okay boss. I get it.'

Patrick looked across the gate at William. He was hunched over his laptop, so close to the screen he looked like he was about to climb in. Rereading Donnie's summary of Aftel's accounts, Patrick guessed. A two-day trip to see poppy fields was going to be a hard sell.

The flight to Delhi was unusually bumpy. Patrick was sitting alongside a large Indian family, all nervous flyers who took it in turns to gasp and swallow as the plane punched through darkening clouds. An hour in, when the seatbelt sign finally allowed, Patrick unbuckled himself and walked stiffly down the aisle towards William. He crouched down next to the reporter and made what he thought was a pretty convincing case for the poppy trip. William let him finish before looking up from his laptop.

'No!'

'It's only two days, William, we could—'

'Who's organising it at that end?' William interrupted.

'Rob said some captain would help arrange things.'

'Remora?'

'Yeah, that's the one.'

'Thought so. No way. Forget about it.' William shifted awkwardly and the entire three-seat row creaked and moved.

'Okay,' said Patrick. 'Maybe we can talk about it when we get to Kabul?'

'Whatever. I need to work on this.' William pulled a sheaf of papers from underneath the computer, and Patrick recognised the photocopied Aftel accounts, now annotated in the margins with an indecipherable mix of scrawl and Pitman shorthand. Carver read and typed all the way to Delhi; after he got off the plane, he fell asleep in a corner of the sweaty arrivals hall while they waited for their connecting flight. Once on board again, he ate the over-sweet pastry offered for breakfast and then slept some more, only waking up as they made their descent into Kabul. Patrick, by contrast, was too excited, wired and worried to rest at all. He watched a subtitled Bollywood movie, read the Eric Newby book that Rebecca had bought him and wondered about how he could possibly reconcile the contradictory expectations of Mariscal and Carver.

Once through passport control and customs at Kabul, William stopped and scanned the arrivals hall, looking at the faces, half-expecting to see Karim. But his translator wasn't there. He noticed instead a small-framed Afghan man in a grey suit holding a board that said *BBC*.

On the drive to the BBC house Patrick drank in every detail, while William dozed. Kabul looked strangely familiar, but it took him a while to realise that this was because he had been watching news footage of these grey low-rise buildings, ragged marketplaces and broken roads for years. He recognised the dusty yellow haze, pockmarked billboards and packs of wild-eyed kids selling petrol in old Fanta bottles. At the house, he was given the room which most recently had belonged to Vivian Fox. He was grateful for it. Vivian had tidied up thoroughly before leaving, and he was sure the place looked about as good as it was ever likely to. He noted some of the home comforts various BBC staff had thought to install over the years. There was a Teasmade on the bedside table and in the drawer underneath a Bible with a camouflage cover. On the wall next to a battered wardrobe hung a faded print of Turner's *Westminster Bridge*. A garish pink lampshade was balanced on the single lamp that lit the room. The place reminded Patrick of the dreadful seaside guesthouses where he and his parents had spent their summer holidays – apart, that was, from the thick strips of gaffer tape forming an X over both windowpanes; to protect against shock-waves, he assumed. He lay down on the single bed and smiled. The BBC house in Kabul. A hell of a long way from Streatham High Street and the *South London Press*. Vivian had left half a dozen shower gels, soaps and shampoos at the bottom of the cupboard, and he used the most neutral to wash the journey from his body and hair in the en suite shower. He changed clothes and went looking for William's room.

'You smell like a girl,' Carver said, his nose twitching, as he opened his door and immediately handed Patrick his laptop before letting him in. 'How about you bash out some notes for me? I want to try and get the whole thing straight in my head. We need to get something new on the radio soon, keep the story warm.'

'I take it you haven't reconsidered the poppy trip, then?' Patrick asked, though he knew the answer.

'Don't keep bleating on about poppies, Patrick, just tell Rob that we're busy with something else, something more important.'

Patrick took a deep breath and drew himself up to his full height. 'I don't think I can do that, William. Rob won't buy it. He's made it very clear. He'll pull the plug and call us both back to London if we don't give him what he wants. I don't understand why we can't do the poppy thing, file that, get everyone off our backs, then get on with Jabar. Where's the problem with that?'

William gave Patrick an even look and was about to speak when there was a gentle knock at the bedroom door. Carver opened it to find Karim Mumtaz standing in the hall, smiling nervously, his hands pushed deep in his jacket pockets. Patrick watched with interest as Carver stepped forwards to embrace Karim, then stopped himself half way. Instead he put his hand on Karim's shoulder and said something Patrick couldn't understand – a Pashto greeting, he assumed. Karim appeared at least as embarrassed as William. Carver ushered Karim into the room, sat him down and introduced Patrick before asking Karim what he'd been talking about in his cryptic phone message.

The young man recounted the story of his visit to the morgue and the revelation that Jabar had been killed not by the bomb but by a shot to the head. He downplayed what had happened to him afterwards and his injury, but at William's insistence he gave some detail and grudgingly raised his shirt to show the thick white bandaging strapped around his waist. As he listened, William paced up and down the small room, increasingly angry and at the same time determined. When Karim had finished, Carver removed his spectacles and cleaned them on his shirt tail, then asked Patrick to type out some notes while he and Karim pieced together what they knew. There was only one chair in the room and Patrick was reluctant to take it; instead, he picked up the laptop and sat on the floor.

'Get it all down, Patrick, leave nothing out.'

Fazil Jabar was an Afghan politician who faced both ways. He had signed up to the NATO counterinsurgency programme but that might have been expediency, or even a deception, because he was at the very least friendly towards the Taliban and, more likely, directly connected to them. Jabar wasn't just a politician, he was a businessman, working with a group of Afghan players who were hoping to win a new mobile phone licence – the third and last network the government planned to allow. He was killed along with his son and bodyguard in a bombing at Savi's tailor's shop on Passport Street. The bomb was a sophisticated device and expensive, but in the event it wasn't the bomb that killed him; he had been shot in the head. There had been a wedding taking place across the road from the explosion, but so far there were no useful witnesses. A British man called Richard Roydon had had an appointment at the tailor's shop just a couple of hours before the bomb went off. He appeared to have had a number of appointments around the same time as Fazil Jabar. Richard Roydon was a former

Royal Marine who had worked at the British Embassy and more recently was involved in private security. Finally and surely not unrelated: Afghan bandits of some sort had attempted to kidnap Karim and were desperate and dangerous enough to chase and shoot at him in a public place.

William stood and stared over Patrick's shoulder at the neat list of facts, then sat back down. 'We've got all that and we've got my contact in London, Dr Berry, and a report into this UK company that's in the running for the telecoms licence, Aftel. There are some interesting things in there but I want to call Donnie and ask him a few more questions before we draw too many conclusions. Is that everything?'

Karim got up from the bed and rubbed at his bandaged waist. 'We also have the tailor, William, Mr Savi. The police told us he was killed in the bombing but the body is missing.'

William nodded. 'Yes, the tailor. God knows what's going on there. There's a serious story in all this, I'm sure about that, a big bloody story. But we don't have the right pieces yet, nothing we can put on the radio, anyway.'

Karim gave Carver a questioning look. 'Maybe if you put something on the radio some more pieces will come?'

'Maybe. Any other ideas?'

Patrick was still sitting cross-legged on the floor; he'd listened carefully to his two new colleagues, pleased to feel included, searching hard for any opportunities to contribute.

'That wedding,' he asked. 'Was it filmed by anyone?'

Carver glanced at him, interested. 'Why?'

'If it was, maybe it's worth getting hold of the tapes. It's possible something useful was caught on camera . . .'

Karim gave an encouraging nod. 'This is a good idea. If there are tapes, I can get them from Baba, I am sure.'

William shrugged. 'Worth a shot.' He stood up from his chair, stretched and spoke in a tone that implied a consensus had been reached. 'So that's what we do, we get hold of that film and I'll take a look at it while you two go and do the poppy trip. A military embed is probably the safest place for Karim to be right now.' Patrick inhaled slowly; Rob wanted Carver on the facility, not him and Karim.

William continued: 'Paddy can collect the audio from the trip and I'll cut it and add a voice track when you get back. Mariscal won't know the difference. He gets his story and I get to work on mine. I'll take a look at the wedding video, presuming there is one, chat to Donnie, and I also want to speak to the Ambo again. Let's see if I can make some real progress while you're away. Okay?'

The question expected no answer. Patrick sucked at his teeth. 'What do I tell Rob?'

'Tell him he's getting his story. Just don't tell him how.' Carver clapped his hands together. 'Now, how about a glass of beer and a Chinese takeaway?'

14 The Wedding Video

DATELINE: BBC house, central Kabul, Afghanistan, July 4th

William swept the detritus from the previous night — the remains of a Chinese meal and eight bottles of American beer — across his desk and into a white plastic shopping bag; the first couple of bottles landed gently on a mess of noodles and rice, the rest clattered noisily on top. He winced. Patrick and Karim had left at around midnight. They'd had two beers each and he'd drunk the other four. Surely four beers couldn't account for this thumping hangover? Glancing around the room, he noticed that the duty-free bag he'd stowed at the back of his cupboard was now by the side of his bed. Poking from the top was the distinctive red cork stopper and broken wax seal that belonged to his favourite bourbon. He resisted the temptation to open the bag and examine how much he'd drunk. Too much. He checked his watch: nearly noon. He had wasted half the day.

Karim and Patrick had been more productive. Karim had called Baba before breakfast. The restaurateur was only too pleased to do his 'BBC friends' a favour. He had immediately called Ali and ordered him to deliver not just the unedited tapes of the wedding but his camera as well, so he could be sure William would be able to watch the film. Patrick had met Ali in the reception area of the BBC house. It was clear he wasn't too happy with the arrangement but that Baba had given him no choice. He agreed to come back that evening, by which time, Patrick promised, William would have watched everything and discovered whether there was anything useful on the film. Patrick then took the camera up to Carver's room and knocked, recoiling a little as the door opened and a warm smell of sweat and sweet-and-sour pork balls hit him.

William dispatched Patrick, switched on his computer and waited while it did its irritating corporate singsong. When the desktop had loaded, he went straight to his music files and scrolled down, first to Cambridge and then to Fauré. He sailed the cursor over the *Requiem* until he found 'Pie Jesu', then hit play. It still surprised him that a crappy piece of plastic like this could conjure up a perfect soprano, but here it came, from somewhere at the rear of the machine, a single note on a King's College organ and then the perfect sound of a boy whose balls hadn't yet dropped. William rearranged his own slightly sticky crotch. He considered taking a shower but quickly rejected the idea in favour of getting on. He plugged a jack from the back of the digital camera into his laptop and drummed a nervous rhythm on the table while he waited for it to find and recognise this new source. After a few seconds a tiny camcorder-shaped logo appeared in the bottom left of the screen. William put his hamlike hand over the mouse. He clicked, and the film began to roll.

God it was boring. William watched, increasingly glassy-eyed, as an apparently endless stream of well-dressed Afghans marched up Baba's garden path, some grinning and gurning at the camera, others pretending it wasn't there at all, blushing or hiding their faces in mock horror. Unless the bomber had decided to crash the wedding, this was no good at all. The only consolation was Ali's fondness for certain female wedding guests; if there was even a hint of cleavage or leg to be seen, then Ali wasted no time moving to a close-up. Carver rewound a couple of these sections for a second look, but it was cold comfort. He was cursing Patrick's suggestion and close to giving up altogether when the camera position suddenly changed. Now he was looking down an almost empty Passport Street, the camera pointing in the direction of the main road and waiting, he assumed, for the imminent arrival of the bride and groom. This was better.

'Now let's have a look at the whole street. Pan round, Ali, you bastard. Pan round.' The whispered appeal worked. Ali swept the camera round, and on the other side of the street Carver saw the tailor's shop and, parked outside, a blue Toyota car. He rewound and watched this section twice, making a note of the time code before letting the tape play on. It got better. In the next shot the bridal car – a long, white 1980s Mercedes – drove carefully up Passport Street – 'keep going, keep going' – before slowing to a stop just beyond Baba's front gate. William held his breath. The bride and groom stepped from the car, and as they did, in the distance, no more than fifty feet away, a stocky figure in a suit could be seen leaving the tailor's shop. Carver pressed pause. He wound the film back sixty seconds and set the controls to play at half speed. He could feel his heart pumping harder. Looking down at his left hand, he saw that his fingers were crossed; he uncrossed then recrossed them, before pressing play. In the foreground the young couple stepped delicately from the car, laughing shyly, their arms linked. In the background, the burly man closed the shop door firmly behind him and walked away quickly, his head down.

'Come on, you tosser, look up. Everyone looks at a wedding.' As William spoke the man glanced up. He looked at the wedding car, the bride, groom and the waiting crowd, but he didn't clock the camera, not straight away at any rate. William pressed pause. 'Got you, Mr Roydon, whoever the hell you are.'

Patrick's room was only feet away, but William didn't want to leave the screen in case the shot somehow disappeared. He texted Patrick, who seconds later rapped on the door. 'Come.'

Patrick had shaved and was dressed in what William recognised as every newbie's first field producer outfit: a starched khaki travel jacket with no sleeves and more pockets than you could count.

'What the hell are you wearing?'

'Er—it's—well—it's my new jacket. Lots of pockets. Good for carrying stuff.'

William shook his head. 'Never mind. What are you like with computers? Photoshop and stuff like that?'

Patrick shrugged. 'I'm all right. Pretty good, I guess. I used to help with page layout at the *South London Press* sometimes, when people were filing late and we were close to deadline.'

'Perfect, go find another chair.'

Patrick went and got the chair from his room and Carver placed it hard next to his and began muttering urgent instructions. 'We need to enlarge and enhance that bloke, save it, then make one sequence from a few other bits and pieces. I've written down the time codes.' Patrick quickly got to grips with the laptop and William's recent versions of the Photoshop and Final Cut software; within a few minutes he had a reasonably clear image of the stocky man's face and inside ten minutes, a neatly edited sequence. William couldn't sit still. He stood and hovered at Patrick's shoulder while he worked. 'Not bad. Good in fact. Leave it at that.'

'Wait a minute, I'll just frame the big bloke properly. Upright and tight.'

'I beg your pardon?'

'Upright and tight, like a vicar's daughter. That's what the picture editor at the paper used to say.' Patrick smiled.

'Whatever. Okay, that's good. Now, save the sequence and that single shot as a separate file to my hard drive, then email yourself a copy of each, yeah?'

'Sure!' Patrick was enjoying his new usefulness.

William turned away from the desk and gazed out of the bedroom window for a moment, before turning sharply back. He grabbed Patrick's shoulder. 'On second thoughts, don't use email.' Digging deep into his hip pocket, he brought out a rectangular piece of plastic. 'Drop it all on this memory stick and transfer it to your own laptop that way. Take a copy of all my notes too, but don't forget to give me the stick back afterwards. Baba's cousin can have his camera back, but tell him we need to keep the original discs for a while. I'll buy him some new ones'

'Okay, boss. Got it.'

'What time are you being picked up?'

'Three-ish, they said.'

William looked at his watch. 'The Army don't do "ish". If they said three, it'll be three, more likely a few minutes early. You'd better move.' He watched as Patrick copied the files to the memory stick and then tried to decide which of his many jacket pockets was the safest place to stow it. Carver turned and looked out the window. Had he ever been as green as this kid? Or as keen? If he had, he couldn't remember it. 'Paddy, by the way, thanks. That was good work.' But when he turned to look, Patrick had already gone.

Back in his room, Patrick checked the time. He had twenty minutes — time enough to copy the files, pack away the laptop and some clean clothes in his rucksack, wash his face and brush his teeth. His head was spinning. He felt like he'd spent years waiting, wanting to live a life exactly like this one, but now it was happening, everything was moving too quickly and he was having trouble taking it all in. He stood at his bedroom window and tried to peer out, but a thick layer of dirt and the gaffer tape crosses made it all but impossible. The unpainted putty where frame met glass was dry and missing in places. He pulled the window open as far as it would go and leant out. It felt like he'd placed his head inside an oven. He saw laundry lines and thick black power lines strung in seemingly haphazard fashion between the tightly packed grey concrete homes. Over to his left he could see one of the VIP and press hotels, the Intercontinental. Around its high perimeter fence were stacked piles of sandbags and large steel security cages filled with rubble – guarding against car bombs or suicide attacks, he assumed. Patrick took a deep breath and then regretted it; he'd read about Kabul's lack of clean water and poor sanitation in his BBC briefing notes, but now he could smell it for himself – the powerful whiff of human sewage. He would get used to it, he was sure. He closed his eyes and listened to the thrum of generators, traffic noise, the occasional shouted greeting and also, from somewhere, birdsong. He opened his eyes and looked around: no tree, no scrap of green, no bird anywhere, but birdsong nonetheless. Taking his mobile phone from one of his many jacket pockets he scrolled through recent calls, found Rebecca's number and pressed dial. There was a long silence, some static and then a female voice, speaking in Arabic and then English informing him that he had no service and should contact one of several providers to 'maintain connectivity'. One of the providers the recorded message mentioned was Aftel. Patrick made a mental note to mention this to William. He considered emailing Rebecca instead, but then rejected the idea; it was her voice he wanted. He would wait until later, beg or borrow an army satphone, and call her on that.

15 On the Bagram Road

DATELINE: BBC house, central Kabul, Afghanistan, July 4th

The vehicle sent to take Patrick and Karim from the BBC house to Bagram was a soft-skin; a regular white Chevrolet SUV with some minor alterations but no armour plating, no guns. The men inside wore US Army fatigues. They introduced themselves as Sergeants Monneghan and Trout. Monneghan didn't look any older than twenty, Trout was in his thirties, and both had neat military buzz cuts. Patrick was reminded of Action Man – or perhaps, in Trout's case, of Action Man's slightly overweight older brother.

Trout glanced down at a printed A4 sheet in a clear wallet: 'And you guys are—let me see now, Carver and Reid, right?' Patrick corrected him.

'In fact, it's Reid and Mumtaz, sir. Carver is sick.'

'Sorry to hear that. All right. Let's go.' The sergeant didn't particularly care. He'd been told to pick up two BBC journalists and as far as he was concerned, he had two. Monneghan pulled out into the traffic unnecessarily fast, spewing a cloud of dust and diesel smoke over the street stall outside the BBC quarters. Trout spoke a short sentence of code into the radio and received a crackle of unintelligible vowels and consonants in reply. 'So Reid and Mumtaz, yes?' He turned to look at Patrick, his accent southern and slow.

'Yes.'

'Cool. They're waiting for y'all up at the airport. Y'all head off from there by chopper. Better get ready for some hanging around. Those bastards never fly on time. It'll take us an hour to get to Bagram, so make yourselves comfortable. Mind if I put a little music on?'

Patrick recognised the road they were on from the previous day, driving in from the airport. They had only travelled a few kilometres when, leaning forward, he saw what looked like a temporary roadblock of some kind, which the traffic in front was slowing to meet. As they approached, he could see through the petrol haze that the checkpoint was manned by four soldiers, or perhaps they were police, wearing an odd mix of uniform; grey camouflage jackets and mismatched trousers.

'Who are these guys?' he asked, but neither soldier replied.

Instead Monneghan tutted and swore under his breath. Trout looked at his colleague and smiled. 'The Afghan National Army in all its freakin' glory.'

Patrick could see him rest a hand on the revolver on his belt. The Chevy crawled forward, tailgating the car in front. When it reached the front of the queue, the ANA soldier nearest to them held up his hand, an apologetic smile on his face. Monneghan cursed and brought the SUV to a halt.

'Look at this. These fuckers are never gonna be able to run a country, they can't even run a roadblock.'

Trout turned to Patrick. 'That's off the record, by the way.' He grinned.

Two of the Afghan officers strolled towards the Chevy, both smiling and holding up their hands as if to acknowledge the lunacy of being made to stop a US Army vehicle. Patrick felt Karim shuffle in his seat. The Afghan soldiers were almost at the Chevy and now Patrick too felt nervous and suddenly nauseous, a cold sweat on the back of his neck.

'What's happening?' he whispered to Karim. The fixer looked directly ahead, his reply no louder than a whisper.

'I'm not sure, maybe nothing. But if something bad happens, stay close with me.'

The Afghan officers came alongside the Chevy, Monneghan punched stop on the CD player and Trout wound the automatic windows down.

'Good morning friends,' said the man at Monneghan's door. 'Accept our apologies. We were told to stop everyone, even our good allies. Can I ask where you are driving to?'

'Where the hell do you think we're driving to? I'm on the airport road, aren't I? I'm driving to fucking Bagram. I'm taking these VIPs up there, and thanks to you, I'm late . . .'

But the Afghan wasn't listening. He was looking past the American soldier into the back of the SUV, staring hard at Karim. Patrick saw him nod in the direction of his colleague, who was standing at Trout's window, and on this signal both men calmly lifted handguns from their sides and in almost the same moment pushed the barrels of their revolvers downwards into the necks of the two Americans and fired. Inside the closed car, the shots were close to deafening. Patrick pitched forwards and grabbed Karim's leg with one hand. He was aware of liquid on his face and in his panicked state assumed he'd been shot. He instinctively put his other hand to the wound, but found himself intact. His palm came away coated in the blood and flesh of one of the American soldiers. Then he heard screaming; an animal sound more terrifying than the gunshot. One of the Americans was still alive.

The Afghan gunmen wrenched open the SUV's front doors and

without attempting to conceal their crime from the growing line of traffic, pulled Monneghan's body and the still-screaming Sergeant Trout out on to the road. A third shot made Patrick jump again and the screaming stop. The gunmen jumped into the front of the vehicle. Patrick instinctively started to feel around for the door handle, but there was no time. The two Afghans who'd previously remained at the roadblock had now lifted it and were running towards the Chevy. The smaller of the two pulled open Patrick's door and punched him in the side of the face, sending him sprawling into Karim's lap. He leapt in just as the fourth man got in next to Karim, sandwiching the two together and shouting loudly in a language that Patrick couldn't understand. He saw Karim nodding vigorously, trying to keep eye contact. Then he felt Karim's hand on the side of his head, pushing him gently down into the footwell.

Karim got on to the floor alongside Patrick and whispered in his ear: 'Keep down, don't talk, or they say they will kill us.'

The new driver started the car and pulled hard left on the wheel. The Chevy lurched forwards and Patrick felt vomit rise in his throat as the SUV's rear wheels bounced over the body of one of the dead Americans. As they accelerated down the wrong side of the Bagram Road there were several more sharp turns and Patrick bounced left and right. His body knocked against the leg of the soldier sitting above him, prompting a half-hearted kick in the ribs.

16 *Vaffanculo!*

DATELINE: Deppington, Oxfordshire, England, July 4th

Mariscal lay low in the bath listening to his heart, its dull beat moving the water above his chest. He watched the tiny ripples and counted the seconds between one plodding thud and the next. An unlit cigarette was stuck to his lower lip. He sighed deeply and heard his heartbeat slow. This was the closest he had come to a feeling of contentment for several days. He closed his eyes, then opened them again as the impatient chatter of his mobile phone sounded from the bedroom next door. He called out to his wife. 'Lucy? Lucia, are you in there?'

There was no response. Rob hauled himself from the bath and stepped gingerly on to the white bathmat. The only towel left on the towel rail was too small to make it all the way round his midriff and so he held it in place with one hand while using the other to help him on his way across the wet floor from en suite to bedroom. Lucia was standing with her back to him, straightening the counterpane on the bed and ignoring the angry ring of her husband's telephone. Rob muttered an oath and tiptoed round his wife, catching the phone just before it vibrated itself off the bedside table and on to the floor. He glanced at the screen: unknown number. Normally he'd let a call like that go straight to voicemail, but these weren't normal times. He swept his finger across the screen.

'Yeah?'

'Mr Mariscal?'

'Yeah.'

The voice at the other end of the phone was clipped and official; a woman's voice. 'I have the Foreign Secretary for you, Mr Mariscal.'

'You do? Fantastic.'

'Can you take the call?'

'Do I have a choice?'

'I beg your pardon?'

'Nothing. Yes, I can take the call.'

'Hold the line please.'

There was a series of clicking sounds as the line bounced around Whitehall and then the familiar northern growl of the serving Foreign Secretary. These calls were not unusual; quite a few senior politicians liked to speak to Rob before agreeing to do an interview the following morning.

'Rob. All right? How are you?'

'Not too bad, thank you, Foreign Secretary. You?'

'Good, good. Busy. Too busy. But we do our best. Listen, your lot have been talking to my lot about an interview tomorrow, but you know how I like to 'ave a word with the organ-grinder and not just leave it to the monkeys. You got a minute?'

'Yes.'

'Good. So, brass tacks. What kind of elephant traps have you got in store for me tomorrow morning?'

Most of Rob's available attention had been elsewhere for much of the day, but he had a kept enough of an eye on the news to know what kind of direction a lead interview on Afghanistan would have to head in. 'Well, we'll have to talk casualties – ours, theirs. Then equipment, what our boys need, and what they haven't got.'

The Foreign Secretary snorted. 'They've got plenty of everything, Rob, but it's never enough. Chuffing generals always want a bigger and better train-set to play with, don't they? Sometimes mum and dad have to say "no" and put up with the tantrum.'

Rob smiled. 'Well, if you'd like to say that tomorrow, Foreign Secretary, please go ahead.'

A basso chuckle rolled down the line. 'You'll be lucky. "We're doing absolutely everything we can for our brave boys." That's what you'll get and you bloody well know it.'

'Fair enough. Then we'll have to ask about exit strategy and dates, I guess.'

'If you ask me when the Army's coming out, I'll just dead bat it.'

'I know you will, but you know we have to ask it anyway.'

'Yes, yes. What else?' The Foreign Secretary liked to negotiate to the last full stop and he didn't mind how long that took.

Usually Rob was happy to oblige – he enjoyed the cut and thrust of these conversations – but his heart wasn't in it tonight. 'Maybe a bit of Israel or the wider Middle East, if there's anything going on, but that's about it, I think. I'm happy to throw you an open-ended one, if you've got something you want to put out there?'

The Foreign Secretary laughed again. 'Really? What is this, my bloody birthday? Or are you going soft in your old age? No, I don't need any open questions, thank you very much. I know you, Rob. There's always a catch. I'm sure you've got something up your sleeve. But don't you worry, old son, I'll be ready for you. See you in the morning.'

The line went dead. Rob removed the towel from his waist and dabbed the phone dry before gazing at the blank blue screen. The

Foreign Secretary was wrong; he had nothing up his sleeve. He walked back to the bathroom. The water in the tub had cooled but the bath was still more inviting than anywhere else he could think of, so he put the phone on the side and climbed back in. In his haste to take the call, he'd dropped his cigarette into the water and flecks of brown tobacco now floated among the bubbles. He swished them away, unfolded his pale frame, and stretched out. Using his big toe, he turned the hot tap back on, whipping his foot away just in time to avoid scalding it.

The rush of water was louder than Lucia's footfall and when his wife appeared at his shoulder, he jumped. She spent some minutes tidying up around the sink, putting toothbrushes, toothpaste and a cake of soap back in the correct place, before turning to face her husband. Mariscal moved his arms from his sides and cupped his hands self-consciously around his genitalia. He tried to make it look a relaxed and natural position, but the apprehension on his face, and the positioning of his hands, made him look like a naked footballer about to defend a free kick. In another time, at an earlier point in their relationship, the sight of Rob like this – vulnerable and absurd – would have reduced Lucia to fits of easy laughter. But the smiling and laughing stage of their marriage seemed to be behind them. He observed his wife; her long white linen trousers and red heels, her loose denim shirt, untucked. Dark hair tied up. No jewellery. Rob had always been impressed by how good she could look with so little effort. He knew that part of the trick was that his wife looked different. His original and originally affectionate nickname for Lucia had been the Camel, and it was obvious why: the high step, huge eyes and exaggerated grace, together with the ability to look exotic and out of place no matter where she happened to be; and especially here, Rob thought, especially in this picture-postcard English village.

Before she was Mrs Mariscal, she was Lucia Vivendi and there was even more life in the woman than the name. Roman by birth and in temperament, she had been working as the London stringer for an Italian news agency when Mariscal met her, in the *Today* programme green room early one May morning. He fell for her heavily and immediately, but the feeling wasn't mutual. Rob had never wanted anything as much as he'd wanted Lucia. Nor had he ever had to work as hard at anything as he had at courting her.

'What did the Foreign Secretary want to talk about?' Although she'd lived in England for nearly two decades, Lucia's Roman accent was strong and she pronounced every word in every sentence with great care. Rob used to think this sounded sexy. Now it made her sound stern.

'Oh, you know, the usual. He's on tomorrow. Wanted to know what we'd ask him 'bout Afghanistan, Israel, Middle East, that kind of thing.'

'And you told him?'

'I gave him a few clues, yes.'

Lucia nodded. The smile was not a warm one. 'Maybe the children and I should try and talk to you about those places? Israel, Afghanistan?'

Rob knew exactly what was coming but found himself unable or unwilling to do anything other than assume his usual position, on one side of an old argument. 'I'd love to talk to you about Afghanistan, Lucy, what would you like to know?' It was well-trodden ground but that didn't stop them returning to it again and again. The argument revolved around what Lucia referred to as Rob's 'perverse pattern of attention'.

'What I'd like to know, Rob, is how you manage to be so interested in these things that are happening thousands of miles away? But at the same time, you are totally disinterested in what's happening here, right in front of your face? How do you manage that?' The question was rhetorical. Rob wasn't expected to say anything and he knew he shouldn't.

But tonight, he couldn't help himself. 'It's "uninterested".'

'What?'

'It's "uninterested" not "disinterested". Disinterested means impartial, like—'

'*Vaffanculo*!'

Rob heard the angry ricochet of high heels on the hard floor as she stormed from the bathroom. 'I wish you *would* fuck me, Lucy. Maybe that'd help. Maybe that's what we need . . .' he shouted after her.

Lucia either didn't hear or chose to ignore him. Rob heard her shout down the stairs to their two daughters. When she was angry her Italian accent grew more pronounced and both girls answered quickly.

Rob felt strangely elated by the row. He was glad that Lucia had picked a fight and glad to feel the heat of an argument. Back in the old days, they argued all the time. It was a game or, at the very least, a shared hobby. They fought long and loud and bitterly, but they always made up and it was the making up that Rob most looked forward to. These days they rarely fought and they never made up. Rob placed another unlit cigarette between his lips. Yes, he'd take the heat of an argument, however short-lived, over whatever it was they had at the moment. Polite small talk, cold silences; the marital equivalent of a never-ending nuclear winter.

He and his wife had made two mistakes. One mistake each, at least, that was how Rob saw it. The marriage wasn't a mistake. They were both happier married than they had ever been before. The first mistake was having children, and having children had been Lucia's idea. The change came two years into married life with the arrival of a daughter, and then, just over a year later, another. From Mariscal's point of view, the time, attention and affection Lucia then had available for him was halved and halved again. He knew this wasn't how a father was meant to react to the arrival of his first- and second-born, but he couldn't help it, it was how he felt; short-changed and cheated.

So the children were Lucia's mistake. Leaving London was his. Moving to the country had been all Rob's idea and it had taken him a long time to talk his wife round. She'd been born in a great city and had lived happily in several others. She had nothing against the English countryside but no particular affection for it either. Mariscal started with all the usual arguments: better schools, fresh air, more room for the kids to grow and play, less dog shit. When these arguments made no impression, Rob ordered an unnecessary office subscription to *Country Life* and started bringing the magazine home each week, leaving it lying around where Lucia was bound to find it. At first she recycled the magazine as soon as she saw it, but slowly the rich, rolling lawns, loggias and turquoise swimming pools drew her in. She began to browse, then graze and before long she was scouring the magazine's colourful pages looking for the Mariscal family idyll hidden somewhere inside.

The cracks started to show almost as soon as they had unpacked and redecorated. The village was pretty – and the house was perfect – but the people were a problem. Through his regular visits to the village pub, Rob realised long before Lucia that their new neighbours were a collection of the humdrum, the worn out and the undeserving rich. 'There are none so mean as those who are given money without grafting for it.' He remembered his dead father's words but he remembered them too late; he wondered how long it would take Lucia to reach the same inevitable conclusion.

After she'd finished fixing up the house and had settled the children at the local school, Lucia started to devote more time to exploring the village. One of her earliest and most enjoyable discoveries was the local charity shop. She recovered and recycled bagfuls of designer clothes donated to the shop by local ladies bountiful and began to wear these clothes in public. Twice in Rob's presence she had worn a hand-me-down dress to a local dinner party. Each time she drew admiring comments from the outfit's original owner and her husband. When she refused these compliments and pointed out that you could wear just about anything with her frame, Rob knew that as far as Lucia was concerned, she was just stating a fact. He also knew that that wasn't what most of the women heard. Weeks later, when Lucia wondered out loud why there were so few new donations hanging on the charity shop rails, Rob feigned ignorance. He knew that his wife's new friends would rather burn a thousand pounds worth of designer gear in a brazier in their back garden than see it worn by someone else to greater effect. And this was the sort of place he had brought his new family to. When he allowed himself to think about it, he felt profoundly guilty. So he didn't think about it. Instead, he spent more time at work and therefore more time in London, eventually arguing that it made more sense for him to stay in town during the week and just return for weekends.

All these things had happened, like most things happen, incrementally, and it was nearly three years into their new life in the country when Lucia woke one Wednesday morning and realised she was effectively marooned. If she had wanted, she could have ordered and organised a return; her father was wealthy and would have happily put his hand in his pocket and paid for the family to return to London. He had been against her relationship with Rob from the outset, against the marriage, and most vehemently against the move to 'nowhere'. But asking for his help meant admitting a mistake, and also the children were in school now – they had good friends, even if she didn't. She would make this work and if she couldn't do that, she would settle for making everyone else believe that she had made it work.

They were better in company and so weekend guests, friends and family were encouraged, almost bullied into visiting. From their arrival on Friday evening to their departure on Sunday afternoon, Lucia put on a bravura display. Fuelled by red wine and the occasional gift of a gram of cocaine, she was the happy hostess, the dutiful wife. She cooked and served and laughed and played after-dinner games. She got her old record player out, piled a dozen Italian and English forty-fives on top of the machine's mechanical arm and danced alone until others joined in. As the late nights turned to early mornings, she might go so far as to run a hand through Rob's ragged hair, even sit on his lap, her arm flung casually around her husband's neck. Sometimes these performances were so convincing that even Rob himself believed something might have changed, only to find his Paisley pyjamas back outside the spare room come Sunday night. So he would catch the first train back to London on Monday morning and stay there till Thursday or sometimes Friday. He told himself and others that this was the perfect arrangement. But without Lucia's day-to-day influence, the loose threads of his life had started to fray. His personal life became messy, and his financial situation fraught.

When Lucia found red bills and reminders in the bureau drawers, where Rob had shoved them, she would pay them without comment. In time, she transferred the direct debits from his account to her own, again without asking any questions. Not even the most obvious one, the one that Rob asked himself on a regular basis: why can't a man earning eighty grand a year pay his own way and provide for his family? The answer was that Rob was living beyond his means and borrowing unwisely. He travelled everywhere by black cab, he ate meals and took meetings in restaurants that he couldn't afford, and he bought round upon round of drinks. Two weeks out of four, these days, the cashpoint would refuse to serve him. He drew the line at borrowing money from friends but instead borrowed from people he didn't know at rates he didn't bother to understand. He was neck deep in trouble and wading deeper, and the longer Lucia refused to judge him, the more judgemental Rob thought his wife had become.

The phone rang again, inches from his ear. Rob grabbed it with a wet hand and tossed it across the floor. It landed safely in a pile of his discarded clothes and continued its muffled call. Whoever it was, rang off before the message service clicked in, but seconds later the phone rang again. Rob ignored this call too, but when the caller tried a third time he climbed from the bath.

'Hello?' he snapped.

'Hello, Rob, what's going on? Screening your calls this evening?' Graham spoke more slowly than usual. Slow enough, Rob thought, that a third person might easily listen in and perhaps even make notes.

'I was in the bath.'

'Oh, I'm sorry. I didn't mean to disturb.'

'Well you have. What do you want?

'Just a chat.'

'Yeah? Have you got another home movie you want to show me?'

'Oh that, yes, I'm sorry about that, Rob. It's nothing personal, you know that, it's just business.'

Rob felt a sudden surge of anger. 'Really? Well it feels pretty fucking personal to me, Graham.'

He had watched the DVD that Graham had handed him as soon as he got back to his office. It took him a few moments to work out what he was looking at: a neat little room, a folding chair, a single bed, all shot from somewhere up high, around the ceiling. The room rang bells but it wasn't until he saw a blurred version of himself wander into frame that everything fell into place. The positioning of the camera was perfect. Rob watched himself smoke a cigarette, drink coffee, undress clumsily and then climb into bed. You hardly saw the woman's face. Most of the time the camera caught only her back and the back of her head until the moment she stepped into bed and you saw Rob fumble with the clasp of her white bra and the curve of her right breast.

By contrast, Mariscal's every groan and gurn was caught on camera. Watching it back, again and then again, he couldn't decide whether it was a blessing the sex act lasted so short a period of time, or an additional embarrassment. He had ejected the disc and hidden it deep in the pages of the *Oxford English Dictionary*. They had him over a barrel. If Lucia ever saw the film, he was finished. It's one thing suspecting that your husband is screwing around. It's quite another to sit down in your living room and watch it on wide-screen.

Graham gave a nervous cough. Rob thought he heard him cover the phone and whisper something. When he came back across the line he was talking at a more conversational speed.

'Listen, Rob. A question for you. Why on earth would a good-looking twenty-year-old girl chase and seduce a knackered old hack like you? Did you ever wonder that?' He waited for an answer but Rob had none. 'No, I can't think of a single reason either.' Graham stifled a laugh. 'Here's a piece of advice for you, Rob, going forward: if it seems too good to be true, then it probably is.'

This barb found its mark. Rob spat back down the line. 'You know what I wonder, Graham? I wonder whether the Foreign Affairs Select Committee knows that you're spending taxpayers' money honey-trapping senior British journalists?' As he spoke arcs of spittle flew from his mouth. At the other end of the line he heard a chortle.

'The amount of stuff that committee doesn't know could keep every paper shredder in Whitehall busy from now till kingdom come.' Graham paused. When he spoke again he sounded a good deal more serious. 'I hope that was a joke, by the way, Rob. Not some ham-fisted threat?'

'Yeah, it was a joke. It's all a fucking joke, isn't it?'

'That's the spirit. Anyway, I didn't call to pick a fight. I have some news.' His voice slowed again, back to dictation speed.

'You'll hear this officially within the hour, but one of your journalists has been kidnapped on the outskirts of Kabul.'

The colour drained from Mariscal's face. 'Oh, shit! William. Who by?'

'No. Not Carver. Turns out Carver didn't take you up on that kind offer of the poppy trip. He sent Patrick Reid in his place. It's Reid they've taken; Reid and your local translator. A chap called Karim Mumtaz.'

Marsical felt his stomach tighten. 'Shit,' he whispered, 'Patrick? He's as green as it gets. Just a kid. So where's William?'

'Carver's still in the BBC house. Right as rain and still a royal pain in the arse as far as my lot are concerned. That's where you come in.' Rob switched the phone from one hand to the other. He guessed what was coming. 'You'll get a call pretty soon from work. They'll ask you to go and manage things from the Kabul end and you'll say "yes".'

Mariscal was silent; he was thinking about Patrick.

'Did you hear me, Rob?'

'Yes I heard you. They'll call. I'll say yes.'

'That's right.'

'Then what?'

'We'll talk about the details later but basically, you're to get close to Carver, find out what he's got. That'll do for starters. We need to know everything, Rob.'

'Fine. And you'll work on getting Patrick back?'

'What? Yes, we'll do everything we can. The more you deliver, Rob, the more we'll be able to do. We're going to have to trust each other if we're going to resolve this one. Do you understand?'

'I understand.'

'Good man. And Rob, don't forget, when you get the call, when your boss tells you what's happened, remember to act surprised.'

Rob had been back in the bath for less than a minute when the next call came. He checked the screen: private number.

'Hello?' The hesitant voice at the other end belonged to Lance Fletcher, Rob's boss, the BBC's Head of News. He took a moment to clear his throat and finish chewing whatever it was that he had in his mouth.

'Hello?' Rob almost shouted.

Fletcher swallowed and then spoke. 'Sorry Rob, you've been engaged so long, I didn't expect the call to go through.'

Why call then, Rob wondered. 'I'm sorry, Lance. Got a lot of family stuff going on. How are you?'

'Fine, fine. I'm fine, Rob, thank you. But, er, listen mate. I've got some rather bad news. Are you sitting down?'

Mariscal looked down at his wet, marble-white and water-wrinkled body. 'Yeah.'

'Good. Look, there's no easy way to say this. I've just heard that one of your producers has been kidnapped. Patrick Reid. It happened earlier today, just outside Kabul.'

Mariscal pulled himself up in the tub and exhaled slowly, emitting a soft wheeze. 'Oh my God. That's terrible. That's—oh, fucking hell, Lance, that's—'

Fletcher took a gulp of air. 'For Christ's sake, Rob, don't *you* start to panic. I've got enough of that going on at this end. It's going to be fine. The Embassy in Kabul is on the case. They reckon it's probably just one of those opportunistic things, grab a westerner, demand a ransom . . .'

'Right, yes, that makes sense, Lance. Okay . . .'

'Reid had a translator with him, an Afghan chap and I'm afraid they took him too.'

'Karim Mumtaz.'

'That's right, Mumtaz. You know him, do you? He's freelance. Not on the BBC books so not our responsibility, strictly speaking.'

'That must be a big relief.'

'Sorry?' Fletcher had a talent for not hearing the words he didn't want to hear. ''Fraid I didn't catch that, Rob. But anyway, this isn't just a courtesy call I'm making here. I need to ask you something.'

'Right. What is it?'

'We need you to go out there and oversee things. Be our eyes and ears on the ground, deal with the Embassy, and the press. Do you think you can do it?'

Rob paused. Counted to two, three. Long enough for Fletcher to think a decision was being made. 'Sure.'

'Really?'

'Sure. I'll go.'

'Good. You don't need to think about it, talk to the little lady?'

'No, I'll go, I want to go. He's my man and it was my decision to send him.'

'That's the spirit,' Fletcher said cheerfully. He had obviously been expecting an argument. 'You're a good man, Rob. A good man.' He paused, weighing up whether to reveal his hand a little further. He couldn't see why not. 'Seeing as how you've been so good about this, Rob, I don't mind telling you, that this idea – the idea to send you out to manage all this – it came right from the top. The very top, Rob!' He warmed to his tale. 'I've got to admit, I was a little surprised when they asked for you. Usually a job like this would go to a more senior fellow. Like me, perhaps. But I sure as hell didn't want to go and now I hear how keen you are, it makes perfect sense, doesn't it?' He chuckled down the line. 'They usually know what they're doing, up there at the top of Broadcasting House, don't they, Rob?'

Mariscal could not have disagreed more profoundly with this analysis of senior management, the group Fletcher often and lovingly referred to as 'the higher ups'. In Rob's experience, the higher ups rarely knew their collective arse from their elbow. As for this decision? Good or bad, it was not of their making. 'Couldn't agree more, Lance. I'll pack a bag and get the office to start sorting a flight right now.' He could sense Fletcher nodding away at the other end of the phone line: a problem was being dealt with, action taken, responsibility delegated – the Head of News was happy. Now was the time to ask.

'There's one thing though, Lance. A bit of a favour really. Could I have a quick chat with you before I fly off? Face to face?'

There was an audible inhalation of breath at the other end of the phone. Rob waited while Fletcher made a calculation. It was obvious that Mariscal wanted something. Probably money because that's what he usually wanted. Fletcher wasn't in a position to give Rob another pay rise, but refusing to meet the man would be poor form, particularly now. He would have to say 'yes'.

'Sure Rob, no problem at all. Call Sally first thing and she'll sort it out.'

17 Captivity

DATELINE: Outskirts of Kabul, Afghanistan, July 5th

The first thing Patrick did was measure the room. The width of one hand was about four inches, three of those to the foot, so by placing his palm on the cool concrete and turning it across one wall, then the next, he calculated the size of his cell. seven feet and a few fingers long. Just five feet across. That gave him thirty-five square feet of floor space. And most of that was already taken up by a metal camp bed. He sat on the folded grey blankets, which served as a mattress, and surveyed the other items in his cell: a white plastic picnic chair and a red bucket. His life was suddenly very simple. He was expected to sleep on the bed, sit on the chair and crap in the bucket. He had no idea what else was expected of him; nothing, it seemed. Nothing other than to wait. Patrick couldn't stand up straight in the room – the ceiling was too low – so every now and then he would shuffle about hunchbacked in his filthy black cotton ankle socks, the only footwear he had left since his shoes had been taken from him along with his rucksack and laptop. He knew prisoners sometimes had their shoelaces taken from them, but the shoes as well? These were the things that Patrick thought about as he waited.

It was hot; at least ninety degrees, he guessed. Sour grey sweat marks had formed under both arms and down his back. He had removed his travel jacket long ago and considered stripping off his dirty white shirt and trousers several times since, but pride and an instinct for self-preservation stopped him. He didn't want to look any more vulnerable than he already did. Letting the men who had taken him see his skinny frame and pigeon-chest was an invitation to beat and abuse. Even with his clothes on, he knew he looked far from invulnerable; his blond hair was plastered to his head and now both legs had developed that excruciating under-exercised itch and his feet were starting to cramp, even though he'd only been locked up for—for how long? A day? He imagined he could already feel the muscles in his legs beginning to waste, so he lay flat on his back on the strip of floor between the bed and the wall, hoisted himself up on to his elbows, lifted his long legs into the air and started to pedal. Keep going. That was the important thing. Don't panic. Don't crack. Keep going.

The cell looked larger from upside down, but no less dismal. The walls were made from rough-cut concrete blocks and painted an uneven grey. There was no window, no ventilation, no sockets, no light fittings. The steel door was also grey but with black skid marks and dents from repeated kicks and punches, and as he stared at it from his upside-down position, it moved on its hinges. Just a little. And with each movement of the door came a dull slapping sound.

'Who's there?' he called out uselessly, rolling himself back on to his knees. He crawled tentatively forwards and put his hands to the metal frame. The slapping sound continued. A slap followed by a rapid, quieter patting. What the hell was it? Patrick put his ear on the ground. He closed one eye and with the other looked through the slim gap between door and floor and then recoiled, gasping, as a lump of coarse mortar landed just the other side of the divide and was scraped up with a trowel. The slapping sound continued. They were cementing him in.

'*Stop*! Please stop. *You're insane*! I'll talk to you. Just ask me. What do you want to know? I'll tell you anything you want to know. Oh God,' he faltered, 'who are you?' Patrick kicked hard at the door with the sole of his foot. He felt a sharp pain travel up his leg, stopping at his knee. He staggered backwards and sat down heavily, the legs of the white picnic chair splaying under the sudden weight. He pressed the heels of his hands deep into his eye sockets and struggled for breath. Piss darkened his trousers. It dripped through the slats of the chair and pooled on the cement floor beneath him.

18 Next of Kin

DATELINE: Peckham, south London, SE15, July 5th

Peckham Green Primary School had seen better days. At least Rebecca hoped it had, or else the people who'd built it should have been arrested. But despite its crumbling gunmetal-grey walls and a floor plan that broke every ergonomic rule, Rebecca loved her classroom. And she loved it best at this time of day. Before eight, it was quiet and orderly with a slight smell of floor cleaner and chalk. She took the marked homework books from her bag and placed each carefully on the desk of its owner. She fetched a box of pencils from the store cupboard, sharpened them in the electric sharpener and placed one next to each homework book. For the care Rebecca took she might have been preparing for a Cabinet meeting or a peace summit at Camp David. Once finished, she stood behind her desk and took a long, satisfied look around. After finishing her coffee she wrote the day, month and year neatly in the top right-hand corner of the old blackboard that had been back in service ever since someone had broken in and stolen the interactive whiteboard. Rebecca didn't condone theft but this was one break-in where, as far as she was concerned, the vandals had done the school a favour. She rubbed the chalk from her fingers with the hem of her skirt and listened. The school was coming to life now. She could hear scooters, bike tyres on the tarmac and the thump of a football on the playground wall. With squeaking trainers and the loud dragging of chairs, her students slowly filled the room and found their places. She looked at them. Thirty-four pairs of expectant eyes looked back. A few months ago the class had watched her in a different way. When she started they watched, waiting for her to slip up, to crack and then scarper like several substitute teachers before her. They didn't doubt it would happen. But Miss Black had stayed and now the word in the staffroom was that the Year Six Problem had been solved.

'What's with the books on the desk, Miss?' Charlene hadn't touched her homework book or pencil. She was staring at them, suspiciously.

'I thought I'd spoil you all a little.'

'I like it better when you Frisbee them, Miss.'

'I'll chuck them to you next week, then, Steven.'

'Okay. Can I sit at the back of the class next week?'

'We'll see.'

'My dad says you put me here to keep an eye on me, 'cos you think I'm lazy.'

'I put you there because your surname begins with the letter B, Steven.'

'My dad says teachers always put the thick kids at the front.'

More difficult: how to reassure Steven without informing him that his father was an arse. 'I'm afraid your dad's wrong on that one, Steven. If your dad came and sat in my class, I'd put him in the same spot because his surname also begins with B.'

'Are you sure you're not discriminatin' against me, Miss, 'cos I'm black and a Muslim an' that?'

Rebecca took a long draw on her now empty coffee cup. 'Do me a favour and hand me your lunch box, please, Steven.'

'Why?'

'Come on.' The boy passed his Chelsea FC lunch box up from under his desk and Rebecca opened it. 'You see this, Steven? This is a ham sandwich. Do you know what that tells me?'

'I like ham?'

'Yes. But it also tells me that you're probably not a Muslim. How often do you see Mohammed with a ham sandwich?'

'His mum probably can't afford the ham.'

'Mohammed is a Muslim. A proper one. And as you know, he's also my best and most favourite student.'

Mohammed lifted his head and gave Rebecca a despairing look. 'Aw, Miss—'

'Sorry, Mohammed. Just trying to teach Steven something. I'm not picking on Steven because he's a Muslim. Steven isn't a Muslim. I'm picking on Steven because I think if he tried a bit harder, he could go far. And I'm not talking about the Bluewater shopping centre.'

Steven blushed and opened his exercise book. First battle of the day won with no casualties. Maybe it was going to be a good day.

The class was busy pulling at rubber bands with Newtonian measuring devices when the Year Five teacher knocked on the door. Rebecca waved him in. 'Morning Mr Harris, how can we help you today?'

Ben Harris walked quickly to Rebecca's desk and answered softly. 'Morning. Listen, the Head's asked me to cover your class for a few minutes, he needs to see you.' There was a formality to his manner that Rebecca didn't like but she nodded, explained the situation to the class and left the room, closing the door behind her. Halfway to the Head's office she realised she was still holding a new piece of chalk in her hand. She knocked at the door and was called in immediately. He was sitting behind his desk, looking somewhat stiff and very pale. Then Rebecca saw the policeman. Her first thought was of her parents, and only afterwards of

Patrick. She was surprised to realise it was the second thought that shook her harder. She refused the offer of a seat and stood while the policeman told her that her 'partner', as he put it, had been kidnapped by terrorists 'identity unknown' just hours after arriving in Kabul. There was no reason to believe he had been harmed and the Foreign Office, the Embassy in Kabul, the British military and the BBC were all working together 'doing everything possible'. Rebecca took an unsteady step forward. She put her hands down hard on the headmaster's desk for balance and felt the stick of chalk break in her fist. She felt sick. Then she started speaking, quickly.

'His mobile wasn't working but I thought maybe he just hadn't set it up properly. I don't know how you'd make his lousy mobile work in Afghanistan anyway, so I thought it wasn't working or maybe he'd just turned it off. And I knew he'd ring me from a landline once he'd got himself sorted, I knew it might take time so I just thought—' The policeman interrupted. She was talking nonsense, she knew that, but she didn't want to stop talking, because what would she do then?

'I'm sorry Ms Black. But I need to ask you something. On his risk assessment form at the BBC he listed you as his next of kin.'

'Right?'

'Just you. So, we were hoping you could help us inform Patrick's parents?'

'They don't know?'

Outskirts of Kabul, Afghanistan, July 5th

Patrick stayed slumped in the white plastic chair for a long time, the heels of his hands pushing against his tired eyes, cold urine stinging at his thighs, a dull pain in his knee from kicking uselessly at the metal door. He felt frightened, helpless and ashamed. After an hour he heard some movement and then a voice from the other side of the sealed door. He jumped to his feet too quickly and had to put a hand on the wall for support.

'Pat-rick Reid?' The voice was deep and heavily accented.

'Yes?' He tried to sound strong, but his voice was weak.

'I am going to ask questions, you answer them. Yes?'

'Yes.'

'Do not lie. If you answer the questions with honesty then the men will take the cement away, open the door and give you food, some water. If you lie, then we will leave things as they are. You will be unconscious in two days and dead not long after that. Do you understand what I say?'

Patrick swallowed. He was hungry and he didn't want to die.

'Yes. I understand.'

The questions all concerned the killing of Fazil Jabar. Why was he investigating the killing? Who was he working for? What had he discovered? There was a pause after each answer and he was frequently told to repeat himself or speak up until it seemed to Patrick that he was talking very loudly indeed, shouting almost. He told his interrogator that he and Karim were both working for the same man, an important British journalist, William Carver, who believed that Jabar had been murdered not by the Taliban but by someone else and for mysterious reasons.

Where was William Carver? In Kabul. At the BBC house. But he would be heavily guarded by now. Patrick didn't know this for a fact but it seemed likely and it might help discourage this group, whoever they were, from going after William. There was another pause. Patrick got the impression someone was making notes or maybe relaying his responses to a third party.

'Who is Karim Mumtaz?'

This was the most difficult question so far. What sort of answer might help keep Karim safe? That he was simply a young Afghan paid to translate for Carver? Or that he was more important, a

200

BBC employee, someone whose life the Corporation would value? Patrick assumed that downplaying Karim's importance would make his captors more inclined to cut him loose.

'He is an ordinary Afghan. William Carver paid him to act as his translator on this trip. He knows very little.'

There was another pause. A long conversation in Dari which Patrick only heard half of. He was certain now that his interrogator was taking instructions down a phone line from elsewhere.

'That is enough. Perhaps more questions later.'

He heard the sound of footsteps retreating and shouted out: 'Wait, what about the food? Some water? I told the truth.'

But the man was gone. Patrick knew he had to try harder to hold himself together. He climbed out of his piss-wet trousers and hung them off the side of the camp bed to dry, then looked again at the cell. There was no obvious ventilation but somehow, from somewhere, he could smell cooking and, more faintly, excrement – from similar cells to his, perhaps, or a nearby toilet. He started walking again. Walking and counting. He counted the drips from water pipes he could hear but not see, he counted the steps he took up and down the cell, his head lowered but still brushing the ceiling, and he counted the dents in the metal door. As he was counting these, the door moved on its hinges. There was a scraping sound and his heart lifted, the cement was being broken away. His honesty was about to be rewarded. He felt an unexpected surge of gratitude.

Patrick's first prison meal was a torn piece of flatbread, a boiled egg and a mug of hot, sweet black tea. It was delivered by one of the gunmen, who, either out of fear or disgust, kept as far from Patrick as he could. The man opened the door gingerly, kicking some of the loose cement out of the way with his sandalled foot. He motioned with his Kalashnikov for Patrick to move to the back of the cell. Then he bent and slid the tin plate across the floor. The egg rolled off the bread and across the filthy concrete. Patrick moved instinctively to retrieve it and the young guard reacted by barking some incomprehensible order and unslinging his rifle, pointing the barrel directly at Patrick's heart. Patrick dropped the egg and put his hands above his head. Both men stared at the fallen egg, which had split open and lay in two bright white-and-yellow pieces on the dark floor. The guard sniffed, put his gun back behind his shoulder and left, locking the door noisily behind him.

Patrick took the egg, wiped it on his shirt and stuffed it greedily into his mouth. He ate and drank everything he'd been given and then resumed his walking and exercising. For an hour or longer he worked hard to tire his body before finally lying down on the hard bed, pulling the dirty blanket over his face and escaping into sleep.

19 Two Plus Two Equals Five

DATELINE: BBC house, central Kabul, Afghanistan, July 5th

On the roof of the BBC house in downtown Kabul the producer of the *Ten O'Clock News* was writing two names on large cue cards to ensure John Brandon didn't get them wrong during his live broadcast. In capital letters he wrote *PATRICK REID* and *KARIM MUMTAZ*. William Carver watched, grim-faced. The kidnapping of a BBC journalist and his translator was the lead. In a few minutes Brandon would tell millions of Britons everything he knew about the circumstances and possible reasons for the kidnapping. This would not take long because Brandon knew very little. Not unusual, William reflected, but in this case no one else knew much more. Not even William himself, and the thought annoyed him. He watched while Brandon had a tissue tucked into his collar and a producer dabbed at his broad forehead with powder. Carver had never understood why anyone would want to watch, work in or appear on television news; identikit men and women in identical suits telling the same stories using the same punchy clichés. What mattered was that they looked good and the backdrop looked bad.

'You've got some devastation in the back, yeah?' Brandon was talking to his cameraman, who raised a thumb in reply. It was pretty easy in Kabul; to western eyes, virtually the whole city looked devastated. Brandon took a look over his shoulder and nodded, apparently satisfied. Four minutes to go. He sat back down. The presenter was wearing his trademark white suit over a white shirt. He sat close to his broadcast point, relaxed, one thick leg resting across the other, arms crossed loosely, smiling broadly. The top three buttons of his shirt were undone, allowing colleagues a generous view of his thick pelt.

In a business where many of his peers waged daily war against male pattern baldness, Brandon was proud to be hirsute. Even now, although his shirt cuffs were gathered neatly at the wrist with plain silver cufflinks, William could see a few sprigs of black arm hair spilling out. A feather of dark hair sat on top of each meaty knuckle. William recalled the conversations he used to have with Rob Mariscal about journalism; print versus broadcasting, radio versus television, vertical versus horizontal. Horizontal journalism waited upon events and then reported them. It waited for reports to be published, speeches made, elections held, wars waged and disasters visited. Vertical journalism set its own agenda; it was active, investigative and trouble-making. Horizontal journalism stood on the roof of a house in Kabul, adopted a serious tone and speculated wildly about the fate of Patrick Reid and Karim Mumtaz. Vertical journalism should be doing something else. As he chewed this over, he noticed Brandon rising to greet someone. Looking back over his shoulder he saw Captain Remora picking his way across the roof, tiptoeing around cabling and arc lights. As Remora drew closer he held up a hand to placate Brandon and to indicate that he'd be right with him before bending close to Carver's ear. His breath was toothpaste fresh.

'I've come to brief John and a few of the others but the

Ambassador's downstairs in his car. He wants to talk to you. Can you go down?'

''Course.'

William pulled himself to his feet. Back to vertical, back to work. As he walked towards the stairs that led from the roof he could hear Remora's confident voice. He turned and saw Brandon listening attentively, his producer scribbling notes.

'John, you're absolutely the only one who is getting this. You can say that official sources have told you that every possible effort is being made to contact the kidnappers and find out what their demands might be. You can say that we suspect a Taliban group, probably the one linked to the killing of Fazil Jabar. Remember him?'

William stopped in at his room and grabbed his bag from the side of the bed, paused to gather his thoughts, then made his way to the front of the BBC house where two SUVs were parked either side of a black armoured Lexus. Ambassador Lever was sitting in the back seat. When he saw Carver he signalled to a British sergeant holding a general-purpose machine gun to let him pass. William opened the heavy door and climbed in. 'Look at all this security, you must feel very flattered.'

'I feel very stupid. Rolling around Kabul like this. Still, one Briton kidnapped in a day is embarrassing; two would be careless.'

William nodded. The cool air-conditioned car was a welcome respite from the hot Kabul night. 'Well. What do you know?'

'We're making every effort to contact the kidnappers but we don't have many leads. Taliban we guess but—'

Carver interrupted, raising his hand. 'I heard the official version upstairs, Ambassador; Captain Remora is helping Brandon learn his lines. Tell me what you really know.'

Lever cast his eyes downwards and stared at the top of his Panama hat, which was resting on his lap. 'Mr Carver, the official version is the only version I've got. I'm sorry. We're in the dark. Like you.'

'Two of my closest colleagues have been kidnapped and you can't give me anything more than the official line?'

Lever sighed. He glanced at his driver, the only other person in the car and separated from them by a thick plate of glass. 'It looks like the roadblock had been set up specifically to catch *that* vehicle. It hadn't been in place long, according to witnesses, and obviously the entire gang disappeared as soon as those poor American soldiers were dead and your colleagues had been taken.

'It was manned by men wearing Afghan National Army uniform, or something like it. Maybe they'd stolen the uniforms or maybe they were ANA doing a bit of freelance work or doing someone a favour. There are bad apples, as you know.'

'There are whole barrel-loads of bad apples . . . as you know.'

Lever frowned. 'We've also had a report of an abandoned SUV, up to its roof in water, to the north-west of the city somewhere. There's a fair chance that's the one involved in this, I'd have thought. So we are monitoring phone chatter, we're tapping up informers, we're keeping the Foreign Office and your Director General in the picture. We're doing everything you'd expect us to do, Mr Carver, and if you have any other ideas, we'll try those too.'

'If you think this kidnapping is linked to the killing of Fazil Jabar, how about you try a bit harder to find Richard Roydon, speak to him. He might know something useful.'

Lever scoffed. 'What on earth makes you think that?'

William hesitated, weighing up how much he wanted to tell this man, at this point. 'All right. I'm going to be candid with you, Ambassador. I trust you – not completely, but enough. I told you about Roydon's appointments at the tailor's, same sort of time as Jabar's, over a number of weeks.'

'You told me, yes.'

'Well I now know for certain that Roydon was on Passport Street on the evening of the bombing, driving a blue Toyota. I have proof.'

'What kind of proof?'

'Film and photos from the scene.'

The Ambassador lifted his eyebrows. William ignored him and continued. 'I think he armed the explosives and placed them. They were packed inside a suitcase and it was a professional job but I think he screwed up. I don't think the bomb killed Jabar outright. I'm pretty sure he had to go back in afterwards and finish the job. Fazil Jabar wasn't killed by the blast, you see, someone put a bullet in his head. Karim was investigating all this last week, and a gang tried to kidnap him the very same day he discovered this information implicating Roydon. So what do you think of all that?'

Lever turned his hat slowly in his lap. 'I think it sounds like a lot of far-fetched nonsense. What could Roydon's motive possibly have been? Or am I to believe he's simply gone insane?'

'No, not insane. I'm guessing his motive is the usual one: money. While I was in London I met a contact of mine. Someone who knows quite a bit about some of the dodgy deals being done out here. He explained the Aftel connection.'

Lever grinned but the smile didn't reach his eyes. 'The Aftel connection?'

William paused. He was about to go significantly further than he'd originally intended, to tell Lever more or less everything he knew. It was a risk but if it could help Patrick and Karim . . . 'How much do you know about Fazil Jabar's business dealings?'

'Very little.'

'He wasn't just a politician, he was a businessman as well, and I'm told he was the main obstacle that stood in the way of Aftel winning a telecoms licence worth billions of pounds over the next few years. I assume you've heard of Aftel?'

'Yes.' The Ambassador's impatience was obvious now; his irritation too.

'And that you knew they were in the running for this licence?'

'Yes, of course. I know them, they're a good, solid British firm. The parent company is in the Footsie100. But it's just ludicrous – and, I'm afraid, thoroughly naive – to try and link Jabar's death to Aftel. Aftel's parent company competes for licences all over the world. It's what they do. It's routine. They win some and they lose some.'

'They don't lose many. So you knew Jabar was involved in the rival bid. How about you? Were you involved?'

Lever looked William in the eye. The Lexus continued to cool and condition the air nicely but the Ambassador's face was increasingly red. 'I'm the Ambassador. Naturally I have an involvement. That's part of my job, helping British businesses abroad. That really shouldn't surprise you, Mr Carver. So, yes, I met some of the people behind the British bid. It was, it still is, a good bid, for all sorts of reasons.'

'Yeah,' said William, dismissively, 'that's what my contact said. A good bid, but not the winning bid. Not until the bomb went off, anyway. My source says that Jabar getting killed was good news for Aftel. Billions of pounds worth of good news.'

'That's a horrible way to think about anyone's death, Mr Carver, dreadful. And it hardly amounts to proof that anyone connected to Aftel had anything to do with the bombing. Frankly, I find it impossible to believe that a rather unimpressive ex-Marine like Richard Roydon could be part of some grand plot, as you seem to be suggesting. I think this is a conspiracy theory too far, Mr Carver. You're adding two and two and getting five.'

'Really? I've been through Aftel's accounts,' said William, 'and a couple of years ago it was just a twinkle in its parent company's eye. Barely existed; it was an idea more than anything else, shares were trading at twelve pence. Now they're worth over a fiver and rising. Imagine if you'd been in at the beginning of that, how much you might make. And do you know what else I found in those accounts? The name of the company Aftel employs for "security and technical services": Rook.'

The Ambassador said nothing for some time. 'So are you pointing the finger at one of the biggest mobile phone companies in Britain, Mr Carver, or just its subsidiary? Or just greedy Mr Roydon?'

'I don't know. There are still a lot of things I don't know.'

Ambassador Lever gazed out of the window. 'Well, I'm not a journalist, but if even a small part of what you say is true, and you can prove it, then I'd have thought you'd have quite a scoop on your hands.'

'Maybe.'

'May I ask how your London contact is in a position to know these things he's telling you?'

'No, you may not ask.'

'Will he go on the record?'

'Perhaps. If I need him to.' Carver dug around in his blazer pocket and found two sticks of chewing gum. He offered one to Lever, who declined with a barely visible shake of the head. William waited. It seemed there was something else the Ambassador wanted to say.

'Mr Carver. The Aftel bid. It isn't just good news for UK business, you know, it's good for Afghanistan too. As I said, I've had some small involvement and I know what the British bid promises. It isn't just about advancing UK plc; it's much more than that. Good, solid jobs for men and women, especially women, they have a commitment. Proper pay, healthcare, pensions, childcare. The sort of employer Kabul needs. A good example. A step forward. Do you see?'

Lever seemed rather desperate that William saw. 'I see. I'd better go, Ambassador. If you get any news about Patrick and Karim, please tell me first.'

'Indeed.'

Carver got out of the car and closed the door behind him. Lever watched him walk back into the BBC house before removing the phone from inside his jacket pocket. Its screen glowed green. He lifted it to his ear. 'Hello? Did you hear all of that?'

'I heard.'

'How much of what he says is true?'

'Some. Quite a bit, in fact. I'm almost impressed.'

Lever's head slumped forwards, his chin touching the knot of his tie. 'Jesus. What have I done?'

'You've done what you had to do. Hold your nerve, Ambassador. This contact of Carver's is annoying but no more than that, and apart from him, we've got everything in hand. Everything.'

Outskirts of Kabul, Afghanistan, July 5th

By the morning of his third day as a prisoner, Patrick felt filthy. He was desperate for a shower or at least a shave, and he would have paid a month's wages for a clean pair of cotton socks.

After a bread-and-water breakfast, he was escorted from his cell but only as far as a toilet cubicle at the other end of a corridor of similar cells. As far as he could tell, none of these were occupied and he could still find no sign of Karim. The toilet room was little more than a hole in the ground surrounded by a breezeblock wall stuck together by untidy cement-work. There was a shower curtain attached at the front of the cubicle for modesty and two buried breezeblocks on which to plant your feet while you crouched over the hole. As he defecated he watched a cockroach saunter around the rim of the hole. It was disgusting. But still he took his time, grateful to be looking at something other than his cell. The toilet was clearly closer to the street because by leaning close to the wall he could just make out the sound of children shouting and playing and even a ball being kicked. It seemed astonishing that normal life could be taking place just yards from where he was, and he took some comfort from the fact.

With a mix of gestures and shouts, the guard let him know that he should bring his bucket with him and, now, that he should empty it. He threw the contents down the hole, making sure some of his cold piss washed a few of the roaches down at the same time. The guard pointed his gun at a standpipe. Patrick refilled the red bucket and, leaving the tap running, splashed water over his hands, face, neck and armpits until something was shouted at him and he was marched back to the cell. The door was locked behind him. Patrick put the bucket back under his chair and resumed his steady walk up and down.

'Well. Now you know some more about where you are. And a change is as good as a rest.' He wasn't sure when he had started talking to himself. He wondered whether it was a bad sign; whether his internal monologue was no longer internal. Seconds, minutes, hours passed. He tried to count them and whatever else he could find that was countable. He received and ate another meal, almost identical to his last, and continued to exercise. It felt like early evening when the door to the cell opened again.

Patrick instinctively stepped to the back of the room and put his hands by his sides, but instead of the regular jailer and a plate of tasteless food, he saw a new face. This man was leaner, older and clearly more senior. He wore a long black beard flecked with grey and a black turban. The man nodded, looked around the fetid cell, then gestured for an underling to bring something in. A bucket of steaming hot water, a scrap of towel and a piece of soap were placed on the floor, and next to that, a plate with a round of bread and an orange which looked so ridiculously bright and beautiful and out of place that Patrick at first wondered whether he was imagining it. Finally a pile of clothes: a dark shirt, camouflage trousers and a pair of black army boots.

The turbaned man spoke: 'Wash and put on the clothes. We leave tonight.'

It was either very late or very early when Patrick was woken by a kick, first to the camp bed, then his bare feet, which were hanging over the end. As his eyes adjusted to the darkness, he could see that the turbaned man was standing over him.

'I told you, be ready. Put on the boots.'

Patrick struggled to a sitting position and jammed his feet into the boots. They were a couple of sizes too small. He tied them loosely and stood. The man muttered a few words of Dari to Patrick's regular jailer, who gestured that he should put his hands out in front of him. Patrick held his hands out, fingers clasped together as though in prayer, and the jailer fastened his wrists together with a plastic cable tie before placing a black hood over his head. He was manhandled out of the cell, up at least one flight of stairs, tripping several times, and through a series of metal-sounding doors. A draught of fresher, cooler air told him he was nearly outside. He took several deep breaths while he and whoever was now escorting him waited for something to happen. They were joined by another two or maybe three people from inside the building, and then there was the sound of a large car slowing and stopping. Patrick was led on to the street and to what must have been the rear of the vehicle before being bundled into a car boot. Another body was already curled up in the back, breathing hard.

'Karim?' Patrick whispered hopefully.

'Yes, but please, be quiet. Wait.' Karim cowered, waiting to be hit in the face with a rifle butt or shouted at. But nothing happened. So he continued, leaning as close to Patrick as he could. 'Are you hurt?'

'No. My hands are tied and I'm blindfolded again. But I'm okay. You?'

'Me also.'

The boot and car doors were slammed shut and the vehicle took off quickly, causing Patrick to slide hard into his colleague. Closer now, the two captive men exchanged quiet words. Karim first.

'I don't know how long this journey will last so I will tell you what I know.'

Karim knew a lot more than Patrick, some of it overheard and the rest guessed at. The men holding them were not simple bandits or a criminal gang, he thought. They were too well organised and the questions they asked were too focused.

'They seem to be as interested in who killed Fazil Jabar as we are, and they know less. They asked you questions, yes?'

'Yes.'

'What did they ask, what did you say?' There was a touch of panic in Karim's voice.

'Like you say, they wanted to know what I knew about Jabar's killing and who we were working for. I told them I knew very little, that neither of us knew much, that we worked for the BBC and for William Carver.'

Karim's voiced loosened a little, his body relaxed. 'Good. I said the same. I might be wrong but I don't think they intend to kill us. Not right now, anyway.'

Patrick took a deep breath. He reached out his shackled hands and took Karim's fingers in his. The young Afghan let his hand be held.

Patrick slept on and off throughout the long drive, lulled to sleep by the vehicle's motion, then jolted awake at a sudden turn or stop. He sensed that Karim did likewise. The journey seemed to take many hours and when the car finally came to a halt and the engine was turned off, he felt sure it must be morning. They were hauled out and made to stand upright. When his hood was removed, Patrick recoiled at the stinging brightness. When he reopened his eyes, the green of the surrounding land took him by surprise. There were fields on every side. He had come to expect all Afghanistan to be yellow or grey, but those colours appeared only in the ribbon of road up which he assumed they had just travelled. They were on high ground, the highest point he could see in any direction. Standing in front of them and obviously in charge was the man in the black turban. He put a piece of bread in his mouth and ate, waiting patiently while Karim looked around and tried to get a handle on their situation. It seemed as though they were being handed over from one group to another. The group in front of them comprised the man in the turban and four others, all younger and all carrying Kalashnikov rifles. The men wore either desert camouflage trousers or combat jackets of the sort the Americans preferred. This by itself would suggest they were Afghan National Army. But they also had thick beards of various hues and black and white scarves associated with the mujahideen. Karim read the various clues and decided to play safe.

'*Salaam alaikum.*'

The leader smiled. '*Wa alaikum salaam.*'

'*Khoob hasti?*'

'I am well, yes.' The man in the turban switched easily to a halting but competent English. He took a hunting knife from his belt and stared at the blade in a way that suggested he would like to use it. There was a dark strip of material wrapped around the four fingers of his right hand, a makeshift bandage. 'You remember me?'

Karim's stomach lurched as he recognised the bandit who had

tried to drag him into the car outside the morgue, whose hand he had crushed. 'Yes, sir.' He looked at his feet.

The turbaned man glanced at his bandaged hand. 'Be calm. If I wanted to kill you for this, you would be dead already.' His face was expressionless. He moved closer to Karim and Patrick; close enough that they could smell his breath.

'I will speak in English for the benefit of your friend. We are going on a trip now. There is someone who wants to talk to you and soon I will take you to him. He has paid a large amount of money for you and he would like to have you alive, but if you try and escape I will kill you. You' – he jabbed Karim in the chest with the hunting knife, just hard enough to draw a little blood through the shirt – 'Ugly face. You I will enjoy killing. Do you understand?'

Karim was still looking at the floor. He nodded and Patrick did the same.

'But my commander does not want you to be cheated. You were meant to see the poppies and so you will. We have some business there anyway.'

Patrick nodded again.

The man strode past the pair and up to the vehicle that had brought them, an old black Mercedes saloon with curtains drawn inside the rear window. He passed a bundle of some sort in at the passenger side and waved the car away. Turning his head, Karim heard the man mutter something and a respectful '*Baleh, Mirgun*' in response. The driver performed a neat three-point turn and disappeared down the dusty road.

As he walked back towards his prisoners, the man in the turban lifted his hunting knife again and both Karim and Patrick cowered. The man laughed before grabbing their outstretched arms and deftly cutting the cable ties binding their wrists. He led the way up from the road and towards the brow of the hill, Karim and then Patrick following, and behind them, keeping a few paces back, came the rest of the bandits. At the very rear was the youngest of the group, who was carrying Karim's and Patrick's backpacks and the laptop case. Once at the top of the hill, Patrick could see down over the neighbouring valley and across acre upon acre of poppy fields.

'Faster, we have a long journey.'

Patrick turned and whispered to Karim: 'Who is he, do you have any idea?'

'No. His men call him Mirgun but this name means nothing to me.'

Before long they had left the path and were walking across the fields; the poppies they moved through were waist-high. Mirgun walked ahead, treading carefully to avoid damaging the crop. Karim and Patrick followed, trying to place their feet directly in the man's footsteps. A few metres behind came Mirgun's men. After an hour of weaving through the tall plants, Mirgun found a clutch of poppies which seemed to particularly interest him and he stopped. He shouldered his rifle, bent and stared closely at the poppy heads before selecting one, cupping it in his palm, the stem passing between ring and middle finger. Patrick looked at Karim and shrugged. Poppies swayed in the soft breeze all around them. What made this one special? Mirgun plucked it and held it under Patrick's nose.

'This is *ghozah*. You want it plump, like a new wife.' He smiled broadly, revealing an incomplete row of tobacco-stained teeth. His smile was genuine. Enthusiastic. From his shoulder bag – a thick, colourful carpet stitched at two sides – he pulled a less threatening, short-handled knife. 'Three blades, you see.'

The stubby instrument had three carefully sharpened blades protruding from a filthy wooden handle. Mirgun took the poppy head and cut into it. The moment the knife went in a white fluid seeped out. He scored the crowned heads of a dozen poppies and as he cut he explained the process. He spoke in Dari now, nodding at Karim to translate. The poppies would be left overnight, allowing the sap to harden, and then this could be collected tomorrow, slowly scraped from each poppy head. The farming was intensive, involving many people, sometimes entire extended families, and it was hard work. Opium wasn't the easy choice but it paid well. Some local farmers had tried to concentrate on other crops such as wheat, but for many that wasn't enough. Patrick could not imagine why Mirgun was telling them this. But the journalist in him couldn't help but be interested. Poppy farming had several advantages, Mirgun said, the plants grew in poor soil and the opium was worth enough that it could be sold and the money used to buy wheat and other food to feed a family and leave a little over.

'The more NATO try to destroy it, the more it's worth,' Karim said quickly, trying to keep up with Mirgun. 'The better it is for the drug men and the harder it is for the farmer to say no. And anyway, everything else is gone. The fruit. We used to have the finest apricots in the world before the Russians blew up all the trees. Silk, Karakul skin from a special sheep, very soft. Almost all gone. He says that the Americans paid Afghans to farm opium when the Russians were in charge; now they say it must stop and they spray the fields with poison. Sometimes they spray opium fields, sometimes they miss.'

Mirgun waited for Karim to finish translating before glancing up at the position of the sun in the sky and speaking sharply to his men and then to Karim. 'He says we are in a hurry now. Time to go.'

Mirgun headed diagonally across the field to where there was a narrow dirt path between that crop and the next. They walked in single-file, Mirgun gradually increasing the pace. The walk was downhill but Patrick's boots were too tight; his feet hurt and it was getting hotter all the time. He needed water but none had been offered. The group walked without a break for another two hours and as they walked the reds and the greens of the poppy fields were gradually replaced by scrubland and then the yellow and grey colours Patrick had previously come to associate with Afghanistan. In the distance he saw a wadi and beside it a man with three heavily laden mules. Mirgun signalled for the group to stop. Walking ahead, he waved his rifle in the air and the man raised a hand in reply. Patrick and Karim were allowed to sit and did so gratefully, their shirts were heavy with sweat. Patrick loosened his boots a little more and drank thirstily from a water bottle which one of their guards had thrown to the ground between them.

After a brief rest they were ordered back to their feet and marched to the mules. Patrick noticed that his laptop case had been strapped to one of the animals. Mirgun walked from beast to beast checking that the bags they carried were intact and securely attached. He took out his hunting knife and slid it easily into one of the yellow plastic sacks. Digging his fingers into the slit, he removed a pinch of sticky opium, first smelt and then tasted it, nodding approvingly. He walked back towards Patrick and held the black resin in front of his nose for him to sniff.

'It's good. Now you have seen everything and now we go. I will deliver you to the General. I deliver him two men and three mules – we'll see what he likes best.'

'The General?' asked Karim, softly.

Mirgun had turned away but now he turned back sharply. He wiped the resin from his fingers, lifted his arm high and brought his open hand down hard on Karim's ear. The sound was loud enough to draw the attention of the other men, who turned and watched with amusement. Karim's knees buckled but he stayed standing. Mirgun leant closer and shouted in the damaged ear. 'Are you deaf and ugly?'

Karim said nothing. Hot tears sprung to his eyes. The man slapped him again, on the same ear.

'Well? Are you deaf?'

Karim tried to gather himself. 'No, no. I understand. We are going to see the General. You are taking us there.'

Mirgun relaxed. 'That's right. So, don't waste time. Let's go.'

Karim lifted his hands and wiped the tears from his eyes. He allowed himself to be shoved along in the direction of the mules. Mirgun put two of his men in charge of one animal each before taking the third mule and pulling it down the incline into the dry river bed. They resumed their march, Mirgun followed directly by Patrick, then Karim, and behind him the men and the other mules.

Karim's ear was throbbing now and he had to concentrate hard in order to walk straight. As soon as he could, Patrick dropped back to walk alongside him shoulder to shoulder.

'What happened? Why did he hit you?'

Karim cast an anxious look in the direction of the man in front and lowered his voice. 'This man he spoke of, the General, he is a myth in Afghanistan, a monster. He fought against the Russians thirty years ago, he was the most feared mujahideen leader.'

Karim's balance was still a little off. He veered right and the young bandit behind him stepped forward and encouraged him back into line with the butt of his rifle. As he staggered on, Patrick grabbed his arm in both hands and tried to walk in step, propping him up.

'You're sure this General they are talking about is the same man?'

'Not sure, no. The General was a ruthless fighter but also a drug dealer. He supplied his own men but mainly he sold to the Russian Army. The story was that he got Russian soldiers so addicted – first to hashish, then heroin – that they were swapping their own weapons for drugs. The heroin he sold was stronger than anything anyone had seen before. Pure white heroin, too good to be local. Some said the Pakistanis were supplying him. Or the Americans. Part of their cold war against the Russians.'

Patrick gave his colleague a sceptical glance. 'It all sounds a little far-fetched, Karim.'

'Don't be so sure. This is Afghanistan. The most unlikely thing is usually the truth. When the Russians left, the General didn't come to the city, he stayed away from politics, stayed in the mountains. Everyone here knows the story. He bought and sold drugs and weapons, he became a warlord and a drug lord, one of the biggest. He was like America's mafia. Untouchable, feared, rich.' Karim took a glance over his shoulder. The young bandit was several feet away, but he lowered his voice anyway. 'Maybe ten years ago something happened. He just disappeared. People say it was because of his wife; she was murdered by the Taliban. He only ever had one wife, a great beauty. Beautiful in the way only an Afghan woman can be beautiful. After this happened, he went mad, killed many Taliban, then killed his guards and his friends and then himself. That's what they say.'

'But no one's sure?'

'No. He disappeared, that is sure. And the palace he built with all the opium money, that has gone, destroyed. I have seen the ruins. But no one has seen him or heard anything apart from rumours for years. He is just a story now. A thing you say to scare your children.'

'A bogeyman?'

'Yes, something like that.'

Karim let go of Patrick's arm and pulled himself upright, lengthening his stride. Patrick tried to keep pace.

'So either these men are trying to scare us with a story, or they are taking us to see a ghost.'

Karim gave a mirthless laugh.

'What's funny?'

'Ghost is correct. That is one of his other names. The Soviet soldiers gave it to him. They called him General Doushki. The Russian word for ghost.'

20 Ships and Towers and Temples

DATELINE: Parliament Square, London, W1, July 6th

Climbing the steps to street level at Westminster underground station, Dr Berry stopped and checked his grip bag. There were the sandwiches, wrapped neatly in greaseproof paper, and the silver thermos flask. Thank goodness for that, he'd been getting a little forgetful recently; keys lost, tickets mislaid, that sort of thing. He put it down to stress. His employers had reached the same diagnosis and suggested – insisted, in fact – that he take a couple of weeks' gardening leave. Alongside his packed lunch were several newspapers and a thick manila envelope with the letters *HMSO* printed on the back. It was strictly against the rules to remove documents from the office but what else was he supposed to do with two weeks off? He loathed gardening.

For two days his wife had repeatedly chided him for hanging about and getting under her feet at home, so this morning he'd decided to take the train into town; he would have lunch in his usual spot and then take a wander around the National Gallery. It was a sunny day and all the benches on Parliament Square were already occupied. The civil servant picked a patch of grass close to a tree that he particularly liked and set about making camp. He stooped and put a hand to the turf; although the air was warm, there was still a little dampness to the ground. He would use one of his many newspapers as a blanket. From this position, Berry had a clear view across the square. There, in between the House of Commons and Portcullis House, he could see a section of Westminster Bridge, a corner of County Hall and the huge Coade stone lion who guarded the south side of the Thames. Westminster was the pick of London's bridges as far as Berry was concerned. Majestic in its own right, but made doubly so through its connection with the Wordsworth poem, a poem which he'd had to learn by rote as a child and had never forgotten. He muttered a few lines now, while arranging the pages of his *Financial Times* into a makeshift picnic blanket.

> *Earth has not anything to show more fair:*
> *Dull would he be of soul who could pass by*
> *A sight so touching in its majesty:*
> *This City now doth, like a garment, wear*

Despite the crisp air, the modest exercise involved in laying out a newspaper and sitting down had left Berry's back wet with sweat and his shirt stuck to him. 'What is wrong with you, man?' he muttered under his breath. He removed his glasses and wiped his face with his sleeve, then took the tail of his shirt from underneath his jumper and cleaned the condensation from his spectacles. Putting them back on, he took in the view.

The catalpa tree he sat beside was tall and handsome, its branches reaching up and out for every piece of London sky. To the left of that was the Abbey and then the Palace of Westminster itself, from somewhere inside of which a twist of smoke curled upwards from an unseen chimney. Then came Big Ben, which drew the eye upwards and encouraged you to check your watch against its accuracy. Berry did so. The time was twelve forty and young men and women from the various government offices were descending on the square to eat a quick lunch and hold their faces up towards the sun. A group of office girls strode past him and one paused, letting her friends walk on ahead before smiling broadly in his direction. At him, in fact, or so it seemed. Berry hesitated, unsure of whether this young woman was being friendly or perhaps found him amusing, a figure of fun. The latter seemed more likely. He smiled back regardless and was rewarded with a wave, which confused him still further, flustered him in fact and he looked quickly away. Only after the girl had gone did Berry place the face; he remembered that she had worked for him briefly, a temporary replacement for his secretary when she was away nursing her dying husband a year or two ago. Her name? Her name was Maria. He remembered that she had come with a slight health warning from civil service personnel but that he had found her pleasant and hard-working and had given her a good reference. He nodded to himself – the reference, that would be why she'd waved.

He took his sandwiches from the bag and unwrapped them. Coarse paté with sliced cucumber on buttered wholegrain bread. He ate and enjoyed the view while tourists poured across Westminster Bridge in both directions.

> *Ships, towers, domes, theatres, and temples lie*
> *Open unto the fields, and to the sky*

That didn't sound quite right. He'd missed a bit. What was it?

> *The beauty of the morning; silent, bare*

That was right, but then what? As he sifted his memory, Berry became aware of a shadow at his shoulder. Looking up from his sandwich he saw a tall man standing above him carrying half a dozen shopping bags from a variety of sport shops and department stores. The man looked down and nodded. Berry nodded back and waited for the man, obviously a tourist, to speak, hoping that whatever enquiry he was about to make could be quickly dealt with.

'Hello, sir. Beautiful day.'

The accent was strong but hard to place. Swiss or somewhere Scandinavian, perhaps.

'Lovely,' Berry said without conviction. He looked at the stranger. The man reminded him of a model in an outdoor sports catalogue. Healthy-looking, handsome, early thirties, with an open, almost childlike face and close-cropped blond hair.

'You mind if I sit down here?'

Berry minded very much but wouldn't dream of saying so. The square was getting increasingly crowded and he would have to share his view; to do otherwise would be unmannerly. 'Public space and all that. Go ahead.'

The man smiled and put his bags down a few feet from Berry. From one of the larger carriers he pulled what at first appeared to be an umbrella but on closer inspection Berry recognised as a shooting stick. Incongruous, the civil servant thought, but sensible nonetheless, given this damp ground. Trust a Scandinavian to come prepared for all eventualities. The tourist unfolded the shooting stick, planted the sharp end in the ground and unfolded the canvas seat before sitting down with a satisfied grunt. Berry went back to his lunch, pouring himself a cup of sweet tea from the thermos. He took the newspapers from his grip bag and leafed idly through *The Times*; he'd bought all the serious papers this morning, as he had every morning for the last few days, combing them for any mention of Aftel. He'd been through today's editions thoroughly on the train but there was nothing, nothing on the radio either, apart from the dreadful news of William Carver's producer and translator being kidnapped. Berry assumed that this made it even less likely that Carver would pursue the Aftel story, that his ham-fisted attempt at whistle blowing had been a complete disaster. He heaved a sigh and stared across fondly at that corner of County Hall. He'd worked there once, a long time ago, and visited it when it briefly became a rather *outré* art gallery. Who owned it these days, he wondered? It used to be the Japanese, maybe it was the Chinese now? He knew that sort of thing wasn't supposed to matter anymore, but it still mattered to him. Out of the corner of his eye he saw the tourist stand and start fumbling with his shooting stick, folding it away and cleaning a clod of earth from the spiked end. Having done this, the man set about picking up his collection of bags. Berry looked away but the next moment there was a curse or exclamation – the clumsy tourist had tripped over one of his own bags and lost his footing. He took a step in Berry's direction before planting the shooting stick sharply in the ground in an attempt to stop himself falling on top of the civil servant. In doing so, the oaf had grazed Berry's bare leg between ankle and calf.

'Bloody hell!' Berry exclaimed, leaning forward to examine his injury.

There wasn't much to see – a small nick, a little blood, no more than that – but the tourist was horrified. 'Oh my goodness. I am so sorry.'

A couple of other picnickers looked across, briefly interested. Berry didn't want any fuss. 'Don't worry. It's nothing, really.' He took a white handkerchief from his trouser pocket and stuffed it between skin and sock, a modest makeshift tourniquet. 'There. Look. All fine.'

The tourist looked and smiled, apologetically, Berry thought. He retrieved his bags, nodded once in the civil servant's direction, and then walked away, keeping his back to the small group of onlookers who had witnessed his embarrassing stumble. The civil servant waited until the man had gone, then removed the handkerchief and dabbed gently at the scratch – it really was nothing, just a flesh wound. He would tend to it later but right now he was a little tired, the heat was getting to him. He leant back on his elbows, stretched his legs out and looked at the view across Westminster Bridge.

> *The beauty of the morning; silent, bare*
> *Ships, towers, domes, theatres, and temples lie*
> *Open unto the fields, and to the sky;*
> *All bright and glittering in the smokeless air.*

That was it. Now he just needed the last little part, but first he needed forty winks. He would lie back and rest and then the poem would come to him, those last few lines, no doubt about it. He looked up at the sky. There were a few high clouds skating quickly across London, on their way to somewhere better. Berry lay down; his pupils were already dilating. He felt a small jolt pass up through his ageing body. He closed his eyes, and died.

From the other side of Parliament Square the tourist watched. Dr Berry looked like a perfectly respectable middle-aged man, a hard worker taking a well-deserved nap in a sunny London square. It might be hours before anyone tried to wake him. The man set off in the direction of a cheap motel where he could check in and out electronically without seeing anyone. He knew exactly where he was going. Part of him would have liked to have gone back, sat down and enjoyed the view that Berry obviously enjoyed so much. Over the few days he had spent following him, he had come to rather like the quiet civil servant. He respected the satisfaction the man seemed to get from simple pleasures and hard work. On the way back to his hotel he stopped at the only unvandalised phone booth at Piccadilly Circus underground station. He dialled a number from memory and his call was answered immediately.

'Yes?'

'Your leak is fixed.'

The voice at the other end of the line breathed a sigh. 'Thank you.'

21 Expenses

DATELINE: New Broadcasting House, Portland Place, London, W1, July 6th

Rob Mariscal arrived in the office just as the programme debrief was breaking up. Underneath a whiteboard filled with illegible scribble were the several exhausted individuals who had worked all night to put that morning's programme on air. Complexions were the colour of cold porridge. A handful of the early arrivals were playing a game of tip-and-run cricket in the corridor between two rows of desks – the cricket ball was scrunched-up pages of the *Daily Mail* mummified inside layers of yellowing sticky tape; the bat was a cheap-looking junior model with a ladder of dents up both sides. As Rob wandered through the outfield, Martin Mainwaring connected well with a loose ball and set off up the wicket. Rob ignored the various shouts of welcome and made straight for his glass-walled office. The collector tray on the printer just outside his room was broken and the machine was spewing sheet upon sheet of newswire copy on to the floor. Stories carpeted the ground. Stepping through them, he turned and bellowed at no one in particular: 'Can some fucker fix that?'

The clock on his wall, like every other clock in the newsroom, was synchronised with Greenwich. He had an hour before his meeting with Fletcher. Plenty of time to work out a plan. He pulled out a notebook and quickly filled the page with names and numbers. He wrote the names in capital letters down the left-hand side of the page; first a couple of familiar high street banks, then several credit card companies, a few other loan providers and finally two short Christian names; local lenders who did most of their business around the pubs and betting shops of Fitzrovia. Next to each name he wrote a figure. Most of these numbers were five digits long. He added them all up and looked at the total before tipping the pencil on its end and rubbing it out. He did the sum again but came up with the same number. Excluding his mortgage, which Lucia had been paying for the last six months anyway, Rob owed just under £230,000. The water had risen from neck height to somewhere around his chin. He wondered how Fletcher or indeed anyone else could help him now.

The Head of News lived at the top of the shiny new part of Broadcasting House. Rob decided to take the lift. He didn't want to arrive sweaty – and five floors had the potential to do that to him these days. The glass elevator climbed noiselessly through the building and deposited him on the eighth. It was probably a much healthier working environment up here than down in the bowels of the building, but there was something about the eighth that made him uncomfortable. With high ceilings and windows, it was strangely uncluttered and every item of furniture looked brand new. Most of all, it had a weird stillness to it. There were quite a few people up here, but they didn't seem to move much. The boil and bubble of the newsroom seemed a long way away. Rob strode across the carpeted floor in the direction of Lance's secretary.

'All right, Sally? Beautiful day. I'm here to see the boss man.'

Sally didn't like Rob and made no attempt to pretend otherwise. Mariscal wasn't sure what he'd done to earn her contempt.

'He's with somebody. You can sit over there.' She pointed a painted fingernail at the only uncomfortable-looking chair in the room, next to the water cooler. He sat only briefly; the chill from the cold-water cylinder gave him the shivers.

'I'll stand,' he announced, unnecessarily. Sally nodded an acknowledgement without looking up.

Rob stared at the side of her head. She had nice hair. Clean. Maybe he'd made a pass at her at some party or other, though he had no memory of it. It could be she just didn't like his personality, plenty of people didn't. He wandered over to the coffee station and helped himself to an espresso from the expensive-looking chrome machine. A patchwork of postcards was pinned to a corkboard above it. His Italian geography was sketchy but it seemed that almost every card came from either Umbria or whatever region was next door to Umbria. He wondered if this was a game. Perhaps the people working here all sent similar postcards to each other by way of a joke. Rob had never sent a postcard to work, jocular or otherwise, nor did he remember ever receiving one. He removed the drawing pin from one of the cards, flipped it over and read *For Lance and everyone*. Skipping through the detail, which concerned a long walk to a monastery and a glass of lemon liqueur, and moving straight to the finish, Sally had written her name in a large curling hand and cross-hatched the bottom corner of the card with kisses. Rob wondered whether Sally's feelings for her boss were in any way requited? He wondered whether Lance had even noticed? Just then, he heard Sally mutter his name and he was ushered in. Whoever Lance Fletcher had been meeting with had dematerialised and there he was, alone, poring over some papers. His thin grey hair, half-moon glasses and exhausted-looking cord jacket gave him the look of a headmaster scared of the school he was supposed to be running.

Rob let him finish his reading and looked around. On a side desk, positioned so visitors might properly appreciate them, stood a collection of silver-framed photographs and a small golden cup celebrating victory in a Surrey squash tournament (1996/7. Mixed). The largest photo was of Lance himself, wearing an incongruous Hawaiian shirt and standing on a sun-bleached jetty. He was smiling and struggling with both hands to lift the glistening tail of a huge fish up over his head. The fish was longer than he was. Out of focus and standing slightly behind Fletcher's right shoulder was the black man who had no doubt located, hooked and probably hauled the huge fish all but the last few feet from the bottom of the ocean.

'That's a big fish, Lance.'

Fletcher looked up and removed his glasses. 'One of the proudest moments of my life, Rob, landing that leviathan.'

'I'm not surprised.' He turned his attention to the other pictures. 'How's Glenn getting on these days?' Standing inside one of the silver frames was a young man on a red clay tennis court, blond, with perfect skin, perfect teeth and a perfect tennis swing, too, by the look of it. A more recent incarnation of Glenn had spent a few weeks on a 'work placement' at *Today* arranged by Rob at the behest of his father, after Glenn had expressed a vague interest in journalism. Contemporary Glenn had mousy hair, a serious acne problem and the surly attitude that sometimes goes with it. Rob hadn't minded the attitude so much as his obvious sense of entitlement. When Lance called for a second favour and asked for Glenn's application for a researcher's job to be shuffled to the top of the pile, Rob complied. Glenn got an interview but that was as far as it went. Mariscal hadn't been on the board but he'd made sure that the brief news quiz that began the interview was rigorous enough to screen out idiots and interlopers.

'Oh, he's all right. He was a bit upset he didn't get past that researcher board, but he seems to be getting over that. Personnel told him it was a strong field.'

Rob nodded. 'Very strong. He came close, they tell me.'

'It's a different world now, isn't it?' Fletcher said sagely. 'I remember my first BBC interview, straight out of Oxford. I walked into the editor's office and he threw a cricket ball at my damn head. God knows how, but I caught the thing and he offered me the job there and then.' Fletcher gazed wistfully out of the window at the spire of All Souls.

'But you asked about Glenn, didn't you? It looks like he's settled on law. He's about to start a second degree.' Fletcher delivered the happy news with the same tone he might have used to announce that he was donating a second kidney. Rob winced in sympathy and Fletcher nodded silently. Both men considered the spire.

Rob took a swallow of air. 'Can I put my cards on the table, Lance? I'm off to Kabul tomorrow, as you know, and I'm sure you're busy too. I don't want to take too much of your time.'

Fletcher nodded slowly.

'I won't beat around the bush. I'm in trouble, financial trouble. The mortgage, credit cards, a few other loans. It's all got a little out of hand. You know how it can be . . .'

Fletcher's stony face suggested he had no idea how it could be.

'So I need some help, Lance. Some kind of loan, to help me start climbing up out of this hole.'

Fletcher ran his soft palm over his hairless chin. 'How much do you need?'

'In total?'

Lance nodded.

'Well. Just south of £230,000 would make everything okay.'

Fletcher removed his glasses. Perhaps Rob was joking. He looked directly at Mariscal. It was clear he wasn't. 'That's ridiculous, Rob, impossible. How did you think I could possibly help you with that?'

'I know the Corporation can't lend me that kind of money but I've spoken to my bank. I called them half an hour ago and they want to help me. The thing is, I'm at the absolute limit of what I can borrow – on my current salary, I mean. But if I could get an extra ten grand or so on my annual pay, that would be enough to reschedule everything. Roll all the debts together and get a better rate. Do you see what I mean?'

Fletcher looked again at the church spire. 'I understand, Rob. I do. The problem is, you're at our limit as well. You're right at the top of the pay scale for your grade. Your head's banging on the ceiling, in fact.'

'How about raising the ceiling? Or changing my grade?'

Fletcher shook his head. 'You know I can't do that, Rob. There would be a riot.'

'No one else needs to know.' Rob knew that Fletcher had quietly and efficiently ironed out all sorts of problems in the past. Those problems weren't so different from his. Some had been caused by his own presenters. Rob had helped in several of the clean-up operations; infidelities had been swept under the carpet, deals made with newspaper editors. Rob decided to push the point. 'You've made bigger problems than this go away, Lance. I've helped you do it.'

This choice of words got Fletcher's attention, containing as it did, both flattery and threat. 'I'm not sure that I have, Rob. I've worked to keep our little corner clean. But no one's ever come to me needing a quarter of a million pounds before.'

This rounding up of Rob's debt to a huge-sounding sum shook him slightly. He fell silent.

Lance continued: 'You've had three pay rises in three years. No one else at the Corporation has been treated so well. The only way for you to squeeze any more money out of the BBC is either to apply for the Director General's job or drop dead.'

'What?'

'I'm just joking, Rob. I was thinking about your death-in-service benefit. You've been with us a long time. If you popped your clogs now, at your age, you'd get—' Lance fell silent as he executed a calculation in his head. 'Well, it would to be at least three hundred thousand, probably a bit more.'

Mariscal said nothing.

Lance took this as defeat, and maybe it was. 'Rob. I'm genuinely sorry I can't wave a wand and make this all okay. But there might be something.'

Rob lifted his head to listen.

'You're doing us a favour, taking on the Afghan trip. How about I advance you £3,000 in cash, and as well as that I'll nod through any reasonable expenses you rack up out there. All right?'

'What about the unreasonable ones?'

Fletcher smiled. This was more like it. 'I'll turn a blind eye to some of those too.'

'All right, Lance, thanks, I appreciate it.'

22 Singing Sands

DATELINE: Dashti Margo desert, Afghanistan, July 6th

Patrick lay completely still, trying to make sense of the haunting sound which seemed to be coming not from one direction but from all around him; it was music of some sort, but from where? He reached over and nudged Karim, who was curled up like a child, trying to sleep, his thin jacket scant defence against the desert cold. Patrick tugged his sleeve.

'Karim. Can you hear singing?'

The young man had heard nothing. His head and face were covered by a scarf and only his deep-set brown eyes and forehead were showing. He pulled the wrapping from one ear and a cascade of fine sand fell to the ground.

'What is it?'

'Do you hear?' Patrick asked again, doubting himself. 'Can't you hear music? Singing, in the distance?'

Karim lifted himself to one elbow, turned his head, and listened. 'Yes, I hear it. It's the sand.'

'The sand?'

'Yes. Sometimes the sand in this desert will sing. Different sounds in different seasons. Sometimes it is like drumming, or like a man in pain, and sometimes it is a low boom, like thunder. You have this in the west.'

Patrick heard this as a question. 'No, I don't think so.'

'Yes, you do. My father was a musician, he told me about Sand Mountain in America. It sings in C. And in Morocco the dunes are G sharp. My father went to Morocco once.'

Patrick craned his neck in the direction of the sound. It was clearer now, moving and beautiful. He wished he had his tape recorder. Instead he tried to find a word to describe what he was hearing, a word he could use to describe it later to his parents, or even better, to Rebecca.

Karim listened too. 'The noise you hear,' he said smiling slightly, 'is really the noise of a slow avalanche. You are lucky to hear it. My father called this the "sounding sands". He loved this sound, this music.'

After a full day's march, Mirgun had reluctantly allowed the group to pitch camp and sleep for a few hours on the edge of the desert. The sounding sands had woken Patrick early and the sky was only just turning from black to deepest blue. The stars were still bright, brighter than any he had ever seen before. As he watched, a comet cut across the sky, leaving a long tail of burning gas and dust in its wake. He looked around the makeshift camp; he could not see Mirgun but his men were crouched by the fire, feeding the embers with fresh kindling and preparing what Patrick hoped might be some sort of breakfast. The mules were tethered together a short distance away, relieved of their heavy packs of opium. He got to his feet and from that position spotted Mirgun, lying flat on his back on top of a nearby dune, staring straight up at the sky through a pair of night-vision goggles. Even kidnappers and murderers, it seemed, liked to look at the stars. Patrick tried to stamp the cold out of his numbed feet. The previous day had been hard. When they had finally stopped and

Patrick had removed his boots, both his feet were blistered and bleeding. He had wrung out his socks and a steady trickle of blood had run through his fingers into the sand. How would he manage another march? Mirgun had told them there was a long way left to walk, across miles of desert and into the mountains. He felt sick just thinking about it.

Breakfast helped. More flatbread, warmed over the campfire, but also a few of the apricots which, Karim insisted, were the best in the world and almost extinct. They washed them down with cup after cup of hot and heavily sugared mint tea. Sustained by this food, and Karim's stories and observations, Patrick made it across several kilometres of desert and scrub. Six hours into the walk, the light suddenly changed and Patrick looked up to see that the gorge they had been walking through, their eyes cast down, had opened up into a broad valley. Snow-dusted mountains tore at the sky beyond. The last leg of the journey was a punishing uphill trek during which Mirgun allowed only one short stop for more tea. Eventually the combination of altitude sickness and exhaustion overcame Patrick and he fell to his knees at the side of the road, vomiting, the edges of his vision fading to black. Mirgun cursed the young man loudly but waited for the vomiting to subside before ordering his men to lift him on to the mule. Three hours later, Patrick arrived at the General's compound, slumped on top of a few hundred kilos of raw opium.

It was a scene from antiquity: half a dozen mud-baked houses at the foot of a sheer cliff. Karim was shown into one of the houses and was given water to wash with and green tea to drink before being ordered to help unpack the exhausted mules. Patrick was also given tea. But he was offered no water to wash with, nor a room to rest in. He was simply left alone to crouch painfully on the stony ground.

An hour passed and while Karim was unwrapping and weighing opium in one of the houses, Patrick sat outside. The sun was going down and it was getting cold. He was thinking about asking for a blanket and lying down on the hard ground when Mirgun returned and gestured for him to follow. Patrick was led between the mud houses and towards what appeared at first to be little more than a long crack in the cliff-face. As they drew closer, Patrick saw that the gap was just wide enough for a man to walk through. Mirgun ducked his turbaned head and disappeared. Patrick followed, but stopped just inside to allow his eyes to adjust to the darkness.

'Come. The General is waiting.'

Patrick heard Mirgun's impatient voice but he could not see him. Slowly his vision improved and the rough-hewn sides of a corridor carved into the cliff came into view. Putting out his hand to steady himself, he felt the cold, wet wall and then he saw Mirgun and just ahead of him, a string of bare unlit light bulbs disappearing into the mountain beyond.

'Quickly!'

Patrick rubbed his hand dry on his trouser leg and followed. He had to stoop every few feet to avoid hitting his head and as a result moved much slower than Mirgun. Up ahead, he heard his escort curse him in several languages. Patrick wondered how many men must have worked to carve such a passage. And for how long? As they walked on the air grew gradually warmer and Patrick caught the smell of strong tobacco smoke and the faint sound of conversation. A few steps further and the corridor opened out on to a huge, high-ceilinged cave lit by candlelight and warmed by a great central fire. The floor was softened by a patchwork of richly coloured rugs. Sitting and in some cases sprawled on these rugs were at least a dozen men, who were smoking, drinking, and talking. When they saw Mirgun, the conversation ceased and they all sat a little straighter, mumbling respectful greetings.

'*Salaam alaikum . . .*'

Mirgun ignored the men and led Patrick around the fire and

into a second, smaller room, separated from the central chamber by a heavy burgundy curtain. This space was lit by several standing candelabra and filled with ornate furniture. In one corner Patrick saw a huge copper bath flickering brightly in the candlelight and, just visible at the near end of it, a man's head.

The bathing man lay very still. Patrick let his eyes adjust to the gloom and looked around: a four-poster bed, a dining table empty but for a silver samovar decorated with Imperial eagles, several large armchairs; all the furniture seemed too big for the room, and packed too closely together. Minutes passed, and nothing happened. Patrick heard hushed conversation from the room next door and noticed that Mirgun had gone. Now he felt utterly alone. When the bathing man suddenly stood, a significant waterfall sloOshed from the sides of the copper bath and crashed to the floor in a soapy wave. The man stepped from the steaming bath. 'Chapan!' The shout brought forth a toothless old man who pushed through the curtain with a towel and neat pile of white linen. The man ignored the towel but lifted from the pile a large shirt, which he dropped over his head. He adjusted the wide sleeves, pulled the front down over his groin, and waved the old man away. Then he stepped forward into the candlelight. His thick black hair was plastered to his head and a great glistening beard covered his jaw. His nose was long and a little off straight, and his dark eyes flashed over Patrick in the dim light.

'So. Mirgun has brought me a journalist.' The voice was deep and the accent strong but hard to place.

'Yes, sir. I am a journalist.' Patrick found the sound of his voice strange; it was almost lost in the dark space. 'You speak English?' he asked, unnecessarily.

'I speak a lot of languages. Which language would you like to speak? Dari? French? Farsi? Russian?'

Patrick stammered. 'N-no, sir I—I'm afraid I only speak English.'

'Of course you do. You are an Englishman. Why would you need to speak another's language?'

The question expected no answer and Patrick was grateful for that. The General strode over to the samovar, which was, Patrick now noticed, bubbling away in the middle of the dining table, fuelled by a small silver oil burner at its base. 'Tea?' Without waiting for an answer, he filled two glass cups, held in ornate silver holders, and offered one to Patrick. 'Sit down then, Englishman.'

Patrick did so. He was tired and hungry and confused but he drank his tea down and tried to gather his thoughts before speaking. 'Why have I been brought here, sir?' he asked as firmly as he could.

The General observed him over the rim of his cup. 'You don't know?'

Patrick paused. He was overwhelmed with a sudden fear that this one answer could spare or condemn him. But he didn't know what the man opposite wanted to hear. 'I only know what your man, Mirgun, told us. He said that his boss, I mean you, that you wanted to talk to us. Karim and I. That is all. That's all I know.'

The General nodded. 'Mirgun is not his name. Mirgun is his job. It means "master hunter".' The General rose and refilled his cup from the steaming samovar. 'Do you know what the Mirgun was hunting?'

'No, I don't know.'

'He was hunting your friend. The Pashtun with the broken mouth. What did you call him?'

'Karim.'

'Yes, Karim. Karim has shown an interest in something that also interests me. Mirgun only took *you* because *you* were with him. You were in the wrong place at the wrong time. Or the right place at the right time. We shall see.'

The General stood again. The shirt he wore was dry now and it billowed like a main sail as he moved towards Patrick. This made the man appear even larger and more formidable than he already was. He took Patrick's cup, refilled it, and returned it before sitting back down on the chaise. He watched Patrick drink, saying nothing. Patrick felt compelled to fill the silence.

'Mirgun, the master hunter, I mean. I think he asked me questions after we were kidnapped. Back in Kabul.'

'Yes. I listened to his questions. And to your answers.' Patrick could feel sweat at his neck and the small of his back. As he had suspected, the previous interrogation had been relayed down a telephone line for the benefit of this man.

'Well, then, you know that Karim and I both work for the same person. For a British journalist who doesn't believe the Taliban murdered Fazil Jabar.'

The General nodded. 'William Carver.'

'That's right. William thinks someone else killed Jabar and he's trying to find out who.'

'Good, that's good.'

Patrick wasn't sure what was good; the fact that William was investigating Jabar's killing, or the fact that this story squared with the one he had told Mirgun back in Kabul.

'What else?' the General asked quietly.

Patrick scratched at his neck and gazed around the room as though looking for the thing he had forgotten. 'I think I've told you pretty much everything I know. I'm quite—well, I'm quite a junior guy, sir. And I've only been in the country for a few days, so I don't know much.'

The General looked faintly confused by Patrick's convoluted speech. He walked slowly to the table and put down his empty teacup. He turned to face Patrick again. 'Should I consider you honest, Mr Patrick Reid?'

'Yes, sir, I am.'

'In my experience, many Englishmen are not honest. Maybe you are different?'

Patrick nodded warily.

'How old are you?'

'I am twenty-six.'

'And you have worked a lot with your William Carver? Here and elsewhere?'

'No, this is my first assignment with him. My first trip to Afghanistan. My first assignment ever, in fact.'

'Really?'

Patrick nodded. He thought perhaps he could see something like amusement in the General's dark eyes. 'So then, you know nothing about this country.'

'I know what I have read. What I've heard on the news.'

'As I say. Nothing.'

The General circled the table, tapping his fingers on the varnished wood. 'Then why did they send you?'

Patrick hesitated. 'I'm not sure.'

The General sighed impatiently. 'There is always a reason.'

There was something about the General's manner which encouraged Patrick to be candid. Something beyond a simple fear for his life. 'I think my boss thought William might trust me, that I could make a connection. He can be a difficult man. He usually works alone.'

'Is he a good journalist?'

'Yes, I think so. It's all he cares about, getting to the truth, I mean.'

The General ran a hand through his beard. 'The truth.' He shouted out a few words in Dari and within seconds Mirgun strode back in, ignoring Patrick and nodding respectfully in the direction of his master. The General issued a series of instructions and Patrick could tell from Mirgun's face that the command he was being given was an unwelcome one. When the General had finished speaking, Mirgun nodded a curt acknowledgement and left.

'Mr Reid. I have made a decision. I will be honest with you and then you will be honest with me. You are interested in the truth, like your friend William Carver, so I will show you some truth. Tomorrow I will take you on a tour. A few hundred kilometres, a few hundred years. After that we will talk some more.'

23 A Clean Slate

DATELINE: BBC News Centre, Portland Place, London, W1, July 6th

Mariscal had an hour to spare before he needed to set off for the airport and he couldn't face going back to his own office. He needed to take stock. He walked slowly down nine flights of stairs to the basement and then through a maze of corridors to a little-used smoking area he knew, close to the loading bay at the back of the building. Collapsing on to a tired green sofa, he let out a yelp of pain; a thin layer of foam barely cushioned the hard wood beneath. Mariscal rubbed at the small of his back and cursed. In retrospect, the idea that Lance might help him clear his arrears had been naive. He wondered whether he might have exerted more pressure somehow. Threatened resignation; threatened something. The offer of three grand plus expenses was a generous one but that wasn't what Rob was thinking about now. He gazed over the loading bay up at the cloudless blue sky above London. There was a regular stream of planes heading in the direction of Heathrow, and as he watched, some painted pretty vapour trails across the sky. The part of the conversation that had caught his attention and was now firing his imagination had nothing to do with the three thousand pounds or the promised expenses. It was Fletcher's mention of the death-in-service benefit which interested him, and the more he tried to not to think about it, the harder it became to think about anything else. The new vapour trails were clean and clear, like chalk lines drawn on a blue background; the old ones spread and blurred, becoming cloudlike before disappearing altogether. Three hundred thousand would clear the slate. Every creditor on that dreadful piece of paper would be paid off and gone. Lucia would have money left over. She could pay off some of the mortgage or buy herself something expensive. Rob couldn't remember the last time he'd bought his wife anything better than an apologetic bunch of petrol station flowers. He would be dead, of course, but right now that didn't seem like such a bad thing. His home life was miserable. Work was a slog. He was only really happy for as long as he was drinking and nobody could drink all the time, not even him. Perhaps now was as good a time as any.

Rob would die, not a hero, but hardly a nobody. Professionally, he was respected, revered even. Lots of people hated him, yes, but not everyone. Far from it. He was not unloved. No. His current standing wasn't bad. It could easily be worse, and as he thought about it, one truth became increasingly clear: the longer it went on, the longer *he* went on, the worse it would get. His kids would grow older, start to understand him a little better and then, inevitably, judge him. And he wouldn't emerge from that courtroom smelling of roses, that was for sure. Better to be a benign absence than a malign presence; if his own childhood had taught him anything, it had taught him that. And it wasn't as if he hadn't thought about suicide before. He'd thought about it plenty. Mariscal had always been happy to tell pretty much anyone who asked about his various sexual fantasies. But his most secret, and now he came to consider it, possibly his most erotic fantasy centred not on sex but on self-slaughter. He even knew his preferred method; and what was that if not the beginnings of a plan? When Rob imagined suicide he imagined a high building and a long fall. Toppling into thin air and letting gravity do the hard work. Waking up dead. He had simply to walk to the edge of any building taller that ten storeys: his Kabul hotel, perhaps? And fall. He had no problem with heights, and the theatre of it appealed to him. He imagined beautiful women screaming and covering their children's eyes while their menfolk watched, slack-jawed, astonished by his speed and trajectory.

An hour later, Rob Mariscal stood, bag in hand, outside the old Broadcasting House building. He spotted what looked like his regular car, a black Ford C-Max, parked neatly in a disabled bay next to All Souls Church. But as he walked closer he saw the shadow of a passenger already sitting stiffly on the back seat. He turned away and squinted into the sun, scanning the street for his ride, feeling a flash of irritation. His driver Colin had texted to say he'd arrived. Where was he? Rob had pulled out his phone to call either Colin or the office and shout at someone when he heard his name being called in an odd stage whisper. The voice was familiar. He turned back towards the Ford and saw Graham's boyish face at the rear passenger window.

'Good afternoon, squire. Heathrow, Terminal 3, isn't it? Can I offer you a lift?'

Rob picked up his suitcase and strode over. 'This is my bloody car.' He wrenched open the back door, annoyed by Graham but even more so by his own petulant tone.

'My car as much as yours, old chap. After all, I pay my licence fee.'

Rob pushed what he hoped was the sharp edge of his suitcase in the direction of Graham's knee and climbed in after it. The back of his shirt was already wet with sweat, the black cotton sticking to his shoulder blades. He felt as if he was at the end of a long day's travel, not just setting out; had hoped the drive to the airport, and the flight that followed, might provide him with some peace and quiet. But one look at Graham's face told him that wasn't how it would be. The driver edged out of the side road on to Portland Place and headed north. Neither man spoke until they were picking up speed on the Westway.

'Almost silent, these, aren't they?' said Graham, feeling the door trim like a prospective buyer. Rob wasn't interested and didn't pretend to be, but the driver took the hint and reached for the radio. An inoffensive piano sonata filled the car.

'Ah, lovely.' Graham smiled warmly. 'Good idea, Mr Blake.'

Rob looked up. Who the hell was Mr Blake? Colin the driver nodded an acknowledgement and Mariscal stared at the floor. What did it say about him, that this man had been driving him around for five or six years and he had never thought to ask his surname? Graham pulled a silver hip flask from his jacket pocket and popped the top off.

'Sharpener?' he asked, waving it under Rob's nose. Mariscal refused with a shake of his head despite the fact that he was gagging for a drink. He looked again at Graham. There was something not quite right about him today. The usual dark suit, black shoes, but then Rob noticed the open-necked shirt. Graham looked wrong without a tie. Incomplete.

Graham took a sip from his hip flask and spoke softly and fast. 'So, first off, some good news. You'll be turning left on the Delhi leg. We've bumped you up.'

Rob gave a grudging smile. This was good news. He'd been dreading eight hours in economy on one bloody mary and a glass of red wine. Now he could look forward to travelling horizontally and anaesthetised.

'What's the catch? Let me guess, you're coming with me . . .'

'Unfortunately not. You might not believe this, but I rather wish I were.'

Rob shrugged.

'I told my boss that you could use a travelling companion but they weren't buying. You'll be met by someone at the other end.'

'Oh yeah? By who?'

'He'll introduce himself.' The sonata finished and a female voice took over. Mariscal listened. Her voice was low but clear and carried well. He wondered how she would sound delivering news. Then she stumbled over the introduction to an oboe concerto and he lost interest.

Graham nudged his arm. 'Your first foreign trip for a while, isn't that right?'

'First trip for years. I used to travel. Did a load of stuff with William just after he arrived on the programme. Good stuff. The Middle East, Central Africa, India, all around. But it's been a while. Just, you know, holidays.' Rob did not consider holidays to be the same as travel. In fact holidays were pretty much the opposite of travel, especially since the children had arrived. As far as he could see, family holidays consisted of packing up all the people in your house, and as many of the home comforts as you could carry, and simply transporting them to somewhere a little hotter, at considerable effort and expense.

Graham looked across. 'Where did you go to in Central Africa? The Congo?' The reverential way in which the man from the ministry uttered the word *Congo* made it clear that he believed the place rich in mystery and dark-heart allure.

Rob nodded. 'Yeah.'

'What was it like?'

'It was a shithole.'

Graham was not so easily discouraged. 'I'd love to visit the Congo. And Rwanda.'

'Yeah, been there too.'

'Do you know that fantastic Kipling quote?'

Rob shrugged. He suspected he was going to hear the Kipling quote no matter what he said.

Graham pulled himself up in his seat: '*There are two kinds of men. Those who stay at home and those who do not. The second are the more interesting.* What do you think of that? It's got to be true, hasn't it?'

'Sure. I'm guessing that you haven't travelled much, Graham?'

It was a mean remark but Graham ploughed on, undeterred. 'No, you're right, I haven't. At least, not yet. I'm told there might be more opportunity once all of this is over, if it goes well. So you see, I'm relying on you, Rob.' His tone was jovial but Mariscal had had enough.

'You're blackmailing me, Graham. That's what you're doing. Remember?'

'Not so loud,' Graham said, tilting his head towards the driver.

'Why the fuck are you here anyway?' Rob hissed. 'You've got my phone number.'

'The personal touch. I like to do things properly.'

'As far as I'm concerned, it's all a bit too personal already. Next time, use the phone or a dead letter drop or whatever else you wackos use to communicate.'

Colin glanced in the rear-view mirror, then quickly back at the road.

'Colin. Whack this up a bit, will you? I love this one,' Rob barked. The driver did as commanded and turned up the volume. Rob leant closer to Graham, his mouth just an inch or two from his ear.

'What's all this really about, then, Graham? What's William done that's got you lot so riled?'

Graham was silent for some time before he replied. 'It's to do with the last report he did for you.'

'His last piece? What? The bomb in that tailor's shop,' Rob muttered, trying to recall the details. The piece hadn't been particularly memorable. He had to dredge pretty deep. 'Some Afghan politician gets blown up by the Taliban?'

'Something like that, yes.'

'Something like that? It sounds pretty straightforward to me.'

'It's a bit more complicated than that, Rob. British interests are involved.' Graham knew he sounded pompous. He also knew he'd said too much already.

'What sort of British interests? Military? Political? Commercial?'

Graham shuffled in his seat. 'I don't know much more than that, and I've already told you more than I should.'

Rob gave Graham time to settle before changing tack. But he was a journalist by instinct; he'd try again. 'I don't want you to give away any state secrets, Graham, but I need some guidance. Why are you sending *me* to Kabul? What's my job? What am I supposed to do? I could do with a few clues before I get on that plane.'

'You're supposed to do what you should have done after our last discussion. Put Carver back on the leash and keep him off the radio. Our contact in Kabul will fill you in. Just be co-operative, do what he tells you and this will all work out just fine.'

'And what about Patrick Reid?'

'What about him?'

'Where does the kidnapping of Patrick and Karim Mumtaz fit in to all this?'

Graham took another pull on his little silver flask. 'The truth is, we're not sure. But the Embassy will take the lead on the kidnapping. You just concentrate on Carver.'

Rob watched the hard shoulder flash by. He let the black macadam of the road and the green of the verge blur together, focusing his eyes only when a piece of road kill flew by. The bloody remains of a fox, guts spilt and tail gone, pummelled so thoroughly by the relentless traffic that it appeared two-dimensional. A little further along, a dead crow lifted a wing and waved him on his way. Some sort of omen, perhaps, but Rob didn't believe in omens, good or bad. What did he believe in?

After a while Graham grew uncomfortable with the silence. He hummed along with the radio for a while before clearing his throat, the overture to another announcement.

'I nearly forgot. There's one more bit of good news, as well as the upgrade, I mean. After all this is over, if everything goes off all right, we'd like to offer you a job.'

Mariscal gave a mirthless laugh. 'I thought I was already working for you, Graham. I'm certainly not doing all this for the *craic*.'

'No. A real job. There's a position coming up in one of the departments – rather a big job, actually – Home Office, Head of Strategic Communications. How does that sound? Sounds quite grand to me.'

Rob flinched. 'A press officer?'

'No. Head of Strategic Communications. If you don't like that title, I'm sure we could tweak it a bit. What about Director of Information? Public Liaison Executive? You can make up your own job title as far as we're concerned. Within reason, naturally.'

'I don't want to be your press officer, Graham.'

'Suit yourself.' Graham gazed out of the window a while. 'It's a shame, though. It'd be fun and the money's good.'

At the mention of money, Rob's hand went to his hip pocket and the reassuring bundle of twenty-pound notes. He'd already spent twelve hundred of his three thousand advance. Some had gone into the Portland Place branch of Lloyds to keep a couple of credit cards at bay. A larger sum had been collected by a shaven-headed man in a shiny grey suit.

'How good?'

'You'd start on a hundred and twenty thousand. Civil service pension and all that sort of thing, too. The perks are pretty good.'

Rob looked closely at Graham to make sure his leg wasn't being pulled. 'Are you messing with me, Graham?'

'Certainly not, that's the pay scale. And that's nowhere near the ceiling. Plus the pension. As I said, gold-plated.'

Rob removed his hand from the cash in his pocket and folded his arms. He'd always suspected that every man had his price, but he'd never tried to work out his own. Now someone had done it for him. Rob's price, it seemed, was precisely one hundred and twenty thousand. Plus pension. And he didn't have to kill himself to get it. He just had to—how had Graham put it? He had to be co-operative.

Graham saw that he had Rob on the hook and was smart enough to stay quiet for a while. They were in traffic now, queuing on the sliproad that would take them off the motorway and on towards Heathrow. He nudged Rob's arm. 'Nearly there. So, just think about it. Take your time. The job comes with a corner office overlooking the Mall, nice and bright and with a great view of the park. Your missus would be very impressed, I'm sure. Just let us know, in due course.'

Rob nodded. The man who wasn't Graham knew a lot about him. His successes, failures, his many weaknesses and most recently his sexual proclivities. All of this was written down in a file somewhere and so it was reassuring to learn that there were still some things Graham didn't know. He had absolutely no idea what might impress Lucia.

PART THREE

24 A Single Shot

DATELINE: BBC house, central Kabul, Afghanistan, July 7th

William recognised the feeling the moment he woke. A vague nagging sensation, which started at the back of his mind before spreading like a drop of ink in a glass of water until it was impossible for him to think of anything else. He was missing something, but what was it? He sat up in bed. With Patrick and Karim gone, the Embassy official in charge of securing their release and Mariscal on his way, William had nothing to do apart from continuing to pursue the story.

What was he missing? His gaze fell on the laptop and alongside it, a tidy pile of discs, the wedding tapes that Ali had reluctantly shared. He'd watched the tapes; he'd seen the car and the mysterious Mr Roydon, he had copies of all that. That wasn't it. What else?

He looked at the discs again.

'Some time after the blast.' It was William speaking, but the voice he heard in his head belonged to Karim. 'He was killed by a shot to the head, some time after the blast.' He heaved his heavy frame up from the bed and powered up his computer. He sat down in the chair, naked but for his boxer shorts, and found the relevant disc. Then he fast-forwarded through the endless wedding ceremony and incomprehensible speeches to the moment the bomb went off. A few dozen people were dancing around Baba's large dining room with big smiles on their faces, then there was a loud bang and the sound of glass shattering. Ali seemed almost to have dropped the camera but he had left it running, filming the floor and the wall. There was a moment of shocked silence, then the sound of Baba shouting something, issuing an order. Then Ali was following his cousin out of the house and into the garden, still holding the running camera but capturing nothing useful. A blur of grey and green as Ali followed Baba through the garden and out into the street.

On first viewing, William had found nothing useful in this section. Now he watched it again; he watched it several times before it occurred to him not to watch but to listen. He turned the volume up as high as it would go. The film was a blur – feet and garden and gravel – but the audio was clear. As Ali moved through the garden there was a bang. It was obvious now, but William had somehow missed it previously; filtered it out, assuming it to be something to do with the explosion. Perhaps masonry falling, or a piece of timber cracking. Now he became interested. It sounded like a gunshot. He transferred the section on to his laptop as a sound file and phoned Sergeant Chaundy.

'Let's have another listen.' Chaundy held the headphones hard over his ears with both hands, closed his eyes, and concentrated while Carver played the sound file again. Urgent steps, water, and then a single gunshot. 'Play it again. Bit louder.' Carver turned the volume up as high as the laptop would allow. Chaundy closed his eyes again, listened and nodded before removing the headphones.

William looked at him anxiously. 'What does that sound like to you?'

The sergeant sighed. 'I hear a man or a heavy woman walking on gravel or shingle.'

'Yes. It's a man, or men.'

'Then I hear water, moving water. A stream?'

'A fountain.'

'Right you are, a fountain. Distressed people somewhere close, they're screaming.'

'A bomb's gone off.'

'Okay. Then the gunshot.' Chaundy looked at Carver, wondering what exactly the old hack wanted from him.

'Definitely a gunshot?' William asked, holding the sergeant's gaze.

'No question. It's a little distance off, though, twenty yards maybe.'

William looked at the soldier, a ballistics expert and a thoroughly decent man. 'All I want to know, Sergeant, is whether you can tell from that audio file what sort of gun that is?'

Chaundy leaned towards Carver. 'I thought you was going to ask me something tricky. That's a P226. A Sig Sauer. I'd know it anywhere. Fired my own often enough.'

'You're sure?'

Chaundy frowned. 'Of course I'm sure. You know how new mums say they can pick out their own baby's cry from a hundred other screaming babies? Well I'm like that with guns. No two the same.'

William smiled. He'd always liked Chaundy. 'Sergeant,' he asked, as if a thought had just come to him, 'who carries Sigs?'

Chaundy didn't hesitate. 'We do,' he said. 'British Army, it's replacing the old Browning. Been rolled out in Afghanistan first, so a load of us carry those.'

'Who else?'

'Out here? No one.'

'Private security people?'

'Nah. Or they shouldn't do, anyway.'

William rolled his shoulders and pulled himself up straighter. 'Sergeant, I'd like to be absolutely sure. I trust your ear, completely, but is there a more scientific way to check that shot's a—what did you say?—Sig Sour?'

'A Sig Sauer. German. Or Swiss-German, rather. I'll tell you what,' he offered, 'you bring your little recording machine up to the firing range right now and we'll shoot a few guns. Pound to a penny the bang on that tape is the same bang as the Sig. You can record the shots and take a look at the sound waves. That might prove something? Although I'll tell you right now, technology won't trump the trusty Chaundy ear. You'll see!'

Carver liked the idea. 'Thank you, Sergeant, that'd be great.'

Chaundy led the reporter to a large gun-locker and took a small silver key from his pocket. 'Where's your little brown friend, by the way?' he asked, distractedly, as he removed a selection of weapons from the locker. 'He gave me a rather nice bottle of French brandy a while back. All you ever give me is grief.'

25 Meeting Mr Roydon

DATELINE: Kabul International Airport, Afghanistan, July 7th

Waiting in the customs queue at Kabul airport, Mariscal became aware of a flurry of activity at the front of the line. Two men, dressed in what Rob took to be the uniform of the Afghan police, were asking a thickset man in a crumpled business suit to remove his sunglasses.

'Why? I've just flown two freaking days to get here, and I'm tired. If I wanna wear my sunglasses, I'll wear my sunglasses.'

One of the policemen looked down at a document he held in his hand. 'You are American?'

'Yeah, I'm American.'

The policeman nodded and moved on down the line, his eyes flitting between what Rob now recognised to be an A5-sized photograph and various nervous-looking passengers.

At that moment, the younger of the two officers caught Rob's eye. He looked him over carefully before nudging his colleague and tipping his head in Rob's direction. The older man looked hard at Rob and then back at the photograph. He strode over and addressed Mariscal in careful English. 'Excuse me, sir, is it possible

261

that we might talk?' The phrase sounded recently learnt and rather over-rehearsed.

'Okay. Do you want to talk here?'

'No sir. In private.'

'Okay.'

It sounded to Rob as though he and the policeman were taking turns reading from a foreign language phrasebook. Neither of them was doing particularly well.

As the pair escorted Rob past the slow-moving queue, he saw an antique conveyor belt jolt into life and the first few bags from his flight appear from a hole in the wall.

The policeman saw him looking. 'Do not have worry. Your bag will come to you.'

They were walking more quickly now, crossing the baggage hall and heading in the direction of an unmarked set of double doors.

'Am I being arrested already? I've only just arrived.'

The policeman turned and looked at Rob, surprised. 'Arrested? No sir. You are VIP arrival.'

Rob was ushered through the doors and then marched down an uncarpeted corridor before arriving at a door marked Longe.

'This is the lounge?' Rob asked.

'Yes sir,' said the officer. They waited while the younger policeman fumbled with half a dozen different keys attached to a chain on his belt. The older man was still holding the photograph and Rob saw it was an enlarged black and white print of his BBC security pass, an unflattering mug shot. Finally the key was found and the door opened. The inside of the room was empty save for a rectangular wooden table with black plastic bucket chairs on either side. In the centre of the table sat a bottle of mineral water with a faded label and next to that, two dusty-looking glasses. The policeman gestured in the direction of the nearest chair. 'Please. Your friend will come soon.' Mariscal did as he was told and as soon as he'd sat down, his escorts turned and left, closing the door firmly behind them. Rob heard a brief debate take place between the two and then the sound of the key turning. 'I'd hate to be an unimportant person,' he muttered.

Mariscal rested his chin in both hands and stared at the bottle of mineral water. The seal appeared unbroken but the water was obviously undrinkable. Cloudy, with small water bugs dancing up and down the sides. He wondered how many interrogations this particular bottle had witnessed. He decided, if offered a drink, to go for tea.

After fifteen minutes the key turned again and the door snapped open. A smartly dressed westerner in his late thirties filled the doorway.

'Hello, Robert. I'm sorry to keep you waiting.' The man was business-like. His accent obviously London, north London, Rob thought, and quite strong but dialled down for the moment. 'So the Afghan coppers found you all right? Got you through customs nice and quick.' He took a confident step forward and offered a large tanned hand for Rob to shake.

'They did, yeah. I'm not used to the VIP treatment.'

'Well, better get used to it. You've got an important job to do.'

'I missed your name,' Rob said, and the man smiled fleetingly.

'I didn't say my name, Rob, did I? Not yet. But, seeing as you ask, it's Roydon. Like the place.' Mariscal knew of no such place but he let it go. He looked at the man. He was tall, six feet three or maybe four, and broad. Everything about him seemed large, even the features gathered closely together in the middle of his wide face. His unusual looks created the impression of a friendly man, jovial even. Until you took a good look at his eyes. Rob held Roydon's gaze and tried to figure out why the man's eyes chilled him. They were, he realised, completely devoid of emotion; they were blank.

Roydon walked once round the room, taking everything in,

before dragging a chair from under the table and sitting down, one long leg folded inelegantly across the other. He nodded at the bottle on the table.

'I don't like the look of that, not one bit. We'll get a proper drink later, after we've had a chat. What's your preference: Scotch or Irish?'

'What?'

'Whisky. What d'you prefer? Scotch or Irish?'

'Jameson's, I guess,' Rob said.

'Right. Good call, Jameson's it will be. Not now but later. Scout's honour.'

Roydon was wearing a suit, a Prince of Wales check with a blue satin lining. It looked bespoke to Rob's inexpert eye, but tailored in an unusual way. In Mariscal's experience, most men vain and moneyed enough to have a suit made to measure did so to ensure it flattered. Roydon's suit did the opposite. It seemed designed to disguise his size, baggily shrouding his obvious strength. Something about the man reminded Rob of pre-fight pressers with boxers or post-match interviews with suited footballers in wide ties.

'I like your suit.' Rob attempted a smile.

Roydon cast a glance downwards, though he knew exactly what he was wearing. 'Thank you. It's hand-made Prince of Wales, but I'm sure you knew that. I like good clothes. I admire quality.' He nodded at Rob's creased black shirt. 'That, for instance. That is a nice shirt. Though it looks like it's had a long day.'

'It was a present from the wife.'

'Which designer?'

'No idea,' Rob replied, honestly.

'No idea? Really? Why don't you have a look? I'd like to know.' He smiled and stared hard at Mariscal. 'Go on.'

Rob stared back. He saw a slight twitch in Roydon's muscular neck and looking down at the man's hands he noticed the corner of a blue tattoo, just visible beneath the cuff at his wrist. Rob realised he felt intimidated. He unfastened three buttons at the neck of his shirt, and dragged the collar round so he could squint at the label. 'Alexander McQueen,' he offered quietly.

'Very nice. Your wife has good taste, Robert. In clothes, at least.'

Roydon stood and made another slow circuit of the room, talking as he walked. 'What a terrible business that was.'

Rob was lost. 'What?'

'Alexander McQueen. Don't you remember? His mum died and he went all to pieces, lots of drugs, lots of drama. Topped himself in the end.'

'Oh yeah. I remember. Sad,' Rob said without conviction. Why were they discussing the world of fashion? Celebrity suicide? It was ridiculous, surreal. He wanted to get away from Roydon, away from this oppressive room.

Roydon stopped and looked at Rob again. His eyes, still, utterly blank. 'Sad? Perhaps. But he was weak. Artistic people tend to be weak, I've noticed that.' He sat down again and pulled the chair as close to the table as his bulky body would allow. 'We could chat all day, couldn't we? Natter away. But we should get down to business. So, how much do you know?'

'Well, not much. Graham told me—'

Roydon jumped in. 'Graham. Who's Graham?'

'My contact in London. Your colleague, I assume. My—my—'

'Handler?' Roydon suggested, then nodded, as if Rob's assumption was reasonable but not necessarily accurate. 'Carry on. Graham told you what?'

'He said that my job would be to keep an eye on William – William Carver, my reporter.'

Roydon nodded again, slowly. 'And?'

'He said that the last story William filed from here, a report on the murder of some local politician – Jabar – he said it had caused problems. Problems for British interests. I've no idea why. The story wasn't a big deal as far as anyone in London was concerned.'

'He told you quite a lot, didn't he, old "Graham"? Stole some of my thunder. I might have to have a word with Graham, next time I'm in London. Well, I guess I'll tell you the rest. Fill in the gaps, is that all right with you, Rob?' The question didn't require an answer. 'So. Let's see, your man Carver is sniffing around a story that he doesn't really understand and that certainly doesn't concern him. Fazil Jabar was a nasty piece of work. Corrupt, strong Taliban connections, all sorts, not a nice bloke, in short. His "murder", as you put it, was no bad thing. In fact it was a good thing.'

'Meaning what? We had this guy knocked off?'

Roydon banged his hand down hard on the table. The bottle of mineral water and Mariscal jumped together. 'No! No, Robert. That's not what I said. Is it? Not at all. Did you hear me say that?'

Rob waited. Watched the bottled water settle and let his pumping heart slow. 'No.'

'No. Look, if we're going to get along, you and me, you have to listen to what I say, right? No reading between the lines. No jumping to conclusions. That won't help anyone. Will it?'

Rob shook his head.

'All you need to know is Fazil Jabar got killed. That was no bad thing but the circumstances got messy. Carver reached the scene before the place had been cleaned up and he found some things. Stole some things, I should say. There were loose ends and Carver picked up on a couple of them.' Roydon waited until he was sure that Rob was taking all this in. 'Our problem is that Carver is like a dog with a bloody bone and there's a chance, a small chance but a chance, that his investigation might fuck up a very big contract that's about to be awarded. What do you know about the telecommunications business?'

Rob shook his head. 'Almost nothing.'

'No problem. Doesn't matter. You don't need to know much.'

'But, from what you're saying, it sounds like this whole thing is about money.'

Roydon sighed. 'Everything is about money, Rob.' His wide face broke into an amused grin. 'You, of all people, should know that.'

Mariscal ignored the jibe and tried to focus on the story. 'So William's figured out what? That Jabar's death was connected with this deal?'

'I don't know exactly what Carver's figured out. That's why you're here, ain't it? But I don't want him digging any deeper into Jabar and, most important of all, I don't want him putting anything – nothing at all – on air. You put a muzzle on William Carver.' Roydon was on his feet again. He seemed incapable of staying seated or still for more than a minute. 'You people are so naïve, you know that, don't you? Did you really think we'd spend billions of pounds, lose hundreds of good men trying to drag this shitty country out of the Stone Age and then just walk away? Out of pocket and nothing to show for it?'

Rob listened, light-headed. What sort of strange story did Carver have a hold on here? The hack in Mariscal wanted to know more and goading Roydon seemed the best way to get him to talk. Curiosity trumped fear.

'Shouldn't you, the Army, the Embassy, whoever you are, be concentrating on winning the war rather than going around touting for business? It's a little undignified, don't you think?'

Roydon grinned. 'You do both, or neither. Take a look at the history books, Rob. The best time to invest is when there's still blood on the streets, it's obvious. Everyone understands that. Just ask the Chinese.'

'And the British Ambassador? He knows all about this—activity?'

Roydon put a finger to his collar; the first nervous gesture Rob had seen him make. 'He's evangelical about it in fact. So don't start thinking that you're being dragged into some black ops shit, or whatever else your over-active imagination is conjuring up. We're working for UK plc out here, that's all. If a few more Taliban get killed in the process, that's all good. They're the enemy, after all, and we're at war.'

Roydon sat back down and leant in towards Mariscal, his voice quieter now, calmer. 'The Afghan communications minister will make a call on who gets the telecoms contract next week. All I'm asking is that you keep Carver quiet for that long. After that, he can do what he likes. He can stand stark bollock naked on the BBC roof and shout the story to the world, for all I care. That's all we're asking for, Rob, one week. Do you understand?'

'Okay, I get it, one week. And what about the kidnapping? What about Patrick and the translator, where does that fit in with all this?'

Roydon looked at his hands. 'I don't know what we're dealing with there. Some of my lot think it's a coincidence but I don't like coincidences so I'm assuming there's a connection. Either way, you don't need to worry 'bout that, we're dealing with it, reaching out to the kidnappers and so on.' He tugged his left sleeve up from over his wrist. Rob saw an inch more of the blue tattoo and an expensive-looking watch. 'I'd better make a move, you need to start cosying up to Carver.' He stood to leave.

'You're not travelling in with me?'

'No. That wouldn't be clever. I think your mate might've made me already. I don't want to do him any favours. There's a cab outside and your bag's in it. The driver will take you to the hotel or the BBC house, wherever you want to go.'

Roydon rapped on the door, which was opened immediately. 'I'll head off first. You wait five minutes. This copper will show you to your car. And Rob—' Roydon reached inside his jacket and pulled out a business card, entirely blank except for an international mobile number '—report to me twice daily on this number. Starting this evening.'

'What if I don't have anything to say?'

'Call me anyway. Make me feel loved.' And Roydon was gone.

On the cab ride into the centre of Kabul, Rob replayed the conversation in his head. All he had to do was hold William up a bit, keep him quiet for a week. He didn't have to spike the story for ever. Maybe that wasn't so bad – it was understandable, forgivable, even.

26 One Hundred Kilometres, One Hundred Years

DATELINE: Hindu Kush, Afghanistan, July 7th

Patrick did not see Karim again that evening. He was taken back to the large communal cave and given a plate of goat stew, some bread and two grey American Army-issue blankets. There were patches of fleece in the stew but he was too hungry and tired to care. He ate it all, then wiped his plate clean with the bread and ate that as well. After the meal he looked for a place to sleep in amongst the other men. He lay awake for some time, watching the fire burn down, before pulling the blankets close and falling into an uneven sleep. His dreams were vivid and filled with violence. He woke once to find that the creeping cold had caused the men to shuffle closer together in their sleep. The strong smell, which he assumed must have woken him, came from the doddery old servant who had brought the General his shirt. He was tightly swaddled now, his rear pressed against Patrick's chest. The old man let go a juddering fart. Patrick struggled out of his blankets and got to his feet, hurrying away from the smell. He picked his way through the crowd of prone and snoring men and walked back down the corridor and out into the night. The frozen air woke him instantly. It was still dark but the brightness of the stars had dimmed a little. He guessed that dawn was still an hour or two away. The moon was bright enough to see by and, looking around for a place to piss, he saw one of the General's men crouched near an open pit, defecating and then grabbing a handful of dirt and dust to wipe his behind. He walked past Patrick, pulling up his baggy pants as he went, and nodded.

'*Salaam alaikum.*'

Patrick relieved himself a safe distance from the edge of the pit before walking quickly back to the warmth of the cave. He found a new space on the other side of the fire, where he hoped there might still be a little heat. He wrapped himself tightly in his blankets and was asleep again in moments.

'Wake up, Englishman.' The General stood over Patrick, nudging him in the small of his back with his boot-tip. 'The horses are ready.' Doushki was wearing combat trousers tucked into tall boots, a long black shirt with mother of pearl buttons, and over that a leather jerkin. The foul-smelling old servant was waiting outside holding two sets of reins. The General's horse was at least eighteen hands high and powerful, a beautiful brown stallion. Patrick had to walk round this animal to find his own ride. Standing in the shadow of the stallion, almost underneath it, was a grey-bearded donkey with sad eyes and strange crosses cut into both its nostrils. The General saw Patrick examining the animal. 'She is my best donkey. We cut the nose to help them breathe.' He glanced at Patrick to see if he understood. 'The bigger nose means she can take in more air. When we are in the mountains, the air is thin. You see?' He took several deep breaths through his own nose to illustrate. 'The donkeys still take most of our opium over the mountains. They are better than the cars or truck for that.' The General patted the beast's flank affectionately. 'This animal has made that trip maybe five hundred times. She could do it all alone if I loaded the pack and showed her the path.'

Patrick nodded. He wasn't sure why his kidnapper was treating him like this, more like a guest than a hostage. But civility was a cause for hope. He knew he had to reciprocate. 'Incredible. What is her name, General?'

'What?'

'I wondered, what is the donkey's name?'

The General studied Patrick briefly before answering. 'She does not have a name. She is a donkey.' He turned his attention to his own animal. The old man had meshed his fingers together and held them cupped alongside the horse's big belly; Doushki nodded at him, placed a booted foot in the outstretched hands and swung easily up into his saddle. The stallion was immaculate. The richness of its brown coat was emphasised by a hand-woven white blanket with silver detail and a highly polished coal-black saddle. The horse was snorting in the cold air and seemed excited to feel its owner climb into position. They were a good match. 'This is my Buzkashi horse.' Patrick stared at the General blankly. 'Buzkashi. It is a sport, like your polo. But instead of a ball, we use a goat.' Patrick struggled to imagine how such a peculiar and incredibly cruel game might work. 'The goat is dead, obviously,' the General added.

'Right.'

'The Taliban ordered Buzkashi "*haraam*". Forbidden. They ban it.' Doushki made a rasping noise at the back of his throat and spat a mouthful of green phlegm on to the frosty ground. 'That is one of the things that is wrong with the Taliban. No fun.' He made a light clicking sound with his tongue and the horse stepped forward, tugging gently at the reins as it turned and circled. Patrick made eye contact with the old servant and smiled. He lifted his foot for a boost. The Afghan stared at the foreign boot for a moment before turning and walking away.

'I don't think your man likes me.'

The General smiled. 'He is Hazara. He likes no one.'

Patrick struggled on to his animal, found his balance, and the two men set off past the mud houses before joining a thin animal trail. Patrick wondered briefly about escape, but looking at his donkey, the landscape and the rifle Doushki had slung across his back, he quickly saw how futile any such attempt would be. As they rode, the General talked.

'So, Mr Reid, your small Pashtun friend told you something of me?'

Patrick nodded. 'Yes. He did. He told me you were a legend, a myth—that you didn't exist.'

The General smiled. Taking both reins in his left hand he slapped his right palm hard on his broad chest; the noise was loud enough to echo off the cliff-face around them. 'Did he? Well you can see that he was wrong about that. What else did he tell you?'

Patrick looked up at Doushki and took a chance. 'He told me you were a war lord, a drug lord, and that you went insane.'

The General gave him an amused glance. 'Insane? Yes, I hear that people say this, but how can I disprove madness? I would be the last to know, is that not right?'

Patrick smiled nervously. 'I guess so.'

'I have done many bad things or ordered other men to do them for me. Some of these seem wrong now, but they seemed right at the time. Or if not right, then necessary. Do you understand?'

Patrick nodded uncertainly.

'It does not matter if you understand or not. It doesn't matter whether any man understands!' Doushki spoke loudly into the empty landscape, and the sudden volume startled his horse into a trot. The General cursed and gave the reigns a mighty tug to bring the stallion under control. 'And the violence is not over, Mr Reid. More people will die. Maybe me, maybe you?'

The creeping, sickening fear which had stalked Patrick ever

since his capture rose again in his throat like bile. Doushki jabbed a heel into the flank of his great horse, circling Patrick's donkey before riding on a few metres. They travelled in this order and in complete silence for some time. When he finally slowed to allow Patrick to catch up, the General's mood had changed again.

'Look!' Doushki pointed in the direction of a dirt road running parallel to their own trail before turning south. 'That road there. That is the road to Ishkalit. He who has not seen Ishkalit has nothing seen.'

Patrick nodded and waited for the General to make the turn, but Doushki ignored the road and they continued on their way. After an hour or more in the saddle the General stopped his horse and took a strangely shaped water bottle from his saddlebag. He handed it to Patrick. 'This is called a *mashk*. A gift from my wife. It holds enough water to get you from one end of our country to the other. Drink.'

Patrick steadied himself in his saddle and held the bag with both hands. His throat was dry. He drank deep and was shocked to find that what he was tasting wasn't water but some sort of wine. He spluttered and gagged but managed to keep the liquid in his mouth. He swallowed with a grimace.

The General smiled. 'Good. That is better. You need strong bones and hard flesh to live in these mountains. *You*. You are young but already you are soft.' To illustrate his point he jabbed Patrick in the side with the toe of his boot. 'Soft, like a girl. You will leave here tougher than when you arrived. And wiser too. That is my promise to you.'

An hour ago Doushki had been threatening to kill Patrick; now he was talking about his safe release. Patrick didn't know whether his host was insane, but he was certainly unstable.

They stopped next at a fast-moving stream spanned by a bridge made from tree trunks and carpeted in shining moss. The General spoke softly, almost kindly. 'The water here is superior, it flows straight from the high glaciers. You must not drink it when you are too hot, but now it is okay. ' He jumped down from his horse and tethered it loosely to a nearby sapling. Picking his way across the rocks, right to the edge of the stream, Doushki knelt down and scooped up handfuls of clear water. He threw the first of these over his face and down the back of his neck and then drank from his huge cupped hands. The sun had not yet climbed high enough to reach into the steep-sided valley and the light was blue-yellow. Patrick tied his donkey to the same small tree and followed Doushki to the water's edge. They drank their fill of fresh water and gazed at the valley and the mountains beyond in an almost companionable silence.

'Have you ever seen a more beautiful place, Mr Reid?'

Patrick shook his head.

'These mountains. This land. And all the history. You can feel the history here . . Do you know your history?' The General did not wait for an answer. 'Alexander the Great, the Byzantines, Mongol Khans, Queen Victoria's brave, stupid soldiers. All of them were here, they rode through this valley or the valley next to this. Can you feel it?'

Patrick muttered that he thought he could, his voice weak and cautious.

'My ancestors. Maybe yours too? Who knows?' General Doushki stepped back a few paces. Bending his knees he descended stiffly into a crouch, then fell back into a sitting position and smiled widely at the younger man. 'So. Now you must hear my story.'

Patrick nodded. He realised that he wanted to hear it. He had never met anyone like this man.

Doushki's story began in the early nineteen eighties. He told Patrick how, aged just fifteen, he had left his family in Kabul and walked into the mountains to join the mujahideen and fight the Soviets. 'The Russians were killing my country. Killing the animals.

Killing the people. At the beginning I just wanted to be shown a gun and taught how to shoot it. I killed my small number of Russians but my superiors saw I could be more useful doing other things. I was smart, quick to learn. I picked up languages easily. My English is perfect, yes?'

'Yes. Yes it's good.'

'Yes. And I have never been to England! Also, I looked very innocent then. I was young, you understand.'

Patrick could not imagine the man next to him looking young or innocent.

'The mujahideen were using drugs to fight the war. Not just to fund it, but to fight it. My job was working in the markets close to the Russian Army camps, selling cannabis and later heroin to the soldiers who were off base for a half-day or whole-day pass. I made money for myself too, of course. I was a Holy warrior and a baby capitalist. Most of the Russian soldiers were not much older than me. They were thousands of kilometres from home, bored and terrified. It was easy to sell drugs to them.'

Doushki boasted that before long the Russians were trading their guns for drugs, and Patrick remembered Karim telling him the same thing.

'Imagine that: an army selling its own weapons.'

Before long, he became interested in the production as well as the distribution of the opium. 'We learnt how to make white heroin and I began to sell this. Better than cannabis, much stronger, and the Russians already had the needles in their medicine kits so it was easy for them to inject. The commanders saw what was happening and they told the politicians and they said no Russian should stay in Afghanistan more than nine months.' Doushki grinned. 'But you can do much in nine months.'

The General took his *mashak* from the saddlebag, lifted it high into the air and poured some more wine down his throat before passing it to his travelling companion. Patrick took a sip and returned it. He tried to remember what Karim had told him about how Doushki's drugs operation had worked.

'But you had help, General? Is that right? The Pakistanis? The Americans?'

'The Americans. The Americans were trying to do to the Russians what the Vietcong did to them in Vietnam. Americans learn the hard way, but they do learn. American equipment came in through Pakistan, the Pakistani Inter-Services Intelligence agency, so if people found out, journalists like you, the Americans could deny everything. The Saudis would pay some of the big bills. A lot of people were involved in those days. It was an interesting time.'

'Part of the cold war?' Patrick offered, and Doushki laughed loudly.

'Cold for you, maybe. Not for us. But yes, it was all part of that. The French had the original idea. Did you know that? Operation Mosquito. A mosquito would defeat the Russian Bear. Look it up if you do not believe me.'

The General explained how, with the help of his supporters in the west, he set up sophisticated labs turning opium into morphine and then into heroin. Swathes of land were opened up for poppy farming. 'We took the drugs out of the country and brought the guns in, arming the mujahideen. At first I told myself I was doing it for the Afghan people, for a free Afghanistan, but that was not the whole story. I was becoming rich and I enjoyed it. But most of all, I enjoyed the chemistry.' Doushki picked up a stick from the ground and sketched a line of barrels in the dirt with arrows between. 'Raw opium stinks. Any customs official with one working nostril can smell it. A dog will find it in seconds. So to move it around, we needed to turn the opium into bricks of morphine. We would dissolve the opium in vats of hot water and add a fertiliser. This leaves the morphine floating at the surface. You scoop out the morphine, heat it again and mix it with ammonia until it turns solid. Then you press it into moulds, dry it in the sun and you have it: bricks of dried-out morphine weighing less than a tenth of the raw opium.'

The General persuaded the mujahideen leadership that they could do better on their own, that he could turn the morphine into heroin without the help of Pakistan or the French. 'By the end of the decade, just my group alone was turning out seven hundred kilos of crystal heroin every month. When the war finished and the Soviets ran away, we, the Peshawar Seven – that's the big seven mujahideen groups – were producing over eight hundred tons of opium a year.' He paused and looked into Patrick's eyes. 'Eight hundred tons! Where do you think all those drugs went?'

'West?'

'The West. America, Germany, France, London. So now you can have another war – instead of cold war, a war on drugs.' The General rubbed away the drawings in the dirt with the palm of his hand and stood.

Patrick looked up at him. 'General. Why are you telling me all this?'

'Am I boring you? Be patient. You will see soon enough.'

He struggled getting back on to the stallion, but once on, looked absolutely comfortable. He touched the horse's flank with his heel and it broke into a steady trot. Patrick's animal did its best to keep up.

'After the Russians fled, after we won, some of my comrades – mujahideen leaders, drug dealers – they flew them to America to get a special thank you from the President. Coffee and tea at the White House with President Ronald Reagan: did you know that? But that was all we got. After Russia left, you all forgot about Afghanistan. America cut the aid. Many Afghans, they begged the West to help build a safe new country but no one was interested.' Doushki slowed his animal to a walk. 'It was obvious what would happen . . . the vacuum would get filled with drugs and terrorism.'

Patrick felt a little fortified by the sweet red wine. 'With groups like yours.'

'Yes. With groups like mine. With men like me. And men worse than me. Afghanistan fell off the map for years and years right up until the Taliban came along and then you started to pay attention again. Too late. Much too late.'

They rode on without speaking for another hour. The land grew flatter and greener but there was not a soul to be seen. They skirted around two small villages and both appeared deserted. It was deathly quiet; all Patrick heard were the heavy hooves of the horse and his donkey and the wind whipping at their backs, pushing them onwards. Eventually, in the distance, he saw what looked like a burnt-out farm or family home.

The General pulled his stallion to a halt and waited for Patrick to draw level. 'That,' he pointed at the ruin, 'is the only good thing I ever did. It is a school. I built it.' He shuffled in his saddle. 'All my ghosts are gathered here.'

They rode on a few yards.

'Children from many villages came. Boys and girls I built it because my wife asked me to. This is where she worked. And where she died. You should never love anything too much, Mr Reid. It makes you weak.'

From this distance it was possible to have some idea of what the school must once have looked like; enclosed on four sides by neat dry stone walls and with a space for a playground at its centre, it was well planned and neat. Off to the right, a steady stream ran through what had once been an orchard and was now a collection of burnt tree stumps.

The General stared at the scene and smiled. Patrick guessed that his host was seeing a living, working school, not the burnt-out scene of a bloody massacre. They moved closer still and it became obvious that the classrooms and outbuildings had been well built. The fire had blackened and baked every surface but it had failed to destroy. Brick walls still stood and even some of the roof and rafters had survived. At the stone-wall perimeter, the General jumped down from his horse, tied it to the broken gatepost and walked across the playground. Patrick followed, and as he drew closer he saw the walls, pockmarked with bullet holes, and at his feet, shell casings, rusting green in the overgrown scrub. The General stopped outside one of the classrooms and put his hand on the blackened door. Looking carefully, one could still make out the decorative detail, carved into what now looked like a slab of charcoal. 'This door was mahogany, decorated by craftsmen in Herat. All the doors were like this.' He traced a section with his finger. 'Passages from the Koran. About learning and wisdom.' The General kicked at the door with a heavy boot. It swung on its one remaining hinge and fell with a bang, a cloud of dust billowing up from underneath. 'You can do good things. That's what she said. You can do good things, even with bad money.' The General walked across the door and into the classroom; the tables and chairs had been reduced to half-burnt firewood but somehow the blackboard was intact and still had writing on it. Patrick moved closer, examining the delicate script. 'Do not touch that.'

Patrick jumped. 'I won't. I wasn't going to—'

The General was at Patrick's shoulder; his eyes followed the line of writing. 'You can look at it. But do not touch it.' He was staring at the writing. 'My wife, she taught the children poetry. She loved your English poets best, she read her favourites to the children and she would read them to me too.' He moved away from Patrick, mumbling some lines under his breath:

> *Though I am old with wandering*
> *Through hollow lands and hilly lands,*
> *I will find out where she has gone,*
> *And kiss her lips and take her hands*

The men returned to their horses and the General brought out some food and a flask of sugary tea. They sat and ate in silence. There was birdsong and the sound of the stream, and apart from that, nothing. After the meal, the General tidied the food away and poured them each a metal shot glass of a thick bitter liquor. 'My wife's name was Gulbahar. It means "The Rose of Spring". They raped her and then they shot her in the head.' Patrick stole a glance at Doushki. His eyes were wet but he would not cry. 'I found the men who did this. Six men. Me and the man you call Mirgun found them.'

Patrick waited. 'What did you do?'

'We tied them up and gagged them, then castrated them, one at a time.' He finished his drink, winced and poured another. 'We left them to bleed for a while and then we burnt them alive. They would not tell us which Taliban leader gave them the order to destroy the school, to kill the teachers and pupils. Maybe they thought of it all by themselves.'

Patrick looked at the General. The day seemed to have taken its toll; he seemed older and smaller than the giant Patrick had seen yesterday, rising from a copper bath. 'And killing those men, it helped?'

The General looked up from his metal shot glass and stared hard at Patrick. He nodded. 'Yes, it did. For a while.'

27 Hog Heaven

DATELINE: Intercontinental Hotel, Kabul, Afghanistan, July 7th

Carver was sitting on a beaten-up banquette at the entrance to the press hotel bar. He would rather have been in the bar but he wanted a clear view of the lobby. Rob Mariscal was already an hour late, and he was getting fidgety. He had a menu in his hand and was considering killing time with a second lunch. He'd had phone calls from the office in London and from Captain Remora telling him that Rob was on his way and he'd passed a message back saying he'd meet him here at the Intercontinental. William was, as always, early. He had dressed hurriedly in jeans, white shirt and jacket, and his laptop bag was slung over one shoulder. He hadn't let the computer out of his sight since Patrick and Karim had disappeared. It sat on the toilet seat while he showered and under his pillow when he slept. It wasn't just the pictures of Roydon he was protecting. William had written up every piece of information he had about the killing of Fazil Jabar and the events that had followed. He flipped open the laptop and reread the last lot of notes he'd made; they summarised his meeting with Chaundy. The soldier was convinced the gunshot on the tape came from a Sig Sauer, and indeed when William compared the wave form created by the bang on Ali's tape and that of Chaundy's Sig, they did look identical. But what did it prove?

Someone had fired a gun not long after the explosion, and the weapon was probably the same weapon that British forces in Afghanistan used. Richard Roydon might have fired the shot, and if he had, then the fact that he possessed such a weapon might mean that he wasn't as ex-military as William had been told – but there were too many mights. It was all speculation. Nothing in William's notes added up to proof that Roydon had fired the shot. Or even that the shot had killed Jabar. He had evidence that Roydon had been in the area, but again, so what? If William had the bullet, then he might really have something, but he didn't have the bullet. And even with it, he would need Roydon's gun to prove the match. He removed his glasses and cleaned them on his shirt tail. Who was Roydon anyway? Even if William could link him to the killing of Jabar, the trail went no further.

'Tenuous.' Tenuous was the word. Everything he had was tenuous. Interesting but inconclusive. It seemed to Carver that the most solid thing he had was his own gut feeling that he was on to something important. But that feeling had been wrong before – very wrong and not very long ago. Looking up, he saw the stocky figure of Dan Riley on the other side of the hotel lobby. He powered down the computer and slipped it back in its case. William took the menu from the table in front of him and raised it to head height, but the American had already seen him and was heading in his direction. The two men had avoided each other since their tense encounter a fortnight ago. It seemed Riley had tired of this game; the American now stood directly over William.

'If you're gonna hide from me, you'll need a bigger menu.'

William nodded an unenthusiastic greeting and put the menu down. Riley was wearing his usual uniform of denim shirt and worn jeans. He was carrying more cameras than usual and he unshouldered these carefully and placed them on the floor. 'I need a drink. Can I buy you a drink?'

'I thought you were on the wagon?'

'I fell off. What do you want?'

Carver looked at his watch; he had nothing else to do, nowhere else to go. 'A beer?'

'You got it.' The American strode round the corner to the bar and returned quickly with two tall beers. 'It's dead in there. Freakin' barman was asleep on the counter. Where is everyone?' William shrugged. 'He only had that low alcohol shit, so I asked him to put a shot of vodka in these.'

'I'm supposed to be working.'

'So am I. Here's to your health.' Riley raised his glass but got nothing in return. Using his drink-free hand as assistance, the American lowered himself slowly into the seat alongside William. They sat in silence for a time. It was obvious Riley had something to say. But he wasn't saying it yet. They sat and drank until, eventually, William spoke.

'How's that job with the Army going?'

'The embed?' Riley grimaced. 'You can call it what it is. It's an embed. Well, it's all got a bit complicated, takin' a good deal longer that it was meant to.'

'How come?'

'Well. That's the question.'

Riley put his drink down and looked at his hands. William noticed a slight tremor. 'I just got back from four straight days away. I was supposed to photograph the offensive. Up in the north. The final offensive they were calling it.'

'It didn't happen?'

'Oh it happened. But it turns out it wasn't final and it was mostly offensive to anyone who gives a shit about basic human rights.'

'And that's you?'

The old American shrugged. 'Yeah, who knew? Me and the Army are having a little disagreement over who gets to keep what pictures. There's some stuff in there they don't like very much. I'll tell you about it one day. But not today. You've got enough going on, I'd say.' Riley took a long pull on his beer and shivered as the cold alcohol rolled through him. 'So I only just heard about the kidnapping. I wanted to tell you I'm sorry. Really sorry.'

Carver glanced up at him. 'Thank you.'

'You're close to the both of them?'

Carver didn't rush to reply. He thought about his missing colleagues. 'Close? I don't know. Patrick, Patrick Reid. He's new and I was kind of bounced into having him but we were getting along all right. He came up through local papers.'

'Most of the good ones do.'

'But this is his first ever send.'

'Really? Poor guy. And your translator I think I might've met. The kid with the harelip. Karim, isn't it?'

'Karim Mumtaz. He's been working for me for years. Working with me, I should say. He's not just a translator. He's a journalist in his own right. A good one.'

'Well if you think he's a good journalist then he must be a very good journalist.'

Carver gave a sheepish smile. 'Thanks Riley.'

They drank to Karim and to Patrick and when their drinks were finished they decided they needed another. This time William went to the bar. When he got back the older man was fiddling around with one of his cameras. He had removed the lens and was blowing gently at the thread. Carver put his drink down in front of him and was about to make some small talk when Riley broke in:

'William, before we go any further, I didn't just wanna talk about Patrick and Karim. I also wanted to apologise for what I said before. For giving you a hard time about Iraq. I was being pompous and I need to say sorry and eat a little crow.'

He glanced up to see if William was interested in hearing this apology. 'I wanted to say it before too many drinks went down.'

William nodded. This was uncomfortable for both of them.

'Thanks. I appreciate you saying it, but the truth is, I only flared up because you had a point.'

Both men felt the air around them clear. Carver necked the rest of his drink and sat as far back as the banquette would allow. The American was a poor substitute for a priest but then William was a poor excuse for a penitent. He'd wanted someone to hear this particular confession for a long time.

'I argued for that war. I wanted it. I swallowed all the stories the Iraqi exiles fed me, I believed the conventional wisdom, I helped propagate it. I even trusted the spooks and the official sources, God help me.' William's head was bowed but his eyes remained open as he stared at the floor. He felt Riley nudge him with an elbow.

'Don't beat yourself up too hard. It was a lapse, that's all. Can happen to anyone. Hell, it did happen to most people.'

'That's true. But I wouldn't accept that as an excuse from anyone else, so I don't think it excuses me. I was naive and they used me. I let them use me. I let that happen.'

Carver scanned the lobby. 'I think about Iraq a lot, you know. Too much, probably. I mean, it's gone now, hasn't it? It's done. But I'm still not sure what upsets me most. That they took us into the war on a big filthy lie. Or that once we swallowed it and they got the war they wanted, they messed it up so badly.'

Riley nodded sympathetically. 'You never thought of quitting?'

'Not really, or not until recently, anyway. Just before I came out here, they called me in. One of the BBC bosses asked me if I wanted to chuck in the towel.'

'Early retirement?'

'Yeah, big cheque and an early pension. I said I'd think about it. I'm still thinking about it.' He paused. 'What's retirement like? Would you recommend it?'

Riley gave a mirthless laugh. 'Oh, it's fantastic. You sit about all day doing nothing, play some golf, watch TV. You'd love it.'

William smiled. 'But you got yourself down to Florida, didn't you? Nice weather, new friends. That doesn't sound so bad?'

'Oh yeah, that's true. I've made a whole load of new friends since I retired. The trouble is, I don't like a single one of them.'

William stifled a laugh. 'What about—what's your son's name, again?'

'Harry. Yeah, I got lots of time for Harry now, but Harry doesn't have a lot of time for me. He gave me three hours a couple of Thanksgivings ago.'

'That's tough.'

'Not really. I wasn't there for him when he was young and he's not there for me now I'm old. It's fair enough. He sends me pictures of the kids, two grandkids I got – boy and a girl I get all the pictures framed, stick 'em up on the wall in the condo. I got quite a gallery going now. Can you stand another of these crappy beers?'

'Sure. I'm sorry, Riley, this place is a dive. I'd suggest we go somewhere better but my boss is supposed to be meeting me here . . .' He looked at his watch. 'An hour ago. When something serious like this happens, the BBC always fly some suit over. Mariscal's the suit.'

Riley saw Rob first. 'Talk of the devil and the devil appears. I'm guessing that's your man?'

Mariscal swept into the hotel accompanied by a clutch of other journalists, including John Brandon, who had been kept in Kabul to see how the kidnapping story played out. Brandon was in one of his many white suits, and with the bright Afghan sun at his back, he appeared luminous, especially standing side by side with Mariscal, dressed as always in black. Brandon reflected every ray of available light, while Rob absorbed it. William recognised most of the other people around Mariscal. The only face he hadn't seen before belonged to a woman; long-limbed and angular with pale skin and a black bob. She was wearing khaki trousers and what looked like a flak jacket. Rob had an arm slung casually around Brandon's shoulder and was whispering something in his ear – something extremely amusing judging by the look on the TV man's face. William looked away. The group gathered around the reception desk. In time, Mariscal unhooked himself from Brandon and surveyed the lobby. When his gaze fell on Carver he grinned and waved, the wave becoming an urgent gesture signalling that William should stay put. Rob made his excuses to Brandon and company and strode across. As he drew close he glanced back over his shoulder before pulling a ridiculous face, a wide-eyed look of comic horror for William's entertainment only.

'Carver! Thank God. Save me from those fucking people.'

Rob grabbed William's proffered hand and clasped it in both of his. 'You looked like you were having a good time.'

'I was crying on the inside, mate. Crying on the inside. They've been boring me rigid for over an hour.' Mariscal looked at his reporter. William's hair needed a cut and a wash too. His gold-framed glasses were dirty. Stubble had worn his shirt collar to threads. His eyes were bloodshot. 'You're looking good, man.'

Rob turned to acknowledge William's companion. 'Hello. I'm Rob Mariscal. I'm—' He paused and took a long look at the older man in front of him. 'I know you, don't I?'

'Dan Riley. We met once before. You were with William in the Balkans. Or somewhere like that.'

'Riley! I don't believe it. I heard you'd quit. Or died.' Mariscal shook the American's hand vigorously before taking a step back and staring at this odd couple. 'I need to take this in. I'm in Kabul with Carver and Riley, two of the best fucking journalists in the world! I'm in hog heaven. Hog fucking heaven. Have you guys had a drink?'

Rob didn't wait on a reply but headed straight for the bar, leaving William and Riley little option but to follow. They gathered up their bags and the cameras and trailed after him. Mariscal had found a corner table as far from Brandon's party as it was possible to get and was arranging three chairs in a tight circle around it. 'Sit, sit. My round. I was feeling a bit jet-lagged before but I'm right as rain now. We'll have one or two here and then go somewhere else and eat, yeah?' He left and returned with a strange mix of drinks: two large whiskies, two white wines, one red wine, a half pint of vodka and three beers. 'I got a selection.' He arranged the drinks around the table and sat.

'So tell me, Riley, what's changed? Does Carver still pop off for a piss whenever it's his round?'

The American laughed. 'Ah, he's not so bad. I remember he bought that big round of drinks that time. Biafra, wasn't it?' He winked at William. Mariscal slapped the table joyously, jolting the drinks, and William flushed slightly.

'I'll tell you what hasn't changed,' said William sharply. 'You're still always bloody late. Where have you been? Your plane landed bang on time. I checked.'

'Ah, I'm sorry. I got dropped at the BBC house, I thought you'd be there.'

'I left you a message saying where I was.'

'Didn't get it. I dropped my stuff and I was coming to look for you but Brandon found me and dragged me off to some bar he knows, the Frontline Club?'

'Yeah. I know the place. He calls it that. It's got a proper name.'

'He wouldn't let me leave. I was stuck between him and that

bird from German telly.' Mariscal turned and pointed indiscreetly at the long-limbed woman who was already looking in their direction and threw him a dark look in return. Rob gave a friendly wave and the woman turned away. 'I think she's got her eye on Brandon. He was giving her the pick of his anecdotes. Some of them were all right. Have you heard his story 'bout—'

William broke in: 'I've heard all of them.'

'Fair enough. Anyway, he was giving her the whole show and she was lapping it up.' Rob looked again; the woman had her hands folded behind her head and her legs crossed in front of her. All elbows and angles. 'I'm not sure I'd risk it. She looks like one of those spiders with the homicidal mating habits. She'd fuck you, but she'd eat you straight afterwards and I bet she'd enjoy the meal more than the preliminaries.'

Carver brightened at this thought. 'Maybe she and Brandon should get together.'

Riley laughed. 'You guys have been ragging on poor Brandon for years. It's so freakin' English. You're both just jealous. You wish you had his talent.'

Rob choked on his white wine. 'He can keep his talent. I wish I had his agent.' Brandon had written a number of books cataloguing his adventures in the middle of or around the edges of various wars, revolutions and natural disasters. They all had grandiloquent titles stolen from the literary canon and amusing anecdotes stolen from other hacks. His success irritated Rob, who had once harboured literary ambitions of his own.

'I don't know how he does it, but he sells books by the bucket-load. He's a crap journalist but he's a bloody good brand.'

Riley stood his ground. 'He wasn't always so bad, was he? I remember when he was just starting out, he was good. He used to tell it like it was. Nice and simple.'

Mariscal, growing ever more animated, was bouncing in his chair. 'Exactly, exactly. That was fine. It was only when he started larding the facts with opinion. And when he got so grand he wouldn't go find anything out for himself.'

It surprised William how quickly they'd fallen back into the old habits and routine, being foul about everyone else but kind to each other. It was a rough kindness but a kindness nonetheless. He couldn't resist giving Brandon a sharp-toed kick of his own. 'You need to head up to the roof tonight, Rob, and watch him do his telly two-way. Every name he needs to remember is written on a big piece of card and held up in front of his face. I'm not joking. Go and ask him who the president of Afghanistan is – or Iran or even Pakistan – and I promise you, unless his wife whispers it to him, he'll have no clue.'

'His wife?' Rob looked again at the group on the other side of the bar. The petite woman sat performing the role of human shield between the German television journalist and Brandon looked familiar. 'That's his wife? I thought she was his researcher?'

'She was his researcher, then his producer, mistress and eventually wife. The circle of life.'

'The circle of life. Fantastic.' Rob jumped to his feet. 'Fuck it. I'm going to go buy them all a drink, make up for all the bad things you two just said.'

Mariscal headed off to do just that and William watched him go. He was running about fifty watts brighter and a hundred miles an hour faster than anyone else around. William's guess was, Rob already had a couple of whiskies inside him before he'd arrived at the hotel, but he also knew alcohol wasn't what was fuelling Mariscal's energy and velocity.

Dan Riley knew it too. When Mariscal got back to the table and next paused for breath, he jumped in: 'So, when were you last in the field, Rob? Been a while?'

'What? Oh yeah, it shows then, does it?' Both men nodded and Mariscal slowed. Checked but not chastened. 'I don't know what's more difficult to believe. That I'm back, or that I stayed away so fucking long. I'd forgotten what it's like. I forgot how everything here is brighter and faster and funnier than back home. What was I thinking?'

'You were thinking that you fancied a big fat pay rise and an easy life.'

Rob winced. 'I remember you used to say you'd prefer the electric chair to the editor's chair.'

'I don't remember saying that.'

'Well, you did.'

William found himself warming to Rob again; wanting to trust him and to welcome him back, but something still niggled, although he wasn't sure what. 'So how did you get in from the airport?'

'Taxi. The Embassy sorted it out.'

'That was good of them.'

'Yeah.'

'But you haven't met with them yet?' William asked.

'Them?'

'Embassy officials.'

'No. You first. Them later. I'm due at the Ambassador's residence tomorrow. He's out today . . . Ambassadoring. Have you had much to do with him? Lever, isn't it?'

'David Lever. I've met him, yeah. A couple of chats, one dinner.'

'Dinner? That's nice, I hope you supped with your long spoon. What was it? Safari suits? Spotted dick served by a native?'

William smiled. 'A bit of that, but not too much. I think he might be all right. I don't like some of the people around him, but I like him.'

'You think he can get our boy back for us?'

William put his drink down a little firmly and it rattled on the table. 'Boys. Not boy. They kidnapped two of our people, Rob, remember?'

Mariscal pushed his own glass to one side and gave William a contrite smile. 'I'm sorry. That was stupid, insensitive. It's just that, in spite of the circumstances, it's really good to see you and it's great to be here.'

'It's all right, Rob, I get it. But Patrick and Karim need you more than I do. You need to put some pressure on. I don't think the Ambassador or anyone else here has a clue why they were taken or by who.'

Rob nodded thoughtfully. 'Haven't they seen this kind of thing before?'

'They've seen Taliban kidnappings, plenty of those, and that's what they're telling everybody this is. But I'm not sure they believe it.'

Rob looked at William carefully. 'Have you got any ideas?'

Carver shuffled in his seat. 'No, not really.'

Mariscal paused a beat, then lowered his voice and took a chance. 'It couldn't have anything to do with that story you were working on?'

William looked up suddenly. Rob had pushed too hard, too soon. 'What's that supposed to mean?' William closed up like a sea anemone poked with a stick, folding his arms tightly across his large chest. 'I have no idea why Patrick and Karim were taken, Rob, or how best to get them back. That's why you're here, isn't it?'

'Yes.'

'You're the suit, you're the BBC's duty of care personified. I hoped you'd have some ideas.'

Mariscal nodded. He knew William well enough to know that backing down now would simply fuel his suspicions. 'Yeah, that is why I'm here. Represent the family, represent the BBC, put some pressure on the Embassy and keep London in the picture. I'm going to do everything I can, William. I've never met Karim but I'm sure he's a good bloke. And I know Patrick is. I hired him, remember?' William unfurled himself slightly. 'All I'm saying is that the more I know, the better. And don't forget, I'm still your editor. If you're working on a decent story, then that work should continue, and p'rhaps I can help. We've done all right together in the past, haven't we?'

William gave Rob an even look. He could think of no real reason to distrust him and with Patrick and in particular Karim gone, he could use some help. 'I'll think about it. There are a few things I'm looking at. But I don't think we should talk about it now. I'd prefer we didn't.'

Mariscal nodded. ''Course.' Course.' He looked around the dank hotel bar; the place had filled up a little and the air was thick with tobacco smoke. 'Listen, there's nothing we can usefully do till tomorrow. How about we have one more here, then go get some food? It's on me. Where do you go for a decent meal around here, Riley?' Rob looked at the American; it seemed he would be more likely to have an answer to this question than Carver.

The old man shrugged. 'Not a clue. I've been eating army rations and room service only. You could ask Brandon. He probably knows a place.'

'Good idea, great idea.' Rob almost jumped from his chair.

Within a minute, William and Riley heard the sound of angry shouting and turned to see some kind of fight taking place at the other table. As they watched, Brandon got to his feet, upending the table and most of the drinks in the process. Mariscal was backing away, hands raised in surrender but laughing uproariously. 'A joke, mate. Jesus! I was only having a joke.' Brandon was looking around for something to throw. He picked up an empty pint glass and launched it, sending it arcing through the air. Mariscal ducked just in time. When he turned to face William and Riley, he was laughing loud and hard.

'Time to move on, I think.'

'I'm guessing Brandon didn't know a place to eat?'

Rob smiled. 'I forgot to ask him.'

'What did you say to him?'

'I bet him a tenner he couldn't tell me who the president of Pakistan was,' Rob said grinning broadly. 'It seemed to upset him.'

William smiled back. 'Look. I know a place. Somewhere that does food.'

Rob stared out of the taxi window watching ancient-looking figures navigate the dark labyrinthine streets around them. He could smell the warm air, hear dogs yapping, traders shouting, horns blaring. Groups of men crowded outside cafés. They stood smoking over open gutters surveying the road. They played backgammon by candlelight. The three men subsided into a content silence as the taxi trundled deeper into the city.

It took half an hour of driving and another half-hour of walking, seemingly in circles, to find the place William was looking for. Rob and Riley tried to persuade William to give up on the adventure several times. The alcohol was wearing off and Rob realised, to his annoyance, that he was missing the security of the press hotel. Finally William led them down a narrow side street, its name painted in broken red script high on one wall and near impossible to read. The gutters were filled with detritus swept or blown from the main road, but William marched purposefully on before finally stopping in front of a large, unmarked door with a polished brass handle and studded with rivets.

He squinted through his glasses. 'I think this is it.'

'You think?' Riley couldn't hide his irritation. The long walk had exhausted him. His knees hurt. William knocked twice, turned the handle and went in. The other two followed. A doorman of some kind sat facing them behind a wide wooden desk. He barely looked up from counting a pile of dirty Afghani notes. He had a lean, pockmarked face and thin lips, which moved slightly as he counted. William let him finish. When he had bound the notes with a rubber band and locked them in a small steel box, he stood. He was wearing jeans, a long Afghan shirt and a pillbox hat.

'Gentlemen. I can help you?' The question was directed at William.

'Good evening. Is the big man around?'

'No. He's dead.'

'Oh, right. Sorry to hear that.'

The doorman shrugged. William tried again. 'How about Neelap?'

'She is here. I know your name?'

It seemed the doorman's questions all came dressed as statements. Carver caught the inflection. 'Carver. William.'

'Carver William. Yes. She knows you?'

'Yes.'

'And she knows your friends?'

'No.'

'Okay.' He peered at a notebook on his desk, as if it might reveal the identities of the strangers. Mariscal nudged William's arm.

'You're sure this is a club? It looks a lot like a brothel.'

The doorman heard the question and answered it before William got the chance. 'This is not a brothel. This is the club. You prefer a brothel?'

'No, no,' Mariscal offered, hurriedly.

'Okay. So you stay. It is early. There will be some nice girls here later, and you can dance.'

Mariscal smiled enthusiastically at the man. 'Great. Good. And food?'

'Yes. Some girls dance. Some girls cook.'

Riley nodded. 'The trick is to find one who can do both,' he deadpanned under his breath.

The doorman escorted the three men through what looked like

an empty cloakroom into another room beyond. It was a large space but not large enough to justify the grandiose decoration. Pieces of antique furniture crowded the room. In one corner there was a huge, domed birdcage in gold, too big for any bird but especially unsuitable for the motionless sparrow-like creature which was currently in residence. There was a Venetian mirror on one wall, the glass slightly yellowed with age, and William stood in front of it for a moment, combing and flattening his thin hair with the fingers of his right hand. The most striking feature hung at the far end of the room: a pair of ceiling-to-floor heavy red velvet curtains on a thick brass pole separated this antechamber from whatever was happening on the other side. Each man picked a piece of furniture and sat. Rob slumped back into an armchair and reached for the heavily decorated box of cigarettes on the coffee table next to him. He flipped the top open and looked suspiciously at the brightly coloured cigarillos stacked neatly inside. 'Fancy fags.'

The air was already thick with the smells of incense, cigarette smoke and good dope. Rob was sure no one would mind. He picked a long, thin emerald-green number and lit it. He pulled heavily on the filter and a quarter of the thing turned to ash. He set about seeing if he could kill an entire cigarillo in one drag.

Mariscal was lighting a third cigarillo when a red-headed woman dressed in what looked like a black one-piece swimming costume under a diaphanous white skirt walked from between the curtains. She clapped her hands together in delight, and when she spoke her voice was unexpectedly deep.

'William! More younger and more handsome than ever.'

Carver hoisted himself upright and embraced the woman. 'Hello Neelap.' He kissed both cheeks delicately. 'How are you?'

Rob and Riley exchanged bewildered looks. No one could describe William as young or handsome, yet Neelap seemed genuinely delighted to see him. The woman turned to examine William's friends. She was more striking than beautiful, in her late forties or early fifties, with a comfortable outline and a commanding presence. She offered her hand a little imperiously, and both men took it meekly and introduced themselves.

'I am Neelap,' was all she offered. She turned again to Carver. 'I did not know you were back in Kabul, William. You must tell me next time. Only the cheap champagne is cold.'

'I'm sorry, I will, next time. The doorman says the big man died. I'm sorry.'

'Yes. You didn't hear? He hangs himself. We do not miss him, don't be sorry. The big man was—what is the right word?'

'A bastard?' William suggested.

'Yes. A bastard.'

'So you're the boss now?' William asked.

Neelap smiled, lifted Carver's hands to her mouth and kissed them. 'William, I was always the boss.' She nodded at Mariscal and Riley. 'Gentlemen you are welcome because you are with William. I'll get my man to show you to a table and you can order food. But you are a little early, so you will have to wait.' She fixed her dark eyes on Mariscal. 'Please go ahead and smoke more cigarettes. I usually advise my customers against too many, but with you, I make an exception.' She disappeared back through the curtains from where the sounds of a band tuning up could now be heard.

'What is this place? And who the hell is she?' Mariscal was impressed.

'Neelap? I did her a favour a couple of years ago.'

Rob wondered what sort of favour would make a woman like that so incredibly grateful to a man like William. 'Like what?'

'She lost something. I helped her find it.'

Rob mused. 'Well it wasn't her sense of humour, still no sign of that. Her dog?'

298

'Her son,' William snapped.

'That'll do it.' Mariscal was satisfied.

The pockmarked doorman brought American beer and a spirit which turned cloudy when diluted with water. Two rounds later and the room had filled with other customers. Neelap returned to find the three men sharing one chaise.

'I will take you gentlemen to your table. We have a good table for you and the dancing starts soon.' She ushered them through the curtains and into the next room, which was in fact a covered courtyard. Rows of circular tables, two deep, were arranged around a square dance floor. At the back stood a raised wooden platform, fringed with faded purple crêpe paper, on which half a dozen musicians were playing a kind of samba with western brass instruments.

Riley nodded in approval. 'Say, Mrs Neelap. The authorities, the police, they're okay with all this drinking and frivolity?'

'You can ask them yourself, they will be here soon.' She gestured to the empty tables. Sure enough, slowly more men arrived, some in pairs and a few with women. When the courtyard was almost full, the show began.

Rob watched as the band exchanged the brass for Afghan instruments. They cleared their chairs, unrolled a long patterned rug across the stage and took up positions sitting cross-legged in a line with tabla drums and a variety of other percussion instruments in front of them or on their laps. The musician at the end of the row held some sort of small lute or sitar. The youngest member of the band took a handful of flour from his shirt pocket and rubbed it gently into the skin of the drum before offering some to his colleagues. Then they began. Starting with a single, simple phrase from the lute, repeated again and again but building in volume, the band switched easily from western to eastern music. They had been playing for ten minutes when the red curtains at the other end of the courtyard parted and the crowd turned in their seats to greet the dancers. One by one, eight women wove between the packed tables to the stage, collecting, as they went, coloured handkerchiefs thrust in their direction by excited members of the audience. The women dropped these favours in a pile at the rear of the stage, behind the musicians, and formed a line at the front. The music stopped. They wore long dresses, which began high at the neck and reached down almost to the ankle. Beneath, they wore matching trousers but no shoes. The dresses had long billowing sleeves. Only the women's faces, hands and feet were exposed. Each dress was identical in design but a different colour: rich red, bright yellow, blue, green, purple. All were embroidered at the hem and neck in silver thread. The music resumed, building slowly, and the women began to dance. At first they moved only their arms and hands, drawing delicate patterns in the air; then, as the drums and strings grew faster they became more animated, moving their hips, shoulders and finally their feet. The music grew faster still and the dancing more elaborate. The crowd roared its approval and the men clapped in time to the now thunderous sound.

Mariscal was losing himself in the spectacle, almost entranced. It was unlike anything he had seen before – hypnotic, and even more so when the women retrieved the handkerchiefs they had collected and used these to emphasise the astonishing speed and elegance of their choreography. Later, each woman took turns to dance a slalom through a line of her fellow dancers. Finally, the dancers took centre stage in pairs and danced alongside each other, facing the audience, seemingly in competition.

The three men were so captivated that when their hostess reappeared at their table it took them a moment to register her presence.

'You are enjoying the dancing?'

The men nodded and Riley managed a couple of words.

'It's wonderful.'

'So what will you eat? There is steak, but the meat is horsemeat, and there is chicken. Or rabbit, but only if you order now, rabbit is popular tonight.'

They ordered and as Neelap turned to leave Rob reached for her arm.

'Listen, the girls. Can we meet them?'

'They are not whores,' Neelap said matter-of-factly, 'if that's what you have in mind.'

Rob reddened. 'Not at all. That's not what I had in mind at all.'

'My dancers just dance, but some speak English. If there is a girl you would like to invite to your table for a drink then tell me and I will arrange it. There will only be talking. If you touch one of the dancers, these men here,' she nodded towards the other customers, 'they will probably kill you.'

Rob nodded. He could feel himself sobering up a little more every time Neelap spoke. 'I understand.'

'The girls drink only champagne.'

Rob glanced at the menu. The champagne started at a hundred and twenty dollars. He thought of Fletcher. Any reasonable expense. 'That's fine. Let's have a bottle now, just for us, to go with the food.' He tapped the page. Neelap smiled.

'Of course. William, I hope we have time to talk later. Alone?' She didn't wait for an answer.

Riley shot William another questioning look, which the reporter ignored, but as soon as he had eaten his food he stood abruptly and made his way back through the red curtain in search of his hostess.

The dancers were followed on stage by a magician who, at the climax of his show, pulled what appeared to be a rat from the pocket he had just shown to be empty. The audience applauded wildly but some recoiled from the rodent, its tail whipping furiously, mouth snapping dangerously. Rob looked at the remains of his rabbit dish and wondered if the surprising popularity of the dish might have forced the magician to improvise.

The snake charmer who followed was booed from the stage when his snake was revealed to be a benign and underwhelming creature. William had been gone for at least half an hour. Rob caught the eye of the pockmarked doorman.

'Sir? Hello. Neelap promised she would ask a couple of the young ladies, the dancers, to come and join us. Can you arrange that for us?'

'You like to talk to dancers?'

'Yes.'

The doorman tipped the champagne bottle on its axis and saw that it was empty. 'You need another bottle?'

Rob shrugged. 'Why not?'

'You will wait here.'

The champagne arrived promptly with clean glasses and another chair, but still no dancers. Rob opened one bottle and poured large glasses for Riley and himself. He took a gulp and grimaced.

Riley smiled. 'You're not paying for the champagne, remember, you're paying for the company.'

'Well I hope my girl's got some fucking good anecdotes because this fizz is shit.' Looking around the room, he saw that every table was now taken. Rob surveyed the smiling, shouting, animated clients, enjoying the good humour. Then he saw him.

The odd man out wore a red fleece jacket, zipped up to the neck, with a pink roll of fat spilling over at the collar. He was nursing a small beer and, unlike every other client apart from the three journalists, he was white. Rob looked away but he could feel the fat man's attention focused on their table and on him in particular. He decided he needed to distract himself somehow. 'Riley, say these dancers do turn up and they are interested in doing a bit more than practising their English. How would you go about claiming for that on expenses?'

Riley gave it some thought. 'Fixers' fee, I guess. It's been a while but fixers' fee covers everything, always has.'

The two men started swapping outrageous expenses stories: the BBC man who claimed the overseas private school allowance for three sons even though he was childless; the correspondent who bought a baby grand piano; an American bureau chief they both knew – the undisputed champion – who had bought a house in Santa Barbara on the proceeds of a currency scam he ran in Tehran.

William returned before the promised dancers appeared. He looked at the fourth chair. 'Are you expecting company?' His face was flushed but he still had a firm hold on his laptop.

'Dunno. We asked for two dancers but they never arrived.'

Riley climbed unsteadily to his feet. 'I'm going to the rest room. I'll have a word with the doorman on the way back. Chase up our order. But if they don't show soon, I'm heading home. I'm getting a little old for all this. What time is it, anyway?'

William looked at his watch; the digital numbers swam a little before his eyes. He held it up for Riley to read. 'Jeez.'

Mariscal pulled his chair closer to William. 'Neelap had a special present for you did she?'

Carver ignored the innuendo. 'No. We had a bottle of the good champagne, and some cake.'

'Just cake?'

'Yes. She has a husband, Rob. She's a friend, that's all. Anyway, she's not my type.'

Mariscal pondered this: William had a type. 'What is your type?'

William took one of the clean glasses and filled it for himself before topping up Rob's. 'I suppose what I mean is, I'm not her type.'

Rob turned his drink slowly in his hand. He wasn't good at the sort of conversation that this was turning into. He looked over at the stage. The band was winding up for the night. The crowd was thinning too. But the man in the red fleece was still there, an inch of beer at the bottom of his glass. Rob turned back to the table and watched William gulp his champagne down in one draft.

'Okay, then,' William said, putting the glass down a little unsteadily and pushing it aside, 'I don't think your dancers are coming for that chat. How about we have one instead?'

Mariscal did his best to appear relaxed.

'You want to talk about your story?'

'Maybe. If you still want to hear about it?'

'Of course, I want to help, any way I can.'

'Right.'

William eyed Mariscal. If he was ever going to get this story straight and put something on the air, he needed help.

'So you remember the tailor's shop bombing I did that little feature on? The Fazil Jabar killing?'

Rob waited a credible amount of time before indicating that he recalled the story. 'Yeah, yeah I remember.'

Carver explained to his long-time colleague what happened in the aftermath, about the appointments book he took and the name in it, about his hunch.

'The bloke's name is Richard Roydon. Turns out he's a former Marine, some kind of freelance mercenary now. He did some work for the Embassy a while back, but he got kicked out.'

Not kicked far, Rob thought.

'I'm pretty sure he's working for this British company, Aftel. They're in the running for a huge telecommunications contract that's about to be awarded. And now that Fazil Jabar is dead, they're the front runners.'

Mariscal raised his eyebrows. 'Wow.' He quizzed William about the details of the story, what he knew and what he suspected, and Carver told him everything. Afterwards, he exhaled loudly and slowly shook his head. He appeared to struggle to find the right words. 'It's incredible, William. Absolute dynamite. But are you sure you can stand it up? What's the solid evidence? A story like this needs to be copper-bottomed.'

William put the laptop bag down on the table in front of him and counted off the solid evidence he had with the fingers of one hand. 'So I have pictures and film of Roydon at the scene of the bombing. I've got evidence that Jabar was killed by a bullet, not by the blast. I think I've identified the shot as coming from a type of gun only the Brits use out here. I've got paperwork that links Roydon with Aftel . . .'

'Flipping heck, William, you have been busy.' Rob eyed the black computer bag. 'And you've got all that on the laptop?'

Carver nodded.

'You've got a lot.'

'Yeah. But it's not enough, is it?'

Mariscal shook his head. 'No, not yet. It's not quite cooked. If I was back in London, in the editor's chair, and you were selling me this, I'd be asking for a bit more. Even if I wanted to go ahead and run it, the lawyers wouldn't let me. Too much risk, not enough evidence. I mean, you might have it bang on but it's all a bit circumstantial, isn't it?'

William nodded. He didn't want to hear this, but he knew it was correct. 'I know. I've got lots of elements but nothing that stands up without me holding it up. I've got a good idea what's going on but I can't prove it. Not yet anyway.'

'Unproven doesn't mean unprovable, mate.' Rob smiled encouragingly. 'And there's no real hurry, is there? If you get it right, it's a huge story. Your biggest yet, maybe? You just need to take a bit of time.'

Rob's mobile was vibrating in his pocket. He ignored it.

'I don't have time. The telecoms contract is decided next week,' William said quickly. 'I need to lift the lid on all this before then, or it's pointless. And it's not just that. You asked before about

Karim and Patrick. Whether them being taken had anything to do with what I was working on.'

'Go on.'

'I think it has. I can feel it in my gut. I don't know what the connection is, but I'm sure there is one.'

'Yeah,' said Rob quietly. 'I think you might be right.'

Carver placed an open hand on the computer case. 'Patrick has copies of most of what I've got.'

Mariscal looked up sharply. 'What?'

'Paddy has the Roydon photos and other bits and pieces. I got him to back them up to his laptop but he buried them pretty deep in the hard drive.'

'Really? So there are back-ups. That's—that's good. Sensible.' His phone was vibrating again, jumping around silently inside his pocket. Rob tipped the last of the champagne into William's glass. 'I'm going to wet myself if I don't take a slash. Can you give me a minute?'

William nodded.

Standing just outside the men's room, with one eye on the corridor, Mariscal checked his phone. Four missed calls and one message. He pressed last number redial and Roydon answered immediately.

'About fucking time. What's going on?' the spook snapped.

Rob was angry enough and drunk enough to snap back. 'I've been busy, all right? Working. Now listen,' he hissed, 'have you got some twat in a red fleece following me?'

'Yes.'

'Why? What do you think I'm going to do?'

'I don't know. That's why I've got someone following you.'

There was the sound of a chain being pulled and flushing water from one of the toilet stalls. Rob lowered his voice. 'I can't talk now. I'll call you when I'm back at the BBC house. Half an hour.'

Roydon cleared his throat. 'Okay. Fair enough, Rob, half an

hour. But don't go forgetting why you're here, or who you're working for.'

'Yeah, yeah. I got it.'

'Indulge me, remind me who you're working for?'

'Her Majesty the Queen.'

'Don't dick me around, Mariscal. Who are you working for?'

'I'm working for you.'

'Good boy. Talk in a bit.'

28 Telling the Truth

DATELINE: Hindu Kush, Afghanistan, July 7th

General Doushki and Patrick made the long journey back to the compound in silence. The General was slumped in his saddle and he held the reins loosely. Watching from behind, Patrick wondered whether his abductor might have fallen asleep. If he had, it didn't matter, the huge old horse knew the way. He thought again about escape but it was an exercise in fantasy. He knew he wouldn't survive alone for long in this desolate place.

It was dusk when they finally reached the base. The General was helped from his horse by Mirgun and went straight to his chambers without a word. Mirgun showed Patrick to one of the mud-built shelters and told him to wash and change his clothes. He nodded to a pair of desert camouflage trousers and a black shirt as well as clean socks and underwear on a camp bed in the corner of the room. Patrick wondered who had organised this comfort. Karim, maybe? He felt guilty; he had thought little about Karim that day. Mirgun raised two fingers and told him he was expected to be in the General's rooms in two hours, for food.

Patrick asked if Karim would be there, but Mirgun ignored the question and left.

After washing and changing his clothes, Patrick lay down on top of the bedding on the camp bed. He fell asleep with a head swimming with images, details and unanswered questions. Most significantly, why General Doushki had chosen to confide in him in this way and, more worryingly, what might be expected in return. He was woken by one of Mirgun's men, who roused him from sleep by shaking his shoulder. When Patrick opened his eyes the man used his rifle to gesture towards the door.

Dusk had turned to night and Patrick was cold. His stomach gave a loud rumble of hunger. He shivered involuntarily as the guard hurried him through the compound, back to the cliff-face, and through the dank corridors to the General's quarters. The furniture had been moved into the corners of Doushki's room to create a space in the centre. In this space were seven men, including his host, sitting in a loose circle, reclining against colourful cushions. At the centre of the circle was the silver samovar and space for what Patrick sincerely hoped would be a significant meal. He took the place in the circle that had clearly been left for him, between an elderly Tajik with a dyed-orange beard and a young Afghan with a scar that ran from the corner of his left eye to his chin. Patrick nodded respectfully in the direction of his neighbours and at the General, who had regained his colour and looked revived by his rest. He was ignored. After a few moments a woman in a gold-embroidered kameez, headscarf and veil entered the room carrying a bright white bundle. All eyes turned to watch her as she walked through the gap between the General and Mirgun and into the circle. With a certain amount of ceremony, she unfolded the four corners of the bundle to reveal the most promising meal that Patrick had seen in several days. She stretched out the sheet to create a tablecloth and then turned her attention to the contents. Inside were several rounds of steaming hot flatbread and a lamb broth of some sort in a large clay pot. The woman arranged the food carefully on the cloth and went off for more. She returned with a bowl of steaming rice and then with eight silver plates, which she set carefully in front of each man. Patrick briefly caught the woman's glance as she placed the plate in front of him. He saw only her eyes and a high forehead, but it was enough to tell him that she was young, maybe his age, and attractive.

The men ate hungrily and spoke little. After the meal the young woman cleared the plates and replaced them with several shisha pipes. Some of the men smoked, some lay back and rested, others spoke quietly to their neighbours. No one tried to engage Patrick in conversation. After she had provided pipes for whoever requested them, the woman reappeared with what was clearly a special shisha, taller than the others and with goldleaf patterns on the green glass. She prepared it in front of the General and handed it to him with tenderness. He leant forward and kissed her hand. As the woman left, Patrick looked up; the General was staring at him intently. He was, it seemed, expected to speak.

'The meal was excellent. Thank you.'

'Good.' The General continued to hold Patrick's gaze.

'Your new wife is a very good cook,' he said uncertainly. He felt the other men were waiting to see how Doushki would react to the intended compliment.

The General paused for a moment and then laughed loudly. The others joined in.

'That is Noor. Not my wife, my daughter. She dislikes wearing the veil but if she doesn't then my men stare—' He paused. 'Though in fact, these animals stare anyway.'

Patrick nodded. He noticed Mirgun looking uncomfortable, even irritated by the exchange. The men sat and smoked and appeared relaxed, but the moment the General got to his feet, they did the same. It was clearly their cue to leave. Approaching him one by one, they bowed their heads and murmured respectful thanks. Patrick prepared to do likewise but when he approached, the General waved him away.

'Sit with me a little longer, Mr Reid.'

They waited for the other men to leave. The General indicated that Patrick should sit in the place vacated by Mirgun. 'Noor,' he called gently, 'please will you fix us the opium pipe?' The young woman reappeared at the curtain and spoke sharply to her father in Dari. He responded in the same language and tone before turning back to Patrick.

'My daughter is in league with my doctor. They are trying to kill me.' He raised his voice but the tone was playful: 'One small pipe, Noor. Not for me, for our guest. Mr Reid helped deliver this opium. He carried it across Afghanistan.' After some minutes the pipe arrived. Patrick took the smallest possible pull and tried not to inhale, but even so he felt high after just two shallow draws. Doushki watched him and smiled.

'So now it's your turn.'

'My turn?'

'Yes. I have shown you much today, told you much. Now you must tell me something.'

'What do you want to know?'

'I want to know who killed Fazil Jabar.'

'Again? General, please, I would like to help you——' Patrick smiled involuntarily, the effects of the opium kicking in.

But the General's mood was changing quickly, like the mountain weather, and his dark look wiped the grin from Patrick's face. 'I told your man, Mirgun. I told him everything I know about Jabar, back in Kabul. You heard all of that.'

'I don't believe you told us everything. I hope you didn't, because if you did I've wasted a lot of time trying to do the correct thing.' Doushki took a long drag on the opium pipe. He leant back and closed his eyes.

'I could have had you tortured as soon as you arrived, but I don't always hold with torture. After a good day and a good dinner, a man might tell you something. After torture he will tell you anything. True or false. So tell me something true, Mr Reid.'

Patrick tried to remember what he had said before and what more he might offer up now. He tried to recall the conversation in William's room. He had told Doushki everything he remembered. He had told him the little he knew about Richard Roydon, about the missing tailor, the bomb, the bullet and Aftel. The only piece of information he had kept to himself was the existence of a couple of files buried deep in the hard drive of his laptop.

'Some of this is new, but I am afraid it is not enough. Who is this Roydon? Who does he represent? If he killed Fazil Jabar, then who gave the order?'

'I swear I don't know, General, that's what William Carver is trying to work out. That's what he's working on right now. I am telling you everything I know, General, everything.'

Doushki sank back down into the heap of cushions behind him and sighed. 'I believe you.' He stared at the ceiling. 'And that is a shame.'

Patrick didn't dare respond. Putting the pipe to one side, he noticed that his hands were shaking. Doushki lay very still, staring at the roof of the cave for what seemed to Patrick like an awfully long time. Then he lifted himself wearily to his feet and waved to Patrick to follow.

'Come.'

The neighbouring room was empty now apart from Mirgun, and just behind him, Karim. Patrick saw the young translator sitting on a wooden chair and his heart lifted briefly until he realised that Karim was tied, fastened at ankles and wrists to the chair's frame. Patrick managed a smile and Karim returned it but his eyes were wet, his face frightened. Doushki looked fleetingly at Karim before turning to Mirgun and speaking in a slow English.

'Mr Reid has told me what he knows but it is not enough. We will have to appeal to William Carver directly.' Mirgun nodded.

As usual, Karim understood what was about to happen well before Patrick. He started to twist and buck in the chair, but the ropes were too tight. Patrick saw Mirgun take the hunting knife from his belt, he saw the silver blade flash briefly in the candlelight and then disappear, buried up to the hilt in Karim's chest. Karim gave a stunned gasp and then sat looking straight ahead, blood bubbling from his misshapen mouth. Patrick shouted something, or he thought he did, but no sound reached his ears. As he watched, Karim's brown eyes lost their brightness, then their focus, and then they died.

Doushki turned to Mirgun. 'Cut off the head and send it to Kabul. Tell William Carver he has two days to tell me everything he knows about Fazil Jabar, or I will cut off another head.'

29 Bomb

DATELINE: BBC house, central Kabul, Afghanistan, July 8th

William Carver finished shaving. His old Braun was making a range of unusual straining sounds, so he removed the top of the electric razor and examined the contents. Inside, a silver cylinder of rotating blades was clogged with grey dust. He tipped the contents on to his palm. Like dandruff, he thought, or ashes, and lifting his hand to his nose he caught a definite whiff of crematorium. He shook the thought from his head, twisted the ancient brass tap on the bathroom sink to full, and washed the dust from his hand and down the plughole. Then he dug around inside his wash bag until he'd found a strip of Seroxat. He popped one on to his tongue, dipped his head and took a long gulp of water from the tap before swallowing. Standing back up he caught a look at himself in the bathroom mirror. He couldn't remember ever looking in a mirror and being pleased with what he saw, but this morning was particularly unpleasant. Ashen-faced, red eyes and blotchy.

'Too much booze.'

The trip back from the club was a blur. He remembered that he had kissed Neelap before leaving. She had offered her cheek but he had attempted a kiss on the lips. He recalled the sweet taste of her lipstick. And now he remembered how she'd recoiled, smiling but obviously disgusted. How could she not be? He cupped his hands to his face, covered his mouth and nose and breathed out. No wonder she flinched; he stank.

'Champagne.'

William brushed his teeth and gargled with water, cursing the drink and the club and his drinking companions. How had they got back to the BBC house? He was unsure. He recalled the kiss and the taste of lipstick. He remembered that but not much more. He would have to ask Mariscal.

'Mariscal.'

William wished Mariscal had not asked so many questions, and he wished he hadn't answered so many. That part of the evening was reasonably clear: Rob firing questions at William and William answering every one, high on booze but also on the attention.

Rob had been so enthusiastic about his story. 'Could be your biggest scoop yet!' He had implored him to take his time and get the Jabar story absolutely right; had offered, repeatedly, to help. In the old days Rob had never really been one for detail. But last night he had obsessed over the smallest component of the story. Why? Perhaps becoming editor had made him more punctilious. It was possible.

Carver's gut rumbled. He needed food. Food and some painkillers.

Mariscal was already in the small kitchen, standing over the stove, stirring at something in a saucepan. He grinned knowingly at William, removed the pan from the heat, and held it out for him to look at. 'Scrambled eggs. You still like those, don't you?'

William nodded.

'Good. There's naff all else.'

William removed his glasses and rubbed his eyes; the kitchen was bright and this seemed to be making his headache worse. 'I'm surprised you found anything. I haven't bought any food. Where'd you find eggs?'

Mariscal gestured to the fridge. 'Big Tupperware box in there. Found some fresh bread, too. We're in business.'

'That'll be the Tupperware box with Brandon's name written on it.'

'That's the one.'

Carver looked his watch. 'We better eat this quick, then. He's usually up by now.'

Rob smiled. 'I wouldn't worry. Don't you remember seeing him last night? He was in a worse state than you.'

William tried again to dredge up details of the journey back from the club. Nothing.

'He rolled in about the same time as us. Hammered. His producer, or wife or whoever she is, was having to hold him upright. He kept shouting names at us. It was funny. "Musharraf, Bhutto, Zardari." Pakistani presidents past and present. I don't think he'll be up for a while. I'm surprised you are, to be honest.' Mariscal spooned a pile of scrambled egg on to two pieces of white buttered toast and put it down on the small Formica table, along with a fork. 'There you go. Tea's on the way.'

He cracked three more eggs into the saucepan and mixed these with milk while the kettle boiled. Once it had, he made William a mug of strong tea and stirred in three sugars. 'How're you feeling?'

'Bad.'

Rob reached into his back pocket and pulled out a brightly coloured cardboard box. 'Try these.' He tossed the box on to the table alongside William's food. On the front was a cartoon drawing of an oblong pill with arms, legs and a smiling face. A speech bubble attached to it read *I kill pain* in several different languages. 'They're Lucia's. She's had a headache for most of the last ten years. They're Italian, triple strength or something . . . illegal in most of the rest of Europe.'

This was a good enough recommendation for William. He popped two of the pills from their foil and plastic strip and swallowed them with a mouthful of sugary tea.

'You only need to take the one.'

William held up his mug. 'Too late.'

Mariscal shrugged. 'Oh well. Guess that'll take care of your next hangover, too.'

'Never again.'

William looked at his breakfast. The hot scrambled egg was melting the butter, softening the white toast. As he lifted his fork he felt a wave of gratitude wash over him. 'Remind me what you're doing today, Rob? Seeing the Ambassador, is it?'

'Yes. Due there in—' Rob looked at his watch. 'About an hour.'

'You better make a move.'

'No need. They're sending a car.'

'Really? You're getting all the VIP treatment, aren't you?'

'It's about time I got some of that. So how about this for a plan: I meet the Ambo, get the latest on what they're doing to find Karim and Patrick, chivvy them along and come back and run all that by you around lunchtime.'

William nodded, his mouth too full of food to form words.

'Then I thought we could run through the Fazil Jabar story properly, beginning to end. Maybe I could have a look at the wedding video?'

Carver looked up from his plate, finished chewing, then swallowed. 'I've watched it a hundred times already.'

'Yeah, but you never know, fresh pair of eyes and all that. Worth a try?'

'Guess so. Is there any more of this?' He gestured to his now empty plate. Rob was about to transfer some food from his own plate to William's when they were interrupted by a sudden, frantic shouting from the reception next door.

'Quick, everybody get out. *Out now!*' It was a woman's voice and when Mariscal and William turned to look, they saw Brandon's wife, her thin face contorted by panic, staring at them from the doorway.

'A man in a motorcycle helmet just dropped a box on the desk. I tried to talk to him and he just ran off. It looks like a big bloody parcel bomb! We've got to get everyone out—'

Mariscal raised a hand. 'Okay, we'll help.'

'I've woken some people, but John's upstairs and he's out cold! I don't think I can move him; can you two try?'

Mariscal looked at the woman. He knew her name but couldn't place it. It began with a T. Tracey, Terri? Barefoot and wearing only a white cotton nightdress, she had a small pot belly, he now noticed. Pregnant, perhaps. ''Course, I'll go up and get him. You run outside with William. You okay with that, William?'

'Sure. Hold on a sec—' Carver slung the laptop case over his shoulder and reached across for Rob's plate of scrambled eggs.

The woman stared at the plate. 'You're bringing that?'

'Might as well.' With his free hand he took the woman's elbow and led her out through reception. The brown package was sitting on the counter. Carver hadn't seen one before, but he guessed that this could be what a parcel bomb looked like. As he walked past, he leant closer and saw his name written in thick black marker pen on the side of the box. He shrugged.

The door to Brandon's room had been left ajar. Rob walked in and saw the legend lying sprawled face down in the centre of the bed. He shook his shoulder for a while, and then his head, before taking his ear between thumb and index finger and pinching it hard. Nothing. Rob then noticed the empty glass jug on Brandon's bedside table. He went and filled it with cold water from the bathroom tap before returning and pouring it slowly over the television presenter's head. This worked.

'What the— Who— What're you doing here? Where's Tanya?'

That was it: Tanya.

'She's downstairs, John. It looks like there might be a bomb in reception; we're clearing the place.' Once he'd processed this news, Brandon moved quickly; he shuffled from the bed and then staggered from the room wearing only his pyjamas and still dripping water. Rob followed but then paused in the doorway. Rather than heading down the stairs and out of the building, he climbed another floor, in the direction of his own bedroom. Once inside he closed the door and looked around, temporarily unable to recall why he needed to be there. He saw the A4 notebook by the side of his bed and remembered that was it, he'd stayed up late making notes based on everything William had told him about Jabar. He looked at the notes now, a mess of arrows, underlinings and large scrawled question marks next to the parts of the story that needed more detail or clarification.

He flicked through the pages. Was he going to simply give this to Roydon? Or talk him through it? Write all the information back down in clear capitals, perhaps, and hand it over in return for his thirty pieces of silver. Yes, he realised, he probably was. He sat down heavily on the unmade bed and put his head in his hands. Outside, he could hear commotion, people making their way out of the BBC house and into the street. Rob was in no hurry to follow them.

This would be better, this would be perfect, he thought. A heroic act, a huge explosion. Much better this than a mysterious fall from the roof. How would the story go? He'd gone upstairs to help rescue a colleague . . . the famous John Brandon. Having saved this household name, he'd taken a brief detour to get something from his room. Stupid, but lots of people do it.

While he was in his room, on the way back out of the door in fact, the bomb had gone off, killed him instantly. Instantly and hopefully painlessly, he thought. He looked around. The walls and ceiling of this dreadful little room would be redecorated with his blood and gore. How would they know it was him? Dental records. That's right. Rob had always rather liked that idea, the thought that all he would leave behind were a few teeth and some silver fillings. That was a proper disappearing act, erasing yourself in some style. He stood and walked towards the window. Stopped and waited. He shifted his weight from one foot to the other and then back again, and closed his eyes. The house was now silent, the only sounds came from outside – police sirens inevitably heading his way. This bomb had better do its thing quick or the disposal boys would be on it.

Still nothing. Nothing at all. He heaved a sigh and opened his eyes, walked back to the door and out, closing it slowly behind him. Mariscal strolled out of the BBC building into the morning sunlight, his fate back in his own hands. Shame.

William was standing with an empty plate in one hand and a laptop bag in the other.

'What took you so long? I thought I was going to have to come back in and get you.'

'But you didn't, I notice.'

William shuffled his feet. 'No need, was there? There's no bomb in there, I can feel it in my gut.'

'What is it, then? Fan mail? It's got your name written on it.'

'Yeah, I saw that.'

'Has someone called the cops?'

'Yep and Brandon called the Army press bloke, Remora, direct. I'm sure he'll be here any minute with the whole bloody cavalry.'

Tanya was standing a good fifty feet from the front of the BBC house, surrounded by colleagues who were listening to her attentively. Brandon cast a long shadow and she'd been standing in it for some time; she was enjoying telling people what she'd seen.

'It looked so suspicious. I was coming through reception, on the way to get John's breakfast, and I saw this bloke jump out of an SUV, right outside. He was in a car but he was wearing a motorcycle helmet and what looked like army gear. He was carrying that big box out in front of him . . .' She gestured in the direction of the BBC house. 'He pushed the door open, plonked it down on the counter and walked straight back out.'

The sound of sirens drew closer and a small convoy of vehicles turned into their street, sending dust billowing up behind. Remora had brought some Afghan police as well as a British Army bomb disposal unit. The unit included four men with a variety of hand-held electronic devices and two sniffer dogs. The Afghan police cordoned off the house and moved the journalists and onlookers back a little further, while the bomb disposal unit went about their business.

They had been waiting on the street for about an hour when Remora came and found William. The Captain looked pale. 'Will you come with me, please, Mr Carver.' There was no explanation, and unusual civility.

Mariscal and Carver could feel the eyes of their colleagues on them as they followed Captain Remora back into the house. The parcel was sitting in exactly the same position as before, but now it was open at the top and several incisions had been made to one of the sides. Two of the army explosives experts were sitting on the staircase, talking quietly, their green helmets with long visors held in their laps. They stopped speaking when they saw the two journalists. Remora looked at William as if he had something he wanted to say. He opened his mouth and then thought better of it. Instead he signalled to the two officers, who stood reluctantly and walked back over to the box. One reached in and removed an envelope, unopened, with William's name on it. He handed it to Carver. Then he reached in again, his colleague holding back the flaps of the box, and lifted out a plastic carrier bag. The handles of the bag were stretching with the weight. He placed the bag gently on the floor and looked at Captain Remora, who nodded. The soldier rolled the sides of the carrier bag down, and stepped back.

The severed head had been wrapped tightly inside several black plastic bags and secured with brown tape, but an incision at the top revealed a glimpse of black bloodied hair and forehead. William pushed past Rob and stumbled to the front door, where he fell on his knees. He vomited a viscous mess of digested egg, toast and warm tea on to the street outside. When he returned, and after a short discussion, it was agreed that the officer would cut the bag open just enough to allow identity to be established. The officer pulled the black plastic away from the top of the head so that he could cut it cleanly. This done, he took a scalpel and cut the plastic, pulling it back until most of the face was visible.

Captain Remora took a handkerchief from his pocket and wiped the blood from Karim's face. William took the briefest possible look. While cleaning his face, Remora had closed Karim's eyes but his broken mouth remained slightly open.

Some of the many dead faces William had seen over the years had appeared peaceful. But not Karim. Karim looked young and scared. Carver turned away. When he tried to speak his voice broke but he continued, determined to finish his sentence. 'That is—that is Karim Mumtaz. He is—he was, my translator.'

William walked across the reception and back upstairs to his bedroom. He would give the envelope to the military police soon enough, but he wanted to look at it first. He closed his door and sat on the bed, turning the letter in his hand before carefully opening it. Inside, on white copier paper, there were a few lines of English written in careful capital letters.

WILLIAM. I HAVE TOLD THEM ALL I KNOW ABOUT THE KILLING OF FAZIL JABAR BUT THEY WANT MORE AND SO THEY WANT TO MEET YOU. IF YOU REFUSE OR LEAVE THE COUNTRY THEY SAY THEY WILL KILL ME THE SAME WAY THEY KILLED KARIM. THEY WILL CONTACT YOU SOON. PLEASE HELP THEM. I DO NOT WANT TO DIE.

William read it several times before transcribing the words into his notebook. Opening his bedroom door, he saw Mariscal coming up the hall. 'I was bringing this back.' He handed Rob the letter.

'Can you give it to Remora? Tell him I only touched the edges of the envelope and paper.'

'Sure.'

'Thanks. And Rob, when you see the Ambassador, can you ask if I could talk to him too, some time soon?'

'What else can I do?'

'Nothing. I need to lie down, just for a while. Then I need to try and find Karim's family.'

Carver closed his bedroom door. He stowed his laptop under his pillow and took a bottle of sleeping pills from a drawer in the bedside table. He made a brief tally of the drugs he already had in his system: two anti-depressants, two painkillers, a fair amount of alcohol. That was all, and most of that he'd probably puked up downstairs. He shook out a handful of sleeping pills, no more than three or four, and tipped them on to his tongue. He found the Maker's Mark under the bed, uncorked it and took a swallow.

30 Diplomatic vs Kinetic

DATELINE: British Embassy, Kabul, Afghanistan, July 8th

Mariscal's cab nosed slowly towards the black metal gates of the Embassy and stopped. The sentry box was empty and the gates locked. The driver kept the car engine running and waited, tapping his fingers impatiently on the steering wheel and glancing regularly in his rear-view mirror. Rob remembered that the British Embassy had been targeted by suicide bombers twice in three years; the driver didn't want to hang around. After a few moments he turned in his seat and gave Rob a questioning look. Rob shrugged. He wasn't happy to be dropped outside a locked embassy and left there. The driver checked his watch, tutted and then muttered something in Arabic just as two Gurkha guards appeared from behind their sentry post. Then Rob noticed Roydon walking towards them across the yellowed lawn. He carried a bulky-looking black sports holdall and was wearing a light grey suit and a thin tie. Raising a free hand, he waved in Rob's direction, beckoning him from the car. Rob shuffled across the back seat and climbed out of the cab. The mid-morning heat hit him full in the face and he immediately felt a prickle of sweat at the back of his neck. His hangover had turned nasty in the last hour and it seemed that his headache was beyond the reach of even Lucia's painkillers.

He reached into the pocket of his black suit and found his wallet, while Roydon looked on. Rob took out two Afghani notes and was about to hand them to the driver, when Roydon intervened: 'One of those is plenty.' The cabbie took the money and flung a dark look at Roydon before putting his car into reverse. Rob looked through the gates and down the gravel drive towards the Ambassador's residence. It was a modest-looking villa flanked by thin strips of lawn. Off to the right, a Union Jack hung limply from a white-painted pole.

Roydon leant in close. 'I heard what happened to the Afghan kid. Nasty. You all right?' He had no real interest, you could hear it in the question.

'I'm fine.'

'Good. Be grateful it wasn't your boy Reid. So I thought we'd have a little chat on our own, before we bother the Ambassador,' Roydon said. 'Let's take a walk.'

Rob looked down the street. It was deserted. Roydon sensed his unease. 'Don't worry. Safe as houses round here and these two will keep an eye on us.' He nodded towards the Gurkhas. 'Ugly little fuckers but as hard as nails, aren't you boys?' They smiled thin, cold smiles. Roydon set off down the road, swinging the sports bag at his side. 'Gurkha versus Mossad . . . Who d'you reckon is gonna win that?' Rob shook his head. 'Most people would go Mossad. Mossad versus anyone and most blokes would say Mossad, but I'm not so sure. Tricky fuckers, Gurkhas – clever, and difficult to kill. Robust. Is that the word?' Roydon looked at Mariscal. This question required an answer.

'Er, robust, yeah. Or durable?'

'Durable. Durable. That's the one. You are the man for the right word, aren't you. Gurkhas are durable. Mossad are flash but maybe a bit flash in the pan with it.' Roydon switched the holdall from one hand to the other. It brushed at Rob's leg.

'What have you got in there?'

'Odds and sods. So, tell me about last night. Had a good time, did you? Get your dick wet?'

'No, it wasn't that kind of place.'

'Ah . . . Shame. My bloke said it looked a bit boring. Mainly for locals and politicians, I've heard. I know somewhere you'd like better. I'll take you there, once all this is over. My treat.'

'Great,' Rob mumbled.

'You'll like it. This old bird runs it, real hospitable. She's got about a dozen girls in there. She calls them her daughters. No sign of a father, but I guess that's no surprise; imagine being dad to a house full of whores. You'd die of shame.'

Rob wondered briefly whether it was possible to die of shame.

'There's a girl down there, the youngest one, skinny like a rake. There's nothing she won't do for twenty dollars. Or if there is, I haven't thought of it yet.' The two men reached a junction and Roydon paused. He turned to Mariscal. 'So, what does Carver know?'

Rob sighed. It was time for him to perform. 'William's got some pictures of you outside the tailor's shop just before the blast. He's got your name in the appointments book. He's got a post-mortem that says Jabar was killed by a bullet fired from close range and a recording of a gunshot that some army expert he knows says is a Sig.' Rob glanced sideways at Roydon. 'I take it you've got a gun like that?'

Roydon cocked his head. 'I might do, but he'd need a bullet for that to be a problem and I don't think he's got one of those, has he?'

Rob nodded reluctantly. 'No, he hasn't'

'Well then, no big deal.'

'Then he's got a load of documents on Aftel. Something that

links Aftel with Rook Security . . . That's where he thinks *you* come in, though he's not sure.'

'Good, the longer he's not sure, the better for us.'

Rob looked again at the man and wondered who the *us* Roydon referred to really was.

'And he's got Aftel accounts and company reports, that kind of thing. Someone in London's been helping him. He wouldn't tell me much about his contact but he reckons he might persuade him to go on the record.'

Roydon smiled. 'I think he'll find that tricky.' He slowed his pace. 'So where's he got all this stuff? The snaps of me and all the rest? Has he been sending it back to the office, someone else at BBC HQ?'

'I doubt it. William's not exactly a team player. It's all on his laptop, which never leaves his bloody side.'

'So everything's in the one place, Carver's computer?'

'Two places. That's good practice and he's a good journalist. He's got duplicates of everything on Patrick's laptop too. That was William's idea of a backup.'

'Reid has copies, too?'

'Yes.'

Roydon stopped and gazed back along the street. He bent, untied, then retied his shoelace. He took his time, chewing the new information over. 'That's annoying. There's a chance Carver suspects you, isn't there? In which case he might be bullshitting. Laying a false trail. What do you think?'

'He trusts me.'

Roydon gave an ugly laugh. 'Yeah? Better journalist than a judge of character, then, isn't he?'

They walked back to the Embassy gates. Rob's head was pounding. 'I need to get out of this sun.'

Roydon smiled. 'Sure, we'll get inside. That's good work, Rob, comprehensive. I'm proud of you.'

Mariscal looked away. A heat haze rose from the yellow road. 'Thanks. So do I get my bag of silver now or later?'

'Don't be melodramatic Rob, doesn't suit you. So that's everything is it? That's all Carver told you?'

Mariscal paused. 'I think so. That's all he's got that's solid. But he's got a load of unanswered questions. The thing he's really hung up on is the tailor, Mr Savi.'

Roydon's face shaped itself into something like confusion. 'What do you mean?'

'He doesn't know what happened to Savi. His corpse didn't arrive at the mortuary with the other bodies. Seems like the tailor just disappeared.'

Roydon scratched at his chin. 'Probably the blast did for him. Pound to a penny the Afghan ambulance boys just dropped whatever was left straight in the incinerator. Let's get you inside mate, you look like you're melting. I'll introduce you to the Ambassador and then I need to make a quick call.'

The Gurkha guards unlocked a large padlock, removed the thick steel chain, and pulled the Embassy gates open just sufficiently for Roydon and Mariscal to walk in, relocking again straight afterwards. The two men walked up the dusty drive. On the wall beside the door was a shiny brass plate announcing this to be Her Majesty's small corner of Kabul. Roydon rapped his knuckle on the door and within a minute it was answered by the Ambassador himself. He nodded briefly at Roydon and smiled at Rob.

'Good morning. Mr Mariscal, I assume?' The Ambassador's hand was cold and dry, his handshake firm.

'Yes, sir.'

'A pleasure, please, come in.' He stepped to one side to let his visitors pass. Lever wore a cream suit and white shirt. His sandy-coloured hair was thinning but carefully combed. The Ambassador ushered the men down a long hall, and as he walked, Mariscal glanced left and right at an array of gold-framed oil paintings crammed closely together along both walls. Lever noticed Rob's interest. 'Please excuse those dreadful paintings, Mr Mariscal. They're the pictures the bureaucrats who look after the Government Art Collection saw fit to send me,' he explained. 'I have to put them somewhere; I hang them in the hall so I don't have to look at them for any length of time. Dark and dreary little English landscapes, every one. The best that can be said for them, Mr Mariscal, is that they help keep homesickness at bay.' Lever stopped and waved a finger at the nearest picture. Through the oily gloom, Rob could just about make out a water mill and alongside that, a wisteria-clad cottage. 'Stick a representation of my ex-wife in the foreground there, and I'd never want to see England again.' They moved through the hall and turned right, into a small library. The Ambassador led them on through a dimly lit dining room to the rear of the residence, where he pulled aside some heavy curtains, drenching the room in light and revealing French windows overlooking a surprisingly verdant garden.

Lever put his shoulder to the door, shoved it open and walked out. Rob followed. Stepping into the light, he felt he'd been transported. Kabul was gone, and in its place the sort of view one might expect to find when staying at a good English country house hotel. There was a flagstone patio, cast-iron garden furniture painted glossy white with green candy-striped cushions, and a blue Spode tea service set for three. Out beyond the flagstones were a series of raised flower beds planted with a variety of different tulips and, in front of these, a green lawn that was being watered by a complicated arrangement of sprinklers.

Mariscal toed the edge of the grass and gave an appreciative nod. 'It's a beautiful garden. Must be a lot of work for someone.' He felt the Ambassador arrive at his side.

'Isn't it? Magnificent. I can take none of the credit. It's all Mrs Ansari's good work. She's my housekeeper.'

Roydon, who had wandered away to make his phone call, now

reappeared and stepped in between the two men, draping an arm around each. Rob felt Lever bristle and pull away. Roydon ignored this and used the free hand to point towards the centre of the lawn. 'It's a bloody waste of good space, if you ask me. You could fit a decent-sized helipad in there, no bother.'

Lever did his best to ignore Roydon. He turned to Mariscal. 'Those raised flower beds are built up around old ammunition boxes, the compost is made from shredded Embassy documents, among other things. The garden is a peaceful place, don't you think? Maybe the most peaceful place in Kabul.'

Rob noticed a churned-up patch of rich red ground at the side of the house. 'Vegetables as well?'

Lever smiled broadly. 'Oh yes. And fruit. Mainly melons and squash. We were just putting up some new netting this morning. Mrs Ansari is at war with the local hedgehogs. They decimated her last little crop. Absolute beasts. She'll win though, she'll win.' He shepherded the two men to the table. Rob took a seat and his host set about pouring the tea. Roydon sat too, and reaching into his holdall pulled out a half-bottle of whisky.

'How about a sharpener before we get started on the tea?'

The Ambassador shot him a disapproving look. 'It's a little early for me, thank you.'

'It's never too early for a good glass of whisky, Ambassador. Mr Mariscal has already had to unwrap a decapitated head this morning; a stiff drink's exactly what he needs. And this is Jameson's. Rob likes Jameson's, don't you, Rob?'

Mariscal was having difficulty understanding the relationship between these two men, but it seemed obvious who was in control. Both men were waiting on his response. He wanted the drink, but he didn't want to offend his host. 'A cup of tea first, and perhaps a whisky to follow? Thank you. It has been a difficult day.'

Lever sighed, chiding himself. 'It must have been dreadful. I apologise, I should have suggested a drink myself. How is

Mr Carver holding up? I gather that he and his translator were close?'

'He's badly shaken by it, I think, Ambassador. He went straight to his room. I get the impression he was as close to Karim as he gets to anyone these days.'

'I understand.'

'He'd like to see you again, Ambassador, if that's okay? After he's had some rest.'

'I'll ask Mrs Ansari to contact him and arrange that.'

Rob was aware of Roydon shifting uncomfortably in his seat while listening to this, but he kept his counsel. Lever rang the small silver dinner bell that sat alongside the teapot, and in moments an attractive, middle-aged Afghan woman appeared at the French windows wearing a shameez in the same cream colour as the Ambassador's suit.

'Sir?'

'Mrs Ansari. This is Mr Mariscal, from the BBC, and of course you know Mr Roydon.'

The woman dipped her head to acknowledge the two men but said nothing.

'Mr Roydon has brought us some whisky and we thought we might have a glass after we've had your tea. Would you be kind enough to pour some for us, with water and ice?'

Roydon held the bottle out for the housekeeper, but when she tried to take it from him, he kept his grip. An uncomfortable tug-of-war ensued until Roydon suddenly let go of the bottle. Mrs Ansari lost her balance and had to take a step back to steady herself. It was a nasty little game which amused no one apart from Roydon, who laughed loudly. He removed his jacket and hung it carefully over the back of his seat, loosened his tie and rolled up the sleeves of his shirt before pouring himself a cup of milky tea. As he did this, Rob stared at his arms. There was the blurred blue tattoo, the corner of which he'd noticed before, and – more striking still — what looked like a series of puncture marks in the fleshy part of the forearm just below the elbow. The scar tissue formed star shapes, lighter in colour than the freckled and sun-darkened skin around it.

Roydon saw Rob staring. 'Three shots from an AK. One bullet went right through.' He pointed out the entry and exit wounds. 'One I dug out with a bowie knife and the third's still in there. A keepsake. I took half a dozen more in the chest but the flak jacket stopped the lot.'

'Lucky.'

Roydon deposited three heaped teaspoons of sugar into his cup and stirred vigorously. 'Luckier than the kid who did the shooting. I emptied two cartridges into him. When I'd finished, he looked like steak tartare.'

The Ambassador cleared his throat in a manner clearly meant to bring his guests to attention. 'Mr Mariscal, before we begin I'd just like to clarify your role here.'

Rob turned his teacup in its saucer. He spoke carefully. 'I'm here to represent the BBC and to help in any way I can to secure the safe return of Patrick Reid.'

Lever nodded. 'Yes, that I understand. But Mr Roydon tells me that you're slightly more—how can I put it? Involved.'

Rob sighed. He suddenly felt very tired. 'Yes, yes I suppose so. I've been asked by Mr Roydon and others in London to find out about William's investigation into the death of Fazil Jabar. I understand that Carver is caught up in something which has national security implications.'

Roydon dropped his cup down a little too hard on the saucer. 'Caught up? He's put himself in the middle of all this. No one's asked him to stick his nose in.'

Lever held his hand up to silence Roydon, and to Rob's surprise, it worked. The Ambassador folded his hands together and placed them on the table. He leant towards Rob and lowered his voice.

'Fazil Jabar was not a good man, Mr Mariscal. He was corrupt. He had deep Taliban connections. Not just sympathies, you understand? He was an important Taliban ally. He was one of the bad guys. There's no question of that.' Lever glanced over his shoulder. There was no one there. 'The operation to remove Jabar was badly handled.'

Rob felt Roydon shift again in his seat, but the man stayed silent and let Lever tell it his way.

'A number of things went wrong. But that doesn't mean that the aims and objectives of the operation were wrong. Fazil Jabar was an obstacle between where we are now and a better Afghanistan. A perfectly legitimate target. Do you understand?'

Mariscal nodded.

'And you also understand that nothing about this can be broadcast or printed or even hinted at. At least for now. There's too much at stake.'

The Ambassador waited for Rob's reply. Mariscal stared into his teacup. There were a few loose leaves swilling around at the bottom, but they told him nothing.

Roydon reached over and gave Rob's shoulder an affectionate shake. 'He understands. We're at war. Patriotism trumps journalism at a time like this. Ain't that right, Rob?'

'Yes, yes. I understand.'

Mrs Ansari arrived with the whisky. She hooked a few loose strands of hair behind her ear and poured the drink carefully from a decanter into three heavy crystal glasses, which she handed to the men.

Roydon held his glass up to the light and examined it. 'The tide's a little far out on this one, darling. Top it up for me, will you?'

The Ambassador's housekeeper did as requested. Lever waited for Mrs Ansari to withdraw before raising his drink in his guests' direction. For a moment the men paused, anticipating a toast of some sort, but no one could think of anything to toast and so they just drank. Rob felt the alcohol burn at the back of his throat and then a wave of warmth and sweet relief as the whisky reached his stomach and began to journey through his bloodstream. They sat in silence for a time. Lever refilled the whisky glasses, pouring Rob a full finger more than Roydon or himself. He spoke a little more forcefully now.

'Let me tell you what my own position is, Mr Mariscal. As far as I'm concerned, Patrick Reid is the number one priority. My job is to get him back, *sospes*.'

A look of confusion clouded Mariscal's face. '*Sospes*. Have you forgotten your Latin? Safe and sound. Our objective is the return of Patrick Reid, safe and sound and soon as.'

Lever reached into the pocket of his cream jacket and pulled out a piece of A4 paper folded into four. He flattened it out on the table in front of him and Rob saw that it was a photocopy of the note that had been delivered that morning to the BBC house, together with Karim's severed head. The words were upside down from where Rob sat, but he had no trouble reading what was written. There was a light breeze blowing now, not enough to bring any relief from the heat but enough to lift the corners of the photocopied note. The Ambassador placed the decanter in the middle of the paper to hold it firm and sat back in his chair. 'We have this, so at least we're not flying blind any more. We know what the kidnappers want. A rendezvous with William Carver. A meeting.'

Mariscal sat forward in his seat. 'With a view to what? Some sort of prisoner exchange, you think?'

Lever shook his head. 'It doesn't say that. Just a conversation. And I don't see what they gain from swapping William for Patrick. One western hostage is as good as any other, I would think, if it was hostage-taking and ransom money they were interested in.'

Roydon stirred. 'The Taliban don't take Brits for ransom. They take them to top them. Every time.'

'Well, regardless of whether that's true or not, we won't pay a ransom. It's out of the question. But there are other things that might be tried, other deals that could be done. At present it seems like the only way to secure Patrick's safety is by putting William Carver in harm's way. I'm reluctant to do that, at least until we've explored every other option.'

Rob could feel Roydon's growing unease. 'What are you talking about? There are no other options.'

'There are always options, Mr Roydon. And that's why we're here, to talk them through.'

'That's not why I'm here. I don't see that there's anything to talk about. It's simple. We wait for them to get in touch. Agree to the meeting. We go in, get your bloke back, and kick the living shit out of the other lot. Simple.'

Lever pushed the decanter aside and picked up the photocopied piece of paper again. 'Mr Roydon, you know as well as I do that we have a rather bad track record with that kind of thing. It's highly dangerous. The kidnappers get killed, sure, but more often than not, so do the hostages, and that's the last thing we want.'

Roydon put a finger to his collar, a nervous gesture which Rob remembered seeing once before.

Lever put the note back in his pocket. 'I'd like to explore diplomatic solutions before you resort to kinetics.'

'There are no diplomatic solutions. We're running out of bloody time.'

'There's enough time for us at least to explore dialogue, Roydon. Make overtures.'

'Fine. Fucking fine.' Roydon necked his whisky and slammed the glass back down. 'Make your overtures. Sing them a fucking opera, if you like. But make it quick, because when that doesn't work, I'll need to agree the meeting, get a special forces operation together and go rescue your bloke.'

The Ambassador folded his arms. 'It's agreed, then.'

Roydon looked darkly at Lever, a flicker of a smile on his lips. 'What are you doing here, Ambassador? In Kabul, I mean? Given that you obviously hate war so much. Why not Paris or Washington or Rome?' He gave Lever no time to answer. 'I guess you just weren't good enough for any of those jobs, were you? Didn't have the right stuff. And now you're here, you want to stay. You want to be left alone to enjoy your pretty little garden and a nice bit of Afghan gash.'

Lever was surprisingly quick to his feet. He stood, took a step around Rob and slapped Roydon hard across the cheek. It was such an old-fashioned gesture that Mariscal had to try hard not to smile at the sight of it. Roydon, too, appeared to find it funny. He grinned as he rubbed his slightly reddened cheek, but his eyes were colder than ever.

'I apologise, Ambassador. Well out of order. Maybe you were right – a bit early for whisky.'

31 Harvard

DATELINE: Hindu Kush, Afghanistan, July 8th

Patrick was under guard and locked inside a room close to Doushki's chambers. Men delivered three meals a day, but since Karim's killing he could eat little. He was losing weight fast. The General's daughter, Noor, visited him on the second evening of his captivity, bringing with her a pile of clothes. She wore a headscarf but no veil. She stood in the doorway a while and stared at Patrick as though deciding whether to enter. Her eyes were a dark amber but as she moved closer their colour seemed changed with the light.

She gave him an even look. 'You are beginning to smell. If you wear these clothes then I will wash the others. I guessed your size. I think you are more my size than my father's.'

Patrick looked suspiciously at the folded shirts and trousers she was holding out in front of her. 'Women's clothes?'

'I wear them for hunting. They will not make you look like a woman.'

The following evening she came again, this time bringing with her a small portable black-and-white television. When she plugged it in to the long extension cable she dragged with her, the single light bulb that lit the room dimmed. They sat in near silence watching what Noor explained was a battle between two Afghan poets trying to out-verse each other. In the gaps between these mysterious contests were adverts, several of them of English or American origin but dubbed into Dari. Patrick noticed that Noor paid closer attention to the ad breaks than to the programmes they interrupted, and that she was monitoring Patrick's reaction to them too. During a breakfast cereal commercial she pointed at the small screen. 'My father will send me to America, to college. Have you travelled to America?'

Patrick nodded. 'Yes, a few times. New York, Washington, up and down the West Coast. Never into the middle, the Mid West.' He spoke quietly, not yet sure how to deal with his visitor, though her presence calmed him.

'I will go to Harvard. It is on the coast of America?'

'The East Coast. That's right. That's the best place to go. I mean, it's got a good reputation. I've not been there.'

Noor nodded, as though he had said something extremely wise. 'In America, I will be fat.'

Patrick frowned. 'Fat? Well, only if you end up living on junk food. They do have salads in America, you don't have to eat hamburgers. I'm sorry, I don't really understand.'

Noor shook her head. 'No. I mean that I see American girls in magazines, on American television. In America I will look fat.'

Patrick smiled. 'Oh, I see. No, you don't have to worry about that. All those girls on television are too thin, or ill. Anorexic? In America you will be, you know, exotic? Beautiful.' He reddened. Noor examined him for signs of sarcasm or insincerity but found none. 'You'll have to beat the boys away with a stick,' he added.

'I do not understand.'

'It's a turn of phrase . . . A thing people say. My mother used to say it to me when I was a teenager, whenever I was going out for the night. She'd say I was so handsome that I'd have to beat the girls away with a stick.' Patrick felt his eyes start to sting. Thinking about his mother, his home, was not a good idea. 'It wasn't true in my case, but it is in yours. You'll be beating American boys away with a stick.'

Noor seemed sceptical. 'My father is going to give me a gun.'

Patrick laughed. 'Fine, that'll work too.'

32 Dying Breeds

DATELINE: BBC house, Kabul, Afghanistan, July 8th

William woke late and with a sore head but also a sense of purpose. It was past seven and the sky outside was darkening fast. By the time he read the text saying that the Ambassador could meet him that evening it was too late and he had already decided that there was something else he needed to do first. He had been too passive for too long. Karim deserved better.

He phoned the Embassy residence and left a message on the answerphone saying he would like to visit the next day, whenever was convenient for the Ambassador but not before eleven in the morning. His second call was to London. The duty editor in charge at *Today* accepted his offer of a morning two-way on the killing of Karim without hesitation.

'How does seven o nine sound?'

'Fine, I'll get the line-up for a quarter to.'

He spent the rest of the evening making notes for the interview; he was determined this would be a fitting tribute to his translator.

*   *   *

The next morning William woke early, ate what was for him a decent breakfast and headed up to the roof of the BBC house with his broadcasting equipment and plenty of time to spare. He unpacked the black plastic flight case, removing the protective foam and lifting the satellite out with both hands and great care. On the back of the sat were printed the words *World Communicator* and indeed this kit had travelled the world with Carver – he'd had it for five years and dragged it across several continents. The satellite itself was not the shiny white dish that many assumed, but instead three leaves of ugly grey plastic hinged one to the other and propped upright by a basic black stand. The World Communicator looked like an ugly grey tea tray, similar to the sort you have to try to eat a meal off if you're travelling economy. Carver unfolded the three leaves and pieced the kit together slowly, attaching the dish to its battery using the shoestring-thin wire, and then to his ISDN box and microphone. This done, he gazed up into the Afghan sky. It was not yet ten in the morning but already the sun was burning hot, which was not ideal as the heat radiating from that direction could sometimes interfere with the satellite's own radiation. He switched the dish on, turned it away from the sun and started moving it around, increasing the elevation and rotating it slowly, waiting for it to latch on to a decent signal. As he did this he whispered to the machine: 'Come on. Do your thing.'

There were four satellites to choose from, depending on where in the world you happened to be, but William knew that from this Kabul rooftop his best bet was either Atlantic East or Indian Ocean; he didn't have a compass on him, so he was having to use the less scientific technique of wiggling it around until it beeped. He stared up at the sky. Somewhere up there, approximately twenty-two thousand miles away, was a satellite which was going to bounce his voice, in crystal clear quality, from here to London. Buildings obviously had to be avoided, and thick trees, but there were also other, less predictable hazards. Clouds were a common problem and even birds; he had once been knocked off air by a huge and beautiful sweep of starlings, which had got in between him and the Atlantic West.

'Hello, this is London. You're through to Broadcasting House traffic. Who've I got?'

'Hello there Brenda.'

'Is that Billy Carver's voice I'm hearing?'

'It is.'

'Lovely! Long time, no hear. So what can I do for you today? Are you going live?'

'Yep. *Today* programme, seven o nine.'

'Ah, back sailing on the flagship, Billy, that's what I like to hear. Better make sure your line's good and solid, then, shouldn't we? Tell me about your breakfast.'

'Okay, Brenda, well this is me and for breakfast I had two toast and butter, one black coffee and four industrial-strength painkillers. How do I sound?'

'Not bad. Do me a favour, though, will you? Move that dish an inch clockwise.'

'Better?'

'No, that's worse. Move it two inches round the other way now.'

'Okay, how's that?'

'Clear as a bell. I think you're hitting that Indian Ocean satellite right on the nose.'

'Thanks, Brenda.'

'Pleasure. I'll plug you through, Billy. You go drop a few words in the ear of the nation like the man said.'

'I'll do my best.'

'Attaboy.'

Carver looked at his notes, adjusted his headphones and half listened to the news headlines that came just ahead of his slot. Before he knew it, it was time. He heard a deep Welsh voice read a tightened-up version of the cue he'd sent over last night, and then: 'Our own William Carver is in Kabul and joins us now . . .'

The text message Mrs Ansari had sent William suggested that he should come to the residence at five and stay for as long as he wished. She even offered to make up a guest room in case he decided to stay the night. He messaged back thanking her but saying that this would not be necessary. William arrived at five on the dot and she met him at the front door.

'Mr Carver. My sincere condolences.'

'Thank you, Mrs Ansari.'

'The Ambassador and I heard you on the radio today. What you said was very moving.'

She placed her hand beneath his arm as she led him to the library. A fire had been lit, more for comfort than heat, William assumed, because the day was still warm. The Ambassador was sitting in his preferred chair and on the low carved coffee table there were some thick-cut sandwiches, a bowl of sugared almonds and a full bottle of Scotch. Lever got quickly to his feet. 'Welcome, welcome. I didn't know whether you'd eaten. Nothing formal, I thought we could just sit here?'

William nodded. 'Thank you, Ambassador, and thank you for seeing me.'

'Not at all, Mr Carver, I'm just glad that you could make it. I was so very sorry when I heard the news about your translator, doubly so after I heard you talk about him on the radio today.' Lever took William's arm from Mrs Ansari. It seemed that Carver was a fragile thing, being passed from hand to hand. It was not unpleasant, and he allowed himself to be led to the chair opposite Lever's. The Ambassador waited for William to speak first.

'They sent a note – I guess you know? They say they want to meet with me.' William delivered his statements flatly.

'Yes, I heard. What do you want to do?'

'I don't know. I need to get hold of Karim's family first. Maybe you can help with that?'

Lever nodded. He patted at various trouser and blazer pockets before eventually finding a scrap of yellow notepaper. He flourished it in William's direction like the winning ticket in the church raffle. 'I had my people ask around. Had you heard Karim talk about this fellow—' he strained to read the name written on it '—Haroun Rashid?'

'Yes, I think so.'

'Good. He's an Afghan businessman, into all sorts of nefarious activities as far as we can tell, but broadly speaking, seems a decent chap. Karim taught him English. Mrs Ansari spoke to him and he's promised to get hold of Karim's family. His aunt died a couple of years back but he says there is some other family scattered around up north.'

'Thank you, that's very helpful.'

'It's nothing. What we *do* need to discuss is Patrick and this proposed meeting.'

'Yes.'

'What are you thinking?'

'Well. Nothing very complicated. I wait to hear when and where they want to meet, and I go. What choice is there?'

Lever paused for a long time before he spoke. 'Let's say you do that, you go, even if you tell them everything you know, everything they want to hear, it's more than likely they'll kill you anyway. You *and* Patrick. I fear that if I allow a meeting to happen, we'll end up losing both of you.'

Carver was crouched forwards in his seat, cupping his whisky in front of him with both hands. 'I know that's a risk.'

'It's more than a risk, it's the probable outcome.' The Ambassador stared at the top of William's head. 'I don't think you should give up on the usual channels. Not yet. I know this is a horrific, horrific thing, but in many ways it is still just a negotiating position. If we can open up a channel of communication with this group, then we can bargain.'

Carver looked up from his glass. 'Bargain with what? I thought the British government refused to pay ransoms. And anyway, they aren't asking for one.'

'There are other ways to bargain. If all this is about losing a contract, well, there are other contracts. Money need not be handed over. As such.'

'Ambassador,' William cut in, 'you told me before that you had some involvement in the Aftel bid.'

'A small involvement, yes, that's right.'

'Why? Why is the British Ambassador involved in something like that? I can see that losing a telecoms contract to a group of Afghan businessmen would be a threat to our vanity, but to our security? I don't get that. I can't understand why Aftel matters so much.'

Lever sighed. 'It's about commerce, Mr Carver. Commercial diplomacy.' He pinched at his forehead. 'You must have noticed. All the talk of UK plc? It's always been a part of what the Foreign Office does, but now it seems like it's almost all we do. Diplomatic missions like ours are judged in commercial terms. A good ambassador is an ambassador who can facilitate business, help land big contracts.' He took a gulp of his drink. 'Point delegations from the Confederation of British Industry in the right direction. Although quite a few of them just want to be pointed in the direction of the nearest, cleanest brothel. Dreadful.' The Ambassador winced.

'So don't do it.'

Lever gave a hollow laugh. 'It's not that easy, I'm afraid. If you want to stay in post, you get on board.'

'And you are that desperate to stay in post, in this post?'

The Ambassador looked away from his guest and into the fire. 'Afghanistan is a good posting for me, Mr Carver. For various reasons, reasons you might have guessed at. I cannot leave. I will not.' He pointed towards the coffee table, the sandwiches and William's empty plate. 'Please have something. Mrs Ansari will be upset if we don't at least try them.' Carver obliged. Roasted lamb, salted butter, fresh mint. 'Also, and I hope you won't consider this special pleading, but the Aftel bid had, has, a lot of good things going for it. If they win, it'll mean good, secure jobs, properly paid. For men and women alike. That sort of opportunity is a rare prize for people here.'

'I understand.'

'Religious freedom, too. Part of the bid is a promise to build a Christian chapel as well as a mosque—to encourage dialogue.'

William nodded. 'Now I see your influence, Ambassador. Don't you think this country has enough religion already?'

'No. Not enough religion, just too much of the wrong sort. Too much fundamentalism. Fundamentalism and ignorance, on both sides. We don't need less religion, we just need the right sort – tolerant and kind.' Carver was shaking his head. 'I know we will probably disagree on this, Mr Carver, but I've become convinced that you can't tackle extremism and fundamentalism with some bleak, soulless secularism.'

'No, better you fight it with a lie.'

There was a moment's silence. The sound of wood settling in the fire. Eventually Lever spoke. 'I don't believe that God is a lie. And I'm pretty sure you don't believe that, either. Even if He was and you decide to take Him away from people, what do you offer in His place? Doubt?'

'No, not doubt, truth. The sooner we diagnose religious belief as a neurosis, label it, treat it and get shot of it, the better things will be.'

Lever considered this position, then cleared his throat and spoke. 'Can I ask you a personal question, Mr Carver?'

William nodded.

'Can I ask again how you came to lose your faith?'

Carver shifted his weight back into the armchair. The ice in his drink had melted and he finished the now watery whisky with a grimace. 'I'll tell you *where* I lost my faith, Ambassador, then you'll probably be able to guess why. It took me a long, long time, but I think I finally gave up believing, once and for all, in Rwanda. During half a dozen visits there, and in the months afterwards. Some of the things I saw in Rwanda were the opposite of miracles. Healthy children disabled and made lame. Women raped and blinded. Farming communities chased off their land and left to starve.' William's eyes were shining now. 'And here's a funny thing, Ambassador – this might amuse you – the last proper theological discussion I had, until I met you, was with a thoughtful, intelligent Anglican bishop, back in Rwanda. I enjoyed our talks. It wasn't until later I found out he'd watched six hundred and fifty of his own flock being burnt to death, locked inside *his* church. The key to the padlock was in his pocket as he watched.'

Lever looked away. 'I understand.'

'Do you? Are you sure? In the last few years I've been to lots of places where God should've been, Ambassador. Places where he was desperately, urgently needed. But I never saw hide nor fucking hair of him.' William realised he'd spat these last words. When he looked up he saw Mrs Ansari standing in the doorway. 'I'm sorry.'

The woman waved the apology away. 'Do not be sorry.'

'In the end I decided to stop believing. Better no God than a callous, uncaring one.'

The Ambassador stood. He walked to the drinks table and refilled his glass. 'I understand, you've been let down by your interventionist God. But have you considered looking at it another way? Couldn't He be working through others? Through good men and women? The likes of Bonhöffer? Romero? Martin Luther King? There are countless, countless examples.'

Carver smiled. 'I see. Is that what you're doing here, Ambassador? Intervening in Afghanistan, doing God's good work because God isn't around?' Lever blushed red and put his glass down a little clumsily on the table in front of him. 'No, no. I would never, ever presume.'

William believed him. Whatever else the man in front of him might be, he was sincere. 'I know, I'm sorry. Again.' He checked his watch. 'I should go, Ambassador. It's late. I promise to call you, soon as I hear anything from Patrick's kidnappers.'

Lever looked a little shame-faced. 'I appreciate that. But I think it's only right to tell you, our people are already monitoring your mobile phone – all calls and messages, in and out.'

William nodded. He wasn't surprised and he felt too tired to feign outrage.

Lever pressed on, trying to stay positive. 'Let's wait for them to get in touch and then try and stall them, maybe we can negotiate. Whatever their next move is, I would rather find a way forward that doesn't put you in harm's way.'

William managed a smile. 'Okay.'

'What will you do between now and then, until the kidnappers get in touch?'

Carver sighed. 'Only thing I can do; keep working, keep plugging away at the story. Try to find the missing pieces of the jigsaw.'

'Will you do me a favour, Mr Carver? Have one more, quick drink before you go . . . Please.' Lever poured a splash of whisky into both their glasses. 'I have a toast.'

'A toast? Okay.'

'To our dreadful bloody jobs. I've enjoyed our conversations, Mr Carver, I really have. I think if it weren't for our respective jobs we might have got along very well. Don't you think?'

There was a dull clunk as their glasses came together and William looked at Lever. 'Hacks and diplomats can't be friends, is that it?'

'I fear not. Maybe in the future, but we are dying breeds, the two of us. It's my job to be loyal, loyal even to wrong-headed policies and ambitious politicians. It's your job to ask awkward questions, uncover uncomfortable truths. That's where things get tricky for us.'

A Land Rover carrying Richard Roydon and a second man waited on the street outside the Embassy with its lights and engine off until half an hour after Carver's cab had gone. Eventually Roydon spoke. 'All right, then, guv'nor, are you ready to go in?'

The man in the passenger seat responded with a brief nod. He climbed out of the car silently. He was slim, a good six inches shorter than Roydon, and wore a pinstriped suit. The pair approached the guards, who stared at the suited man and the black briefcase he carried. Something about him set the Gurkhas on edge. But there was no question of searching a guest brought in by Roydon.

Lever was dozing by the dying fire. The sharp knock on the door woke him with a start and he heard Mrs Ansari's voice, then footsteps in the hall.

'It's Mr Roydon again, Ambassador,' she announced quietly, 'and another gentleman. They are waiting in the hall.'

Lever looked at the clock on the mantelpiece. Almost midnight. He felt a prickle of sweat on the back of his neck. 'Will you show them in?'

Lever's housekeeper hesitated. 'Are you sure?' she half-whispered conspiratorially. 'I can say you are asleep. It is late.'

'No. Thank you.' He gave her what he hoped was a reassuring smile. 'I had better see them.'

'Yes. Of course.' Mrs Ansari quickly cleared the empty glasses from the coffee table and straightened the cushions on the armchairs.

Roydon's companion was wearing the wrong clothes for the

climate, Lever thought. The wrong clothes for the country. Something about the man's dress and demeanour suggested that he'd only recently arrived and did not intend to stay long.

Roydon spoke first. 'Good evening, Ambassador. This is Mr Jones. He's from London.'

'A pleasure to meet you, Mr Jones. When did you get in?'

The visitor ignored the question. 'Good evening, Ambassador. I have bona fides from your immediate superior, if you would like to see them?'

'Yes, please.'

Jones placed his briefcase on the coffee table and clicked open its two gold clasps. Lever could see a thin black laptop, a manila envelope and on top of those a single sheet of cream-coloured paper bearing the Foreign Office crest. Jones handed the letter over and waited while the Ambassador read it.

Lever smiled at the arcane language and extravagant signature of his Whitehall superior. 'It seems I am required to afford you every courtesy, Mr Jones.' He returned the letter. 'So what will you have? Wine? Whisky? Mint tea?'

'All I need is a few minutes of your time.'

The Ambassador sat back down and gestured his visitor to do likewise. Mr Jones sat and was about to put the letter back in his case when he noticed the open fire. He handed the letter to Roydon, nodding in the direction of the grate. Roydon grinned and set about burning the letter, feeding a bottom corner to the small orange flame and watching the white paper blacken. Lever raised his eyebrows.

'There goes your good faith.'

Jones stared at the Ambassador. 'I beg your pardon?'

'Your bona fides, your good faith – up in smoke.'

Jones closed his briefcase. 'I will keep you for as short a time as possible. This conversation concerns Aftel and its bid for the regional telecommunications licence.'

'I assumed as much. I believe we have everything under control.'

Mr Jones nodded his head slowly but when he spoke it was in the negative. 'No. I'm afraid you don't. If you did, I wouldn't need to be here. The Afghan government will announce who has won the contract in a few days.'

'I know.'

'That decision is still in the balance,' Jones declared softly.

'That's not the information I have. Mr Roydon?'

Both men looked at Roydon.

'Too close to call, we reckon. The crooked bastards who're making the decision should go for Aftel, if everything stays just like it is. The fix is in and it should hold. But it's close. Any little thing could tip it back the other way.'

The man from London turned back to Lever. 'I'm here to tell you that this contract must go to Aftel.'

'We've been working on that basis for some time, Mr Jones.' Lever was becoming increasingly irritated.

'There is a lot more at stake than you think, Ambassador.' Jones paused. 'In the light of recent events, it's been decided that I should apprise you of all the relevant information.'

Lever got to his feet, his face coloured. 'This is a joke, an insult! I'm Her Majesty's Ambassador. What sort of information have I been working with until now? Irrelevant information?'

Mr Jones was unmoved by Lever's anger. 'Partial information.' He opened his case again, took the manila envelope out and removed ten or fifteen pages fastened together with a small black Bulldog clip. 'There is a reasonable amount of detail here. You might want to sit back down.'

Lever sat.

'The Aftel project has nothing to do with promoting British business, job creation or anything like that. Or rather, if it has, then that is purely incidental. Cosmetic.'

'What on earth are you talking about?'

'As far as we are concerned, Aftel is an intelligence operation, pure and simple. Are you familiar with the Echelon system?'

Lever shook his head. 'No.'

'In simple terms, it's a huge information vacuum cleaner. It collects around a billion intercepts each day, largely on our behalf and on behalf of the American National Security Agency. The system collates phone calls, text messages, emails, web searches, passenger lists, credit cards. Anything that contains certain triggers – words or interesting sequences of numbers – is sent to Cheltenham and a larger site in Utah, where it's all processed. Do you know how we gather that sort of information at the moment, Ambassador?'

'Good old-fashioned bugging and burgling, I assume? Satellite stations, Nimrods, submarines?'

'That's right, but it's increasingly old-fashioned, inefficient. Last year over sixty billion text messages were sent in Britain alone. You can't expect a Nimrod or SIGINT station to collect all those. But imagine you owned the platform through which those messages were sent.'

Lever saw where this was going. 'If you control the telecommunications provider,' he ventured, 'then you can listen, see or hear as much as you like.'

'Yes. It's easier and more effective than snooping on other networks. If you own the company, you can do as you wish. You can place chips directly inside the fixed line or mobile phone system, if you want to.'

Roydon was still standing, back to the fire but shifting from foot to foot and obviously keen to be part of this conversation. '"Deep packet sniffers", they're called. I've helped bust in to a couple of places so the geeks could set them up on the quiet.'

Jones ignored the interruption. 'They are basic black boxes that hoover up all content, then cross-reference phone calls, texts and emails. Look at who's talking to whom. You can plot that against credit card activity or flight details or any other data you choose. It's immensely powerful.'

Lever nodded. 'And Aftel will do all of this for you? For us?'

'Aftel is, one way or the other, a front. It belongs to us. Setting up here will be like having our own little GCHQ right in the middle of the most dangerous, unstable and interesting region in the world.'

Roydon could not contain his enthusiasm. 'Inside the belly of the fuckin' beast. How about that?'

'And what would you do with all that information?' Lever asked, genuinely fascinated. 'Won't you simply be deluged by data? No computer could process it all.'

'We will mine it. We're generating new and better algorithms all the time. Our computing power doubles every three years. Every person in the wired world leaves a digital trail behind them, like a snail trail; you just have to know how to follow them.'

'And you follow who? Everyone? Doesn't that raise some ethical questions?' Lever observed.

Roydon dragged a chair closer to the two men and sat down. 'It's the old story, isn't it? If you've done nothing wrong then you've got nothing to worry about. If you have, then it's a night flight to Poland for a little light water-boarding.' He laughed.

Lever and Jones looked at each other, seemingly oblivious to Roydon's presence.

Jones spoke first. 'So now hopefully you understand just how important the next few days are – how critical it is that the decision goes our way. Everything that can be done, must be done. Everything.' He put the papers back inside the brown envelope and the envelope back in his case. He snapped the locks shut and stood up to leave. 'I am going to absent myself now, Ambassador. You and Mr Roydon need to discuss some of the contingencies, actions that may or may not prove necessary.'

Lever smiled. 'You're welcome to stay for that, Mr Jones. I have no objection.'

'No. I don't need to know the details.'

'I understand. Well, thank you for the briefing. Will I see you again, before you leave Kabul?'

Jones put out his hand. 'Good evening, Ambassador. I think it's unlikely that we'll need to meet again.'

As soon as Mr Jones had left, Roydon rose from his seat, headed for the drinks table and poured himself a glass of the first spirit that came to hand. It was clear in colour and he drank it quickly. He turned to Lever. 'You should be feeling very fucking flattered, you're in on the biggest secret there is right now. That stuff he told you is highly classified, the highest in fact. You need oxygen at that level.'

Lever was exhausted. 'Can you just tell me what you need to tell me, Mr Roydon, and then allow me my bed?'

'Fair enough. So here's the plan . . .' Roydon poured himself another vodka. 'As soon as the mob who're holding Patrick Reid get in touch with Carver, we say yes to the rendezvous.'

'I just told William that Plan A was to bargain.'

'Then tell *William* Plan A didn't work. It was never going to anyway.'

'And how do you propose to manage the meeting?'

'Manage it?'

'I'm too tired for euphemisms. How will you make sure it doesn't end in a ruddy great firefight, everyone dead, including Reid and Carver?'

'Don't worry. It'll be silky smooth. Special forces, Israeli drones . . . video and SIGINT. The works.'

'I wish I shared your confidence.'

Roydon drained his vodka. 'With all due respect, Ambassador, I don't give a tinker's toss about your confidence. We'll save who we can, kill who we have to. You've got other things to think about.'

'Like what?'

Roydon's eyes narrowed. 'I think you know what. Other loose ends. Loose ends that now need to be tied up. There's no option any more.' Roydon belched lightly into his fist and poured another drink. 'Those lovely hands of yours. Diplomat's hands. I'm afraid you're going to have to get them a little dirty.'

The prickle of sweat had returned to Lever's neck. 'Is that really necessary?'

Roydon nodded. 'It is now. You heard what Jones said, no risks, and that means no witnesses.'

'Why does it have to be me?'

'You know why it's you. You can walk straight in through the front door at Bagram, no bother. You're the British Ambassador. We've been through this.'

'And if I can't do it? If I won't?'

Roydon leant forward and lowered his voice. Lever could feel the heat of the man's breath on his ear and neck. He could smell the sour vodka.

'Then you lose everything. Every single thing. Kicked back to London, all by your lonesome. And who knows what might happen to her, then, eh? Without you here, keeping an eye out for her. Keeping her safe.' Roydon reached for the Ambassador's arm and squeezed it. 'But if you do it, and if everything goes off okay, in a few days it's all over.' He stood and looked down at the Ambassador. 'Confirmed in post for the foreseeable. No questions asked about you or your living arrangements – if you get what I mean?' He turned to leave. 'Don't worry. I'll see myself out.'

Mrs Ansari locked and bolted the front door before returning to the library. She cleared Roydon's glass and removed all other evidence of the men's meeting before returning to kneel at Lever's side. She swept his thin hair back into place and cupped his cheek, staring and smiling gently into his face until he managed to muster a smile in return. She took his hand and placed it on the collar of her shirt. Lever undid her top button and then the buttons beneath, slowly and deliberately, as far down as he could reach. His housekeeper folded her shirt aside and Lever stared; sometimes she wore a white embroidered bra, sometimes a red silk chemise he had brought back from London, but tonight she wore nothing. She took his right hand and placed it on her bare breast. He was always amazed by how pale and soft her skin was there; how completely different from the darker skin around her face and hands. Some nights, when her husband was away driving, they would fall asleep together. Maybe she could stay tonight? It was as if she knew what he was thinking.

'Not tonight,' she whispered, 'but the night after tomorrow I can stay.'

Lever nodded. 'Yes, all right. The night after tomorrow.'

Mrs Ansari looked at Lever. 'You love me?'

There was no hesitation. 'I do. I love you. I would die for you.' This was true. He would die for her. But could he do the other thing?

Jones waited for Roydon in the car. A misshapen moon hung over the Ambassador's residence and the Gurkha guards stood to attention on either side of the high black gates. Jones took a laptop from his briefcase, opened it and then closed it again without turning it on. He switched on the ceiling light and examined the thumb of his right hand. He'd been bitten by something, a mosquito, right on the knuckle and now it was itching like hell. He hated fieldwork. 'The sooner we get out of this God forsaken country the better.'

He looked at his watch: what was taking Roydon so long? It was a simple enough message he had to relay. Once that conversation had taken place and once Jones had made sure Roydon understood what was expected of him, Jones could be on his way. He did some sums in his head. With luck he could be back at RAF Brize Norton by mid-morning and in the office by lunchtime. Not so bad. Out of the corner of his eye he saw that one of the guards was busy opening the gate and then a shadow, which resolved itself into Roydon, striding in his direction. Roydon wrenched open the driver's door and sat down heavily. Jones felt the car's suspension drop an inch as Roydon settled himself.

'Well, how was that for you, then, boss? Worth the long haul from home?'

'It was fine.' Jones put his laptop back in the briefcase. 'You know Lever better than I do. Do you think he understands the situation? Are we all on the same page?' Jones looked straight ahead as he spoke.

Roydon adjusted the rear-view mirror. 'He gets it. So, what now? Home, Jones, and don't spare the horses?'

The man from London looked quizzically at his companion. 'What?'

'Back to the airport, is it?'

'In a moment. I just want to walk you through the next few days, make sure you know exactly what London expects.'

'Right you are, sir,' said Roydon. It was annoying, he thought, having to doff his cap to cunts like this, but it was unavoidable: Jones could end his career with a stroke of his Mont Blanc pen.

'We tell the group that have Reid that we agree to a meeting on their terms, yes?'

'Got it.'

'But we insist on seeing that laptop as well as Reid himself?'

'Understood.'

'They'll get back to us with when and where and so on, and you just agree to everything, yes?'

'Yes.'

'Either William Carver will agree to go along or he'll refuse. Hopefully he'll do the decent thing and agree. But either way, we go ahead. Right?'

Roydon was getting impatient. He was being patronised. 'Right.'

'We want you to lead the operation and I'm authorised to tell you that you need show no restraint.'

Roydon raised his eyebrows at this. He wondered whether the man from London understood what he was saying. 'No restraint?'

The stony look on Jones' face suggested that he did understand. 'The rendezvous will probably not be straightforward. It will not be bloodless. From what I understand, it won't be the first time something like this has happened.'

Roydon knew the incident Jones was referring to and some of the detail. A female journalist had died, together with all her captors. He stared straight ahead, out of the windscreen and into the darkness. 'You want a clean slate, I get that. But I don't much like killing Englishmen, Mr Jones.'

'If the operation goes as we would expect, as we wish it to, then there will be no need for you to do that particular part of the killing, will there?'

'Okay. So what kind of kit do I get?'

'Anything you want. APCs, hummers, hardware, software. Just make a list.'

'Good. And the personnel?'

Jones looked down at his black leather briefcase. 'You're in charge, you put the team together. But no British involvement.'

Roydon shifted uncomfortably in his seat. 'None at all?'

'No.'

'Why not?'

'Because that's what London wants.'

'Well, that's going to cost a packet, Mr Jones, I mean serious money. Double what I had in mind before.' Roydon got the impression that Jones' attention was moving elsewhere.

'Fine, you can go to double.'

'You don't know what the original figure was.'

Jones looked at his watch. 'I don't care what the original figure was, Mr Roydon. Money isn't an issue, do you understand? Now, I think we're done, aren't we? Straight to the airport, if you don't mind. My plane is waiting on the apron.' He lifted his thumb and examined it again. He rubbed gently at the swollen bite while Roydon watched.

'Oh, no. Has one of the local mozzies had a nibble?'

'What? Yes.'

'Monsters, these Afghan mosquitoes. Don't scratch it, whatever you do. Best thing is to stick a lump of ice on it once you're on the plane and keep your fingers crossed it's not malarial.'

The man from London glared at his knuckle. Roydon smiled and started the engine. There was no malaria in this part of the country.

33 Proof of Life

DATELINE: Hindu Kush, Afghanistan, July 10th

On the third night after Karim's killing Patrick managed to eat most of the meal he had been given. He washed, changed his clothes and waited, but there was no visit from Noor. Instead, Mirgun and one of his men arrived, both carrying AK-47s and obviously in a bad temper. They ordered him from his quarters and out into the cold night. He was marched to the cliff-face and then on through the dank corridors, the high-ceilinged reception space and finally straight into the General's chamber. Doushki was standing, waiting on his arrival. He wore a long black shameez, its hem touching the floor. There was no greeting, no invitation to sit. Patrick stood nervously in front of his host.

'If your people wish your safe return, they have a strange way to go about it. They are not professional.' Patrick looked at the floor. Doushki continued. 'We contacted William Carver and your English Embassy intercepted the call. They agree to the meeting with Carver, exactly as requested. All they ask is that as well as *you*, I bring your computer. That is the only condition.' Patrick kept looking down. The General stooped and stared hard into his eyes.

'Why do they ask this?' Patrick had no answer. He wondered what William was playing at. 'If I were them, if they had someone I was concerned about, I would want proof of life: a film or a photograph. Only then would I agree to meet. I would not be asking about a computer.' Doushski dropped down into a low armchair. The upholstery was a deep green and the chair had golden claws for feet. 'It can only mean that there is something important on your computer.' He gave Patrick a questioning look. 'What is it?'

Patrick shook his head. 'I'm sorry, I don't know.'

Doushki looked fleetingly at Mirgun and then glanced away. The blow was unexpected and arrived too suddenly for Patrick to have time to tighten his stomach muscles. The butt of the AK-47 buried itself deep in his gut and he buckled, swallowing for air. One moment he was upright, the next bent double, hands on knees and struggling to breathe. When he attempted to right himself, his body refused and shock made way for pain. With his hands still on his knees he started to gag and then vomit copiously and noisily on to the floor in front of him, and over his own shoes. He spat and stepped backwards, away from what he could see and smell to be his most recent meal, a stringy goat stew. The pain was overwhelming. Patrick was sure the rifle butt must have ruptured something inside; his bowel, appendix or the stomach itself. He fell back into a seated position and grasped at his belly, imagining gastric acids, blood and part-digested food swilling around inside. Then he passed out.

Mirgun looked at the General. 'One blow.'

Doushki called out over his shoulder, in the direction of the kitchen. 'Noor! Take the boy back to his quarters and tend him. You—' He jutted his chin in the direction of Mirgun. 'Carry him for Noor and be careful – we need him for now.'

Mirgun pulled Patrick's puke-covered shoes and socks from his feet before lifting him easily on to his shoulder.

*

Unusually for him, William didn't want to be alone. He'd spent an hour in his bedroom trying to focus on the story, but he'd drunk too much of the Ambassador's whisky for proper work and couldn't concentrate. He wanted company. He called Dan Riley and shortly after that, a cab.

Inside their Kabul base, the US Army had built a passable imitation of a Boston bar-room, complete with heavy wooden furniture, large bowls of cheesy nachos, a blue baize pool table and a Wurlitzer jukebox. It had taken William some time to get there, and it was late and loud by the time he got to the bar. The hundred or so men and half a dozen women inside had arranged themselves in several distinct groups: the Rangers were around the pool table; the Marines at the bar; a couple of Special Forces men were off in a corner playing draughts. A handful of journalists sat at a cluster of tables close to the door. Carver found Riley in a corner booth.

'Thanks,' he said as he took the seat opposite. 'I'm glad you were around.'

'Not a problem.' Riley smiled. 'Drink?'

'Coffee,' William said.

When Riley returned, he slid one of the two black coffees over to Carver and drummed a hand on the table. He glanced around to see if there was anyone who might be able to overhear their conversation, and when he saw that there was no one, he started straight in. 'I was going to call you tomorrow anyway, William. I've got something for you. A lead on your story, or it might be, anyway.'

'Fazil Jabar?' William felt that familiar flutter in the pit of his stomach.

'Yeah. So you know this shitty assignment I'm on?'

'The embed.'

'Yeah, well the latest part of that means I've been hanging out with Mortuary Affairs. Have you heard of those guys?'

'No. An American thing, I guess.'

'Guess so. Anyway, I've met some fucked-up fellows in this war but Mortuary Affairs takes the prize.' William was impatient, but he knew better than to hurry this old friend when he was working up a yarn. Riley explained that this was the US Army unit that dealt with the dead. Bodies of American soldiers and occasionally other nationalities too were delivered to them, and it was Mortuary Affairs' job to go through the uniform and kit and all their personal effects before anyone else could access them.

'It's pretty fuckin' heart-breaking stuff,' Riley said. 'They find photos of the wives, the girlfriends, ultrasound pictures of babies who'll never know their fathers, porn, pictures of cars, half-eaten candy bars, the lot. And letters. Lots of letters. Sent to these dead boys by their mums and dads and brothers, their fiancées. Mortuary Affairs has this rule that they shouldn't read the letters, but naturally they read them anyway. Earlier today, while I was there, they brought in this dead Marine, a young guy, twenty something. They were going through his pockets and they found this stuffed toy, a little blue bear. When you press its foot it plays a recorded message. It was something his daughter had recorded for him back in Greenville, Ohio, or wherever. So they squeeze the bear's foot and this little girl is talking: "Good morning, Daddy. It's a beautiful day. I love you." Again and again; fucking thing gets jammed. "Good morning, I love you" over and over. They're trying to get the damn bear to stop talking, standing next to the kid's dead dad. It's no wonder they're completely fucked up, I'm fucked up and I've only spent half a day with them.'

Riley shook his head slowly from side to side, trying to comprehend something or, even better, shake it away. 'Anyway. I was taking some pictures, shooting the breeze, asking them about the work, and they told me something you got to hear. A couple of weeks ago they got a delivery; it was an Afghan ambulance that'd been at the scene of a bombing somewhere in the centre of Kabul. The ambulance guys said they'd been told to take the dead to the American military mortuary. Don't know why. It was approved somewhere, I guess. So these Afghan guys turn up and say they have two bodies. They drop them and go on their way. So far, so what, yeah? But when my boys start checking the bags, things get interesting. The first bag's fine, I mean the guy's dead – bits missing, blown to hell but normal stuff. Then they get to the second body bag and while they're dragging it off the van it starts wriggling around . . . The youngest guy in the unit nearly shits his pants. They unzip the bag and the guy inside, he's A-okay; I mean, he looks like shit, covered in blood and a little bit barbecued, but he's alive. They figure maybe he was been knocked out cold by the blast, but there's no serious damage. Imagine that? So the guy in the bag starts babbling away, chatting in Afghan and some English but making no sense. He's saying someone killed someone. Mortuary Affairs clean him up, they make a call to let their superior know what's happened and request a transfer to the hospital, you know, and within minutes, they get a call back from some English guy saying they're coming right over. Ten minutes later the Brits turn up and take him away. No conversation, no explanation. Just bundle him into a Jeep and off they go.'

Carver stared at Riley. 'Two weeks ago?'

'Eighteen days. I asked them to check it.'

'I don't suppose you've got anything other than their say-so on this?'

Riley cracked a smile. 'You're gonna love me for this: I got them to make me a photocopy of the incident report.'

The American took a sheet of paper from his trouser pocket and unfolded it in front of William. Carver picked it up. The date matched, June 21st, and there underneath, in dry military jargon, was the story Riley had just told him. At the end of the incident report, after the confirmation that British representatives had collected the 'unidentified middle-aged Afghan', was the standard army sign-off — *Nothing Follows* — and a name, rank and signature. William held the paper in both hands. He read and reread it.

'This is it, Riley. Karim's hunch was right, that's the tailor, Savi, it's got to be. And he's the eyewitness.' William reread the report, silently mouthing every word, then raised his head. 'Did your guys have any idea where the Brits took him? '

'Yeah. I asked them that. The mortuary boys reckon that they called another favour and got him checked in at the Hotel. You know, Bagram detention centre.'

'Do you know anyone who can get me into the Hotel? Soon?'

The American shrugged. 'Maybe. I can ask around. From what I hear, it's been done before. How much folding money you got?'

34 Hotel Bagram

DATELINE: Bagram detention centre, Parwan Province, Afghanistan, July 11th

Carver arrived a full half an hour early. He sat in the shade, squinting into the early morning sun, looking for the man Dan Riley had told him to expect. He could see a big-bellied Chinook lifting slowly towards the horizon, its dark shape clear against the snow-capped mountains beyond. He had arrived at the base at six that morning, leaving three hours to get through security and to the meeting point. Unusually, security had taken less than an hour. But he'd needed most of the rest of the time he had to get to the rendezvous; the guardsmen refused to escort the BBC man to the Bagram detention centre without authorisation, and William had had to call Riley's contact to arrange a pick-up. Sergeant of the Guard, Karl Brella, arrived at exactly nine. He checked his chunky watch, perhaps hoping William had missed the appointment, and when Carver called his name, he made no attempt to conceal his disappointment.

'Mr Carver? Right on time.' Brella was tall, square-jawed and intimidating. His voice, a deep Virginian drawl, matched his physique. William sensed they were unlikely to get along. He knew Brella would have no idea why he had been granted access to a detainee, and he knew Brella would hate the fact he had been. He knew, too, that if Brella ever learned the truth – that his corrupt superior had been paid two thousand dollars to make the arrangements – his synapses would short-circuit. The sergeant marched ahead of William to the reception area at the rear of the building. Three other Marines frisked William and tipped the contents of his bag on to a trestle table. Brella waited for William to pack his stuff, then escorted him through one more set of swing doors to the reception desk. At first sight the woman behind the steel desk looked like any receptionist anywhere – bored and easily displeased. But when the SOG appeared at William's shoulder, she brightened. She stood and gave a neat salute, her hand catching a gooseneck desk-lamp on its descent, almost sending it over the side. She righted the lamp and tucked a few strands of blonde hair back behind her ear.

'Sergeant Brella. I didn't know you were back on base?'

'Just back a couple of days, Gayle.'

William watched the woman process this information, open her mouth to speak, and then, with a quick glance at William, change her mind. 'So, Gayle. This is Mr Carver. He's from the British media.' It was clear from Brella's tone that William could not have been less welcome had he been from the Devil's dining club. 'You got him on your list?'

'Let's take a look. Full name?'

William gave his name and Gayle pulled a clipboard from a drawer and made a big show of running a polished nail down a list of half a dozen names. Carver's name was first on the list, he could see that from three feet away, but she seemed to be having trouble finding it. She was either showing off for Brella or just making the most of her little quota of power. William didn't mind either way. He followed Gayle's finger down the page, reading the names, and when she reached the final name, Carver took a sharp intake of breath. He read it again to be sure and then questioned what the presence of that name on this list might mean; he realised that it meant he had to hurry. Gayle read Carver's name back to him before taking a plastic visitor pass from a tray.

'So, am I your first guest today?' He tried to sound as casual as possible.

'You are, sir. We don't get too many visitors in here.' She took a cursory look inside William's plastic bag, smiled at Brella, and buzzed them through another set of security doors.

The detention centre smelt municipal – chlorine and camphor. The block walls were painted hospital green. They walked swiftly past some empty holding cells, striding deeper into the main building, their steps echoing in the deserted corridor.

'What's this fella to you, then, Mr Carver?' Brella said suddenly.

William quickened his pace to draw level. 'I don't know him personally, Sergeant, but if my information is correct, you might have an innocent man locked up in here.'

'Is that right?'

'Yes. I hope you're treating him properly.'

Brella stopped and faced William, standing a little close. William could smell his toothpaste. 'We meet the standards here, Mr Carver.'

'Glad to hear it. So you never beat the prisoners? Hang them up? None of that?'

Brella's neck reddened. He stared evenly into William's eyes. 'You have quite an imagination. Listen, I don't know whose dick you sucked to get in here—'

'Your boss—' William broke in. '—it was your boss, Sergeant. I didn't suck his dick but he approved my visit, as you know.'

Brella sucked his teeth and spat his reply. 'Mr Carver, I don't care if God Almighty approved your visit. At this moment I'm on duty and in charge of this facility. You'll treat me and this institution with respect. Understood?'

'Understood.' William had enjoyed sparring with Brella, but he knew better than to risk his mission by pushing the man too far.

They completed the last part of their route march through the detention centre in silence. At the far end of the wing they were met by a single guard in creased army fatigues, an assault rifle on his shoulder and a short truncheon tucked inside his belt. The guard saluted a little uncertainly, as if he hadn't been expecting to see anyone.

'As you were,' Brella snapped.

William looked at the guard. He was small and unremarkable and yet there was something about him that made William nervous. He had dark eyes, a wet lower lip, and a name badge that read *Kopek*. Brella put his face hard up against the greasy glass window in the cell door. He was straining to see inside. He turned and ordered his man to open the door. Kopek gave a slack-jawed smile and unhooked a bunch of keys from his belt without comment. He identified the correct key without hesitation, unlocked the thick metal door and pushed it open. Brella went first. The cell was dark and airless and William smelt the prisoner before he saw him. Mr Savi was sitting cross-legged in one corner, his head lowered, his clothes caked in shit. Brella covered his mouth and pushed back past William in the direction of the guard.

'I thought I gave orders to clean him up!' he shouted.

Kopek stepped into the cell to take a look and at that moment Mr Savi raised his head. When the old Afghan saw the guard, he flinched like an animal and shuffled closer to the wall, arms raised. It was one of the most horrible things William had seen. The guard looked at Savi and then spat on the floor.

'Ain't my fault if he shits his pants. He's got the commode.' Kopek pointed to the metal receptacle by the cell door, a foot from a tray of uneaten food. William looked from these to Savi, who was shackled with short chains to the opposite wall.

'Clean him up, Kopek, right now! Then bring him to the interview room,' Brella yelled, a vein throbbing in his thick neck.

Half an hour later, the man sitting opposite William in the white windowless room looked if not well, then at least human. Carver laid the microphone on the table and pressed record. The sergeant's embarrassment at the state in which they had found Savi had had a beneficial effect: he had reluctantly agreed to the use of a tape recorder. Although William had had to agree that the tape was for note-taking purposes only, it was a significant concession. Two mugs of sugared tea and a plate of biscuits had been delivered and William saw Mr Savi eyeing them, interested but wary. Carver took a biscuit, dunked it in his tea and ate. It was Savi's cue to pull the plate close to him and eat the remaining biscuits quickly, one at a time, washing them down with large gulps of the tea. He finished his drink, tipping it high into the air, and then stared at William's. The journalist pushed it slowly across the table to Savi and nodded that he should drink that too. He gave the man a few more moments to gather himself, and then spoke.

'Mr Savi, I am a BBC journalist. My name is William Carver. I am investigating the death of Fazil Jabar. I need you to tell me exactly what happened that evening at your shop. It's important for your safety and for the safety of a colleague of mine.'

The tailor's story came in tentative but workmanlike English. Savi had been doing the final fitting for one of several suits ordered by Fazil Jabar and the politician had brought his son with him to be measured as well. The appointment before Jabar's was with Mr Roydon, an Englishman, who had been back a number of times for alterations on a pinstripe suit. That evening, Roydon had had a black suitcase with him but had forgotten it in the dressing room when he left the shop. Savi had found it and placed it close to the door, expecting his customer to come back.

He couldn't remember the bomb going off. He worked out afterwards that he had been at the rear of the shop measuring Jabar, who must have taken more of the force of the blast though obviously not as much as the boy or the bodyguard, who were in the front. Savi could remember opening his eyes and seeing Fazil Jabar lying on the floor, close to him. He was moving a little. Then he saw Mr Roydon. He assumed he had come to help and he was about to call out when Roydon took a gun from inside his jacket pocket, knelt down and shot Jabar in the side of the head.

The fitting room was filling with smoke and he couldn't remember much after that, but he thought he must have passed out. When he woke, he was trapped inside a bag. He was helped out and cleaned up by some American soldiers, but then handed over to an Englishman.

'What kind of Englishman? Army?'

'I am not certain, sir, but not Army, I think. He said there had been a big mistake. He promised compensation, money, an apology. He said I needed to be kept somewhere safe for a time. And he brought me to this place. And. And then—'

Carver nodded. He glanced at the door. It was still closed, and the green light on his MiniDisc was steady. 'But this man. He didn't give you a name, Mr Savi, not even a first name?'

'No, sir, he did not.'

'But he was definitely English?'

'Yes. English voice. And English clothes, good clothes. A lounge suit, good quality, and a hat, a panama hat.'

Ambassador Lever was walking into reception just as William was leaving. His look of shock and guilt shaded almost immediately to one of resignation. William felt he saw each emotion with perfect clarity. He also saw Lever's right hand move without conscious thought to the pocket of his suit jacket. He wondered what was in that pocket. Pills? A needle? Lever would surely choose the most painless method to kill a man. The most polite way. The hand left the pocket now and was offered up in greeting. William shook it.

'Mr Carver. How good to see you. Am I right in thinking you've found another piece of that jigsaw you were working on?'

'I have, Ambassador, yes.' William held the diplomat's gaze.

'And how is Mr Savi?'

William was only willing to go so far with this game. 'I've recorded an interview with him, Ambassador. I have the whole story, on the record, on tape.' He lifted up the plastic bag containing the tape machine and his notes.

Lever stared. 'I see, yes. I understand.'

'I hope so. Mr Savi's words will soon be available for the world to hear, whether or not Mr Savi is able to repeat them.'

There was a pause, neither man knowing what to say next.

Eventually the receptionist broke the silence. 'Here you are, sir, you're all good to go.' Gayle offered Lever a plastic security badge.

Lever turned and smiled kindly at the young woman. 'Oh, thank you. But do you know what? I shan't be needing it now. You see, Mr Carver's visit makes mine entirely superfluous.'

Brella and Gayle looked at the two visitors, slightly perplexed. The Ambassador was turning to leave. William followed.

'Can I walk with you, Ambassador?'

'By all means, Mr Carver,' said Lever, as though he'd hoped William might ask. They walked for a time, past the coils of razor wire and blast-proof sandbags, neither man uttering a word. The Ambassador was bareheaded today despite the intense heat.

'So, how's that puzzle of yours looking now?'

William glanced sideways at Lever. 'It's coming together. Piece by piece.' He paused. 'The trouble is, I'm not so sure I want to see what I think it's showing me.'

The Ambassador shook his head gravely. 'Uncomfortable truths, Mr Carver. Remember our conversation? It's your job to tell uncomfortable stories. No room for sentiment. You should do it soon, I think, tell the world. No more delay.'

'I could go to air with the Fazil Jabar story now. It wouldn't be the whole story but it would be something.'

'I'm sure it would be riveting. Prize-winning or game-changing or whatever matters to you fellows these days. You should go ahead.'

William looked again at the Ambassador's profile, the thinning hair, the weak chin. He wondered if he knew what he was asking. If nothing else, broadcasting what William knew about the killing of Jabar would end Lever's career. 'There would be consequences.'

The Ambassador gave a short snort of laughter. 'But that's what it's all about, isn't it? What's the point of journalism if there are no consequences? Are you telling me you would rather tell inconsequential stories?'

'No.'

'No, of course not. There was a time, Mr Carver, when I thought that the greatest good for the greatest number would be served by you staying silent. I'm no longer of that opinion.'

'Why?'

'It doesn't matter why. All that matters is that the scales have been lifted from my eyes. I've changed my mind. I think you should let people know what's going on here. Post-haste.'

Carver swapped the carrier bag from right hand to left. The sentry gate was only metres away now and beyond it, the Ambassador's waiting Land Rover. 'I don't think I'm going to do that yet.'

The Ambassador stopped in his tracks; his dust-covered brogues kicked up a little swirl of dirt and sand. 'Why on earth not?' he half snapped, surprising William and himself.

Carver raised the plastic bag and waved it gently as though attempting to guess its weight. 'This information is the only card I have to play with Patrick's kidnappers.'

The look Lever gave him was one of genuine disbelief. 'What? You're not still planning on attending this rendezvous or exchange or whatever the hell it is?'

'I don't have a choice.'

'But you do have a choice. The operation to release Reid will go ahead, with or without you. And I'm pretty sure the outcome will be the same whether you're there or not.'

'What do you mean?'

'I mean they will either free Patrick Reid or they won't. You being there won't make a jot of difference.'

'I don't agree. The men that took Patrick want information from me and I've got it now. It's a chance I have to take. I put Patrick where he is now. I've already got Karim on my conscience.'

'Nonsense.' Lever stared at the floor, then at Carver's plastic bag and the bulging black brick of a recorder that weighed it down. 'Karim would want you to go ahead and tell the story. Wouldn't he? So would Patrick.'

William half nodded. 'Maybe. You may be right, Ambassador. But you're forgetting your Bonhöffer.'

'I beg your pardon?'

'Your man Bonhöffer, you remember? "To save one life is to save the world entire." That's how it goes, isn't it?'

Lever looked suddenly much older, his face dusty from the day's journey, tired and lined. He managed a thin smile. 'Yes. Yes, that's how it goes. To save one life. The hard part is deciding which life to save.'

The Ambassador's driver opened the Land Rover's rear door and Lever climbed in. William watched as the four-by-four drove off, a cloud of dust billowing up behind. He kept his eyes focused on the rear window, but Lever didn't look back.

By the time William had trudged back to his quarters, collected his bags and reached the departure building, the Ambassador was long gone. At the transport office a surly lieutenant told him that his transport back to Kabul could not leave for several hours. '. . . And they've just set fire to the shitters. So you might want to cover your nose.'

There were VIPs on the move and after that Bagram was hosting a service of repatriation for an officer of the Yorkshire Regiment who had been killed while mentoring an Afghan National Army unit nearby. The base was locked down. William made the most of the time. He found a quiet corner and listened again to his interview with Savi, transcribing it as he went in spiderish script. Time passed and eventually he was told that he could hitch a lift out shortly. He was ushered across the airstrip in time to witness some of the Repatriation Service. A padre, in battledress and bands, stood completely still, prayer book in hand, in front of a lectern and ten or twelve lines of soldiers. Carver recognised fighting men and women representing several different British regiments as well as Americans, Danes, Estonians. Some soldiers were dressed in full military regalia, others wore combat camouflage. At the back of the group stood mechanics and technicians in overalls. All stood straight and silent. Silent too were the giant transporter planes, American helicopter gunships, Chinooks and every other piece of American and Allied hardware that usually made the airstrip a deafening place. They had all fallen silent as a mark of respect for one man. The man in question was lying inside a flag-bound coffin on a metal gurney just a few feet from the lectern. The padre was speaking now, through a scratchy PA system, and William moved closer, straining to catch what was being said.

'They shall not grow old, as we that are left grow old. Age shall not weary them, nor the years condemn. At the going down of the sun, and in the morning, we will remember them . . .' And then a single soldier marched from out of the ranks and stood alongside the padre. He lifted a bugle to his mouth and played a note-perfect *Last Post* and *Reveille*.

William jumped as an RAF Hercules standing nearby suddenly started its engines and slowly backed up until its rear ramp was within feet of the coffin and gurney. A six-man bearer party came forward and lifted the dead man to shoulder height. They waited for the padre to join them and then marched their cargo up the ramp, out of the afternoon sun and into the dark hold. As the plane doors closed, some of the soldiers drifted away but the core of the ramp ceremony stayed and Carver did likewise. He watched the plane taxi up the long runway before taking off straight into the sun. Still the padre and soldiers stood and William followed their gaze skywards. He saw the Hercules climb and then turn slowly back in the direction of Bagram, as though the pilot had changed his mind and was planning to land again. William watched mystified as the giant aircraft flew low and fast, back over the black tarmac. As it passed, the mighty plane dipped its starboard wing in tribute to the fallen soldier and to the comrades he had left behind.

35 The Rendezvous

DATELINE: BBC house, Kabul, Afghanistan, July 12th

When it came, the text message was short and to the point.

> MEETING CONFIRMED FOR TOMORROW (WEDNESDAY)
> APPROXIMATE LUNCHTIME. YOU WILL BE COLLECTED
> 0500 AM FROM YOUR ROOM (BBC HOUSE). DO NOT
> TRAVEL ANYWHERE OR CONTACT ANYONE UNTIL
> THEN. GOOD LUCK. LEVER.

William shook the last three sleeping pills from the little brown bottle into his palm and swallowed them with a glass of water from the bathroom tap. He drew the curtains, lay down on his bed and waited for sleep to come, but it would not. He drank the two fingers of bourbon that remained at the bottom of the bottle before lying down again. Still nothing. Finally, he plugged in and powered up his laptop and scrolled through the music files till he found first *Requiem* and then 'Pie Jesu'. He selected play and repeat. The King's College choir sang him to sleep and kept singing through the short night.

He was woken by a loud rapping on his bedroom door. He stared at this watch until the numbers and hands revealed themselves as four ten. William groaned and bellowed at the door. 'They said fucking five.'

There was a snort of laugher and then an Australian accent shouted back: 'Yeah, sorry 'bout that, but the early bird gets the worm, Mr Carver, early bird gets the worm.'

Carver rubbed sleep from his eyes. 'How do I know it's you?'

'Who the fuck else you expecting this time of the morning?' This seemed fair enough. William hauled himself up out of the bed, found his glasses and walked across the room to unlock the door. The Australian accent belonged to a man in his mid-forties with curly brown hair and a hard physique. He had a three-day beard and wore a safari jacket, combat trousers and boots. He looked to William like every other Australian Special Forces man he'd ever met, but he was about ten or twenty years too old for the job. William nodded. 'What are you? Aussie special?'

'Something like that, yeah.' The man had bright green eyes and deep laugh lines that suggested an almost permanent smile. He was smiling now. 'Fuck me, mate, you're looking a little green around the gills. You all right?'

William looked downwards and realised he was wearing nothing but boxer shorts. He moved sideways so a little more of his stomach was hidden by the door. 'I'm fine, just confused. I thought this was a British Army operation?'

The man broke eye contact and looked past William's shoulder. 'It is. More or less. The boss is as British as bacon and eggs.'

'Who's the boss?'

''Fraid I can't tell you that, William, not yet anyways. I'm sure he'll come say g'day soon enough though, eh?' The Aussie checked his watch. 'We can talk about it when we're on the road. My orders are to put the packet in the van. You're the packet, so if you don't mind, get your shit together quick so I can put you in the van. Yeah?'

Carver sighed. 'Okay. Who're you?'

The man's smile brightened. 'All right, that I *can* tell you. I'm Cahill. Pleasure to meet you.'

Carver dressed quickly, splashed water on his face and cleaned his teeth with paste and his index finger. He'd stowed his recording equipment behind the cupboard and a memory stick containing a copy of everything he had was tucked inside the lining of the bedroom curtain. A second memory stick was in his jeans pocket. He took one long look over the room as he closed the bedroom door, checking to see if he'd forgotten anything but also half wondering whether he'd see the place again. He shook the thought from his head and followed Cahill down the stairs.

Halfway down, the Australian took another sideways glance at William and stopped. 'Hey, Billy. You've got a kitchen here, yeah?'

Carver balked at the new shortening of his name but let it go. 'Yes. Behind reception.'

'Good. Let's make a quick pit stop. It's not good to drive on an empty stomach, 'specially if you've been drinking and popping sleepers the night before.'

'What makes you think——?'

'Ah, I know that look, mate. Seen it many times. Mostly in the bathroom mirror each morning.' Cahill smiled sympathetically. 'Let's try and rustle something up.'

The Australian rifled the fridge in the kitchen with great efficiency. He poured William a mug of milk and watched him drink it. After that he constructed a basic sandwich from white bread, a thick layer of margarine and several slices of processed ham and cheese. He pressed the snack down hard with the palm of his hand before passing it to Carver. 'Not the best breakfast I've ever made, mate. I'll cook you something proper at a later date. But at least it'll line the stomach, eh?'

'Thanks.'

'No need to thank me. We're riding together and I don't want you hurling in the back of my van.'

'How far are we going?'

'Can't say, I'm afraid, Billy-boy. The whole operation is "need to know". I don't need to know much and you need to know even less.' While William ate, Cahill took another look inside the various cupboards and the fridge and found a yoghurt. He ripped off the lid and gave it a sniff. 'Wanna wash that sarnie down with a yoghurt?' William shook his head. 'Suit yourself.' Cahill found a spoon and ate it himself.

Looking out past the Australian and into the street, William saw two identical Humvees. The heavily armoured cars shone glossy black even in the early morning gloom, and looked so new they might've been driven directly from the factory that morning.

Breakfast finished, Cahill strode through reception with William a few paces behind. At the main door he put a hand out to halt William and went ahead. He took a moment to check the street, glancing left and right, and as he did so Carver caught sight of a big man in a blue windcheater bulked out further by body armour, who turned quickly away and climbed into the passenger seat of the lead vehicle. He only saw his profile for a split second and then the back of his cropped blond head, but it seemed to William that there was something familiar about the man. He sifted his memory for the faces of British officers he'd met who fitted the description, but found none. On Cahill's signal he walked forwards heading in the direction of the first car but then felt Cahill's hand in the small of his back, steering him away and towards the rear of the second vehicle.

'You're riding with me, mate, remember? Second car is safer, anyway.'

The Hummers looked impressive and William felt reassured at the sight of them. Cahill pulled open the door at the back of the second Humvee and encouraged William to climb up. The back of the oversized vehicle had been stripped bare to allow room for two rows of metal benches to be bolted to the floor, one on each side. One bench was empty and on the other sat three clean-shaven Afghans wearing similar outfits to Cahill's; desert camouflage jackets buttoned to the neck, combat trousers and boots, all looking as new as the car the men sat in. Each man held an AK-47 rifle. The Afghan on the end of the bench nearest the metal wall that separated passengers and driver managed a sheepish smile, the other two kept their eyes fixed on the floor and ignored Carver completely. William sat down on the empty bench and Cahill jumped up and joined him, sitting a little closer than necessary given the amount of room available. In the space between the two benches were a number of green metal ammunition boxes with white stencilled descriptions painted on the sides. William read these and tried to decode them. The boxes labelled RPG and AK were easy enough to guess at, but other sequences of letters and numbers eluded him. Cahill removed a mobile phone from his jacket pocket and pressed last number redial. William heard the call connect but no voice at the other end.

'Packet on board,' he said simply. William heard the growl of the lead car's engine and then that of their own vehicle. Both Humvees moved off at speed. The car bunny-hopped several times in the first hundred yards and Cahill tutted. 'The Safa that's driving us is still finding his feet, and the foot pedals by the sound of it.'

William glanced at his neighbour. 'Safa?'

'South African.'

'Right. And these three?' Carver tipped his chin in the direction of the Afghan men opposite.

'All local. Good blokes, the boss says, but they don't talk much. I can't seem to get their names straight so I call 'em Mary, Mungo and Midge, left to right.'

The three were studying William with some attention now. Cahill grinned. 'I think they like you. Or maybe they're just surprised to see you. The boss thought maybe you'd bottle it.'

William remembered what Ambassador Lever had said about it mattering little whether he agreed to the meeting or not. 'What would you have done if I had? Bottled it, I mean?'

'Not a lot. Keep calm and carry on, as you poms like to say. That was the order.'

'Go ahead? Whether I was here or not?'

'That's it, mate.'

'But what would you have done once you got to the meeting point? Why would they release Patrick without getting me in exchange?'

'I don't know anything about an exchange, Billy. Far as I know we go in and banjo the bastards, grab the other pom and get the fuck out of there.'

William felt his stomach tighten. 'How the hell is that supposed to work?'

'Most of the time when these Talibs see they're overmatched, they turn tail and run for the hills. Seen it myself.' Cahill kicked the toe of his boot against the nearest ammunition case. 'The boss has got enough hardware in these Hummers to start a third world war. Enough to start it and finish it. So, no worries. We're just going to take a nice drive. The chances are, you won't even have to get off the bus.' He reached into a knapsack at his feet and found a battered blue thermos flask. He clamped the flask between his thighs and unscrewed the lid. 'Coffee? It'll help steady your nerves.'

William drank. It tasted filthy; a sour coffee with a sharp alcoholic aftertaste. 'What's in that? Brandy?' he asked hopefully.

The Australian laughed. 'Yeah, something like that.'

William looked around for somewhere to dispose of the remaining half cup and seeing that there was nowhere, drank it with a scowl. Cahill took the empty thermos lid and refilled it. The cup looked like a thimble between the fingers of his big right hand, which he raised, smiling broadly at William and the Afghan soldiers. 'I'd like to make a little toast,' he grinned. 'This is my last job. Last job for your man up front too, last job in Afghanistan. Last fighting job, full stop. I do this, pick up the cheque and then it's straight back to the motherland for me. Kabul to Dubai, Dubai to Sydney. All booked and bought.' He beamed at the Afghans but got nothing back, so he shifted round towards William and nudged him in the arm.

'That's great,' William muttered. 'Congratulations.'

'Thanks, Billy-boy. Plan is buy myself a big dog, a ridgeback or a blue heeler, or maybe one of each. I grew up with dogs but small ones, mongrels mostly. I'm planning on getting a few acres of farmland, too, so I want working dogs. The dogs'll do the work and I'll do the drinking.' He finished the thimble of coffee in a gulp and frowned. 'Fuck, that is nasty. So, yeah, that'll be me. No loud bangs, no nasty surprises, just a nice bit of land and a big old dog or two.'

William nodded and they sat in silence for a while. The Humvee was moving at pace now and the roads had turned rougher.

'I know what you're thinking, Billy.'

'You do?'

'Sure. You're thinking maybe I'll need a woman.' Cahill elbowed Carver in the ribs and gave him a look that suggested William was remiss in not mentioning the possibility that Cahill might want a woman as well as his dogs. 'And you're right, but not a skinny one. I prefer the fuller-figured lady. How about you, Billy-o?' When William failed to answer, Cahill looked him up and down. 'I guess a bloke like you can't be too picky. No offence.'

'None taken.'

Cahill slopped another round of coffee into the cup and passed it across the aisle to the Afghan man opposite. 'Mungo?'

The man took a small sip, then a gulp, before passing it to his neighbours. The vehicle was bouncing around now and the ammunition shifted in the aisle. Cahill leant forward and straightened the boxes. 'I hope this fucking Safa knows what he's doing, these Hummers tip if you turn 'em too sharp. Fact is, they're not half as bloody useful as the Yanks think they are.'

Coffee and nerves had loosened the men's bowels and the smell of petrol and sweat was competing with the sour stink of flatulence. So when Cahill reached deep into his backpack again, this time for a crushed packet of Camels, William was almost relieved. The Australian offered the cigarettes around and every man but William took one. Cahill lit them one by one with a silver Zippo. A fog of smoke quickly filled the Humvee and William had to suppress a cough. Cahill noticed and tried to wrestle one of the small square windows open to allow some air in. He managed to slide it a couple of inches, bringing some small relief. William closed his eyes and pretended to sleep, which seemed to discourage any further conversation from Cahill. They rode on for what felt to William like an hour but when he checked his watch it turned out to be closer to three. He realised that, against all odds, he must have fallen asleep for a time, and when he glanced over at Cahill, he saw he was grinning.

'You're awake Billy-boy, thank fuck for that. You're the first bloke I've met snores louder than a Hummer.' Just then Cahill's mobile phone rang and William felt the car begin to slow. The Australian held the phone close to his ear and put his finger in the other. 'Yeah. Okay boss, you got it. Yeah. No worries.' He tucked the phone back carefully into his jacket pocket then looked at his team. 'It's on.'

His mood and the mood of the van suddenly changed. The South African driver cut the engine and there was quiet for the first time in several hours. Cahill reached beneath the bench and removed a rifle from its clips. The gun was not new and it was clear to William from the way Cahill handled it that this was his personal and preferred weapon. Cahill cradled it in this lap.

'We stay here until we get further instruction. Sit tight.' He directed this information at the Afghan man sat nearest to the driver's window and who William now noticed wore a gold wedding band on the appropriate finger. 'You got that, Midge? Pass it on.' Midge nodded and translated the instruction to his compatriots in a low whisper. The other two nodded at him and then at Cahill, who attempted a reassuring smile. The Australian turned to William. 'You just relax, mate.' But it was obvious Cahill was not relaxed. He fiddled with his gun and then, appearing to remember something, reached for his bag. He retrieved a small brown leather D-shaped coin purse and flipped it open. There were half a dozen white pills inside. He noticed William watching. 'Benzhexol.' He held the purse out so William could see the lozenge-shaped pills. 'You know about these?' Carver nodded. He'd heard stories of soldiers, both American and Afghan, who went into action doped up on anti-psychotics, drugs designed to stop them feeling scared all the time. 'Benzy Boys', the Americans called them. Cahill shook a handful of pills into his palm and offered them to the Afghans, who took one each without hesitation. Cahill took one himself and offered one to William, who refused and then immediately regretted it. He was terrified. The five men sat and waited.

Up ahead of them, in the lead car, Richard Roydon leant forward and looked out of the windscreen. He stared high into the blue Afghan sky. There was a contrail from a plane up around thirty thousand feet, but it was too high and too far away to have anything to do with what was happening down below. He sighed and sat back in his seat. The Afghan driver at his side drummed his fingers on the steering wheel but stopped quickly when Roydon gave him a sideways glance.

'One hundred metres,' Roydon said to no one but himself. A

hundred metres away, up the dirt road, was a dark SUV. Roydon lifted a pair of binoculars and sharpened the focus. There was one man moving around in the front of the SUV, and as Roydon watched, he climbed into the back. He could see several other figures sitting in the car; all but one, he thought, would be heavily armed. The last instruction he'd taken on the satphone had told him to stop one hundred metres from an SUV on this stretch of road. He looked across at the driver and out over the landscape. He knew this wouldn't be the ragheads' only vehicle. They would have another group, better armed and close behind, just in case. Or maybe they had a second unit stationed somewhere in the rear of Roydon's group. That was a strong possibility, too, but not one that worried him unduly. He had the men and the machinery to blast and kill his way out of a corner. But the rendezvous point wasn't perfect. There was high ground to the left, although he had been watching it carefully and he could see no sign of men or movement. To the right it was better, what looked like dried-out marshland – fuck all for miles and miles. His phone vibrated in his pocket and he answered it quickly. The Afghan man at the other end of the line had no time for pleasantries.

'I can see you now, Captain Roydon. Your position is good, stay there. You may call me General.'

Roydon held the phone in one hand and lifted his binoculars with the other. One hundred metres away he saw a figure in the front of the SUV holding a phone to his ear.

'This is what will happen. I will send Patrick Reid from this car and when you see him on the road, you will do the same with William Carver, yes?'

'Okay, General.'

'Once they are both in the open they will walk and meet in the middle. Carver will then walk to us and Reid will remain in the middle, in the open. Understand?'

'Yes.'

'I will talk to Carver here. I will not take him anywhere and he will remain in plain sight at all times. When we have talked, when he has told me what I need to know, he will return to you. Unharmed. And we can go our separate ways.'

'Good.'

'But if you do anything unexpected, then I will kill Patrick Reid. Do you understand?'

'Yes.'

'Good. Stand by.'

The phone went dead and Roydon allowed himself a smile. 'Fucking amateur hour,' he breathed.

Roydon was about to phone through to the second car when he saw a figure stagger from the rear of the SUV. The figure stopped abruptly, as though ordered to do so, two paces from the back of the vehicle, at exactly the place you'd want him if it became necessary for someone in the SUV to kill him quickly. Roydon reached for the binoculars. The man was hooded. He had on a travel jacket, white shirt and a pair of filthy trousers. He wore no shoes, just black socks. He was shaking. The figure was holding a black laptop out in front of him, like a shield. Roydon focused on the computer and enhanced the magnification. The boy's tremble made it hard to focus. 'Stand still, you pussy.' There was a barcoded sticker on the front and the words *PROPERTY OF THE BBC*. Roydon picked up the phone and rang the second car.

Cahill jumped when the phone rang and nearly dropped it in his attempt to answer quickly. 'Yes, boss?' After receiving his brief instruction, he put the phone away and reached into his bag for something. He brought out what looked to William like a bunched-up tea towel, and inside that, a square of mirror, the size of a picture postcard, attached to a car aerial. Cahill moved quickly. He opened the rear door and jumped down, then gestured to William to follow suit. 'Boss wants you to see something.'

Carver shuffled along the bench and stepped down on to the

road, wincing as the blood rushed to his feet. The two men were enclosed on both sides by the doors of the Humvee and Cahill was obviously keen to keep it that way. He extended the car aerial and held the mirror out beyond the black car door, then took his time to find the right angle. He pulled William towards him by the shoulder and encouraged him to look at the image reflecting in the mirror. 'Is that your man? Is that Patrick Reid?'

William squinted at the three-inch-high figure. Patrick was wearing the ridiculous khaki travel jacket that William had made fun of, the one with maybe a dozen pockets, and the white shirt and trousers he had on the day he was snatched. He was holding his laptop and shaking with fear. William nodded.

Cahill put the mirror to one side and retrieved the phone. 'Boss? Carver says it's him.'

Roydon could hear a call waiting tone underneath Cahill's voice. He ended the call to his colleague and connected to an angry-sounding General.

'What is taking so long? You can see Reid, can you not?'

'I can, it's okay, General, don't worry. I'm going to bring your hostage round now, okay? I'm going to bring Carver. You and your boys just sit tight and leave Reid in clear sight. Yes?'

There was a long pause. 'Move slowly, Captain.'

Roydon stuffed the phone deep into his trouser pocket and opened the car door slowly. He stepped out, hands in the air, and walked backwards down the side of his Humvee to the rear door. He knocked twice and then once again, and the right-hand door opened sharply. Crouching inside was a stocky man with pale skin and wiry red hair wearing desert camouflage. Resting under his right hand was a rocket-propelled grenade launcher. Roydon looked at the weapon.

'Armed and ready?'

'Yes, sir.'

'Good boy, remember, they'll see you soon as you step round

the Hummer. Put it right down the middle and don't fuck up, you'll only get one shot.'

The redhead nodded. 'Now?'

Roydon stepped aside. 'Now.'

The man jumped down nimbly, turned and reached back into the back of the vehicle for the RPG. He lifted it easily on to his right shoulder, staying close to the car. The only other person who could see what was about to happen was the driver in the second Humvee. The South African whistled under his breath. With the weapon settled on his shoulder and his hands carefully positioned, the redhead took a deep, slow breath. On the exhale, he took two paces back and then three to his left. He took aim and fired. It was a perfect execution. The grenade entered the front window of the SUV a fraction of a second after it left the chamber, exploding with an almighty crack. Roydon counted to three and then put his head round the side of the Hummer door to see the car in flames and a plume of black smoke rising from it. Then he heard screaming.

The ginger-haired soldier was quickly back at his boss's side. 'You want me to put another one down?'

Roydon shook his head and patted the man on the arm. 'Nah. That'll do for now. Nice work.' He looked back into the rear of his Humvee at three uniformed men, all dark-haired but not Afghan. 'You lot sit tight for the time being. Moshe, pass me an AK.' The man nearest him handed over his own rifle.

The screaming had stopped. Roydon watched the scene from the relative safety of the side of his Humvee before deciding to move closer. Several things had still to be done and he had to remain focused. The SUV was burning furiously and he cursed the smoke and the yellow dust and willed it to clear quickly. As it did, he saw Patrick lying face down to the side of the burning vehicle, a widening pool of blood darkening the sand around where his stomach used to be. Looking around, Roydon saw that the black laptop was close by and apparently little damaged. He gave a grunt of satisfaction and turned his attention back to the burning vehicle. He was looking for a weapon, something belonging to the dead General or one of his men. He would kill Carver with this gun, toss it somewhere close to its owner, near the burnt-out SUV, and then call in the cavalry. After a goatfuck like this, it was almost impossible to unpick who had killed who, and the military police wouldn't want to be out in the open long, anyway. Not way out here in the Talib badlands. They would take his word for what happened when and to whom. Drop the laptop into the fire and the job would be done.

The car was still giving off a considerable heat and it was hard to get close or see anything beyond the thick black smoke. Roydon smelt burning fuel, and even more noxious, a powerful smell of burning plastic or rubber. Burning tyres, he guessed, though looking at what he could see of the car, it seemed at least two of the wheels had been blown clean off. He circled the General's car. He saw a single limb in a ditch a few feet away and moved closer. It was an arm. He stared at it. He was close to it now. It was pink but not the pink of scorched flesh. The arm had been separated from the shoulder completely cleanly, as though with a butcher's cleaver. There was something not right about it. It almost looked like— Roydon felt his stomach turn. He span round and ran back towards the SUV, shading his face against the heat. He saw a burning form in the back seat. It was a man, hair ablaze, his forehead melted into a frown and the rest of the face into a clownlike grimace. Roydon realised he was looking at a clothes shop dummy. His mind turned. Now he'd recognised one mannequin, he realised there were several, all aflame and all melting slowly away in the front and back of the burning car. He started walking backwards, away from the vehicle. His heart was pumping quickly, too quickly. He had to gather himself, think straight. He turned to his right and ran over to Reid's body, grabbing the laptop on his way. He had an idea what he might see when he removed the black hood. Not a mannequin, but not Patrick Reid either. He pulled the hood away and flipped the body on to its back with his foot. It was a young Afghan man, not even a man but rather a boy not yet out of his teenage years. His eyes were open and there was a little breath left in him but not much – there was a hole where his stomach should be and he'd lost a lot of blood.

'*Plar? Ubu plar.*'

Roydon lifted his AK and fired a round straight into the boy's heart. He left him and started jogging back towards his Hummer. The stocky redhead had ignored his order and was standing, rifle in hand, between the burning SUV and his own vehicle. As he drew closer, Roydon shouted loudly at the man. 'Turn the fuck around. We gotta get out of here!'

The red-haired man nodded and was halfway to turning when a bullet hit him in the right temple, just below the hairline. He died where he stood. Roydon jumped at the sound of the shot and briefly stopped. He watched the soldier fold from the knees and fall, then he spun around quickly, surveying the threat. The bullet had come from an elevated position to his right – the cliff-top. He shielded the right side of his head with the laptop computer and tacked left for the Humvee. He could see the bewildered, staring face of his driver as he moved closer, and then heard a familiar sound – the muffled boom and rush of a grenade launcher.

Looking right, towards the mountains, he saw the missile complete the last fifty yards of flight. It came from up high and hit his Humvee expertly, just above the petrol tank. He saw the vehicle lift and his driver thrown sideways by the blast, his head smashing against the passenger side window with enough force to crack the glass, before slumping out of sight. The Hummer blossomed into flame. Roydon stopped running again and dropped into a low crouch. He watched one of his men jump from the rear of the burning vehicle, AK-47 in hand and head down, but a sniper's bullet found him almost as soon as his foot hit the ground. This bullet, like everything else, came from high on the right. Then came Moshe. Clever not to be the first, Roydon thought. The dark-haired mercenary was out and round to the left-hand side of the burning car when the bullet pinged into the metal doors. He held his rifle at the ready and made eye contact with Roydon. He gave him a signal suggesting he might provide covering fire so his boss could move from his exposed position. Roydon nodded. Moshe started to work his way round to the front of the Humvee so he could fire up towards the bluff. He was nearly there when a volley of bullets hit him in the back and he was thrown forward against the front of the Hummer. This round had clearly come from the other side, the dried-up marshland, but when he looked, Roydon could see nothing. He could only wonder, with a calm that surprised him, why he was still alive.

His vehicle was ablaze now. The last member of his group must've been killed when the grenade launcher hit. His only hope was the second Hummer. He shuffled in its direction, moving on his belly with the AK slung over his shoulder and the laptop left behind. In the second Humvee, Cahill was staring at the scene through the small slide door that separated him and the South African driver. The driver put his hand to the ignition key.

'It's a fucking turkey shoot out there, let's move, yah?'

Cahill put his hand through the window and grabbed the driver by the neck. 'No fucking way. Boss said wait, so we wait. You turn that key and I'll shoot you myself.'

The driver mumbled some Afrikaans abuse under his breath but put his hand back on the wheel. 'Okay baas. I guess you're the man now, so what's your plan?'

Cahill took a breath. The anti-psychotics were helping keep the fear at bay but he was still having trouble thinking straight. 'We drive to him. Pick him up, then get the fuck out of here. Let's go.'

'And get an RPG up the arse?'

'If they've got another one, why haven't they used it already? Maybe they only had the one.'

The driver swore again and started the car. He had only just moved it into gear when Cahill heard the deafening sound of bullets and breaking glass. He jumped backwards, away from the hatch, and fell down heavily on the ammunition boxes. The car was still moving slowly and when Cahill tried to stand there was another jolt as the second Humvee drove straight into the one in front and he was thrown down at William's feet. William reached out and Cahill took his hand and rose. He stood and put his head gingerly through the hatch. The South African was dead. His clothes were cut to pieces by the sheer number of bullets fired. His head, almost unrecognisable, was slumped over the steering wheel. There was already a shallow pool of blood in the footwell. Cahill sat down next to Carver and ran his hand over his face.

'Last fucking job.'

'What now?' William rasped, his throat tight with fear.

'Not a lot of choice, mate.' Cahill looked at the three Afghans opposite. 'We've gotta go get the boss. The main man. You understand? Can you translate that for me, Midge?' The Afghan on the end of the line, the one with the wedding ring, nodded and spoke briefly to his countrymen.

'They understand.'

Cahill nodded and looked at William. 'You sit tight, mate. I reckon they're out of rockets; I hope they are, anyway. Move over a bit closer to the door, yeah? If they hit the car with something big, jump out and run like fuck. But until then, you're safer in here.' He turned his attention to the Afghan soldiers. 'Okay, so they're mostly over there—' he motioned to his right '—so keep left. That side, yes? And stay low and whatever you do, keep fucking firing, the more lead, the better.' Midge translated and then nodded at Cahill, who looked in turn at William. 'Watch this. Bet your life the moment they're out the van it'll be hands in the air and guns to the ground. Any bloody money.' Cahill smiled and jumped out, followed immediately by the three Afghans who didn't run or surrender but stayed close to him and started shooting, left and right.

The Australian took the first bullet. It hit him before he'd made it past the side of the vehicle, entering at one side of his neck and exiting the other. He fell back into a sitting position and dropped his gun. Lifting his arm, he tried to cup the blood in his right hand and press it back up against his neck, as though pushing it back in. It was pointless; the flow quickened. When William moved to help Cahill, the man raised his bloodied hand and signalled him to stay where he was. His eyes were wet with tears but he smiled before falling backwards in the dirt.

Outside, the gunfire continued for several minutes before everything fell silent again. Roydon saw two of the three Afghan soldiers die but made no attempt to move from the position of precarious cover that he'd found. There was silence for a time, and then an unexpected sound. It took Roydon a while to realise that it was his phone ringing. He found it buried deep in his pocket.

'Yes? General?'

'Did that go as you had hoped?'

Roydon stayed silent.

'If you want a chance to leave here alive, Captain Roydon, you do this: you drop the gun and you go and get William Carver and you bring him out into the open. That's assuming you have him. If you do not have him, we will kill you now.'

'I have him, I still have him,' Roydon blurted. He stood up slowly and dropped the AK on the ground, walked unsteadily to the rear of the second Humvee and stared into the back. William was sitting pressed into the corner of the vehicle. When he recognised Roydon's face, he made a reach for one of the rifles that was clipped beneath the seat opposite, but Roydon was too quick. He jumped up and punched Carver hard on the side of the head. Then he grabbed his collar and dragged him head first out of the Humvee. He pulled his captive out into clear ground about twenty feet from the concertinaed cars and stood William upright. He took his mobile phone in one hand and pulled a Sig Sauer handgun from the back of his belt, its grip polished to a shine from years of use.

When the phone rang he answered it immediately and didn't wait for the General to speak. 'Okay. Here he is. Now you get your boys to back off or I'll shoot him in the fucking head.'

'Captain, be calm . . .'

It was difficult for Roydon to keep a firm grip on Carver's sweaty collar with one hand while holding his phone and gun in the other. He wheeled around, scanning the high ground on one side and the marshland on the other, trying to work out where the phone voice was coming from.

'I want William Carver. What is it that you want?'

'A car and a driver. A car and driver to take me back to Kabul. Once I'm back there, I'll let Carver and your driver go. You have my word.'

Roydon heard a grunt of laughter.

'Your word? Your word hasn't been worth much so far. Has it?'

Roydon looked around at the many dead bodies and the three burnt-out vehicles. A growing feeling of panic was rising up inside him. 'You get me back to Kabul and we can do business. The Aftel deal isn't done yet. I can help. I can get the negotiations reopened, I know—'

The General interrupted. 'You know nothing. My interest in Fazil Jabar has nothing to do with Aftel or contracts or money. You cannot bribe your way out of this, Captain Roydon. Fazil was my wife's youngest brother. I promised to look after him and you killed him. This is a personal matter, Captain, not a business matter. I am tired of this. Let Carver go, drop your gun, or I will kill you now.'

Roydon scanned the cliff-top. For the first time he saw a glimpse of something, a glint or a reflection.

'Wait, wait. Come down from the cliffs, General, and we can talk this over, like men.'

'You are not a man.'

'Hold on. Just hold on—' Roydon was sweating heavily by now and he had to blink the sweat from his eyes. His grip on Carver felt vulnerable, but William was making no effort to break free. 'It's pointless, General. Killing me would be pointless, it achieves nothing.'

Roydon heard a sigh.

'You are probably right.'

The Englishman heard a glimmer of hope in this response. 'It is true. I am right.'

'But I will do it anyway.'

William heard a shot. He was blinded momentarily, and when he opened his eyes everything was a rosy pink. A mist of blood from Roydon's exploded head covered his glasses. Roydon's dead hand released its grip and William slumped forward, like a puppet that had had its strings cut. He fell to his knees in the yellow dust, waiting for the next shot.

On the cliff-top, General Doushki lifted a hand. One of his men helped him to his feet and took the rifle. His knees and shoulders were stiff from lying flat to the ground for so long and his dark beard was dusted white in places. He looked around for Mirgun, and seeing him, barked an order. His man made an alternative suggestion and the General frowned. 'You would kill a man to save yourself a few hours' drive? No, there has been enough dying today. Take him back.'

Doushki looked down at the carnage he'd helped create. Smoke rose from the vehicles. He counted half a dozen dead. Only one man was standing – or rather kneeling, as it appeared William Carver had still made no attempt to move. 'I will deal with Mr Carver and collect our brother Abdul's body. I will tell his family he died bravely. A martyr's death. Now let us go.'

At ten thousand feet an Israeli-made drone awaited further instruction. The images it captured were being viewed in real-time in the basement of an anonymous-looking grey stone building in Whitehall. Jones watched in silence. He turned to his laptop and a draft press release announcing the deaths of Patrick Reid and William Carver together with Special Forces soldiers during a failed rescue mission a hundred kilometres outside Kabul. Jones closed the file and dragged it towards the wastepaper icon on his screen. His hand hovered there a moment and then he let go. It disappeared with a computerised crunch.

'Hubris,' he said out loud and to no one but himself. He considered his options. Ground bombardment? There was an AC-130 Spectre gunship in the area. He could call in a favour from the Americans and they could level the whole area in one or two runs; kill everyone, destroy everything. But an air strike like that would leave a paper trail right back to Jones, and he would need a good story to explain why it was necessary. He didn't have a good story. It was probably too late anyway. The tiny figures were on the move, jumping into a variety of vehicles and heading off in different directions. The living moved, the dead remained. Jones stared at one shape in particular, arms and legs splayed, head to one side. Richard Roydon. At least he wasn't an issue any more.

So no air strike. Better to clean it up quietly and keep it in-house.

He steepled his hands in front of him and stared. He wore a round pink plaster over the mosquito bitten knuckle, which he'd picked at on the plane until it bled. Unfolding his hands, he returned to the laptop. It took him just seconds to locate the file on His Excellency, Ambassador David Lever.

36 Release

DATELINE: Outskirts of Kabul, Afghanistan, July 13th

Patrick was driven back to Kabul hooded and tied and lying across the footwell in the back seat of an SUV. The drive felt endless; it seemed to Patrick they had been bumping and crunching over the potholed roads of Afghanistan for days.

Mirgun shoved him from the car just a few streets from where he'd first been abducted.

'Goodbye, Englishman.'

Patrick said nothing. He had no idea where he was or what was about to happen. Too afraid to try to loosen the rope that bound his hands or shake free the black hood, he stumbled and then sat down in the road.

Mirgun waited a while and watched. He had the driver rev up the engine a few times and laughed as Patrick flinched, but he tired of that game. It was stifling hot in the late afternoon sun and he needed to move. He nodded at his colleague, and the SUV accelerated away.

Patrick just sat. Local children found him first. A couple of young boys threw some small stones at him from a safe distance and in a half-hearted fashion before a taller girl of ten or so years shooed them away. She walked up to him and pulled the hood slowly from his head, looking straight into his eyes. It took Patrick a while to adjust to the light, but when he did, he saw that the girl was wearing a dirty white shameez, her brown hair was bleached blonde in places by the sun and her eyes were a bright green. She smiled tentatively at him and his eyes filled with tears.

Mrs Ansari had her husband drop her at work an hour earlier than usual. She had told him there was a diplomatic visit she had to prepare for, but that was a lie. Something about the Ambassador's mood and manner the previous evening had unsettled her. He had been quiet to the point of near silence. When she caught him looking at her, it was not the usual appreciation or gentle hunger she saw, but something else. A look that seemed almost apologetic, although he had done nothing wrong. Nothing other than working too late, scribbling away past the dinner hour and then failing to eat what was usually his favourite meal. Overnight, it had come to her. He was sickening. There was a flu virus about and he had caught it. So in her handbag she carried a knuckle of fresh ginger and her own favourite honey. She would make him a hot tonic with some of his whisky. She knew the one he liked; twelve years old with the smell of wet earth.

When Mrs Ansari reached the black gates at the front of the residence, the Gurkha security guards were absent. She let herself in and walked quickly up the drive to the front door. It had been forced open and was slightly ajar. She stepped inside and saw splinters of wood on the hall floor. Reaching for her mobile phone, she then changed her mind and walked straight down the hall in the direction of the library.

'David?'

David Lever was sitting in his armchair, tied at the wrists and ankles. His throat had been cut and the blood had flowed like a curtain over his white shirt and light suit trousers. Mrs Ansari dropped her bag and sat down heavily in the seat opposite. She looked around for signs of struggle but no ornaments were broken, nothing was upended or disturbed. The room was in the same perfect order she had left it in just the night before. She reached for her bag and found the phone. In her contacts, underneath *Embassy David* she found *Embassy Emergency*. She dialled the number and listened to the strange-sounding ringtone. She pictured a big Bakelite phone ringing on a wide desk, far away in a grey-looking London. The man on the other end of the line told her she should not move. But she could not stay where she was. She walked to the kitchen, her domain, and looked around. The little orange light on the dishwasher was flashing. The cycle was complete and ready to be unloaded. Mrs Ansari reached behind the kitchen door for her pinny; a floral thing that David had bought her, 'a little joke', he had said, but she had worn it every day. Lifting it from the peg, it felt heavier than usual and as she went to tie it round her waist, some papers fell from the front pocket on to the tiled floor. She picked them up. There were two envelopes, each addressed in Lever's beautiful calligraphic script. One bore her name, the other that of William Carver.

Mrs Ansari could hear shouting at the front of the house now, and the insistent blaring of a car horn. She remembered that she had locked the gates behind her, so she tucked the letters back in the pocket of her apron. As she passed through the library ,she took one more look at the Ambassador. His hair had fallen forward, exaggerating his bald patch, and she swept it back tenderly. Looking down, she noticed something silver on the carpet, next to the chair leg. A piece of jewellery. She crouched and picked up the tiny crusader cross. She put it in her pocket alongside the two letters and went to open the gate.

37 Debrief

DATELINE: British Army barracks, Kabul airport, July 15th

The shock of release affected Patrick profoundly. When he was finally left alone in his barracks room after two full days of questioning, he sat on the bed and stared out of the window, switching focus between the comings and goings outside on the military base and the gaffer tape crosses on the dirty glass. He had been told that the day after tomorrow, after one last and no doubt equally pointless debrief, they would fly him home. His heart raced as he thought of it. His memories of the last forty-eight hours were vivid but incomplete, like a handful of old Kodacolor pictures. He remembered the young Afghan girl leading him through courtyards full of chickens and being sat down in the corner of someone's living room. He had been offered green tea and drank several cups while a growing group of old men discussed who he was and what to do with him. After an hour a fat man in a grey western-style suit arrived. He was greeted with obvious respect and quickly became the centre of the discussions. When he spoke others became quiet and when he finished speaking heads nodded.

Another hour had passed, and the house, which at first had felt cool, had become warm, heated by the gaggle of men, this informal *shura*. The fat man was feeling the heat. Sweat marks stained his suit under each arm and he regularly dabbed at his upper lip and forehead with a white handkerchief. In time, the to and fro of debate slowed and Patrick sensed a decision had been reached. He was encouraged to his feet and escorted back to the stretch of road where the girl had first found him. His guide this time was the fat man himself, who walked a few paces ahead, waving Patrick forward with his handkerchief. When they reached the road, the fat man handed Patrick a heavy plastic bag and encouraged him in broken English and handkerchief semaphore to lean himself against a low wall and wait. Once Patrick had understood this message and complied, the sweating man slowly withdrew, walking sideways and backwards away from Patrick until with one final wave of his handkerchief he disappeared into a side street. Patrick stood alone and scanned the road. Mud-walled houses, a yellow dirt road and beyond that scrubland and a field of small dusty green-leaved trees. Olive trees, maybe? Or fruit? He wondered what would happen next, whether he was about to deliver himself into the hands of another group of hostage-takers or if he was free, awaiting rescue? Should he wait, or try and find his own way to safety? But these seemed idle thoughts, just something to pass the time. He felt as though he was considering someone else's fate, not his own.

Within fifteen minutes a three-car convoy appeared on the horizon, kicking up clouds of dust. Patrick watched as a strange six-wheeled armoured vehicle approached, sandwiched between two Humvees. The convoy drew closer and when they began to slow and he could make out some of the faces, he lifted his arms into the air. A dozen American soldiers jumped from the three vehicles and took up positions around the convoy, forming a loose heavily armed circle. An older-looking officer in heavy body armour walked towards Patrick, stopping a few metres from him. He removed his sunglasses and shouted. The accent was Midwest and had a hard edge to it.

'Are you Reid? Patrick Reid?'

Patrick nodded.

'Are you armed? Wired?'

Patrick shook his head.

The man stared at Patrick's midriff and at the ground around his feet. His eyes settled on the plastic bag. 'What's in the bag?'

Patrick looked at it. He didn't know. He shook his head.

'Okay. Tip out the bag . . . Nice and slow.'

Patrick did as he was told. A litre bottle of water rolled on to the road along with half a dozen oranges.

After they'd patted him down, Patrick had been marched, almost lifted, and loaded into the back of the mastiff truck. Two soldiers fitted him with a Kevlar-plated jacket and he heard his name being repeatedly shouted down the line by an excited radio operator. The American soldiers were asking him questions but he was unable to frame any answers. He just nodded or shook his head depending on what seemed appropriate. Pretty soon the soldiers tired of questioning a mute and put their music back on. Patrick looked around the vehicle, at the scraps of colourful soft porn torn from the pages of magazines and stuck to various surfaces. He listened to the radio operator shouting their proximity to base above the noise of metal music. A plate of the body armour was resting heavily on a bladder full of green tea.

He had wanted to piss, had wanted to sleep, had wanted to be somewhere else. But he wasn't sure where.

There had been a scrum of maybe twenty journalists at the airport base and hacks of various nationalities shouted questions at him as he was marched from the armoured vehicle to the low-rise reception building. He remembered a long, scalding hot shower and a brief medical examination. He recalled heaped plates of tasteless but brightly coloured food, much of which he could not eat.

Most blurred of all were the hours of questioning which followed. These sessions involved several different interrogators, some American, one English, all asking the same sort of questions, few of which he could answer to their satisfaction.

The most vivid of all his recent memories was a brief phone call to Rebecca. When he was handed the phone and heard it ringing, he wondered stupidly whether she would pick up, not realising that the call would have been arranged. The phone rang three times and then she answered.

'Hello?'

Patrick could not speak. He didn't want to. He just wanted to listen to her voice. 'Hello? Patrick?' The voice was hopeful but full of doubt. He realised that if he didn't say something, she might hang up, thinking that a mistake had been made. He had to say something. 'Rebecca.'

'Patrick!'

Her voice broke and he listened to her cry. Tears welled now in his eyes too and he turned his chair to face the wall, still gripping Rebecca's voice tightly in his hand. The call lasted several minutes but there were few words. They listened to each other saying nothing. They listened to each other breathing.

38 Breakfast at Baba's

DATELINE: BBC house, Kabul, Afghanistan, July 16th

Rob Mariscal swung his naked feet out of bed and planted them on the cold floor. His first attempt at getting upright had to be aborted. He made an inventory of his various ailments. The soles of his feet hurt and his knees ached, and he had a headache, but that was normal. As he brushed his teeth he thought about his wife and about money and about the day ahead. The mysterious Baba had left a message at the BBC house, an almost illiterate note telling Mariscal that he must come to meet him at his 'hotel, restaurant and wedding venue' at eleven 'sharply'. There was no further explanation; just the address and directions and folded inside the note a brightly coloured leaflet advertising Baba's with a starburst that read: *As seen on BBC radio!* He weighed up the possible risks of going to the meeting against the alternative. The alternative was sitting in his room or going out and getting drunk again. The military police would still not let him see Patrick – not until questioning and debrief were complete, they said.

Rob got dressed and was about to leave the room when he saw the letter propped against an empty glass on the bedside table. A cream-coloured envelope addressed to William Carver and written in an elaborate hand. The envelope was heavy and gum-sealed, and so far Rob had resisted the temptation to steam it open. He wasn't sure why. William was missing, possibly dead, and probably wouldn't notice that the letter had been tampered with, even if he ever did get to read it. Mariscal suspected that his reluctance to pry was in part superstition. It was the last letter written by a dead man and it wasn't meant for him.

He remembered Mrs Ansari placing it in his hand. He had no idea how long she had waited in the BBC reception for him to arrive, and he couldn't remember what time of night it was. Late. But he did remember thanking her and her refusing to return his smile.

'I have no one else to give it to,' she'd explained, making it quite clear that she had no trust in him at all and little hope that he might do the right thing. So he had left the letter alone, until now, at least. Now something told him to take the letter with him and so he grabbed it from the bedside table, placed it in his jacket pocket, and left the room.

The cab he had ordered was waiting on the street. The driver said that he knew Baba's well. The trip across the city was quick, and as the car drew up outside the guesthouse, Rob's attention was drawn to a burnt-out building on the other side of the road. The tailor's shop had been thoroughly looted but some burnt rolls of material still lay around in the blackened weeds and scrub outside the shop. The doors and windows had been boarded up with grey corrugated metal. Mariscal stared.

'So that's what this was all about.' But he knew that whatever he was seeing constituted only a small part of the story, and, anyway, the driver was sucking at his teeth, waiting to be paid. He passed over a couple of notes and walked towards the guesthouse. The garden was green and well-kept and reminded him a little of the Ambassador's – much more modest but just as carefully tended and well loved. He walked up the path towards the house, past a three-tiered fountain which was producing a dribble of brackish-looking water. A large man wearing a grease-stained T-shirt, faded jeans and flip-flops was coming the other way. He came slapping down the path cradling a small brown cardboard box. As he came closer, Rob noticed that he also wore a small torch on an elasticised band strapped high across his bald head and a tool belt round his large stomach. The man smiled when he saw Mariscal. 'Ah. You came.'

'Er, yes.'

'Good, good.' The man tucked the box carefully under his arm and looked at his watch. 'Not early but not too late. Good.'

'You're Baba?'

'Certainly.' Baba nodded. 'But you must excuse me. I have a new pump now, and work to do. There is a wedding tomorrow and another the next day.' He crouched down alongside the fountain, pulled the torch a little lower on his forehead, and switched the light on. He placed the box down next to him and started fiddling with a set of keys.

Rob stood and watched, confused. 'But our meeting? Your note? You asked to see me?' he said, irritated.

Baba looked up, the workman's light blinding Mariscal briefly. 'What? Oh! Not me, Mr William. He is inside. He brought me this pump. Maybe he has something for you.'

'William Carver is inside?'

'He is my honoured guest. He is eating. He likes my cooking very much.'

Baba waved Mariscal away and went back to work. Rob realised he was not in the least bit surprised to be told that Carver was alive and well and inside eating lunch. He remembered telling colleagues that the only creatures left alive after nuclear Armageddon would be cockroaches and William Carver. William endured.

And here he was, or the back of him anyway, sitting alone at a dining-room table, his shoulders moving up and down as he chewed on something.

'William,' Rob said quietly.

Carver turned in his seat, his mouth full of chicken. 'Rob. You by yourself?' There was no warmth in the greeting. It was an acknowledgement and a straightforward request for information. Mariscal could tell in that instant that William knew everything.

'Yes.'

'Okay. You want to sit?'

Mariscal sat in the chair nearest to William and leant forward. Carver shuffled his seat an inch further away and kept eating. 'I've spoken to Mrs Ansari. She gave you a letter for me. Have you got it with you?' Rob patted at his jacket and William held out his hand. He noticed it was greasy from the chicken and so he withdrew it, wiped it on a trouser leg, and then offered it again. Rob handed the letter over and William put it down next to his plate. 'Have you seen Patrick yet?'

'No. Soon, they say.'

William nodded. 'Tell him hello from me.' He picked up a chicken leg. 'You can leave now, if you like.'

It was clear that this was what William would prefer. Rob got to his feet and walked to the door. 'Okay. So I'll see you in London, yeah? Take your time coming back. No hurry.' There was no response. 'What are you going to do?' Mariscal persisted in the friendliest tone he could muster.

William turned and gave Mariscal an even look. 'Do? About what, Rob?'

'About everything.'

'I don't know. Not yet.'

Once he was sure that Mariscal had gone, William reached for the letter. He checked the seal on the cream envelope and opened it with a clean knife. Pushing the plates aside, he laid the letter out as flat as the fold would allow.

Dear William,

I realise as I write this that I never got around to calling you by your Christian name. An oversight I think, so if it's okay with you, I'll use that name now. If not now, then when? The main purpose of this letter is to tell you that I don't want you to feel even the smallest scintilla of guilt for what I fear might transpire between me writing this and you reading it. I think you probably carry enough guilt around with you already and I have no wish to add to it. Everything that happened to me I brought upon myself. The numbered key in this envelope is to a locker at Kabul airport. Inside you will find a small amount of money, which I would like you to give to Mrs Ansari. You will also find some papers and a signed affidavit, which I believe might help you to tell your truth. I hope you will believe me when I say that I was trying to be true to something too.

Enough self-justification. I did a terrible thing and I would have gone on to do worse had it not been for your intervention. Intervention. There's that word again.

Your countryman and perhaps, in another life, your friend?
David Lever

William put the letter back in the envelope and shoved it to the bottom of his plastic bag. He heard Baba shouting his name urgently. The fountain had sprung back into life. Water jumped high into the air from the central spout before running fast and free down over the ornate stone. The water went nowhere, just round and round, but it made a pretty noise, and now it was working properly again, it really looked rather impressive. Baba stood alongside, spanner in hand. 'Abracadabra!'

William smiled. 'I think you mean eureka.' Baba flip-flopped his way over and embraced him.

'I mean both, my friend. I mean both. This fountain is going to make me a rich man. Every bride in Kabul will want her picture in front of this fountain, I know it. I will give you a commission. No question.'

'I don't want your money, Baba.'

Baba frowned. 'Not money. I'm not going to give you my money. A meal. I will cook you a good meal, a banquet, every time you return to Kabul.'

'Thank you, Baba.'

'We will sit and eat and watch the fountain and we will toast.'

'Okay, Baba.'

'We will toast your health and my health and my fountain's health, but most of all . . . we will toast our friend, Karim Mumtaz. Yes?'

William Carver attempted a reply but there was a catch in his voice. He nodded firmly and then he turned away so Baba might not see him cry.

39 The Nightmares

DATELINE: Serena Hotel, Kabul, July 17th

They agreed that the best and most anonymous place to meet would be one of the larger hotels. Patrick arrived early but the lobby felt too small and he felt too conspicuous, so he left a message at reception, asking Rob Mariscal to meet him at the pool bar. The sun was already high in the sky. Stepping outside, Patrick felt the dry heat hit him hard in the face. He found an empty table in the shade and ordered a beer from an Afghan waiter in a white tailcoat. When the drink arrived, he sat back in the plastic chair and watched the show.

A platoon of American soldiers had just arrived back from the south and had two free days before flying home on leave. Tattoos adorned almost everybody. The colours were rich and varied but there was a startling lack of originality as far as subject material was concerned: fighter planes, flocks of American Eagles and enough American flags to deck out Washington DC on Memorial Day. The current fashion was for a piece of script written on the calf or up the inside of one arm. Often these were in Gothic English, but sometimes something more exotic: Spanish or Hindu or Hebrew or a Cyrillic script that Patrick couldn't recognise. He guessed the idea was that the words might acquire weight and majesty if written in another language.

Many of the GIs were gathered round the three or four western women brave or foolish enough to have remained at the poolside. None of these women looked particularly attractive to Patrick, but then he wasn't at the end of a ten-month tour. The woman attracting the most admirers was tall and blonde, but she looked strangely desiccated and rather stretched, as though there was not quite enough skin to cover the sharp bones. The smell of suntan oil was heavy in the air. As he watched, another woman removed herself from the pack, strode to the side of the pool and readied herself for a dive. She jumped, folding and unfolding herself like a penknife before entering the water with barely a splash. There were loud whoops of admiration from the watching GIs. Patrick turned away. He was getting his appetite back and he ordered another beer and a hot dog, which arrived daubed with bright yellow mustard. Tearing off a corner of the bread roll, he wiped away as much of the mustard as he could before eating the hot dog in three bites. He washed down the meat with a swig of beer.

'You know those fuckers are low alcohol, yeah? You've got to drink shedloads to feel anything – or feel nothing, depending on which way you're going.' Patrick stood and took Rob's outstretched hand. 'Hello, boss.'

Rob sat down, waved the waiter over and ordered two more beers and two more hot dogs. 'Well, when do they let you go home?'

To Patrick, this felt like the first honest and uncomplicated question he'd been asked in a long time. He drew a deep breath. 'Tomorrow. I can't wait. When are you going back?'

Mariscal looked at his watch. 'Now, today. Last thing I had to do was see you. Make sure you're all right.' The beers arrived and Rob drank half of his in one swig. 'Are you all right?'

Patrick loosened his shoulders, and smiled. 'Yeah, I think so.'

'What are the nightmares like?'

Patrick shrugged but it was clear that Mariscal expected an answer; he wanted to hear it. 'They're all about Karim. Not much about me.'

'Right.'

'I killed him.'

'No you didn't.'

'I didn't stop it happening, I helped it happen. I made them think he was unimportant, disposable. I thought that might mean they'd let him go. I was so fucking stupid.'

Rob leant in close enough that Patrick could smell his breath: tobacco and beer, it wasn't unpleasant. 'Patrick. Listen to me. I wasn't there, but my guess is there was nothing you could've done. Nothing that would've made any difference.'

Rob placed his hand briefly on top of Patrick's, patted it, and then reached back for his beer. 'Did I tell you about the first famine I ever covered? First and only.'

Patrick shook his head.

'No. It's not a story I like to tell too often. I got sent to Ethiopia. My first proper field producer job. I was as green as you . . . greener, maybe. We were doing a walkthrough at this hospital attached to an IDP camp. Displaced people, yeah? Tens of thousands of them, misery everywhere. I got attached to this one particular kid, tiny she was. Starving but bloated, you know how they look? Very sick but her eyes still had this light in them and she looked at me, right at me, she wouldn't stop fucking looking at me.

'After my reporter and all the other hacks had moved along I went back and sat with her for a while, and when I left I gave her all the food I had on me, some bread rolls and chocolate, that kind of thing. I tucked them away under her blanket.

'I went back the next morning to see how she was. In my stupid fucking head I had this idea that she'd be better, maybe sitting up, reading a picture book, talking, something ridiculous like that?'

Mariscal looked down from the table, towards his shoes. 'She was dead. Laid out under a shit-stained blanket. The doctor said she'd eaten the food too quickly. The state she was in, the bread and chocolate I'd given her had burst her fucking intestines. I had killed her.'

They fell into a long silence. The grunts in the pool were hitting each other with blow-up dolls while the real women watched and laughed. Rob looked at Patrick over the top of his glass and nodded. 'You should get home, quick as you can.' He reached around in his pockets, found some notes to pay the bill, tucked them under one of the empty beer bottles and got to his feet. 'There'll be three months extra pay in your bank account by the time you're back. You're to take at least two months off work. Go away somewhere, perhaps? Take that girlfriend with you, what's her name?'

'Rebecca.'

'That's her. Take Rebecca.'

'Okay.'

'Good. I'll see you back in London.' Mariscal walked away but after a couple of steps he turned and glanced back. 'Oh, Paddy, I almost forgot. I saw Carver. He's fine. He said to say "Hello".'

Patrick beamed. 'That's great news. Amazing.'

'Yeah, really great. ' Rob paused. 'He likes you, you know. You should be proud of that, I don't think he's liked anyone for about fifteen years. And he's a good judge of character. Take care.'

With that, Mariscal turned and left.

Epilogue

DATELINE: Highbury Corner, London, N5, September 3rd

Patrick was struggling to remember what went into a Chinese stir-fry. It was one of his favourite meals but Rebecca usually made it. He just ate it without ever paying much attention to what it was he was eating. The shopping list he was writing read: soy sauce, bean sprouts, vegetables (various), wine. He checked his wallet. The wine could be eight quid but no more. They'd gone through a stage of buying twelve-quid bottles in recent weeks but the bonus money was almost all gone now. The warm feeling that normal rules could be suspended was faltering. Patrick was trying to think of what else he might add to the list when he heard the phone ring in the other room. He ran through and picked it up, cradling it between shoulder and chin, keeping the paper and pen to hand so he could continue with his list while whoever this was tried to sell him whatever it was they had to sell.

'Hello?'

'You don't even have a garden.'

'What?'

'How come you get two months gardening leave when you

417

haven't even got a garden? You've got a window box, I can see it, and I'll bet you a tenner there's not a living thing in it.'

Patrick's mouth split into a wide grin. 'William?'

'Which begs the question: what've you been doing for the last month and a half?'

'Resting. Recovering. Stuff like that . . .' Patrick laughed

'Yeah, right. Scratching your balls and pestering your poor bloody girlfriend, more like.'

Patrick dropped the pen and paper and hauled the phone line past the sofa and over to the window. He pulled back the net curtain and there was Carver, sitting on the bench, a hand raised in his direction. He looked the same as ever.

'So, Patrick. I've got a little story. I thought you might like to help me tell it?'

Acknowledgements

The following books were particularly valuable while researching *A Dying Breed*: Steve Coll's *Ghost Wars*, Rory Stewart's *The Places In Between*, Sherard Cowper Coles' *Cables From Kabul*, Ahmed Rashid's *Descent into Chaos*, John Cooley's *Unholy Wars*, Nick Davies' *Flat Earth News* and Eric Newby's *A Short Walk in the Hindu Kush*.

I would also like to acknowledge the journalism of Rodric Braithwaite, Alan Johnston, Christina Lamb, Brian Keenan, Martha Gelhorn, Patrick Cockburn, Robert Fisk and Robert D Kaplan. There are too many BBC hacks implicated to acknowledge them individually but I would particularly like to thank the brilliant producers, reporters, editors and of course presenters that I've worked with at *Today*, and Will Gompertz and Matilda Harrison who read the book at various stages. All characters appearing in this work are of course fictitious. Any resemblance to real persons, living or dead, is coincidence. Be assured that none of the events depicted inside or outside the BBC are based on real life and any insights the characters might appear to offer into the practices of journalism or those of the BBC are purely the product of the author's imagination. This is a work of fiction.

Thanks for invaluable editorial help to Lisa Highton, John Saddler and Fede Andornino, and the whole Two Roads team, including Ben Summers, Susan Spratt, Lyndsey Ng, Ruby Mitchell and Ross Fraser.

Special thanks to my incredible family: Victoria, Jack, Martha and Connie, and beyond N10 to my brothers Euan, Mark and Nick Hanington, my sister Zoe Curtis and brothers-in-law Patrick Scott, Chris Scott and Steve Cotton and my sister-in-law Amber Scott. Finally, thank you to Richard Knight for his invaluable support and advice throughout.

About the Author

Peter Hanington has worked for BBC Radio 4's *Today* Programme for fourteen years and throughout the Iraqi and Afghanistan conflicts. He initiated and ran the special guest editor programmes and has also worked on various special projects including collaborations with the Manchester International Festival and Glastonbury.

He lives in London with his wife and two children.

peterhanington.co.uk

@HaningtonPhan

Stories . . . voices . . . places . . . lives

We hope you enjoyed *A Dying Breed*. If you'd like to
know more about this book or any other title on our list,
please go to www.tworoadsbooks.com

For news on forthcoming Two Roads titles, please sign
up for our newsletter.

enquiries@tworoadsbooks.com

TwoRoadsBooks